TEMI OH lives and works in London.
This is her first novel.

DO YOU DREAM OF TERRA-TWO?

TEMI OH

**SIMON &
SCHUSTER**

London · New York · Sydney · Toronto · New Delhi

A CBS COMPANY

First published in Great Britain by Simon & Schuster UK Ltd, 2019
A CBS COMPANY

This paperback edition published 2020

3 5 7 9 10 8 6 4 2

Simon & Schuster UK Ltd
1st Floor
222 Gray's Inn Road
London WC1X 8HB

Simon & Schuster Australia, Sydney
Simon & Schuster India, New Delhi

www.simonandschuster.co.uk
www.simonandschuster.com.au
www.simonandschuster.co.in

A CIP catalogue record for this book
is available from the British Library

Paperback ISBN: 978 1 4711 7127 7
eBook ISBN: 978 1 4711 7126 0
Audio ISBN: 978 1 4711 8076 7

Typeset in the UK by M Rules
Printed and bound in Great Britain by CPI Group (UK) Ltd, Croydon, CR0 4YY

MIX
Paper from
responsible sources
FSC® C020471

*This book is dedicated to my Grandmother
and my Grand Mother*

*And – lovingly, loyally, gratefully –
to Benedict Douglas-Scott*

THE CREW OF THE *DAMOCLES*

Senior Astronauts

Commander Solomon Sheppard – *Commander and Pilot*
Igor Bovarin – *Flight Engineer*
Dr Margret 'Maggie' Millburrow – *Flight Surgeon*
Dr Cai Tsang – *Botanist and Hydroponics Expert*

The Beta

Harrison 'Harry' Bellgrave – *Pilot/Commander-in-Training*
Poppy Lane – *Head of Communications/In-flight Correspondent*
Juno Juma – *Trainee Medical Officer*
Astrid Juma – *Junior Astrobiologist*
Eliot Liston – *Junior Flight Engineer*
Ara Shah – *Junior Botanist*

Other

Jesse Solloway – *First Alternate Beta*
Dr Friederike 'Fae' Golinsky – *Lead medical officer*

PART ONE

'We will never forget them, nor the last time
we saw them, this morning, as they prepared
for the journey and waved goodbye and
"slipped the surly bonds of Earth" to "touch the
face of God".'

Peggy Noonan for Ronald Reagan

It is just like Earth, Terra-Two. It has turned in silence for millennia on the same spiralled arm of the galaxy. It is enveloped in temperate air, oxygen, nitrogen, noble gases, dark oceans licking empty shores. It's luxuriant with life. Trees burst from the dirt. Electric-blue fish slalom through coral reefs and the wind is heavy with spores that germinate in shadows. Wild, everything, the land and the flowers.

But there is nobody on it.

When we ask 'Why?', they say 'Because we haven't sent anyone yet', although really they're saying, 'Because there is nobody else out there. Not on any of the worlds.' We are the only thinking heads in the universe.

We were taught that, for a while, the universe existed and not one person knew. Stars exploded, nebulae collapsed, atoms crashed together and formed planets, then quiet oceans where single-celled organisms swallowed light and learned to flourish, then more complex life, plants, then creatures dragged their heavy bodies from primordial seas, shook off fins, feathers, opened eyes, but not one of them was capable of awe. Not one of them wondered at the lines on their palm and asked 'How?', or shouted at the stars as we did – for a time – searching for fellow travellers.

We know now that consciousness is rare. It's wretched and magnificent and lonely. It allowed humans to conquer the empty moon, the mountains of Mars, then Europa, Callisto and the rings of Saturn.

They planned the journey to Terra-Two and when they named the six of us how could we say no? We were young. They had hauled us from obscurity to hurl us at the stars, and we were dizzied by shallow fantasies of being the first, of leaving our footprints on the land, pushing our flag down into the dirt, giving it a name, dividing and taming it.

Did we forget about the darkness? Did we shrug off the loneliness and the labour? Did we regret? Of course we did.

We have been told that Terra-Two is waiting for us, and perhaps it still is. Perhaps the sand has washed up on the shores in quiet anticipation of the day we set our soles dancing across it.

Some nights we ask ourselves why we chose to leave everything behind. We used to think we had many reasons, but – really – there is only one.

JESSE

2004–2012

HE HAD DEVELOPED THE habit of tapping his thumb against the tips of his fingers. The index first, three, four, five again and again, perfected to a quick, quiet art. He had read online that it was a test of neurological agility. When the neurons in his brain began to pop out like lightbulbs he would no longer be able to perform this minor feat. Nor would he be able to roll a two pence coin over his knuckles forward and then back in one fluid motion so the penny slid across his lissom hands – another skill mastered over years of staring out the window during tutorials, watching blossoms fall and thinking about death.

Jesse thought about death a lot, in the beginning, with the same detached curiosity roused by the sight of a car accident. He had been told that he would die before he turned twenty.

During a trip to Indonesia, a medicine man had taken his sister's hand and told her she would fall sick but not leave this Earth, and then stared down at the lines of Jesse's own palm and said that in nine years he *would*.

It was only after his sister's preternatural recovery from cerebral malaria that Jesse began to give some thought to how he might die. He'd been eleven, then. Young and relatively healthy, it was unlikely to be an accident of genetics or something insidious and tragic like leukaemia. He hoped that, when death came, it would be quick as a knife. Something as dramatic as a car accident or gunshot wound seemed, to him, romantic but unlikely. Jesse believed that if anything was going to kill him it would be his brain. A tumour, an aneurysm, a sudden unexplained blow to the back of the head.

Whenever his mother or the family paediatrician intervened – promising that he was healthy and unlikely to die – he would remember the sight of his sister's green eyes flying open in that humid hospital room just after the doctors had told his parents there was nothing more they could do.

Jesse sat in class, tapping his fingers and imagining the build-up of intracranial pressure. His anxious, overactive brain swelling like a sponge against the cage of his skull. By the time his family left Indonesia and returned to London, life was like a fickle lover, leaving him guessing and sick and wanting more time.

A few more years was not enough. He might never go to Argentina, never have sex, never ride in an open-top convertible along the California coastline with the wind in his hair and shadows at his back. All these things had never been his and yet he felt as if they'd been taken from him. The future, the freedom to hope for it.

His suffering – made ineffably worse by the fact that no one believed him – grew so bad that by age thirteen he was a morbid recluse. He spun away from his classmates like a satellite in a doomed orbit. Lay in bed, tallying all the time he had already lost, too tired to get up, to cut his nails, to get dressed. His older sister would stand over his bed in her crumpled school uniform and shout, 'Some people have *real* problems, you know.'

But when applications to the Off-World Colonization Project opened up, Jesse saw his salvation.

Like most people his age, he had grown up with dreams of Terra-Two. Built papier-mâché models of the habitable exoplanet in kindergarten. He had been seven or eight when the Search for Life on Terra-Two had started, with unmanned satellites landing on alien shores and sending back images of the verdant earth, clean-water lakes, a thriving ecosystem and no humans. By the end of the twentieth century, many countries had mastered interplanetary travel and set their sights on neighbouring stars. When the grainy footage of this new and beautiful planet was broadcast across the globe, Terra-Two ignited the imagination of every child Jesse's age.

The tabloids had declared it habitable long before NASA issued an official statement, and soon after that the race to colonize T2 truly began.

The UK Space Agency put out a nationwide call for healthy twelve-to-thirteen-year-olds with an aptitude for physics and biology to join a team of experienced astronauts on the twenty-three-year-long journey to the new planet. The group would be called the Beta, and they would be chosen from a pool of students enrolled on an accelerated course of study at the Dalton Academy for Aerospace Science in the suburbs of London. A school founded to train a generation of astronauts, engineers and employees of the UK Space Agency. Jesse was eating dinner one night when he heard that the organisation were looking for people his age. It occurred to him, then, that perhaps he was not destined to die at twenty after all. Perhaps leaving Earth on board a space shuttle had been the prophecy instead.

The application process involved months of interviews and

physical assessments, and several rounds of gruelling exams. Jesse was thirteen when he was finally admitted to the Dalton Academy. The main building was a repurposed sanatorium, the words 'New Addington Home for Incurables' still conspicuously etched into the crumbling stone architrave.

The initial adjustment was difficult for Jesse, who had been the brightest in his school – two years ahead of the other students his age – but was now amongst his academic peers. His days began before the first glimmer of dawn, at 5.30 a.m., with a compulsory run around the training facility, a cold shower before breakfast and then classes that began at 8 a.m and finished at 8 p.m. That first year involved cramming four years' worth of exams – GCSEs and A-levels – into thirteen punishing months. He staggered through those weeks, along with the still star-struck students in his class, only to find that there was no time to rest on the weekends. Saturdays were for training and tutorials, and after lunch on Sunday they were herded into the library for six hours of silent study. With only three weeks a year of summer holiday, months ran drearily into each other. Every vacation, every summer's day, every light-limned afternoon was sacrificed to the laminated textbooks he hauled around like bricks. Scribbling up flashcards. Tackling incomprehensible worksheets. Watching his sister sunbathe out in the garden as he memorized tables of data. Tempted every hour by the mid-August barbecues and the sweet smells of sizzling beef, the sounds of his parents' laughter drifting through his bedroom window as he rewrote and rewrote and rewrote specific biochemical pathways so many times that they became muscle memory.

The stress was sickening, and many of the school's students broke under it. During his first term, Jesse had been grouped with a team of six called an 'expedition', and by the end of the first year one of them had dropped out voluntarily and two had been expelled after failing an exam. When he returned to Dalton the next year, at age fourteen, their initial cohort of 300 had halved. They began studying aeronautics, degree-level physics, geology and propulsion engineering. Two months into the new term, Jesse returned from a weekend away to find that his roommate had been in bed for three days, sheets soaking wet, eyes vacant and haunted. 'I just can't do it anymore,' he told Jesse, 'I can't even move.' He'd been collected an hour later by his parents and a mental health officer. That same year, a boy drowned in the Neutral Buoyancy Lab and, although there was an investigation, Jesse was horrified to find that life at Dalton went on as normal. Classes continued the next day without interruption, although one morning run was cancelled, and the flag above the observatory flew at half-mast for the rest of the week.

In spite of all this, every time his parents asked if he wanted to drop out, Jesse was surprised to find that he did not. He had never been in love, but perhaps this was close to it. He had never wanted anything more than he wanted to go to space. Dalton pushed him to his limits. Each completed chapter of a book was a new triumph of understanding – after staring at a genetics text until the words began to blur he would gain a happy, tentative understanding of Okazaki Fragments or the Shine-Dalgarno sequence, and his heart would rejoice. And etched on the school's front gates were the words, 'It is better to fly like a falcon for half a year than to crawl like a turtle through a lifetime.'

The hope of being one of the six students chosen for the

Terra-Two mission made it into his every waking thought. He plastered his walls with diagrams of spacecraft, manoeuvres and constellations, so he could memorize them as he lay on his back. The prospect sustained him. Kept him running laps across the frosted grounds when his fingers were prickly and numb with pre-dawn cold. He could stand all of it because he knew that leaving Earth was not merely his destiny, it was his only chance to live beyond his twentieth birthday.

The first four years of work paid off. Jesse passed his exams and was selected to be an astronaut candidate in a group the students liked to call 'The Final Fifty'. Everything was different by then. Two hundred and fifty hopefuls had been culled: friends, confidants. Jesse felt isolated. For the first time, he doubted himself. Every one of the brilliant students who remained in his cohort believed that the sky was their destiny also. They could study forty-eight hours straight in their dorm rooms and ace the impenetrable weekly exams. Everyone became more acutely aware of the competition, of the fact that years of toil could so easily amount to nothing. That more than half of them would never make it to the shuttle, would ache forever with private longing, Earthbound and wretched. Students Jesse had once considered friends became cool and suspicious, leaning over his work to smile at errors only they could see. Dalton became a lonelier place, and Jesse began to wonder how much he belonged after all. Every now and then his mind would swell to great heights of tenuous certainty (*of course he would make it, hadn't it been prophesied?*) only to slip again and again into nail-biting anxiety.

When the result finally arrived, it was in the form of a letter, two weeks before graduation. The students chosen for the Beta and the backup crew would stay on and train for ten months until the launch. But everyone else would be discharged, free to seize the rest of their lives. But, what lives?

Jesse opened it alone, behind the Weightless Environment Training Facility, watching the silver July light on the surface of the water, fingers cold with dread.

His name was printed at the top: JESSE SOLLOWAY. The subject heading was 'Off-World Colonization Programme'. The first word that grabbed his attention – the first sickening word – was *Unfortunately*.

LATER THAT DAY, HE saw the six who made it on the BBC news. There was the one everyone suspected: Harry Bellgrave, who stood waving for the crowd in the shadow of the school's boat-house, smiling under a golden coronet of curls. And the weird but determined Ara Shah, who sang in the corridors and came top in most of the botany and hydroponics exams. While she radiated an air of effortless brilliance, Jesse had caught her, more than a few times, hunched over her laptop for so long in the library that she'd look up at the sunrise and blink in confusion as if she had no idea where it came from. There were people no one expected: Poppy, a hyper-polyglot who reputedly spoke twenty-three languages. She was a year older than everyone else and if she gave the wrong answer when called upon in tutorials, she would slip down in her seat, her cheeks flaming the same crimson as her hair. Eliot, the reclusive programmer, with whom Jesse had shared a dormitory for six weeks. Kenyan twins Juno and Astrid, the former studious and dour, the other prone to fits of breathy giggles in the back of assembly. When Jesse saw them all together the first time that day, and every time after, it stung.

'Why them,' he would hiss, 'and not me?' When he spotted them on the cover of *TIME* at a local newsagent's, his stomach turned. He tossed the stack of magazines in the dustbin and the shop assistant demanded he pay for all of them.

His nineteenth birthday was fast approaching, and his escape from death had been snatched from him at the final moment. 'It was amazing that you made it so far in the first place,' his mother reminded him and – after all – it was not a rejection. Jesse had been assigned to the backup crew. This meant that he had to forgo his final summer to train with the Beta. Only, after graduation the school was like a vacant fairground. Disconcerting, to live out his days in this place that was usually hectic with life. Only fourteen students remained, the crew and the backup crew. Practising with them was a miserable experience. In less than a year, they would all be in space. And Jesse's job would be over. He felt like a shadow boxer, learning to maintain a shuttle that his feet would never touch. It had all been for nothing, he'd lie awake and consider. Forlorn insomniac nights as the summer vanished. Occasionally, though, Jesse allowed himself to imagine it, leaving Earth and the risk of dying young behind, his name echoing down the halls of history on everyone's tongue. Neil Armstrong had served as backup commander on the *Apollo 8* mission, he remembered. It could still happen. A member of the Beta could be taken ill or fail to comply with the UK Space Agency and he would be called upon. It could still happen, he whispered with clenched fists into the darkness. But then he would catch himself counting the number of days he had left to live, and the old dread would settle like frost.

POPPY

JULY 2011

T-MINUS 10 MONTHS TO LAUNCH

THE DAY THE NEWS broke she was on her way home from school, and the sun was already setting on her mother's street. The fences were razor-edged in the last of the light and Poppy savoured it as she walked, letting her fingers clatter along the chain-link. She usually found a reason to stay behind after term ended: something she had forgotten, a second drama rehearsal, Arabic Literature homework, an hour frittered away in her dorm after everyone packed up and left. But this time, there hadn't been much to do. It was the final half-term before their class graduated, and the high point of the summer when the air was thick and wet as tar.

As always, Poppy had booked the long train home at the last minute, because it was always a miserable affair, leaving behind the sweet-smelling tree-lined avenues near Dalton and returning to her hometown on the outskirts of Liverpool. Part of an urban sprawl that had been condemned by the city's mayor. She'd taken the coach a thousand times from Lime Street Station, and watched from the window as glass towers slumped down. It took about forty minutes for the bus to wind into ghost-streets of boarded-up shops, Victorian terraces destined to be demolished and post-WWII social housing screaming with spray-paint.

It was downhill from the urine-scented bus shelter to her mother's flat. Poppy reprimanded herself if she ever turned up her nose at the cracked pavements that spewed dandelions and flattened cigarette butts. This was where she came from. The run-down townhouses carved into flats. Where she grew up.

And these people, the teenagers on children's bikes who cat-called and whistled when she past, these were *her* people. For five years, she had believed that when Dalton ended – when she was no longer allowed to lounge in the ivied quad reading books – it was to these streets she would return. To hate this place would be to hate herself, her mother would remind her during every visit home. Her mother vetted Poppy's speech for a new word or turn of phrase, and teased her mercilessly about it. 'Ohhh, Mrs Dalton,' she'd say with a curtsey. 'Too good for us these days,' and Poppy would blush and bite her tongue.

On Monday she had discovered that she had been chosen to go to space. In the quiet week after she found out, Poppy walked around in numbed surprise, certain a mistake had been made. It had been a dream to get into Dalton in the first place, to live and study amongst the neat, brilliant students who were unlike her in every way.

At almost fourteen, Poppy had been four months shy of the upper age limit for candidates, but she had filled out an application – an online test, logic problems, personality quizzes, reasoning and lateral thinking – in a secret moment of longing. Half a million other children also applied. She had been shocked when she was invited for the selection interviews, but knew that her mother would not be able to afford the train fare into London. That might have been the end of it, right then, had it not been for a school teacher who handed her an envelope of cash with a note saying, 'make us proud'. It was the first time she'd ever left her city. An escort had taken her and a coach full of other applicants to Dalton for three more rounds of testing in a purpose-built training facility alongside thousands of other terrified candidates, wearing numbered badges and coded wristbands. They had been the hardest tests that Poppy had ever taken, four hours in a humid silent hall, several writing and coding tasks and one tortuous language exercise that required her to pen a persuasive argument in a language that the examiners had invented, following stringent rules in their devised syntax and morphology. Then came a week of invasive physical exams, blood tests and a comparatively low-tech beep test, which involved running back and forth across a gymnasium at ever-decreasing intervals. Two prospects had vomited on the linoleum.

That had been six years ago. Getting accepted into Dalton had been the greatest achievement of her life, and yet every test she had taken since then was harder than the last. Every week, when their scores were projected up in the school hall, Poppy had been comforted to find that she had achieved high enough to remain on the programme, but never high enough to pose a strong enough threat to the other students, who were bright and driven and strange and already disliked her because of her accent and her age.

When she'd opened the letter to discover that she was one of the six who had been selected for the Beta, she'd been certain

that some mistake had been made. And so, for the rest of the
week, she carried the news around with her like rubbish she
was keen to toss.

The day the names were released publicly, Poppy returned
to her street to find a mob. At first, seeing the road blocked by
cars and news vans, she'd thought there had been an accident.
Reporters thronged the pavement speaking simultaneously
into microphones, and the shuttering lights of cameras burst
like firecrackers at the edges of her vision. Initially, Poppy was
drawn towards the mob with a shiver of intrigue, but it turned
into dread in the next moment when she realized that the crowd
were lining up outside *her* flat, trampling the lawn and banging
on the door.

'Hey—' she approached a young man who had been slouched
on the wall. 'Do you know what's going on?'

'Oh, it's uh—' He looked up at her and took in her white
uniform and her vivid red hair, which was already slipping out
of the loose braid she had twisted it into. 'Oh,' he said again, and
then produced a small notebook from his back pocket. 'Poppy
Lane, how are you feeling about the upcoming mission?' The
sound of her name on this stranger's tongue was unnerving, and
Poppy stepped back. 'Can you just give me a sentence or two?
What are you excited about? What will you miss the most – since
you will never return?'

'I – uh?'

A couple of people standing nearby caught sight of her. *Wait,
is that her? Is that Poppy Lane?*

'Poppy,' shouted a reporter, 'over here!'

'Can we get a picture?'

'Over here!' Camera lights blinded her. When she opened

her eyes it seemed as if people had materialized out of nowhere; there was already a small crowd closing in on her, and more racing towards her, jostling for a better view.

'How does your family feel?'

'Is it true that you speak thirty-two languages?'

'Why do you think this mission has been so controversial?'

Poppy turned away from them and began to run, back down the street in the direction she had come. Just over her head the streetlights were flickering on and when she reached the end of the road she cast a quick glance over her shoulder. But the mob were descending upon her.

The blood beat in her ears. She felt exposed and frightened and far away from herself. The world had uncovered her secret before she had had a chance to fully understand it herself.

'Just a few questions!' A man pulled at the collar of her shirt and Poppy heard the tearing of cotton.

'Leave me alone!' she yelled, pushing him away. But more people were bounding towards her.

'Can I get a picture with you?' asked a woman, grabbing at her sleeve.

Everywhere she looked there were people, their voices slipping into a white-noise of urgent clamour. Sweaty fingers tugged at her blazer and the strap of her messenger bag. She pictured her own face, petrified in black and white on the cover of a newspaper. In a moment of panic, she kicked over a large plastic bin, which crashed to the ground with a heavy thud, the contents flying out. The crowd dilated, giving Poppy enough time to scramble over the fence into the darkness of someone's garden.

She raced around the unlit house and into a narrow alleyway

between the buildings. Hid in the shadow of the high walls. As she unhitched her bag and dropped it on the ground, Poppy noticed a ladder ripped into her tights. Nettles bit her ankles and she waited for the blood to stop crashing through her ears before she considered her next move. Through the bushes she saw the lights of the news vans, reflected off the black windows of the house. The thought of facing that crowd again, of trudging back through them to get to her flat, filled her with dread. She was trapped, and the realization made her heart sink. But the idea of squatting in the gloom of the alleyway until the drifters left the street and the vans drove away made her skin crawl. The cracks in the fence were fluffy with cobwebs, cigarette butts yellowing amongst the leaves and the silvered edges of condom packets.

Poppy spotted another escape. She could run through the alleys and into her own back garden, as she had done with her friends in the past, during humid summers. Just the sight of the overgrown passages reminded her of following the neighbourhood girls as they clambered over fences and marched through bramble, sweeping away cobwebs like the intrepid explorers they thought they were before finally scrambling back over the picket fence and into their shared back yard, rolling into the house filled with laughter.

Poppy lifted her bag and took a route behind the houses that she remembered, creeping through the thorns until her foot struck pavement on the other side of the alley. The street behind her house was quiet, so she climbed over rubbish bins and slipped into the pool of yellow light that illuminated their back yard. Dashing to the door, she stabbed the key into the lock and, finally, she was home.

The only light in their little kitchen was the flickering of the television screen. Poppy's head spun as she recognized her own face smiling back at her over the ticker-tape headlines – *Names of the Beta, the students chosen for controversial interstellar mission, released today.* Like her own, the names of the other students selected had been kept top secret. Poppy's gaze was drawn to the screen as their faces appeared: Juno Juma, the scholar, the prefect, and her twin sister. Ara, who never seemed like she had to cram for exams, as if she was born understanding mathematical constructs like quaternions. Her stomach flipped with joy and relief when she saw Harry's handsome face on the screen. 'He's going too . . .' she said out loud.

When she turned to her mother she noticed the tears in her eyes, then the faded lipstick on a mouth that had begun to sag. A halo of silver hair had appeared at her temples and Poppy wondered when her mother had become an old woman. Maybe it had happened suddenly, between trips to and from Dalton, or maybe an old woman had consumed her mother slowly in the solitude of their flat. Her mother's first words when Poppy entered were, 'Don't go. Please. Don't go.'

Poppy winced at the request.

Their family friend, Claire, sat on the other side of the table nursing a chipped mug of tea.

'How can you do this?' she asked. 'You didn't even tell your poor mam.' Poppy didn't have the energy for an argument, and so she turned on her heel and headed quickly out of the room, but Claire's voice trailed down the corridor after her: 'How can you leave her alone like this, when you're all she has? The ungratefulness of the child who . . .'

Poppy was out of breath when she reached her room and flung the door shut behind her. She slid down it. There were footsteps coming down the hall. Poppy turned the lock.

Poppy Lane. They had chosen her.

In the silence of her bedroom, her heart was pounding. Some part of her had not believed it was really true until the reporter said her name on the news. Some part of her was certain that a mistake had been made, that she would be passed over in favour of some more deserving girl. She had always believed that she would live and die in this council flat.

Poppy Lane. She let herself believe it now. *Mirabile visu*, she thought, *wonderful to see*. Her entire body buzzed with fear and excitement. Muscles tensed around her mouth, lips dawned into a smile she could not hold back, spilled over with laughter that came out thick and fast as quicksilver.

'Poppy.' There was a bang on the door but she wasn't yet ready to open it. 'Poppy, love.'

There was something on the bed, a solid parcel with her name written on it. Poppy stood up and held it in her hand for a moment, noticing the telltale signs, the hard ridge of it, the indented edges – it was a book. When she tore it open she wrinkled her nose in puzzlement. *A Guide to the Zodiac: Decoding Your Destiny in the Stars*. She traced the golden patterns along its thick spine, and then opened the front page, and found the inscription:

I always knew you'd do it, Freckles. You were born to shine. Dad.

She traced her thumb over the word; D. A. D. – her favourite.

'Poppy.' Poppy heard the familiar scrape of metal in the lock, which meant her mother was twisting it open with a butter knife. She appeared a moment later on the threshold in her faded dressing gown.

'Mum, was Dad here?'

'Is that from your father?' Her eyes darted to the book in Poppy's hand.

'Yeah. I mean, it's his writing on it. Did he come here to see me? When I was in school maybe?'

Her mother shook her head. 'That arrived in the mail this morning.' She sat heavily on the bed, taking the book from her daughter's hands.

'Funny thing to get you, eh?' she said. 'But then, he never bothered to learn a thing about you. Probably thinks you're interested in star signs, just like me.'

'Maybe I am.' Poppy had always rolled her eyes at her mother's devotion to astrology. Through the gap in her curtain she could still see a constellation of headlights, bonnets of cars parked in front of their house, idling engines, the rising chatter of onlookers. It was the first inkling she had of quite how different her life would soon be.

'Don't go.' Her mother's voice was thick and Poppy felt her stomach sink.

'You knew this might happen.'

'Did I?' her mother said. 'I mean, what were the chances, like one in a million. I know you're supposed to be clever and you know all those languages but . . .'

'Why me?' Poppy finished for her.

'Right. And I didn't think I'd find out from the Channel Four news.'

'I'm sorry about that.'

'Why didn't you tell me?'

'I don't know.' Poppy cast her mind back to the strange disbelief that had clouded her thoughts over the past week. 'I guess

I didn't properly believe it either. Like, maybe they'd made a mistake or something. It was too good to be true.'

'Too good to be true,' her mother repeated and then her expression broke and she was sobbing fat ugly tears, her face twisted in misery, nose dripping. When Poppy leant over to hug her she felt guilty as a thief. She had nothing good to say to her mother, whose future life she could see suddenly and horribly. She imagined her mother growing old in her dressing gown in their dirty flat, her cholesterol soaring, hair turning coarse and white. If her heart didn't kill her, the loneliness would. When she slipped away in the light of the television the reporters and talk-show hosts on-screen would shout at her corpse for two weeks before the smell became so bad that someone came to find her.

Was it possible to save your parents? Poppy wasn't sure. The only thing worse than watching her mother was *becoming* her, becoming a woman in that house where despair lurked, waiting to swallow her whole.

'Hey,' Poppy leant back as a thought occurred to her. 'Now I'm in the Beta they'll take care of you for life. You know that. They'll pay you. You could move maybe – to a nicer place.'

Her mother choked on her sob. 'Is that why you're doing this?' she asked.

Poppy shrugged. 'I'm just saying, that's one thing. At least there's that.'

'Yes—' her mother sniffed. 'At least there's that. And will they be writing a cheque for nineteen years of my life as well? Giving me all those hours back. For your red hairs in the bathroom sink? For a child I'll only watch grow up behind a television screen? Will they pay me for that too?'

ASTRID

12.05.12

T-MINUS 30 HOURS TO LAUNCH

THE MORNING BEFORE THE launch, Astrid woke up starving.

She'd had a nightmare about the rocket exploding on the launch pad, and all their bodies roasting in their seats. In the dream, the air smelt of rocket fuel and roasting flesh. Astrid opened her eyes at 5 a.m. longing for meat.

The sun was only just rising behind the space centre, and clouds rolled up the horizon, bringing a storm that was scheduled to pass by lunchtime. Her sister and the other girls were asleep, bundled up in their duvets in quiet heaps at the four corners of the dormitory. Astrid tried to climb out of bed without waking any of them, but as her bare feet hit the floor, Poppy rolled over and her eyes flew open.

'Sleeping?' Poppy asked in a whisper. She was wearing her retainer, and her voice was full of metal.

'No,' Astrid said, 'I'm awake.'

'Where are you going?'

'To the bathroom,' Astrid lied. Poppy closed her eyes again and turned away.

They hadn't left the space centre for almost nine days. Nine days of intense training, the twice-daily medical checks and briefings. Astrid felt as if she had not seen the sky for months.

She stepped out into the corridor, looking up and down for any security guards or medical inspectors, but it was empty. The fastest way to the kitchen was via the emergency staircase, so she headed in that direction and rushed down steps, cold as stone under her bare feet, two at a time.

As the launch approached Astrid had developed the strange sense that her stomach was yawning open like a dark well. She woke up every morning weak with hunger, longing for the roasted potatoes soaked in butter her grandmother made at Christmas, blistering hot on the tongue. She wanted to leave the space centre's clinical refectory behind and return to the humid, joyful cave of her grandmother's kitchen, the tiled floor on which she'd played from birth, watching the old woman's wrinkled hands as she set cauldrons of stew bubbling over the fire. Astrid remembered a cornucopia of food on the table, the air so thick with spices that she could taste it. Everyone candlelit and laughing.

The afternoon they'd reported to the space centre had been thrilling, the approaching days rich with possibilities. Yet Astrid had realized, as she waved her father goodbye, that she had traded his earthy espressos for the rancid instant coffee that dripped from machines in the space centre's refectory. She'd chosen macronutrient power bars over the raspberry and white chocolate cookies her mother baked in obscenely large batches. Astrid's mouth watered at the memory of the silky sweetness of the chocolate, shot through with the tart skin of the raspberries.

She remembered the midsummer's day their family made a trip to the Diana Memorial Playground in Kensington Gardens.

Astrid and her sister had been nine or ten, then, and they ate mint ice creams in front of a wooden pirate ship. Their father took a photo, which Astrid still had, the image sun-bleached and overexposed, two brown girls, their tongues green, toes caked with sand. Astrid wanted to eat it all, the sweetness of turning ten. The first time she tasted a lemon and squealed at the acid bite of it, the time Juno – out of spite – had stirred a spoonful of washing-up liquid into her squash and Astrid's mouth tasted so strongly of soap that she cried, in the car, all the way home. She used to think that you could taste the spring, even. That when she grew tall enough to pluck cherry blossoms they would melt in her mouth like liquorice. But spring was almost over now.

Astrid was empty inside and she was running out of time. On the spaceship, their meals would be bowls of macronutrient broth, cereals and rehydrated meats, or vitamin-fortified spag bol, until the hydroponic greenhouse began producing crops. Astrid had seen a spreadsheet of everything she would eat for the next twenty-three years and it turned her stomach.

Astronauts who had gone up before her said that in the darkness something changed in their mouths and foods they loved came to taste like rubber, sapped of every delight. They were known to add liberal amounts of salt and spices to everything in hope of reinvigorating miserable meals. Astrid thought with dread that she had around twenty-four hours left on this rich planet and there were so many things she had never eaten.

She slipped into the cool pantry. The motion-sensitive lights flickered and the clinking sound of it made her breath catch in her throat for just a moment. She looked around. It was nothing like their busy pantry at home, where some shelves were stacked precariously with pots of wildly growing basil and thyme, others with the lurid cardboard boxes of their childhood cereals.

This pantry was more like a laboratory, the food arranged carefully in cupboards marked with all of their names – their portions were tightly controlled by a consultant dietitian – sticky labels loaded with cryptic etchings referring to specific nutritional and caloric values.

Astrid peeled open a fridge, and her eyes fell on the shelf marked Juno. There was her sister's breakfast, glistening with condensation. Cooked salmon and pickled eggs, a salad, soft pearls of mozzarella and sun-blessed tomatoes swimming in oil.

Was it stealing?

Astrid reminded herself that she was running out of time. Thought again about all the foods she would never try. Quails' eggs – spotted ivory treasures the size of olives that she lusted after every time her mother took her to the farmers' market. She wanted to eat a blood orange, with its eerie crimson flesh, which she imagined tasted like rust. For a whole year now, whenever she'd gone off-campus, she'd lingered by restaurant windows, green with envy, as she watched people devour little langoustines, guinea fowl, golden pears. Last Christmas their mother had won an ornate jar of quince jelly at a raffle but dropped it in the car park on the way home. Astrid had stared down at the shattered glass and the carmine splatter on the tarmac as if the jelly might as well be a million miles away. Her stomach ached for it now. For any and everything.

So she ate it all. The egg first, in one briny mouthful, then she peeled the salmon off the platter and dropped slices into her mouth before stabbing her finger into a lump of butter and licking it clean.

Astrid ate magnificently, bits of everybody's breakfast, and then the fruit salad. It would be over a year before the hydroponic garden on the *Damocles* yielded any fruit, so she devoured a whole box of cherries and spat the stones out like tiny bones sucked clean of marrow. Grapes, a generous helping, and then mango that was soft as butter inside, golden as a slice of the sun.

Time slipped by. As she ate, the sky outside grew lighter and the rain began. The racing in her heart only made the stolen feast even richer, sweet with abandon.

There was a noise outside, and Astrid froze midway through tearing apart a crackling loaf of bread. The wind, she wondered, or a security guard making his rounds outside?

Another sound. The door to the refectory slid open, lights flickered on and flooded through to the pantry, where Astrid crouched like a thief.

She was holding her breath, fighting to keep as still as possible though her chest shuddered against the hollow thumping of her heart.

With black terror, she looked around at the remains of her meal. The floor was littered with shreds of tin foil and cling film and a cairn of cherry stones, and a little blizzard of breadcrumbs drifted around her. In the glacial light of the fridge she saw herself, in a nightdress, her fingers stained black by cherries, hair unbrushed, on her knees amongst the mess. The food in her stomach turned, curdled into a sudden shameful awareness of her animal self.

What would she say?

She pictured her sister's nose wrinkling with disgust. And then the fear, again. Would she be punished for stealing? She wasn't supposed to be out of bed before the morning bell. Her mind flitted naturally to the worst thing imaginable: being kicked off the programme, convicted, publicly shamed.

She dropped the bread and darted behind an open door into a shadowed corner of the pantry, holding her breath and praying not to be found.

Her ears pricked up a minute later as the sound of footsteps echoed off the walls. She tried to imagine who might be downstairs so early. One of the cooks with their white hairnets? A security guard who'd heard a sound in the kitchen and come to investigate? The surly dietician? Astrid spotted her sometimes, roaming about the refectory with a clip-board.

Her stomach snarled.

'Hello?' came a voice.

Astrid said nothing, tried to keep still.

But the sound of steps grew louder, marched towards her, slammed the cupboard door back.

'Astrid!'

She yelped and leapt back. Then looked up to find a familiar face under a storm of red hair.

'Poppy?' she gasped, almost with relief.

'What are you doing?'

Astrid glanced around at the pantry, the cupboards she had thrown open, the detritus on the floor. Her cheeks burned.

'I – I . . .' Astrid fumbled for an excuse as Poppy looked about in amazement, and horror. 'Please don't tell anyone.'

It was then she noticed that her friend's eyes were bloodshot and shadowed.

'Are you okay?' she asked. Poppy shook her head, choking back a tear. 'What is it? What are you doing down here?'

'I came to look for you,' she gasped, wiping her nose with the back of her hand. Sniffing. 'You said you were just going to the bathroom and I thought . . . I need to talk to someone.'

'Then talk.' Astrid closed the fridge and they stepped out of the pantry and into the refectory, sat on one of the plastic benches on the nearest table.

Poppy pulled her retainer out of her mouth and placed it in front of her, silver strings of saliva sliding off her gums.

'You won't tell anyone?' she asked. Astrid shook her head. 'I was up all night. And I've been thinking. I can't go.'

'What?' The words knocked the breath from Astrid's throat. Poppy nodded.

'I'm . . . I know the rest of you don't understand this . . . but . . . I'm afraid. And maybe I'm not ready.'

'For what?'

'For all of it.' Poppy's pale fingers were trembling. 'This whole thing has happened so quickly. It feels like yesterday that we were selected and now here we are. Leaving tomorrow. I'm not ready for it, or to spend twenty-three years travelling to a planet that no one has ever been to. And the other stuff too . . . never having children of my own, and—'

'Look,' Astrid interrupted, 'you just have cold feet. That's all.'

'Twenty-three years, Astrid.' Poppy's eyes widened as if she could see every hour they would surrender to the darkness. 'And—' she lowered her voice. 'Do you always believe them, about Terra-Two?'

'What do you mean?'

'That it will be a paradise. That it's as beautiful as they say it is. Like the pictures.'

'Of course, I do. W-why wouldn't I?'

'I don't know.' Poppy shrugged, 'I imagine reaching it sometimes and finding that it's as scarred and desolate as the face of the moon. I think I'd die of disappointment.'

'You just have cold feet,' Astrid said again, gripping Poppy's arm, willing her to stop.

'Do I?' she asked.

'I believe everything,' Astrid said. 'This is an amazing adventure, and we're the first. Like Armstrong and the moon or Igor and Mars. And it will go by quickly. All the years. Like this –' She snapped her fingers.

They both looked up. They'd only just noticed the sound of the rain, the heavy way it was pounding the copper roof of the refectory. Behind Poppy was a glass wall, and a door leading to the courtyard. The sky was twice as bright as it had been just five minutes ago, and the dawn made the clouds light up in peach and bruise-purple. Astrid had never seen rain like it before, the kind that reflected the sun and filled the air with a flaxen light. She might even have called it *beautiful* if the word hadn't curdled in her stomach.

'That's why *you* deserve to go,' Poppy said, turning back. 'You and your sister and Ara. The boys. They made a mistake with me.'

'Don't say that.'

'No . . .' She lowered her eyes, 'It's true. I came because I was running away. And . . . you want to know something?'

'What?' asked Astrid.

'*Moy sekret*,' she said. Astrid recognized the Russian from her GCSE classes. Poppy had an irritating habit of flaunting her language skills at inappropriate times. 'I lied in the personality tests.'

Astrid gazed at her in confusion.

'It's quite simple, actually,' Poppy continued, 'they have specific select-out and select-in criteria. You have to be sociable enough to thrive as a member of a multi-disciplinary team, but introverted enough to do well in the isolated environment of outer space, so you—'

'It's not possible to cheat those tests,' Astrid said. 'They control for lying. Don't you think everyone lies? Or tries to? No one's going to say they're frightened of the dark or enclosed spaces. Everyone ticks "strongly agree" when they read "I function well in a team." But they chose *you* for a reason. You're so good at—' Astrid fumbled for a moment. '... communication. And ... public relations. The crowds love you. You wouldn't have made it through if they didn't know you were right for this mission, Poppy.'

Poppy looked up again at her friend with desperate eyes. 'You think?' she almost pleaded.

'Of course.'

Poppy's talent with languages had long made her the envy of the other students at Dalton. As part of their training, all astronaut candidates were required to display some proficiency in Russian, as the UKSA had strong links with the Russian Space Agency, Roscocosmos. As her classmates took their first clumsy halting steps into the language, Poppy was reading *Анна Каренина* and conducting happy conversations with their engineering teacher. Although she scored below average in almost every other subject, Poppy had excelled in computer science and robotics because she picked up programming languages with the ease of a stamp collector.

Nevertheless, everyone suspected, uncharitably, that the real reason Poppy had been selected for the Beta over so many other competent candidates was because of her good looks. Poppy's role, as Head of Communications, was the most public-facing of the crew. And her face was a delight. Unnaturally symmetrical. Titian hair drawn down her porcelain forehead into a delicate widow's peak. Cartilage of her nose curved exquisitely upwards. Every week for twenty-three years, her role was to appear on the TV and computer screens of children all over the world, explaining thermodynamics and Kepler's laws of planetary motion in twenty different languages.

'And you have doubts too, sometimes?' Poppy asked.

'Sure,' Astrid lied, 'sometimes.'

A tremolo voice rose up from the rain, and Astrid looked up to see a girl outside the window in the courtyard, dancing by herself, dressed in mufti, a crop top and combat boots, a glittering line of bindis dotting her left brow. It was Ara. Singing a song that Astrid had heard her perform before, at their Leavers' Ball the previous year. She had been the first on the dance floor, singing alone, wearing, then, a sequinned dress with a skater skirt that flared up around her thighs when she twirled. She had been like a human disco ball with her bold voice, an inspiration to them all – every girl who had scrabbled the previous fortnight for a date – alone and unashamed.

'She can't go a day without dancing,' Poppy said with a weak smile as she stood up. Prising open the door, she followed just like the other girls had that night at the dance. Ara's siren song, irresistible.

Although Astrid recoiled at the freezing rush of air into the refectory, she watched Poppy skip into the courtyard to join in. Ara took her hand and led her in a dizzy waltz up and down the cobblestones, both blinking fiercely against the rain. Then she let go and sent Poppy reeling, their laughter scattering up the four walls and into every window.

From where she sat, Astrid saw her sister Juno pop a sleepy head from the first-floor window, and was sure she was going to tell them off about the noise, but instead she ducked back inside then appeared in the courtyard a moment later to join them in the dance. Her sister had never been able to dance. She moved awkwardly, with none of the rhythm of her companions. Never able to shuffle off the weight of other people's eyes, and even in short moments of celebration, too nervous to move the way her body quietly urged. But that morning, she could.

Astrid ventured from the table and stood on the threshold between the kitchen and the garden, watching them all in surprise. 'Astrid, come and join us,' Ara urged, spinning around, her arms thrown above her head. 'The air smells so good out here. Like, cool and clean. The day's just begun.'

Astrid hesitated – the storm that had been threatening when she woke up had arrived, and it was violent. Thunder roared overhead, raindrops exploded on the cobblestones and sluiced over the gutters. 'What would you do with this day, Astrid,' Ara called to her, 'if you could do anything at all?' But Astrid remembered that this morning was not a beginning at all. They had been five years in training for this mission and all of a sudden here they were, almost at the end.

It occurred to Astrid, in a disembodied instant, that already this moment was accelerating away from her. In a second, being young and full of laughter and standing with all her friends on Earth would be only a memory. Nothing more than a memory ever again.

When she finally stepped out into the storm everything hurt; the icy needles of the rain, the sharp cold cobbles underfoot, the gnawing hunger in her stomach and a sudden longing to swallow the whole sky, the sound of her sister's celebration and the light shining off their forearms before it all slipped away.

A flash of lightning lanced across the clouds and Astrid spotted faces illuminated under one of the darkened archways on the opposite side of the courtyard. The boys. Eliot and Harry, their faces pale. Harry had his hands open, palms up, as if the rain was made of platinum coins.

Astrid cleared her throat, all of a sudden ashamed and aware of herself. 'Did we wake you?' she called to them.

'We've been up all night,' Harry admitted. 'Both of us. What are you doing?'

'Dancing.' Ara's voice still chimed with laughter.

'Evidently,' said Eliot. 'You'll catch pneumonia or something, in this weather.'

'You don't catch pneumonia – or *something* – from the rain,' Juno snorted.

They all stood in silence for a minute; the sun was breaking through the clouds and its muted light spread across them.

'I want to go into town,' Ara suggested with an excitement that sounded out of place. The exuberance of their last dancing moments had already dissolved on the rain-slicked stones. Harry chuckled, then stopped, spotting no sign of jest.

'Are you serious?' he asked, wiping the wet blond hair from his eyes. 'How would we do that?'

'We used to sneak out sometimes at Dalton. In the early days, when we were thirteen or fourteen.'

'Yeah, but it's pretty much impossible to leave here.'

'I know what you mean though,' Poppy sighed heavily. 'I feel as if we've been indoors for years or something. It's been so much work every day.'

'We don't have much scheduled today,' Eliot said. 'Just the tree-planting ceremony.'

'Is it lame that I'm excited?' Juno said, with a shy smile. They had grown up with pictures of famous and long-dead astronauts planting trees at the British Interplanetary Society, in the Garden of Flight. Pumpkin-orange in their flight suits, sprinkling dirt over the roots as they might over a lover's grave. It was a ritual the Brits borrowed from the Russians, who planted saplings in Cosmonauts' Grove near their launch site in Baikonur. Space enthusiasts still made the pilgrimage to see the 100-year-old oak tree planted by the first man in space. Astrid was excited too. She wondered if, in another century, people might touch the dirt at the roots of her own tree, mouth silent prayers for the other distant Earth that the Beta would be the first to stand on.

'It feels like graduation, almost,' Poppy said. 'Like we're finally real astronauts.'

'We are,' Harry said.

'We will be tomorrow,' Juno said, 'technically.'

'And,' Eliot said, 'the garden will be in town. The BIS is near the Houses of Parliament. We'll see all of London through the window. So you don't have to feel like you're missing anything.'

They all avoided each other's gaze.

'I thought I heard singing out here.' Their flight surgeon, Dr Maggie Millburrow, entered the courtyard, wearing a transparent rain poncho over her lab coat. In the corner of her eye,

Astrid thought she saw her crewmates straighten their backs, grow serious. They weren't sure if they would be in trouble for getting out of their beds so early. But the doctor smiled at them, and ruffled Juno's hair.

'We were just talking about the tree-planting ceremony,' Astrid said.

'I see.' Dr Millburrow smiled a little. 'I'm excited too. The birch I planted died while I was on Luna-Nine. They say it's bad luck, though the mission was a success. Fingers crossed this time.'

She glanced at her watch. 'The kitchen staff have told me that there's been a problem with breakfast.' A pang of guilty nerves made Astrid's heart flutter, and the blood burned in her face. She lowered her eyes, hoping that no one would notice. 'It's delayed by ninety minutes, so your medical checks have been brought forward to fill the time instead. Good to get them over with before the morning briefing. Commander Sheppard and Igor Bovarin have an engagement and so won't be there but we'll see them at 12.30 at the tree-planting ceremony. I have to tell you now though, I've been informed that anyone who does not pass the medical check this morning can't be cleared to travel. Safety precaution. We don't want to take any risks this close to launch.'

AFTER HER MEDICAL EXAMINATION, Astrid found Ara throwing up in the toilet.

'Did they clear you?' she asked, fingering the green 'cleared' tag they had just snapped onto her wrist. Peering around the open door of the cubicle, Astrid recoiled at the pungent tang of vomit, clutching her own stomach. 'Are you sick?'

'I'm not sick,' Ara gasped finally, sitting up to wipe the side of her mouth and waving her own green wristband. 'There were butterflies in my stomach.' Her eyes flitted back to the toilet as if they were actually in there, the butterflies, sunk in the water. Papery wings dissolving in bile. Ara flushed and then got unsteadily to her feet. Closing the cubicle door behind her, she rinsed her mouth out in the sink.

Astrid caught herself examining Ara's reflection in the mirror. She looked a little green and the skin under her eyes was dark. Ara smiled at Astrid's reflection in the glass.

Ara was not beautiful, but had inherited her Indian mother's thick black hair, which fell in heavy waves past her waist and smelt of the jasmine oil she rubbed into it. She had spent years of her childhood in the North, so her tongue still tripped prettily over words like *laugh* and *grass*. In their first year at Dalton, she had told the other students that she could speak to the wind and everyone had believed her or wanted to believe her, because her eyes were black as magic and sometimes when she spoke a gust *did* pick up, knocking leaves across the field.

Astrid watched as her friend lifted her head and eclipsed the sun, which was beaming through the window behind her. She envied Ara. People who knew her had always been certain that she would be selected for the Beta, that she belonged amongst the constellations, although they'd also been mistakenly sure she would be selected to be their commander-in-training.

'This is a great day.' Ara turned to point out the dispersing clouds. 'Can you feel it too, Astrid? It's like being in love, you know. So sweet it's painful, almost ... everything is beautiful, but everything hurts.'

'It's because we're saying goodbye all the time now,' Astrid said. 'It's kind of exhausting.'

Ara turned and leant against the window ledge. 'When I was younger and I fell asleep on car journeys with my dad, I'd wake up in my bed the next day, sometimes with my shoes on under the duvet, and I'd know that he'd carried me. Which I liked so much that sometimes I'd just pretend to sleep as the car turned into our road, so that I could feel him lift me over his shoulder then put me in my room. One time I opened my eyes when my head hit the pillow and he told me that soon I'd be too old to be carried.

'It happened less and less until now – obviously – when I fall asleep in the car, he just wakes me up and I walk to my bedroom. Take my own shoes off.'

'I think that's pretty normal,' said Astrid. Their voices echoed slightly in the little room.

'I know, but the problem is that when I turned twelve I couldn't remember the last time he carried me. I still can't. Probably when it happened I just thought that it was *another* time. The last time I was carried, the last time I saw Brighton Pier, or Trafalgar Square, I didn't know it was . . .'

'What would you have done if you had known?' Astrid asked.

'I don't know.' Ara frowned, her sight turned inwards with thought. Finally, she shrugged and said, 'I don't know. *Felt* it.'

Astrid wasn't so sure. Some part of her was sick with excitement about taking off in the shuttle tomorrow but the same part of her was gutted by grief. When she had said goodbye to her parents, nine days ago, she had known for sure that she would never hug them again. The knowledge had quickened in her an impossible urge to tell them everything that they meant to her.

To thank them for everything. But when the moment came to say it – to thank them for school fees, for her mother's paper-cut Christmas decorations, for every hot meal for her bones and for her beating heart – she had only waved.

'You know,' Astrid said, as Ara climbed off the window ledge, 'sometimes it's a good thing. When you don't know it's the last time.'

JUNO

T-MINUS 24 HOURS

HER BOYFRIEND, NOAH FLINN, had once shown her a graph of the inverse-square law, and pointed to the curve, force over distance, which decreased rapidly at first and then levelled off, like a playground slide. 'As you leave the Earth,' he'd said, 'the force of gravity halves and halves and halves and halves until there's barely anything pulling you back.'

Juno imagined that was how she would feel about him as she hurtled out of orbit. First, the keen pierce of heartbreak, but that would dull soon enough into an endurable ache, then again in ever-decreasing increments until she felt nothing, almost nothing, for him at all.

When their cars pulled up outside the British Interplanetary Society, a throng of reporters were gathered on the pavement and the crew lined up to greet them before heading into the building. Juno had only visited the BIS a couple of times before, for school trips and lectures, or to see the Aerospace Museum. The Edwardian building was like a geometric illusion, modest on the outside but vast as an airport hangar on the inside. Her head reeled as they stepped under the soaring glass dome above the foyer.

'Wow,' Eliot said with a low whistle, looking up.

An art deco chandelier flung refracted stars of daylight across the black marble floor. Juno admired the effect, stretching out her palms to catch the glimmer on her fingertips as the others moved off. 'I always forget how big this place is,' she said, to no one in particular. Through the foyer, the main hall was like the visible edge of an iceberg, arranged in descending mezzanine decks that telescoped down into a dark courtyard, where a life-sized reconstruction of a pre-First World War space shuttle was erected. From where she stood, Juno could almost touch the top of it.

'It's six storeys high.' Juno turned towards the familiar voice, and saw him bounding up the stairs.

'Noah?' she said. His head of platinum curls bounced as he walked. It felt like months since Juno had seen him, although it had only been nine days. He had come along with her parents to drop her and Astrid off at the space centre. After their final dinner, he held her hand in the back of the car and mouthed *Always, I'll always, I'll always love you*, as streets ghosted past.

'How did you know I would be here?' she asked.

'You know, you're kind of famous,' he said with a smile. 'My internship doesn't officially start until next week, but I asked to come in today, at short notice.' He fingered the society's blue crest on his shirt. A rocket and three stars: Earth space, near space and deep space. 'Because I knew you were coming for the tree planting.'

'That's right,' Juno said, 'I forgot that you might be here.'

'Well, I didn't know whether I'd see you, but my manager says that if there's free time I could show you around a little. Maybe, after the ceremony. I'm guessing you chose your favourite tree.' When Juno nodded, he continued. 'You're in good company, because Annie Tyning, the first British woman in space in ...' His blue eyes rolled up in thought, ''53 or '54, chose a wild apple tree as well. It's one of my favourites. I actually really like sitting down there, in the Flight Garden. And thinking about how almost every GB astronaut has touched the ground under me.'

'I think I'd probably do that too. If I worked here,' Juno said.

There was an awkward confusion between Juno and Noah, the kind that comes after saying all your goodbyes once, only to meet again. Their energy was spent and the idea of facing the theatrics of a second goodbye struck Juno as silly now.

'I feel as if I've been waiting here all morning ...' Noah said, rubbing a sweaty palm on the side of his jeans. Under his BIS jacket he was wearing an old mission week T-shirt from their school's Christian Union. Juno knew that it said 'Dare to Believe' in bold letters on the back. 'Is this okay?' he asked, reaching out for her as if his fingers might burn. 'You probably won't catch anything.'

They touched cautiously at first, fingertips brushing. Noah took a quick breath, as if steeling himself to say something. 'Juno ... I wanted to ask you—' He was interrupted by the public affairs officer, who emerged from the press office and shouted, 'Juno Juma!'

'Wait, what about Harry,' Poppy said, getting up from the ottoman near the front desk. 'He's not here.'

'He wasn't cleared to leave today.'

'His white blood cell count was a little low,' Juno explained.

'He's sick?' Poppy asked, eyes widening in horror.

'No,' Juno said, although Harry had gone pale with disappointment when it was announced that morning during their briefing that he would be put in quarantine for twelve hours. 'I mean, probably not. It could suggest that a viral infection is coming on. So they'll probably keep him in the sanatorium until T-minus twelve, and monitor him just to make sure he can fly tomorrow.' Poppy's brow furrowed. 'He'll probably be fine, though,' Juno added.

'Well—' the officer looked down at her iPad. 'The press have set up in the council room. You can change in the library and then the tree-planting ceremony will take place at one.' Juno glanced at the clock opposite. They had just over an hour. 'Plant your tree – I've been told by your flight surgeon to make sure that you wear your gloves; just a precaution – plant tree, final interview before the launch, although this one will be a small one, for the Interplanetary Channel and the society's publications. And then take some pictures. You should be able to leave by three and then your schedules are clear for the rest of the day. Get some sleep. You'll need it. Obviously.'

As they followed the woman around the main hall, Juno lingered behind to take in some of the displays. An oil painting of the inventor Sir William Congreve that she had encountered before in a History of Space Travel textbook. He was a pioneer of British rocketry and the society's founder. The date etched under the gilded frame read 1812, 200 years ago. The Congreve rocket was used during the Napoleonic Wars. Juno had always found it amazing that by the end of that century British explorers were rallying expeditions to the summit of Mount Everest, but 100 years later their grandchildren were scaling the mountains of Mars, embarking for Jupiter's moons and beyond.

Congreve left the bulk of his estate to the society after his death and, in accordance with his wishes, the money was invested and used to fund research into aeronautics and space exploration. Fellows of the BIS had initially conceived of the Off-World Colonization Programme and many of its members were amongst the pantheon of astronauts and scientists employed by the UK or European space agencies.

Juno was humbled by the history of the place. On every wall there was an image that made her shiver with recognition. Sepia-toned portraits of men wearing helmets, mission patches from pioneering flights. There was a Dalton professor – who had delivered a series of lectures on peculiar galaxies – accepting a Nobel Prize. There was the school's provost, shaking hands with a former prime minster. There were framed letters signed by notable MPs, UN council members, US senators, congratulating the society on its achievements.

'The girl is dawdling.' The public affairs officer clicked her fingers from where she stood at the entrance of the library. The acoustics in the main hall were such that the sound was startling as a gunshot. Juno jumped and rushed after the others – her sister Astrid, Ara, Poppy, Eliot and Noah – as they all walked ahead of her. 'I'm sorry,' she said as she reached the entrance.

The library was a cathedral of books, shelves of them stretching into dusty infinity. Juno gasped at the exquisitely detailed painting of the solar system on the vaulted ceiling. Space; black as crude oil and awash with stars.

Nine flight suits were folded on one of the tables. 'Do you want us to get changed now?' Ara asked the officer. But before the woman could reply her phone buzzed, and she pulled it out of her pocket in a reflex-quick action.

Sorry, I need to take this, she mouthed, and left the room.

'What happens if Harry isn't cleared to fly tomorrow?' Noah asked, as Poppy sank down into one of the reading chairs.

'They'll find – whatshisname? – his replacement from the backup crew,' Ara said.

'But that probably won't happen,' Juno insisted. 'They'll infuse him with synthetic white blood cells and he'll fight off any infection extra fast. He'll be completely fine by tonight. Probably.'

They were silent for a while, gazing at the library's oak door, waiting for it to open again. But after a few minutes, Juno gave in to her curiosity and began to wander around the library, examining the different publications while they waited for the public affairs officer to return. Heading down aisles of identically bound astronomical journals, she ran her hands along the sun-bleached spines of familiar volumes on engineering and space physiology. It was reminiscent of Dalton's library, except that on top of almost every shelf were tiny models of defunct space shuttles, their hulls gathering dust.

'That one's *Daedalus*,' Noah said, pointing to a model as he appeared at her elbow. The strange unmanned craft was unlike any other, surrounded by engine bells that looked like a bundle of silver billiard balls all around its outer hull. It was the interstellar spacecraft that confirmed the existence of Terra-Two and broadcast pictures of it back to Earth.

'I know,' she said and smiled at him, her breath condensing on the glass as she stared at the model.

'You'll never believe this. Come look,' Poppy called. She was waving a shiny issue of *Vanity Fair* she'd found amongst the magazines piled on the rack.

'What?' Everyone turned to her, gathered round.

'We're in it,' Poppy said.

'Stop waving it around and keep still,' Ara said.

When Juno leant over her shoulder she caught sight of the headline: MEET THE BETA: THE YOUNG ASTRONAUTS ALREADY MAKING HISTORY. Their faces stared out from the cover.

'I didn't realize that came out this week,' said Juno, her stomach sinking. Her sister was already flipping through a copy and Poppy handed her a spare.

Under the special issue's title were the words 2012: TERRA-TWO COLONIZATION BEGINS. Juno flipped to the in-depth article. The text was spattered with their smiling faces, quotes in bold, pictures of Dalton Aerospace Academy captured in unfamiliar perspectives using a wide-angle lens. There was even a timeline of the selection process – the six and a half years it had taken to arrive at this point.

Harry's quote in bold: 'It's great to fly the flag for Team GB.' Juno stifled a laugh as she stared at his handsome face, blond hair thrown back from his high forehead. But as she flicked through the thin pages, more memories rose like bile. The long day they'd spent showing the reporter around the space centre, then posing for the photographer out near the launch site.

'Why is Poppy always in the middle?' Noah asked.

'Poppy's the cover girl,' Astrid said, and nudged Poppy playfully.

The group photo was a two-page spread. The team posing against a black background that looked like the night sky but was actually a canvas sheet clipped to metal railings erected the previous day. Poppy and Harry were positioned in the centre – as always. Half-moons of digitally whitened teeth waxed inside their mouths. The stylists had twisted Poppy's straight auburn hair into spectacular 1920s style pin-curls, only to discover that whenever she moved they fell out, which was when they would descend upon her again with hairspray and tongs. Harry was standing a little in front of his crewmates in a way that, on the page, made him appear unnaturally large. The photographer had to keep telling him to move back each time he stepped in front of Poppy or Ara, blocking their faces from view.

Eliot slumped in the margin of the photo. The make-up artists had managed to conceal the tangle of blue veins usually visible around his temples, although the photographer's attempt to coax a smile from him had yielded only a pained grimace. Juno flipped to the next page to find that he wore the same twisted expression in another photograph, gazing up at an overcast sky, his pewter eyes giving off an aura of terrestrial melancholy.

'You look gorgeous,' said Poppy. 'Both of you,' she added for good measure, pointing to the corner of the page where the twins stood beside each other, smiling the same lopsided smile. They had been too hot in their spacesuits and had been restless by the time that photo was taken. When asked how to tell them apart, Juno had overheard the public affairs officer tell the interviewer that Juno was 'the slimmer one'. A whispered distinction Juno recognized for the first time that day. She had never noticed the way Astrid's generous hips and bottom made the material of her suit strain ever so slightly against flesh, while Juno's bunched like dead skin around her thighs.

The voice of the public affairs officer sounded shrilly through the walls of the library, snapping Juno out of the recollection. When the officer finally returned she announced that two of the senior astronauts, their commander Solomon Sheppard and the flight engineer Igor Bovarin, had both been delayed at the UK Space Agency, and were not expected to arrive until after 1 p.m. The tree-planting ceremony was going to be delayed by at least an hour.

'What should we do in the meantime?' Ara asked. The officer cast her gaze around the library, as if hoping she might find an answer amongst the publications rack.

'Read?' she suggested.

'Can we see the garden?' Astrid asked.

'Or the museum?' Eliot asked. 'It's just in the next wing over.'

'I can show them around,' Noah suggested. 'I work here. Sort of.'

The woman glanced at her phone, then looked at them nervously. 'I'm not sure,' she said.

'We can't sit here for hours,' Ara said. 'Not when the sun's coming out. Not when we won't see the sky again for twenty years.'

The public affairs officer grimaced. 'Wait here one minute,' she said, brandishing her mobile. 'Let me ask your flight surgeon.' She left the room again, and they listened to the undulations of her voice through the door.

'*We're never going to see the sky again*,' Poppy said mockingly, flapping an arm in the gesture of a prima donna.

'It's true, though,' Ara said.

'Well I wish you'd stop saying it.'

'I wish you'd stop *doing that*,' Noah hissed. Eliot was crouched on the floor, where he had found a lighter someone had tossed near a dustbin. He was sparking and re-sparking it, his thumb sliding over the sputtering flame as he stared, mesmerized.

'It doesn't hurt,' he said, without looking up.

'Still—' Noah twisted uncomfortably. '...it's something about the way you look when you do it.'

'How?' Eliot tore his gaze away from the flame and glanced up at Noah.

'It's just strange, that's all.'

'There's nothing strange about a fascination with flames,' he said. 'Fire is pure energy. Light and heat. Some places in the world, people worship it.' He stuffed the lighter into the pocket of his jacket. 'Besides,' he added, 'you can't be an astronaut if you're afraid of fire. Or if you're afraid of what happens when gasoline meets liquid oxygen. Tomorrow we will be sitting on top of a bomb.'

Noah's lips were white. 'Maybe that's why I'm not an astronaut,' he said quietly.

'She's not going to let us go.' Ara was looking anxious now, chewing on a thumbnail, and beginning to pace.

'Where do you even want to go?' Poppy asked, leaning back in a reading chair to flip through the rest of *Vanity Fair*.

'Where the fun is,' Ara said. This was Ara's catchphrase. On the few nights out they had been allowed over the years, Ara would refrain from making plans and jump on random buses until she reached somewhere exciting – and she always did. She attracted fun things, like an impromptu street party, a marching band. Ara seemed to trip through life wide-eyed, expectant and spoiled on delight.

'I've spoken to the flight surgeon.' The door flew open as the public affairs officer re-entered. 'She said that you can look around the library and this wing of the space museum, for an hour. You must be back here and changed into your flight suits

before your commander and the other veteran astronauts return.'
She looked at her watch. 'One o'clock.'

They all agreed.

Back in the main hall, Juno's crewmates looked as if they
would burst with delight. Ara was laughing, Poppy's face was red.
'One *whole* hour,' she said as if it was something too large to eat.

'Where should we go?' Juno asked, but Noah slipped his
fingers into hers.

'Come with me?' he asked.

'But, the others . . .' When Juno turned back, Ara, her sister
and Eliot were already skipping in the opposite direction.

'Please?' he asked, his knuckles dovetailed into hers. Every
time she looked back on that afternoon, Juno would urge herself
to do something different.

'Let them go,' Noah said.

And she did.

THEIR FEET FELL INTO a familiar rhythm as Noah led her
down the dim corridors and towards the lift that led to the
Garden of Flight. The silence was uncomfortable, so Juno scrambled for things to say to him. 'You know,' she said, 'Everyone's
getting really emotional this morning. About the launch. I feel
as if I'm the only one who's excited. They're only focusing on
the things they're leaving behind but there are so many things
I'll be glad I'll never see again.'

'Like what?' Noah asked, pressing his thumb against the
scanner to hail the lift.

'I don't know. Traffic jams and hailstones.' They stepped
inside. 'I'll probably never have to pay taxes, or stand in line at
the post office.'

'You'll probably never see all that stuff that supermarkets throw out in those big skips at the end of the day and the people who rummage through them for something to eat,' Noah added. 'That makes me sad as hell.' The floor numbers began at zero and descended into negatives, Noah pressed -7 and the door closed.

'Greenhouse gases,' Juno said. Her stomach dropped as they headed to the basement. 'Civil war. Famine.'

'All those things might happen on Terra-Two, you know,' Noah said. 'Eventually. I mean, war kind of happens everywhere.'

'No, it won't,' Juno said. 'We're leaving behind a world where slavery happened. Two world wars. Genocide. A world where people have used atomic bombs. Terra-Two will be different. Better. We will make it better.'

The lift pinged and they stepped out. The Garden of Flight was a dark orchard, densely packed with trees of all different kinds. Lots of silver birches, with bark that peeled like tissue paper. 'Sheppard had a birch tree,' she said.

'All of the Mars Expeditions did. I don't know why. Look here.' He led her to a row of them, like pale sentinels, the names of astronauts carved into a marble stone at the foot of each tree. Juno found the names of the veteran astronauts following them on the mission. Igor Bovarin had the most trees; some delicate saplings, others sturdy and flush with leaves, thick roots swelling from the black soil.

Noah led her to the centre of the garden, skipping over an artificial spring, into a luxurious clearing, lit blue with holographic galaxies projected on the ceiling. The air was heavy with pollen, and Juno trod carefully, so as to avoid crushing the flowers. 'This place is different from the way I imagined,' she told him, looking around at a patch of bluebells, their stems heavy with flowers. 'I don't think I've seen a plant, or anything other than titanium and steel and plastic, for over a week.' Juno laughed. The air smelt deliciously of apple blossom, and juniper, mint and wild sorrel. 'It's still spring here,' Juno said, reaching to break a bunch of cherry blossoms off a branch.

'It's something to do with the climate controls I think. They use these LEDs – like the ones they use on space stations, to keep them growing down here. But, for some reason, the seasons start and finish about a month later.' Flower petals dropped like confetti and gusted across the ground. It looked like the type of wood that she and Astrid used to search for faeries in. Like the wood near Noah's childhood house where he had first asked Juno to be his girlfriend, his cheeks burning, his eyes defiantly hopeful. Or where she'd met him after a dentist appointment, the first person he smiled for after they fitted him with braces – still ashamed of the cages they'd locked his twisted teeth into.

Dalton was a hostile place for friendships. Few romances lasted longer than a summer, but because Juno and Noah had endured, their union had taken on a kind of mystique. The young, star-bound lovers. But, after Noah had chosen to leave the programme, some of the excitement died. Juno sometimes wondered what kept them together now. The tepid comfort of habit, she supposed.

'So—' Noah stopped walking and let her hand drop. 'I got you a gift.' He dipped his hand into his pocket and opened his palm. 'It's a moon rock,' he said, 'in a necklace, so you can't lose it.'

Juno's heart fluttered. 'But that's yours,' she said. She had lost count of how many times she'd seen him turning the little stone over in his hands, or slipping it into his pocket before exams. It was small and grey, shot through with silvery flecks. An actual piece of the moon that Noah's father had left behind when he walked out of his son's life.

Juno was unable to meet Noah's gaze.

'Yes, but I wanted to give it to you. I mean, I know you're probably going to see so many other things on your way. Nothing so pedestrian as the moon, but—'

'Thank you,' Juno said, and kissed him quickly on the cheek. He smelt of sweetened milk and non-bio washing powder. Motes of dust flitted between them, and she memorized his face. His watery eyes, hair like spun sugar.

'Shall I put it on?' he asked.

She turned around and lowered her gaze as he tightened the clasp. The silver chain was cool on her skin and Noah let his fingers linger on the nape of her neck. Juno became aware of the airless intimacy of the garden, of the hair prickling up along her spine.

When she glanced up, though, she noticed something in the corner of the clearing. Nine holes, dug like graves in a row, and the potted saplings, ready to be transplanted into the ground. 'Those are ours,' she said, rushing towards them. Her name was engraved on a marble stone. JUNO JUMA. She knelt down and touched it with trembling hands.

'Do you ever think about what we would be doing if you weren't in the Beta?' Noah asked, his shadow stretching before her.

'Not really.'

'Like, what do you think we would be doing tonight?'

'Noah . . .'

'We might be going to the same university. You'd be studying physiology or medicine and I would be a physicist. Maybe we'd go to Blackwell's and buy all the books on our reading list second-hand, then sit upstairs in Costa blowing bubbles out of straws and making them all burst because we're laughing so hard. When we kissed goodbye in the night we would still have tomorrow . . .'

Her stomach squirmed with the usual guilt. He couldn't know that she had already left him. She wanted to say, *Space, Noah, I'm going to space. How could I choose you?* How could she choose those insipid dreams of his over the splendour of the sky?

As he spoke, she imagined – as she often did – that she was already up there. His hold on her decreasing, like gravity. Soon this residual remorse would be nothing at all.

'Juno?' When she turned to him his eyes were wide with anticipation.

'What?'

'Were you even listening?'

'Sorry. I'm sorry. Please say it again.'

'I said – I said . . .' He took a breath, his cheeks flushing, 'Will you have sex with me?'

She leapt to her feet. 'What? Now?'

'We've been going out for three years—'

'Yeah, and I thought—'

'I know we both agreed to wait but since you're leaving tomorrow, I thought . . .'

'What?' she said, a little more aggressively than she intended. She was prickling all over with panic.

'Well, don't you think that changes things? It's not really "waiting" anymore, is it? We're never going to see each other again.'

'You don't know that.'

'Tomorrow you're going away on that shuttle, and if we see each other, ever, like if I make the Gamma and launch in two years' time, I still won't see you for almost three decades—'

'Two ... and a half ...'

He was blinking fiercely, fighting back tears. 'We love each other.'

'Yes but ...' She could feel her pulse in her clenched fists.

He squeezed his eyes shut. 'Please ... ?'

This was it. This was the reason Noah was here, the thing he'd been steeling himself to ask. What difference did it make, it occurred to her, if she said yes or no? She'd regret it either way. And when she glanced at him, then, in the shade of the old trees, her heart swelled with pity. Juno imagined the day after the launch. Imagined what it would be like to be the one who was left behind on the planet she'd renounced. On a clear night, Noah would be able to see the *Damocles* flicker like another star amongst the constellations. But as it disappeared, he would feel as if it was really him getting smaller and smaller, spinning out in a lonely orbit, sentenced to navigate streets that used to be theirs.

Other astronauts had snatched pieces of the moon to keep themselves from forgetting. To make the goodbye a little easier. Would it be so bad if she gave him this?

'Okay,' she said, taking a deep breath as if bracing herself to dive into cold water. 'We'll do it.'

'Really?' His eyes widened with gratitude.

'It's what you want, right?'

'And you, right?'

Juno glanced at her watch. 'We haven't got long.'

When they kissed that time, it reminded Juno of their first time. There was a photo of them on his mother's mantelpiece, at a Christmas formal, Juno in an ill-fitting satin dress, distracted by the rainbow shards on a disco ball. Noah was photographed gazing at her in an unguarded moment of naked adoration. It had made her cringe even then. He looked the same way that day, in the Garden of Flight. He even thanked her when she twisted an index finger into one of his belt-loops, and then he stepped back to snap open the buckle and tug it loose. The light glanced off it and, for a moment, it was the blade of a knife. 'You don't know how long I've wanted this,' he said, unbuttoning his shirt.

Juno sat down on the grass and watched his fingers, fleet and trembling. He let his shirt flutter to the ground and it occurred to Juno that she had only seen his body a couple of times before: at swimming practice or at the beach. Noah's chest was hairless except for a thin jet of blond beneath his navel. His ribs and collarbones shone through blue-veined skin. Juno was struck by how terribly alien it was. The sight of all that flesh.

The holographic stars cast a spotlight on the clearing. It was an empty stage now, before the curtain, and Juno's nerves felt like ice. Noah lunged clumsily forward, and rolled on top of her, and then his clammy hands were everywhere, in her hair, between her thighs, pushing under the wired cradle of her bra. Juno willed herself to feel the same desire, for just a second. But as Noah continued kissing her face, her neck, urgent and dumb, the blood drained from her. He was made repulsive by his need, his heavy breathing, the sourness of his breath and the fullness in his jeans.

Pins and needles prickled up her fingers. 'Noah ...' She

twisted away from his sloppy mouth. Nettles in the bumpy undergrowth were sharp against Juno's spine. As her muscles went slack she became more aware of the weight of Noah's chest bearing down on hers so hard she could only take in shallow gasps. 'Get off me.'

He didn't.

She looked around wildly, flailing for words to describe her distress.

'Noah ... please. Get off me!' It was too much. She didn't want the weight of him, she didn't want his hands or his lips or any part of his strange body on hers. She shoved him, leapt to her feet in one fluid movement and stood shaking at the edge of the clearing.

There was an awful quiet between them while Juno choked back the acrid tide of nausea in her throat.

'Juno ... ?' Noah's voice trembled. 'Did I hurt you?'

'No.' She looked away, blinking back tears. 'No. I'm sorry. It's me. I can't – I don't know why. It doesn't feel good. It never feels good.'

'You can. It does. You're just ... not letting yourself, that's all.'

'That's not true.'

'It is. I mean, we love each other. And you know, we're basic-ally adults and stuff ...'

'But—'

He grabbed her arm and looked at her seriously,

'You know, Juno, there are worse things in the world than ... doing this. People do worse things all the time.'

'When did you decide that?' she said, then regretted it.

Noah clenched his fists. Juno watched his knuckles turning white.

'I don't know what you want from me. I can't help it. Loving you ... wanting you. It's all the same thing for me. And sometimes I really feel like you want to as well, but you're stopping yourself. I think that you're scared of not having control all the time.'

'That's not true,' Juno hissed. 'I'm not scared. I just don't want to.'

'Really? You don't feel anything at all? Because sometimes you—'

'I don't. Feel anything. That's the truth, Noah. When you're on top of me, I don't feel anything at all. Not one bit of affection, not one soupçon of desire. Not for you. Not for anyone. It's not that I'm scared. It's just that ... sex is repulsive.

'I don't understand why it's such a big deal. I don't understand why you think about it all the time. It's just your body. It doesn't have to control you.'

As Noah got up off the ground she caught a flash of green boxers through his jeans. He zipped them up, fingers still unsteady. 'I can't take this,' he said quietly, as he turned to go. 'Maybe everybody's right and there really is something wrong with you.'

Juno felt the blood rise up in her face – hot with shame and fury and regret.

She called out, 'I don't know what it would change. It won't change anything at all. You'll feel okay for an hour and then you'll feel rotten and I'll *still* be leaving.'

'Maybe that's what it comes down to,' he said, with a quiet rage. 'I love you too much to ever leave you.'

'I wish you loved me too much to ask me to stay.'

Before he disappeared into the darkness between the silver birch trees he said, 'Don't you realize? I always have.'

T-MINUS 22 HOURS

SHE WAS ALONE FOR a long time before someone came to find her. It was the public affairs officer, and when she did the phone in her hand was lit up. Juno thought she could hear the sound of sirens hiss through the speakers. Poppy emerged from behind her, her face streaked with tears. 'Juno!' she shouted, 'Something terrible's happened!'

ASTRID

T-MINUS 22 HOURS

SHE HAD DONE IT once before.

Once, in the gilded foodhall of Harrods department store, Astrid stole a handful of sugared almonds. She had wandered the aisles, her heart clenched with longing, and gazed at the silver fish gutted on shelves of ice, scales resplendent under the chandeliers. Towers of sherbet-coloured macarons. Strawberry truffles. White-chocolate bonbons. Glittering bowls overflowing with crystalized fruit. Astrid had glanced around – uniformed shop assistant temporarily distracted by a demanding customer – and then grabbed a handful of sugared almonds, the size and blue of robin's eggs, and then run, past the guards at the front door, past the throngs of tourists and all the way out into the glare of the midday sun. It had been an easy thing, a little thing, a swift combination of muscle contractions that comprised the theft, all, in themselves, innocuous. Astrid and Ara stole that delicious hour of freedom just as easily.

After the public affairs officer dismissed them, Astrid followed Ara down the corridors and into the Space Museum one floor down, with Eliot racing after them. They headed through the exhibitions, barely seeing them. A tour guide was leading a group of pensioners past an exhibit that featured Edwardian spacesuits. The three of them rushed past into the neighbouring hall, the one with the machine that simulated flight for small children.

'Wait!' Eliot shouted. 'Slow down!' But Ara wasn't listening; she gathered speed, ducking around glass display cases. Astrid followed her as she rushed around the base of a decommissioned space shuttle, almost toppling visitors. So strange, to see these members of the public. Uniformed schoolchildren, pregnant women pushing prams.

'Where are you going?' Astrid shouted, taking care not to slip on the linoleum.

'Somewhere great!' Ara shouted over her shoulder. Astrid followed past the museum's gift shop, up spiralling flights of stairs, their laughter crashing off the marble walls.

'Come back,' Eliot said, just before he disappeared behind another tour group.

Astrid chased Ara through a deserted fire exit and out into the blinding daylight. She didn't realize that they'd escaped until they had.

'This?' she asked.

Ara stopped running and leant on her knees to catch her breath. As Astrid's vision cleared, she gazed around. Ara had led her to the children's playground at the back of the building.

The wooden benches were still wet from the morning's rain, the ice cream stall shuttered, play-horses sunk into the AstroTurf, heads reared as if drowning.

'This,' said Ara, and pointed past the low wall of the play-ground and beyond the road to the wind-whipped river. She said it as if she was giving it to Astrid. 'We have an hour. Let's go for a walk. Let's take what we can.'

'But . . .' Astrid hesitated. 'What about Eliot?'

'He'll find us.'

'We should probably stay indoors.' Astrid glanced back through the fire door at the darkened stairwell.

'Astrid, don't you want to do everything you never did before? Or at least one thing?'

Astrid's arms were prickling with goosebumps.

She wanted to go.

She knew what she should do. She should go back into the building and wait for the other astronauts to arrive. She should rejoin her sister and Poppy and Eliot and plant her sapling . . .

'Astrid?'

. . . and yet, she had only one life. And she was tormented by how lovely the sky was, with the sun spearing through the clouds, and the pavements glittering.

How would she explain it to the Astronaut Office when she returned? Or to herself an hour later? Or in the years that would follow? How would she explain the mistake she was about to make?

Ara vaulted the fence on the other side of the playground and strode into the road, forcing two drivers to swerve, both cursing out of their windows. Astrid had a second, as another car passed, to choose between staying or following. She glanced back at the

Interplanetary Society. The unlit corridor was like a dark maw, leading to a life away from everyone she loved. And, for one wild minute, she didn't want it at all.

She had sacrificed her whole childhood on the altar of diligence and obedience and hard work. So couldn't she steal back this day? This one hour, and keep it for herself?

Astrid chose her friend. She darted in front of a red bus as the lights changed and raced after her.

They grabbed each other's hands, hysterical with delight, marooned on a traffic island amongst the cars. This was the most they had seen of the world in over a week, and the sounds were an assault on her, the roar of tyres on tarmac like waves smashing rocks, her pulse a snare drum.

The green man lit up. Ara dashed across the road and into a throng of people.

'We have an hour,' Astrid reminded Ara as they ran.

The rain had stopped and the wet pavements sparkled in the sunlight. Astrid and Ara ran by the Thames, deliriously free. Months of sprinting across the grounds at Dalton meant that they were at their peak of physical fitness, barely out of breath as the white stuccoed houses flashed past, as Tate Britain appeared and then disappeared behind them. They headed into throngs of tourists in plastic-bag ponchos, photographing Big Ben, the Palace of Westminster, protesters gathered on Parliament Square.

They could see everything when they reached the bridge. The low buildings to their right, clustered around the British Interplanetary Society, then on their left was the London Eye, the South Bank, the Shard like a broken tooth in the distance.

Amongst the crowd, a woman in harem pants was blowing

giant bubbles with two sticks. Astrid watched as rainbows slid across them, and little children bounced with delight at the sight of their own warped reflections. The bubbles were so big that, when they burst, they made a splash on the ground.

'Why do you think the bubbles are so interesting?' Astrid asked.

'Because they only last for a few seconds,' Ara said, as a small girl let out a thrilled yelp, jumping up to touch the shining edge of the thing and missing every time. 'Imagine if, instead of bubbles, that woman was blowing balls of see-through plastic that didn't cost much and lasted forever.'

By the time they reached the South Bank, Astrid was eager to head back. If they ran they could do it in twenty minutes. But Ara was distracted by the busyness. She kept slipping in and out of the crowd, pausing often to look at the street performers. One dressed as Charlie Chaplin doing tricks for pennies, a skinny teenager covering Jimi Hendrix songs. Ara emptied her pockets, chucking coins and a few crumpled notes at him with a laugh. 'It's not like I need them anymore,' she said.

Astrid was distracted by the food trucks, the ones selling foot-long hotdogs, Neapolitan ice cream, nuts that smelt like burnt sugar, boiling in vats of caramel. Only she couldn't eat anything. With each minute that passed, her stomach knotted with dread.

'Ara.' She grabbed her friend's wrist before she could turn on her heel again. 'We have to go.' Her voice growing stern. 'I've had enough.'

The pulse in Ara's wrist throbbed wildly. She shook herself free, and smiled.

'This isn't a game,' Astrid told her. Ara pressed her palms against Astrid's cheeks and brought their faces together, for a second, in a kiss. Her mouth tasted bitter as aspirin and there was a film of sweat on her upper lip. Astrid closed her eyes and, when she opened them again and drew in a surprised breath, Ara was running away.

'Where are you going?' she shouted after her friend.

'I'm not going back!'

All Astrid could see was her red skirt as she raced down the bank, her black hair like a comet's tail behind her.

She headed across the bridge and Astrid had to sprint to keep up, ducking and weaving past people on the walkway and calling apologies after her. She took a sharp turn down a crowded road, past the subway, which was belching steam in the May heat, into one end of Embankment station and out the other, to the crossing facing the Thames. Ara had vanished. When Astrid stopped running, her head was spinning and she pushed a hand against the strain in her chest, dizzy and panting in the humid air.

She groaned in frustration. This was getting away from her. She considered making her own way back to the BIS building, but could she go without Ara?

She headed in that direction anyway, back along the river. They had thirty minutes.

The warmth of the afternoon surprised her. It was late spring and the wind was hot as flesh. Astrid followed Victoria Embankment, where the river was the colour of rust. Then she stood for a long while, trying to memorize the city's skyline, before she heard a voice behind her.

'Juno . . . ?' She felt the cool of a shadow across her shoulders and turned around to find Eliot. 'I mean . . . Astrid. Sorry, it's hard to tell you apart . . . from behind.'

Astrid exhaled with relief. 'What are you doing out here?'

she asked. Eliot looked as if he'd been struck by lightning, his eyes wide.

'I was looking for you, and Ara. We need to get back.'

'You ran after us? All this way?'

'Yes. I lost you in the museum, then I saw you running up the road. Tried to catch up. Lost you on the South Bank.' He swore, leaning against the railings to catch his breath. 'This isn't funny.'

'I know,' Astrid said, and suddenly it wasn't at all.

'What's wrong with you?' he asked. 'You could get in trouble. You could get sanctioned. Or not cleared to fly. Astrid, don't you want to go to space?' The question cut her. Of course she wanted to go. Wanted nothing more. And yet, what was she doing here? Why had she done this foolish and reckless thing? Her own motivations frightened her.

'Let's find Ara and head back.' Eliot glanced around wildly, as if he might find her behind him, or across the road. 'Ara?'

'I lost her. Should we go back without her?' The silence between them, then, was horrible. Going back without Ara didn't feel like an option. 'Maybe she's there already,' Astrid ventured finally. 'This is probably all a huge joke to her.' And she imagined her in the society's library just as they spoke, bent double with laughter. 'If we keep going in that direction—' she nodded ahead of her, back the way they had come, '... we'll probably bump into her.'

She turned around and headed in that direction. Eliot followed without protest. Of all the members of the Beta, Eliot was the boy that Astrid knew the least. He was a year younger than the rest of them, seventeen, although he looked fourteen. His teeth were gappy and small, as if he'd somehow managed to hang on to his milk teeth. He was a robotics genius who had grown up in wales and the only student to be personally head-hunted and invited to join the Dalton training programme after winning an engineering competition run by Imperial College London. Famously, he'd written a computer programme that could predict the probability of a planet bearing 'life'. He'd been twelve when he'd joined and still scored perfectly in almost every exam. However, many had believed he would not be chosen for the Beta because of how poorly he consistently scored in every psychological evaluation and team exercise. He flinched when anyone but Ara touched him, and had to arrange his chips in order of length before he could eat them.

They had almost reached Westminster station when they both heard a scream. A gathering of people by the side of the road. A car accident maybe? A cyclist crushed under a wheel?

Eliot inhaled sharply and turned. Following his gaze to the edge of the river, Astrid noticed that a small group of people were gathering, looking down a flight of narrow steps that led to the Thames.

'What is it . . . ?' Astrid asked, but Eliot was walking quickly, then running, towards the low wall above the water.

'Call the police . . .' one woman said, rummaging in her handbag for a phone.

'. . . an ambulance . . .'

'. . . it'll be too late – there must be someone around here who can . . .'

When Astrid approached, Eliot shoved his phone at her. 'Use it . . .' he barked, then vaulted over the rusting gate blocking the steps that descended into the black water. A couple of people shouted, but none of them moved to stop him.

There was a body floating in the river.

She only recognized it was Ara a minute later, when Eliot emerged from the water gasping and grabbing at the railing. Astrid stood at the top of the steps and watched – gripped with disbelief – as Eliot scrambled and slipped at the bottom, heaving Ara's limp body with one arm and clutching at the railing with the other.

'Help! Help me!' he cried out. Astrid's muscles unglued, and she climbed down as fast as her trembling legs would allow. It was difficult; each step was coated in a slippery green-black slime. Every time Astrid moved, her foot threatened to fly out from under her and she pictured herself flailing, crashing down the steps and slipping into the river.

Eliot was having the same trouble. He was half-blinded by river water and tears and his trainers slipped across the stone. He almost buckled under the weight of Ara's body. Her head was lolling back on her neck, her fingers grazing the ground.

Astrid grabbed onto the railings and reached out her free hand to grab one of Ara's arms, and together they hauled her up to the pavement.

It was only when Astrid let her friend's body fall onto the asphalt that she noticed how thin Ara was. Her waterlogged skirt hung halfway down her thighs, exposing her knickers and the harsh angles of her pelvis.

'Does anyone know first aid?' one onlooker said, but Eliot was already flicking wet hair out of his eyes as he checked for signs of life, her breathing, her pulse. They had learned how to do that in physiology. The memory took on a grim reality then, as Astrid remembered Ara playing dead in her school uniform as her partner checked her pulse. *It tickles*, she'd spluttered, her face red with giggles she failed to swallow down.

'Call an ambulance ...' someone shouted, and three people confirmed that they already had.

'Don't touch her,' another person said, 'looks like she's broken something.' Her body was twisted unnaturally on the ground, one arm bent outwards. Astrid shuddered. It didn't look as if moving her would make any difference – her jaw was slack, eyes yellow and half-open.

SHE DIED IN THE ambulance. It seemed as if she would make it for just a little while, when she was breathing again and puking up the black water, her lips and teeth stained as if she'd been chewing on charcoal, but her heart had stopped before the paramedics could rush her off to the hospital and before they had time to hold Astrid and Eliot back to keep them from watching her body slump on the gurney.

Looked like poison, one of them said; something in her body before she jumped. Her stomach was filled with it.

Astrid had never seen someone die before – Ara was the first. From then on, when she recalled their final day on Earth, her friend's twisted body was all she ever saw. And the message they found later on Eliot's phone. A text that she had sent him, which everyone would go on to consider her suicide note. It was what she had said earlier that day to Astrid, what the reporters quoted: *Everything is beautiful. Everything hurts.*

T-MINUS 15 HOURS

'DID YOU SUSPECT THAT Ara Shah was suicidal?' Dr Maggie Millburrow asked in the car on the way back to the space centre. Astrid sat in the back, squeezing her fists into her eye sockets and trying to scrub away the haunting memory of the previous hours.

'I don't know,' she said through tears.

Whenever she closed her eyes, she played the day back. Had Ara appeared nervous? When they danced together in the storm that morning? Ara's hands had been hot in Astrid's palms and later she'd discovered her being sick in the bathroom. When they had escaped from the BIS building, her pulse had been throbbing through her fingertips. Had she been suicidal then? Or had it happened later when they skipped along the bridge by the South Bank – had the windswept river called after her? Perhaps she had never made the conscious decision to jump. Perhaps the notion had struck her, lightning-quick like inspiration, impossible to refuse until the dark water closed over her head and invaded all the hollow places in her chest.

'I don't know,' Astrid said again, opening her eyes to find the city disappearing in the rear window.

'What were you *thinking*?' Millburrow asked. 'Running off like that?' Astrid had to admit that she didn't know. She could not explain stepping from the safety of the society building and traipsing into London with the thoughtlessness of a sleepwalker. She'd just followed Ara, as she always had.

Astrid was sick with regret. Over what had happened to Ara but also over the very real threat that hung over her and her crewmates – that they would no longer be cleared to fly. That the launch would be delayed. Or suspended.

The UKSA would find someone responsible for what had happened. And, during the drive back, Astrid could not push away the horrified thought that it would be all her fault, that if the mission was suspended and she was kicked off the programme – Earthbound and disgraced – there would be no forgiveness for her. She had already heard whispers about 'breach of contract' and 'criminal proceedings' . . .

When she returned to the space centre, Astrid had stepped out of the car to find a small crowd was gathered in the half-light of the drive. Dr Golinsky – Dalton's lead medical officer – in her white coat, their school's provost, Professor Stenton, and directors of the astronaut's office. Astrid's stomach was heavy with dread as a woman in a grey suit ran towards her. 'You saw it, didn't you?' she asked, the car's headlights illuminating the gooseflesh along the side of her neck. She peered into Astrid's eyes as if she thought that if she looked close enough she might be able to see the incident herself.

'I didn't exactly . . .' Astrid turned her gaze down to her feet. 'I just saw her body. In the water.'

'After she fell,' Professor Stenton said, stepping from the shadow of the doorway, 'it looked like an accident, didn't it?'

'Well, the thing is, I didn't really see—'

'But if you had to guess,' interrupted a man in a lab coat, 'you'd say she fell. She wasn't suicidal.'

'No,' Astrid said. 'I didn't think she was. She seemed happy. And we would have known, right? We're her friends.' She shook her head. 'We would have known if she was unhappy.'

'Exactly.' A public affairs officer stabbed a painted fingernail at Astrid. '*We* would have known. *We* would have detected it. So she must have fallen.'

Astrid nodded. 'She must have . . . she fell,' she said, looking away as if she could see it already. The twist of an ankle, the snap of the railing, Ara's final look of surprise as her soles left the earth. 'I think she fell.' Maybe Ara only realized what happened once her body hit the water.

'An accident,' Dr Golinsky said. 'A tragic accident.'

'These things happen,' said a supervisor, his glasses flashing in the headlights. 'That's the sad thing.'

These things do happen, they agreed.

They announced this to the shouting reporters gathered at the gates, hurling questions through the bars. It was an accident, they said, even at the press conference a few days later, after it was revealed that Ara's combat boots had been discovered under a bench on a bridge, pushed neatly together, the laces tied up, neon pink ankle socks scrunched inside like oysters in a shell.

JUNO

T-MINUS 12 HOURS

AFTER JUNO HAD BEEN driven back to the space centre, she and the rest of the crew returned to a different kind of fray. Reporters were gathered at the gates, their cars parked all the way up the street. The driver had to take them around to a side road and up through a shadowed back entrance where directors, police and public relations officers were gathered.

They were ushered immediately into separate rooms. Required first to give a statement to the police, and then the Astronaut Office, the school's directors and finally to undergo a psychological assessment and mental health screening.

By the time the gruelling round of tests was over, Juno

emerged from the windowless room to find that the sun had set long ago, that night was marching on, and yet the launch felt more distant than it had three weeks ago.

Before Juno was sent for an inspection in the medical exam room, a technician led her towards a cubicle with a bathtub and shower and said, 'Twenty minutes, and make sure to scrub under your nails' before he closed the door,

Juno was glad to climb out of her clothes. The day had been so humid that when she peeled off her T-shirt the air was ripe with the smell of her body. She sat on the porcelain edge of the tub and watched the water gush out of the tap. Her hands were shaking.

She ran the water so hot that it scalded her feet at first. But she gritted her teeth and surrendered herself to it, letting herself slip down until it lapped over her head.

There would be no bath on the *Damocles*. Just as there had been no baths in the dormitories at Dalton. Only spartan shower cubicles and lukewarm water. If she launched tomorrow this would be her last bath before she and her sister could swim into the hot springs in the mountains of Terra-Two.

Although Juno wasn't sure they were going anywhere anymore.

She held her breath under the water until her body screamed for oxygen and then she held on longer still, until the pain of deprivation squeezed her lungs in a vice. Finally, she lost control of her legs, her knees unbuckled and her feet smacked the side of the bath. She jolted upright and came up gasping like a newborn, splashing in blind panic and scrubbing suds from her eyes.

Was there a worse way to die?

She had seen a picture of a drowned boy on the front page of a newspaper the previous June. His head had been half-submerged in water and in the midsummer temperatures putrefaction had already begun. Algae had attached to portions of his little body, multiplied and formed a living layer of slime around the side of his mouth and the hollows of his half-open eyes ...

An hour earlier, when the police had asked her what happened, Juno had to remind herself that she hadn't actually seen anything. By the time Juno, Poppy and the public affairs officer reached the Embankment, it was the chattering throng that had told her what happened.

Someone's just died. Some girl.

The girl. That girl's an astronaut.

Just jumped in.

No, she fell *in. My kid saw her.*

The girl from the magazines. The girl from the news. One of them, anyway.

Looked like an accident to me.

If suicide looks like an accident ...

When Juno climbed out of the bath she felt the ground shift under her feet and she had to reach out for the handrail to stop herself from slipping. The mirror was fogged up, and it was a relief not to catch a glimpse of her own reflection. She had been awake now for almost twenty-four hours and the day was far from done.

'Are you ready?' A little tap came on the other side of the door.

'Yes.' Juno pulled on a white cotton bathrobe and stepped out into the medical exam room. It was filled with the familiar acid smell of antiseptic and the citrus tang of floor cleaner. Two suited flight surgeons stood near a trolley. Juno had been in the same room earlier in the week for a pulmonary function test and a bone density exam. A nurse had clipped her nails down so far that they bled and just before her bath that evening she had been swabbed again for contaminants.

'Can you step into the scanner please?' said the first man, indicating the door. Juno walked slowly towards it, taking care not to let her wet feet slip on the ground.

She climbed out of her robe and crept through the door. The cold of the room was a shock to her bare skin, and the hairs along her forearms stood on end. 'Please hold your arms out and place your feet on the markers below,' buzzed the voice of one of the doctors over the intercom. Juno could not see them examining her naked body on the other side of the wall. She looked at the indicators on the ground and placed her feet upon them, stretching out her arms like a gymnast. Any contaminants that remained on her body would fluoresce under the light.

She had heard the stories about astronauts who were decertified the morning of the launch after failing an eleventh-hour medical examination. In the closed air system of a spacecraft, viruses spread rapidly and threatened the success of a mission, especially during long-term missions such as theirs, where medical supplies were limited and protracted exposure to radiation would eventually weaken their immune systems.

Juno thought about Noah and couldn't help imagining his hands leaving marks on her body, little pockets of bacteria.

She'd heard the Thames described as a 'biohazard'; after heavy rain it acted as an overflow for the city's sewers, and Astrid had come into contact with it. What if Juno was certified to fly and her sister wasn't? The thought of facing the darkness of space alone filled her with panic.

'*Are you all right?*' A voice over the intercom.

'Y-yes.' Juno swallowed deeply and straightened her back. Now was not the time to break down. She was an astronaut. Now was the time to show the supervisors that she could shoulder anything and still do her job. 'I'm fine, sir.'

'*Here comes the flash.*' A mechanical voice counted ... *four, three, two* ...'*Close your eyes.*'

Juno squeezed them shut – *one* – and even then she could still see the flare. Her eyelids lit up pink for a few seconds and the beating capillaries in her retina flickered red. Her nerves screamed for an instant, but she gritted her teeth against the pain. When she opened her eyes again her vision was bleached green and her skin stung as if she had been sunburned.

'*Well,*' came the voice of the second doctor, '*you're all done. It didn't hurt much, did it?*'

Juno let out a breath that she didn't know she had been holding, stepped out into the exam room and pulled her robe back on. 'Only a little,' she agreed as the spots in her vision began to fade.

Outside, the doctors were huddled over a monitor, checking the readouts from the scanner, which were scrolling up the screen.

'Um ...' Juno lingered in the middle of the room, the cold creeping up her calves. 'When will I find out if I'm certified to fly?'

'That depends on the results,' one of them said.

'It depends on whether I was exposed to anything today, right?'

'Amongst other things.'

'Um ... do you think you could tell me—'

'Look, it's not really *our* decision.' The doctor turned around to face her. Above his mask, his tired grey eyes were all Juno could see. 'We just run the tests.'

Juno nodded and left the exam room, water dripping down her neck. She took the shortcut back to her dormitory, via the emergency stairwell in the side of the building, but when she pushed the heavy door open she was surprised to find Poppy and Astrid huddled on the shadowed landing. Poppy was wrapped in an identical bathrobe, and her wet hair hung down her back like rats' tails. Astrid was sobbing hysterically, the kind of desperate wailing that Juno had only heard when they were children.

'You can't let them see you like this,' Poppy hissed. Her eyes kept darting over the banister and down to the exit, as if she was worried that one of the police officers stalking the grounds might throw open the door at any moment.

'You didn't see her,' Astrid wailed, making no effort to wipe away the tears skidding down her cheeks. 'The way she looked when we got her out of the water. She wasn't breathing. We were holding her. And I think she broke something, her arm was all bent back at the elbow, like it—'

'Please stop.' Juno shuddered. Her voice came out louder than expected, every sound amplified up the long stairwell, and both the girls let out a yelp of surprise.

'I'm sorry.' Juno lowered her voice a little and stepped forward. The lights in the hall were motion sensitive and the bulbs on the wall beside her came on with a clink. 'But it's bad enough without you telling us—'

'Bad enough for you?' Astrid glared up at her sister, her eyes bloodshot and unforgiving. 'Where were you, Juno? Where the hell were you?' The last words reverberated off the walls.

'I was . . .' Juno bit her lip. She didn't want to tell anyone about her experience in the Flight Garden with Noah.

'Hey, *you* left *us*,' Poppy said. 'Juno and Noah and me. You and Ara just ran off. I was wandering around the museum on my own looking for all of you before the PA officer told me there'd been an accident and it involved you three. I thought you'd been run over. I was terrified.'

'Okay.' Juno took a deep breath. 'Look, you guys, this isn't the time. We have to do what we have to do.'

'What are you talking about?' Astrid's eyes were raw and swollen from rubbing them dry.

'You know,' Juno said, 'when we practise emergencies in the simulator and eight different things are going on at once and we're sweating bullets . . . the only way to get through it is to think about the next thing. The thing right in front of you. Not what we could have or shouldn't have done. This is an emergency. And we've lost someone. But if we don't pull it together we're not going anywhere tomorrow.'

'That's what I'm talking about,' said Poppy. 'If they see Astrid in this state there's no way they'll clear her to fly tomorrow.'

Juno chewed on her lip. 'Has she had her interview yet?' she asked.

Poppy nodded. 'It went on really long, apparently. They really ripped into her.'

'I'm sorry about that,' Juno said.

'That's not even the worst of it,' Astrid said. 'It was like they didn't even care. They just want to know who's to blame.'

'That's what I'm saying.' Poppy lowered her voice. 'She has to get it together or we're all in trouble.' Her eyes darted nervously up and down the staircases. 'We have to say we had nothing to do with it.' Poppy swallowed and turned to Astrid. 'Say it was all Ara's idea.'

'It *was* all her idea,' Astrid said.

'So ... you just went along with it. Ara always had a way, a weird way of getting people to do what she wanted.' Poppy's use of the past tense was jarring.

'How can you even think about this stuff?' Astrid began to cry again, and wiped the back of her hand against her nose, spreading a shiny trail of snot from her wrist to her index finger.

'Juno – please.' When Poppy looked up, Juno saw that she was on the edge of breaking down as well. 'I don't want to get into trouble for this. I don't want to be prosecuted or forced to stay.'

'Forced to stay where?' Juno asked tentatively, but Poppy's eyes spilled over.

'Here! On this planet. In this country. I thought I did, but I don't. My life isn't *like* yours. I don't have picture-perfect parents to go back to. I have things. Things I thought I'd leave behind—'

The whine of the door opening echoed loudly up the stairwell and all the girls froze. Juno's breath caught in her mouth as she heard the sound of heavy shoes coming up the steps.

'Hello?' called a voice. 'Who's there?'

She saw the top of his head first, his frizzy dark hair, and then he came up to the second landing and spotted Astrid and Poppy huddled like frightened children. 'Girls?'

'Commander Sheppard,' Poppy said with the breathlessness of a schoolgirl.

'Are you hurt?' he asked

It was still strange to see their commander in civilian clothing. Juno was used to seeing Solomon Sheppard wearing a spacesuit or the navy and red uniform jumpsuit of the

UK Space Agency. He was a quiet but imposing astronaut, a former child prodigy and then the youngest man to travel to Mars, where he had scaled Olympus Mons, the tallest mountain in the solar system, with an international team. When he returned they made a movie about his life. The first time Juno had met him was at a scholars' dinner when she was sixteen. Sheppard had returned that summer from another nineteen-month mission and when he'd abandoned his knife and fork at the end of the meal, a couple of the girls squabbled over them like drumsticks tossed out after a concert.

Tonight, however, his eyes were bloodshot with fatigue.

'Nowhere I can touch,' Poppy said quietly.

'Eliot was hurt.' Juno suddenly realized that the last she had seen of Eliot had been in the police car parked on the Embankment.

'He has been treated for the injuries he sustained by the medical officers, and he's currently undergoing a psychological assessment to ensure he can be cleared to fly. As will you, Astrid.'

Poppy nodded, then asked quietly, 'Are we in trouble?' They all looked up. Sheppard's face darkened.

'Yes. A terrible thing happened today. We lost one of our own. I don't think I need to tell you that regulations are set down to keep you all safe. When I heard the news that you *left* the Interplanetary Society, I was beyond disappointed in every one of you. But all I can think is that this has been a trying couple of months for everybody, even for the senior members of the crew who have served on missions before. You're all so . . .' he bit back on a word, 'it's easy to forget that you're just *young* people.

'I don't know what the directors will decide. But if you are certified to fly on the mission after all, I need to know that a breakdown of order like this will never ever happen again. Our mission is about teamwork and responsibility. We need to be able to trust each other, because out there we've only got each other. Our lives depend on everyone following the code of conduct strictly.'

Juno nodded. A heavy knot of shame twisted in her stomach and none of them could look up to meet his eye.

'Anyway, you all have somewhere to be. Astrid, you're late for your medical inspection. Poppy and Juno, dinner has been prepared for you in the refectory. From this moment on I want to know where each of you is, from now until launch tomorrow. The freedom you had here – which you abused today, with tragic consequences – was a privilege and not a right.'

With that, their commander left, and Juno watched as her sister followed him up the stairs, leaving her and Poppy alone in miserable silence. Poppy was clearly as frightened as she; shadows dark as bruises were spreading under her eyes. She was shivering in her bathrobe and her feet were bare.

'What do you think will happen to him?' Poppy asked. She was still whispering as they made their way out of the echoing stairwell and towards the refectory. Juno had to lean in to hear her.

'Eliot? I don't know,' Juno said finally, after a moment's consideration.

'He's being interviewed right now, I think.'

'It's not like we know what will happen to any of us at this point.'

'Well, I'm pretty sure he's a goner,' Poppy said.

Juno cringed at the word. 'Why?'

'Well, his best friend slash girlfriend just jumped into a river.'

'It wasn't his fault.'

'I'm not saying it is, just ...' Poppy lowered her voice conspiratorially, 'everyone thinks he had something to do with it. Him and—' she cut herself off with a startled glance at Juno.

'My sister.' Juno finished the sentence with bitterness in the back of her mouth.

When they reached the edge of the refectory, smells of food, of roasting meat and warm bread, reminded Juno of the emptiness in her stomach. And yet, once she entered, she couldn't bring herself to eat any of it.

'No one is like Eliot,' Juno said, thinking of the way he had looked earlier that day, in the back of an ambulance, river water pooled around his Converse trainers. His eyes shiny and vacant. He was the only member of the Beta that the UKSA had personally head-hunted; it struck Juno as unlikely that he would be kicked off the programme at this late stage.

'But Astrid ... ?' Poppy asked quietly. They shared a frightened look. 'Why do you think she did it? Ran off like that?'

'I don't know.' Juno looked down at her plate. Dinner that night was supposed to be a treat. The kind they served for school dinners on Fridays or at the end of term. Burgers smothered in ketchup with a side of thinly sliced fries. 'All I can think is that Ara must have just convinced her to go. You know that way Ara has ...'

'She can convince anyone to do anything.' Poppy put a chip in her mouth. 'There's a word for it in French,' she said. Juno sighed. There had never been an evening that she was less interested in Poppy's linguistic musings. '*Folie à deux*. Madness shared by two. Like, infectious madness. The kind that makes you make a terrible decision and not think twice about it at the time. Only, all three of them escaped, so *folie à trois*, or *folie à plusieurs* – madness of many—'

'Poppy.' Juno's eyes narrowed with a quick pinch of irritation. 'Would you go without her?'

Juno couldn't even imagine it, going to Terra-Two without Astrid. 'There is no thought more horrible,' she said. They lapsed into a grim silence, like defendants waiting for the jury to return, listening to the sounds of cars pulling up and leaving outside and footsteps in the corridor.

Finally, Poppy flung down her cutlery. Juno watched it clatter across the table. When she looked up, Poppy's face was wet as she shoved her chair back and rushed away.

'Poppy?' Juno called after her.

'Maybe this is just what she wanted,' Poppy shouted back. 'To ruin everything. Did Ara have to do it *this* way? Did she have to take all of us down with her?'

LEFT ALONE IN THE refectory, Juno let her meal grow cold before abandoning it and walking over to the glass doors at the far end of the room. Moths were flinging themselves at her reflection, attracted to the bright lights of the dining room, which seeped out into the unlit grounds and across the dim stretches of land they had skipped across that morning. Through the gloom, Juno thought she could see her own laughing self, dancing with Ara that morning in the rain.

She pulled the door open and stepped outside. The grass, which had baked under the sun all day, filled the air with a hot earthy smell that Juno inhaled deeply, and then she closed her eyes to pray.

Would you go without her?

It was possible that Astrid might not be cleared in a medical inspection. Juno knew that the incubation time of a virus could be anything from one day to a couple of years. Even as she stood in the garden, tiny strands of genetic code could be hijacking her sister's cells or slithering into her bones to lie dormant for months. Rhinoviruses – such as the common cold – could live up to forty-eight hours on touchable surfaces, such as handrails and doorknobs, lift buttons and light switches, counters and coins passed from one hand to another. What lived in London's rivers? Juno rubbed down the goose-bumps on her arms and decided silently that if Astrid couldn't go then she would not either.

A helicopter beat in the air above her head and Juno squinted up at the navy sky, drawn from her worry with a jolt of recollection. The world outside was astir. Everyone in the country was waiting to see if the launch would go ahead.

Juno headed out onto the gravel path behind the space centre, just glad to feel a tepid breeze at her back. As she turned the corner of the building, floodlights exploded behind her and the ground rumbled. Juno spun around in alarm to find herself in the path of an oncoming car, the tyres spinning so fast they skipped sharp little rocks at her ankles. Diving out of the way, Juno tumbled into a darkened patch of shrubbery beside the driveway.

The car came to a violent halt in front of the reception, the headlights drained to blackness, the rumble of the engine faded and was replaced by the muted slam of the driver's door. 'This way.' It was their provost's voice, and Juno crouched down further in the gloom, hoping not to be caught.

A second later, the back door opened and a boy in pyjamas

climbed out. Juno glanced at his angular face with a jolt of recognition. She was sure she'd seen him before, in school perhaps,
but it was difficult to tell in the darkness. He had waist-length
hair and spider-black eyes. She liked the delicate way he moved,
sloping back into the car to pull out a duffle bag and slinging it
over his shoulder. She knew him. *Jesse Solloway?* she mouthed in
surprise. She had trained with him for a few months after graduation. And, although she knew that a member of the backup
crew would be enlisted to take Ara's place, it felt unreal to see
him so soon after Ara was gone. Before she'd even been buried.

'You've got everything you need?' came Professor Stenton's
voice. Juno tried to keep as still as possible. After the events of
the day, she knew she was in disgrace and supposed to be in the
space centre, choking down dinner. If her teacher turned and
found her crouching in the shrubbery it was likely she would
find herself in even more trouble.

'Sure,' the boy said. He turned suddenly and his eyes
found Juno's.

Her heart leapt and she bit down on her tongue.

He smiled conspiratorially, catching his bottom lip on the
edge of a tooth. Juno pressed a finger to her mouth, as if to say
shh. He nodded and turned away.

'Come right this way,' Professor Stenton's voice called out
from the entrance. 'We have so much to do.' The two figures disappeared inside. The driveway filled once more with darkness.
Juno waited for a long while in the gloom before she was certain
it was safe to clamber from her hiding place and return inside.

She walked around the edge of the building and re-entered
at reception. The television was on low. The news was running,
a man speaking into a microphone as headlines rolled across the

screen. There was only one guard on duty. His ID badge read *Edward*. The lanky boy who collected the mail and nodded at them from behind the desk as they came and went.

'Hi, Teddy.'

When he turned from the television his eyes widened with surprise. 'Oh. Hello,' he said. 'Thought you'd be asleep by now.'

'Even if they let me I don't know if I'll be able to.' Although, even as she said it, Juno could feel the tiredness in her bones.

'I bet. If I were you I'd be crapping myself.'

'Really?'

'For sure.' He nodded towards the television, where the camera zoomed in to a live shot of the shuttle at the launch site, dimly illuminated in the darkness. 'All those people watching you. All those reporters.'

'Will you be watching it?' Juno asked.

'Course,' Teddy said. 'Me and my kids. Got the day off. I'm going out to the launch site' This took her by surprise.

'You have kids?' Juno asked, frowning at his patchy stubble and the acne scars faintly visible on his chin.

'Yep.' He laughed at her expression. 'Two. A six-year-old and another who's eighteen months.'

'Wow. How old are you?'

'Twenty-four.'

'So that means ... you had your first child when you were eighteen?' He nodded. 'I'm never going to have children.' The words tumbled out of her mouth before she could stop them.

'Really? Why?'

It wasn't Juno's job to have children. Women would come after her – healthy young colony women whose job it was to grow fat and give birth. But theirs was a pioneer mission. They would land on Terra-Two towards the end of their child-bearing years and start a colony, build the base and chart the land. Perhaps children would come after that, but Juno had been informed that this wasn't her primary purpose. As soon as she was accepted into the Beta she underwent a procedure that slipped a little implant under her arm, and her periods had dried up.

'The mission is my child,' she said. And then, her head full of how heroic that sounded, she said a little louder, 'Terra-Two is my only child.'

Which wasn't entirely a lie. Going to space saved her from every other fate. From marriage and having to sleep with Noah, from the disappointment of motherhood, from a lustreless life. She was going to make a different world, a better world, on Terra-Two. A noble ambition – in her mind – the noblest.

Teddy shrugged. 'I guess that's why you're here then. Cos that's what you want.'

'Yes.' She blinked, and with a sudden ache in her stomach remembered the predicament she found herself in – still unsure if she actually would launch tomorrow. 'That's right.' Her eyes flicked towards the screen again. A reporter was holding a microphone and standing in front of Embankment station, a poor-quality video taken on somebody's phone of Eliot dragging Ara's body out of the water playing over her shoulder. Juno felt the ground shift under her feet, but took a deep breath to steady herself.

'You okay?' Teddy examined her for a moment. 'They're saying it's an accident.' He nodded at the screen. 'That you were allowed on an outing before the tree-planting ceremony and she fell in.'

'I don't know what happened,' Juno said, which was true.

Teddy eyed her knowingly and said, 'Thought so. There's always a difference between what goes on in here and what I hear 'em saying on there. Between you and me, I think someone's going to get the axe.' He leant in conspiratorially. 'And I wouldn't be surprised if it wasn't—'

He fell quiet and his eyes darted to the door as the susurration of people coming out of the conference room filled the hall.

Juno looked around in surprise. She wasn't sure if she wanted to be caught hanging around in reception, so she headed quickly back down the corridor and towards the refectory.

'Juno.'

When she turned, she saw Dr Millburrow.

'Aren't you supposed to be in bed?'

'Umm … I was just having dinner.' Juno's eyes darted towards the door of the empty refectory.

It was good to see Maggie's ruddy face. Of all the senior crew charged with looking after them, she was the most like a friend. Juno had been glad when she turned up in her car earlier that day to take them back home and she was glad to see her now.

'I was just in a meeting with the board of directors and they've come to a decision.' She glanced behind her at the serious-looking men and women in suits who had spilled out into the hall. 'I thought you better hear this from me.'

Juno felt her stomach drop with a jangled swoop of alarm. Maggie was about to tell her that she was no longer on the mission. That tonight they would all pay for Ara's actions with their future.

And then, all of a sudden, a quiet kind of abandon came over her. The kind she had felt in the three horrible hours after Astrid discovered she'd made it into the Beta and before Juno had. In those moments, a colourless life beneath the stars and away from her sister extended before her. Now she felt it again. Juno experienced the dim resignation that sometimes came over her in the split second she realized she was about to drop something; the swollen moment after the shift in weight registers and just before the crash.

'The mission will be going ahead as planned but someone will have to replace Ara. You do realize that, right?' Juno stared at Maggie dumbfounded. Could it be? Could it be that God had smiled mercifully upon her?

'We're going to launch,' she said, and her throat tightened.

'Yes.'

'I'm going to space?'

'Yes, that's what the board has agreed.'

'Oh ...' Juno let out a long breath, leant against the wall to steady herself.

'Are you all right?'

'Yes ...' she gasped. 'Just ... *relieved*.'

Maggie put a hand on Juno's shoulder and her eyes softened. 'It's been a long day, JJ.' Juno nodded. 'Why don't you go up there and get some sleep?' She nodded again.

Maggie leant forward and kissed her on the forehead. For a moment Juno's nose was filled with the sweet lavender scent of her perfume and she exhaled another shaky breath.

'If I don't see you in the morning ...'

'You're supposed to wake us up.' Maggie nodded as if she had forgotten that fact. Juno had grown used to seeing her silhouette in the doorway in the morning, just after the bell rang. She always smelt sweet as fresh bread and woke them all up by leaning down and stroking their cheeks. Like a mother, almost.

Whenever Juno pictured waking up in space she imagined Maggie standing in the doorway and saying, *wakie wakie, girls*, her own eyes bright and ready to face the day.

'Sure thing,' she said with a smile that wilted a little into a grimace. 'I'm proud of you.' Maggie added it as an afterthought, when Juno had already taken a couple of steps down the corridor. She stopped and turned back.

'For what?'

JESSE

T-MINUS 36 HOURS

TWO NIGHTS BEFORE THE launch, Jesse was lying on his bedroom floor listening to news reports from mission control. His sister was speaking to him about attachment, but Jesse was only half listening. He was thinking about the rocket. She kept repeating herself: 'The thing about attachment,' she was saying, crossing her legs in front of her, 'it's not about not caring, it's about not clinging.' The word rang in her throat as if it was a little dirty. 'You know, the way you hold your breath for just a second when you are given something little and beautiful, in the immediate anticipation of losing it. Which – of course – you will.' She said this with a flippant wave of her hand. 'You can't cling on to anything in this life; money, possessions, other people, even the cherry blossoms dry up and drop away. Loving anything is bound to the pain of losing it. Which is why clinging causes suffering.'

'You should write that on a bumper sticker.'

'Are you listening?'

'Mostly,' Jesse said. 'I just don't see what this has to do with me.' His sister rolled her eyes.

That was the last night he ever spent with her. The last conversation they had in person. He would realize this later – with a wrench of pain. She had returned from university the previous week and whipped off a patterned scarf to reveal her stunningly bald head. She'd shaved off her thick waist-length locks, and with them the clutching spectres of unhealthy attachments, her own vanity and the hopes of her weary parents.

'You know what this has to do with you,' she said, and then her voice softened a little, 'it hurts to see you in pain like this.'

She had left the week after he discovered that he was not going to Terra-Two, and returned months later to find that he was still hunched over with the ache of disappointment. For Jesse, not a day went by where he didn't glare at his sleep-swollen face in the mirror and curse his own inadequacy. Not an evening went by without pushing his food away at the dinner table, silently wondering what hateful thing had caused him to fail at the final hurdle. He would never know.

He'd trained with the Beta until January and after he'd been released the six of them had become his new obsession. He bought an issue of every magazine that featured their smiling faces, choked down the breakfast cereals that promised tiny figurines of the shuttle and kept the models themselves in his pockets, which were already heavy with the commemorative coins he collected – the ones with the two earths emblazoned on one side and THE OFF-WORLD COLONIZATION PROGRAMME stamped on the other – and would roll them across his knuckles until his fingers were numb.

'How do I do that?' he asked his sister. 'Since you have all the answers. You talk about worry as if it's a jacket that I could shrug off. Don't you think I want to? Don't you think I want to crawl right out of this anxious body and forget about the space programme and about dying. I can almost imagine how good it would feel. I can almost imagine the vanish of weight. Go on then, Morrigan. Tell me how to do it and I will.'

She was silent for just a moment, her green eyes filled with pity. The radio hissed in the background. 'Oh Jess—' his sister reached out to rub his shoulder. 'Destinies don't change.'

JESSE WAS TOO NERVOUS to sleep that night. He stood up every half hour to limp over to the mirror and check his body for visible signs of disease, not including the shadows under his eyes or the hollows his new restrictive diet had worn into his cheeks. Whenever he closed his eyes, he dreamt of malignance, of cells multiplying in the soft tissues of his body, of spores floating into his open windows and settling in the membranes of his lungs. Sleep was an abandoned hope.

Instead, he thought about off-world colonization. Of the exquisite design of the spacecraft and the people who would be climbing on to it in a little over twenty-four hours.

Over a million spectators were camped out at the launch site, filling the roads and the surrounding fields with their nocturnal celebrations. *It's like a music festival*, one of Jesse's friends had texted, and he could imagine it now. Most of the people would be the amateur astronomers who had developed a sort of offbeat cool over the past few years. They would be parading their homemade telescopes, the astrolabe apps downloaded onto smartphones. Some of them would be schoolchildren with the Union Jack painted on their eager faces, eyes lifted towards the skies waiting for history to be made.

Jesse didn't know, even as he began shuffling through another day, that Ara had already taken her final steps towards the bile-black river.

What he did know was that the shuttle that would carry the Beta into orbit – the *Congreve* – was lit up on its platform behind guards and barricades, and that when it disappeared into the sky the following day, so would the last of his hope.

He was going to die. He was no astronaut. He was no pilgrim, he was no humble dreamer fated for the stars.

JESSE

12.05.12

T-MINUS 12 HOURS

HE HEARD IT ON the radio first. The headline, that the body of an astronaut had been recovered from the Thames in what appeared to be an accident. His nerves quivered as if they'd been struck by a tuning fork.

He rushed down the stairs to the kitchen, where his mother was half-watching *Strictly Come Dancing* on the small television above the fridge. Jesse grabbed the remote from the table and switched to the news. The saucepan hissed as his father set it on the stove. Jesse's heart was racing as he watched the headlines rolling. Saw the words 'ARA SHAH', and 'ACCIDENT' and 'MISSION IN CRISIS'. He didn't even notice that he'd dropped the remote until he heard the sound of plastic crashing against the kitchen tiles and saw the batteries roll under the table. Then he turned around, and began to run.

He stopped outside his front door, standing alone in the cloying late spring air, his eyes stinging. In his sleep-addled mind, he was certain that, tonight, his life was about to change, but he didn't know how. A blood vessel bulging in his brain, about to burst? A car lurching around the kerb, its headlights bright as jack-o-lanterns in the split second before it crushed him into the concrete? Or a call from the space agency at the last minute?

'Destinies don't change,' he told the silent street. At nineteen years he would leave this world, he had been told.

Jesse took a tentative step forwards. The cars were still as sentinels, catching the moonlight, and the air buzzed with flies. Inside the window of every house families crowded before television and laptop screens, like the night before new year. The launch was predicted to be the most watched television broadcast in history. Tomorrow, if it went according to plan, there would be street parties all across the UK. Jesse could already see the sherbet-coloured bunting strung up between the lamp posts in preparation for the festivities.

He started down the street and towards the main road. It wasn't until he reached the corner, the unlit shop fronts and blinking traffic lights, that he began to run. His feet knew where to take him.

He was used to running with no destination in mind. The first few minutes always felt like flying, momentum sending his knees careening up in front of him as he neared the city lights. Then his muscles would begin to clench, heart striking at his sternum, lungs burning, sending hot tendrils of pain through him until he was one galloping vessel of flame.

By then, though, Jesse knew some things about pain. He knew that if he just kept running his heart would keep beating. He knew that pain was just a symptom of being, and he would endure it all – savour it even – if he could only live a little bit longer.

His feet striking familiar pavement, Jesse slowed his pace.

He knew this quiet street, lined with beech trees, illuminated in the sodium yellow of the streetlamps. He had emerged down the road from Dalton. He took a moment to catch his breath, wiping his wet forehead with the back of his hand.

He should have expected the traffic outside, the crush of reporters, the flickering shutters of cameras. During his time there, it had not been unusual to spot a stray photographer lingering by the entrance or pushing a lens through the bars. And today of all days, footage of the school's extensive grounds would flicker across every news channel. Jesse dodged past the swinging heads of microphones, towards the entrance.

It was surprising how little time it had taken for the tall iron gates of Dalton Academy to become an eerie relic of his past. It was even stranger to see the provost, standing in the centre of the throng, just below the school's crest and emblazoned motto: *It's better to fly like a falcon for half a year* ... She was more hunched over than he remembered. Two security guards were pushing the crowd of shouting reporters back. She poked her glasses up the damp ridge of her nose and read aloud from a piece of paper.

'All we can confirm at this time is that there has been a tragic accident involving a member of the Beta ...' Had she said accident, or *incident*? Some reporters had believed that it had been a rusted railing, a twisted ankle, a yelp of surprise. Others, a barefoot dive, a shout of exhilaration before the crash of water.

The only thing that was clear at that point was that one of the Beta was dead. An astronaut had died that afternoon while Jesse had been lying on his back watching the shadows slip down his wall.

'Professor Stenton,' one of the reporters shouted, 'can you

or can you not confirm that the launch will be going ahead as planned?'

'I cannot confirm anything at this moment in time. Our directors are working very hard to—'

'Will you be looking to replace Ara Shah with a member of the backup team? Will they be mission-ready?'

The moment was here. Jesse saw it illuminated before him. 'I will be!' he shouted.

At first only a couple of people around him heard. Jesse leapt into the light, suddenly, horribly, aware that he was still in his pyjamas. Sweat patches were spreading like stains under his arms and as he strained to catch his breath camera flashes blinded him. Jesse leant into the microphone. 'I'm in the backup crew. My name is Jesse Solloway and I'm here to replace Ara. I'm ready to go to Terra-Two.'

ASTRID

13.05.12

T-MINUS 6 HOURS

ON THE MORNING OF the launch, Astrid opened her eyes to an empty dormitory, the beds abandoned, the cool sunlight pouring through the window. She was surprised that Maggie wasn't there, as she usually was, to wake them. Most mornings Astrid leapt out of bed at first bell, and was brushing her teeth in the sink by the time Maggie poked her blonde head around the door to wake the other girls. Astrid sometimes suspected that Poppy and Ara feigned sleep just long enough to feel the back of Maggie's hand brush the hair from their brows.

The night before, the doctors had given Astrid half a dose of valium to stop her from shaking. She had cried so much that, even after the tears dried up, her throat still contracted with rhythmic little *hic*s. The pills had dragged her so deep down into sleep that she missed the first and second bell, but Maggie had not come in to wake her.

Across the dormitory, Ara's crumpled duvet was bundled up as if she was hiding under it and if Astrid looked hard enough she could make herself see it rise and fall. She kept remembering that Ara was never coming back. Everything about her was still there: her socks scrunched by the foot of her bed, the air perfused with the smell of jasmine oil and incense, a smudged handprint on the window where she had thrown it open. She couldn't stay in that room any longer; her eyes kept darting to the door in the vain expectation that Ara might burst through. So Astrid climbed out of bed, pulled on a cardigan and went to sit on the landing outside.

There was so little left to prove what had happened the day before. The bruises forming where her knees had smacked pavement, the soreness and exhaustion that follows a night spent crying, the ache of despair.

'They're at breakfast already,' came a voice. Astrid looked up and was surprised to see Solomon Sheppard, their commander, in civilian clothing, moonfaced from sleep, his afro slightly misshapen.

'Good morning, sir.'

'No, don't get up.' He came up the stairs and stood on the landing in a way that cast a long shadow over her. 'I was just out there.' He gestured towards the courtyard.

'Really, why?'

'I was ...' He hesitated for a moment, 'praying.'

'Oh ...' Astrid looked down, suddenly embarrassed about asking such a private question. 'I didn't know you were a—'

'Sometimes I am. Days like today.' He paused, glanced away too and then said, 'I hope you're feeling better.'

'Kind of ... yesterday was ... a nightmare ...' Astrid exhaled heavily, but then remembered herself. 'I am feeling better, though. Ready for the mission. Of course.'

Sheppard was tall and thin, with skin darker than her father's but not as deeply lined. Astrid had always liked the soft baritone of his voice, and the way he rarely smiled with his straight white teeth, as if he was keeping them a secret. He had been the youngest man – at twenty-six – to land on Mars, and for the first time it occurred to Astrid that perhaps he was *still* young. She had only been eleven back then, and so when she'd seen his face on the news he'd seemed astronomically old, just another adult, like her parents.

'And today?' he asked. 'Underneath it. Don't you feel just a little bit—'

'Excited?'

'Yes,' he said. 'I always do. Before a launch. Especially the first couple of times. I'd be so excited I couldn't sit still. As if I was a kid again and it was the night before my birthday.' He laughed at himself.

'I keep forgetting it's real, actually. Then I remember and feel glad, but whenever I feel glad, I also feel guilty that I get to go and she ...' They fell silent. On her ankle was the friendship bracelet that Ara had woven for her one Christmas when she had no money for a 'proper gift'. It used to have three tiny silver bells on it, so that 'you can have music wherever you go', Ara had laughed, and then rattled the bracelet on her own ankle, 'and so you'll always know where I am.' Over time the bells had come loose and dropped off, each in turn. The pain of it was crushing and fresh every time Astrid thought about it. She'd thought they would all grow old together.

She only realized she was crying again when Solomon looked at her in alarm.

'I'm sorry,' Astrid said, her face burning with shame. She jumped up and tried to duck back into her room, but he put his hand on her shoulder and for just a moment they both froze in surprise.

'Don't be sorry,' he said. A fresh wave of tears from Astrid. He did something she'd never seen him do before. He leant forward and hugged her. And, for half a minute, when Astrid buried her face into his shoulder, she forgot who he was. Her commander. Her once and future teacher. Forgot that she was still in her pyjamas, her feet bare, hair still in the fat cornrows she had tied them in the night before. She liked the way he smelt, distantly, of aftershave. Sandalwood and bergamot.

'I should go,' she said suddenly, leaping back.

'Of course.' He stepped away. Astrid turned and fled down the stairs.

She rushed down the oak-panelled hall of the residential wing of the space centre, hoping to reach the refectory in time to catch the tail-end of breakfast. She had missed lunch and dinner the previous night, and her head was spinning with hunger. But she was surprised on turning a corner to spot the provost of Dalton Academy through the glass pane in the door of a meeting room. Astrid ducked, instinctively: six years at Dalton had instilled an almost Pavlovian dread of the woman.

'... ever recover, quite frankly.'

Who was she talking to? Astrid peered through a gap in the door, and spotted the slight figure of Dr Friederike Golinsky, one of the medical directors. They spoke in hushed voices and as Astrid leant in to listen she noticed Dr Golinsky's uneven intakes of breath, the shuddering of her shoulders. She was crying.

'We all have to make sacrifices—'

'I know, I just thought there would be more time. That the mission would be suspended or delayed, at least, for half a year.'

'Come on, Fae. We both knew that had to be avoided at all costs. And *consider* the costs.'

'But I'm—'

'This is bigger than you!' the professor shouted. 'We all have our part to play, and . . .' Her voice died down suddenly.

'Did you hear something?' Dr Golinsky asked. They both turned towards the door.

Astrid leapt back and stood for a moment, holding her breath. When the soft hiss of voices behind the door started up again, she turned in the opposite direction and headed to the refectory, where the whole crew sat together on a table near the glass wall. They had almost finished eating by the time she entered.

'Glad you could join us,' said Harry. 'It's not breakfast until Astrid arrives.'

'Why didn't you wake me?' asked Astrid.

'We thought that Maggie would wake you,' Poppy said.

'I don't think Maggie will be doing anything anytime soon,' Harry said, gulping down the last of his coffee with a grimace.

'What are you talking about?' asked Juno.

Harry looked at her with wary disbelief. 'Because she's been suspended.'

The words hit Astrid like a jab in the solar plexus. 'What?'

'Yeah,' Harry said. 'I guess they had to blame someone. Dr Millburrow was supposed to be our psychiatrist when we're in space. It was kind of her job to know if one of us was planning to, you know . . .' He trailed off with a shrug.

'It's not fair.' Poppy shook her head, 'None of us knew.'

'True,' said Juno. 'But at least the mission's still going ahead.

There was talk yesterday of delaying the launch. Or decertifying us *all*.'

Harry snorted. 'You didn't really believe that, did you? Delaying the mission would cost millions. Everything's already planned. Hundreds of thousands of people have come to London to watch the launch. There was a lottery for the tickets. The prime minister will be there. What did you think they were going to do? Say, *Hey sorry about that, the launch can't go on because we can't control a bunch of kids*?'

Astrid supposed it was true. And the public had come to love all of them, were captivated by their personal stories of success. It was part of the reason the programme had accrued so much additional sponsorship from private organizations. Swapping the members of the current Beta for other astronaut candidates so soon before the mission would likely tarnish the reputation of the entire programme.

'Okay, maybe not that,' Poppy said. 'But launching on a mission like this before she's even buried ... it just feels like bad luck or something.'

They were quiet for a moment. The refectory was unusually empty, with very few of the space centre personnel huddled over their breakfast or queuing near the coffee machines.

'You should get something to eat,' Poppy said.

Along the opposite wall were vats of juice, hot water for tea and trays of cereal bars. Astrid took a handful and stuffed them in her pockets.

'It's a big day, love,' said the ruddy-faced cook from behind the counter. Astrid flashed her ID and the cook handed over a tray marked with her name. Lots of dried food, toast, chopped bananas – food that was unlikely to turn in her stomach during the launch. The cook winked, and added two oily sausages onto her plate. 'You'll need it,' she said.

'Thanks.'

The cook smiled, then pointed to the cereal bars, inviting her to take more.

Astrid returned to the table.

'Think it's really a good idea to eat all that?' said Harry, eyeing her plate. Astrid sat down beside her sister, who was nursing only a cup of peppermint tea. Harry's tall glass was slick with his usual protein shake – raw eggs whipped into a frothy mixture with warm milk, which he used to suck down with a straw before heading out with his rowing team to the river.

'I don't know how you can eat anything at all,' Poppy said, dropping her spoon with a sigh of surrender. 'Doesn't your tummy feel all . . .' She made a face and Juno nodded.

'You better hurry up,' Juno said, glancing at her watch. 'We're supposed to stop eating five hours before the launch. Which gives you twenty minutes to get that down.'

Harry looked across the long table to where Eliot sat with two empty seats either side of him. He was paler than usual in the morning light, his lips were chapped and bleeding and he stared down at his plate of scrambled eggs as if he could not understand how they came to be there. 'He's got the right idea,' Harry said. 'Don't want to see that breakfast coming right back up again when we launch, eh?'

'Shut up,' Eliot hissed without looking up.

'I'm just saying,' Harry continued, 'won't be so tough in three hours if you're puking your guts up, right?'

Eliot lifted a fork and flicked a few globs of scrambled egg at Harry, who dodged too late and then cried out in fury as the egg splashed his eye. His expression immediately darkened and he swore.

'Please!' Poppy said. 'Please don't turn this into another fight.'

'Tell that to him,' Harry said, wiping his eye with a paper napkin.

'Don't tempt me,' Eliot said, very quietly. 'Not today.'

'Ohh, is that a threat?' Harry wriggled his fingers in mock horror.

'I bet you're happy now.' Eliot's eyes narrowed. 'You never liked her anyway.'

'*Eliot*,' Poppy pleaded.

'It's all right,' he said, slamming his fork down. 'I'm done.' He stood up and left the room, the squeak of his soles echoing off the walls in the silence that followed.

'You can be kind of mean sometimes,' Astrid said to Harry as the door slammed shut.

'It was only a joke,' Harry said, glancing down at Eliot's abandoned plate of food.

'I'm not sure he knows that,' Poppy said. 'He gets really sick in the simulated launches. And I think he's a little embarrassed about it.'

'It's not true, anyway.' Harry lowered his eyes. 'About me never liking Ara.'

'You were always competing,' Juno said. 'You were the only two of us who made it to Command School, and then ... you know, you were picked to be pilot over her. I don't think she ever got over that.'

'Well, I did.' Harry shrugged. 'And Eliot's just upset because flying is something he's not the best at. It's not robotics or computing. The guy needs to be put in his place sometimes. He got it easy, and I know you all think so too. It's never been fair with him. He just waltzed onto this programme and then he gets into the Beta. He doesn't have to really *work*, not like the rest of us.'

'Is that jealousy I hear?' Juno teased.

'No.'

'He was chosen because he's talented. Even though he's younger than us. And when we get to Terra, he'll design and programme robots that we'll depend on,' Astrid said.

'It doesn't really matter anyway,' Juno added, 'how anyone got in. Not anymore.'

'Damn right it matters,' said Harry, 'and now more than ever.' He took a long drag from his glass and slammed it down. 'Am I the only one who thinks it's weird that Eliot wasn't suspended yesterday too?' Juno and Poppy wrinkled their brows in confusion. Harry leant forward. 'He's lying about something. He and Ara went everywhere together, did everything together. They're like conjoined twins for God's sake, and you're telling me that he has *no idea* that she's planning to jump into a river? And yet, he's "conveniently" close by and finds her body?'

'You weren't there,' Astrid reminded him. Her stomach twisted at the memory of Ara limp as a doll in Eliot's arms.

'I didn't need to be,' Harry continued. 'They barely questioned him. He's lying about something and even if it doesn't matter down here, with everyone else and space to breathe, up there—' he glanced at the ceiling. 'I mean, think about it, except for the seniors there will be no one but the six – I mean, the five – of us for the next twenty odd years. We've got to rely on each other. Trust each other. I couldn't trust a loner like Eliot Liston.'

'His parents are dead, you know,' said Poppy. 'Both of them.'

'How does that change anything?' asked Harry. 'It's not like any of us can go home for the holidays anymore.'

'It's not true, that they're both dead,' Juno corrected. 'His mother died, I heard. And his father walked out on him.'

'No I heard it was cancer and a car accident.' Poppy lowered her voice. 'He's lost literally everyone he loves.'

There was a moment of silence and then Juno took a sharp breath, as if she'd suddenly recalled a dream. 'Someone new is coming. To replace Ara.'

'Are you sure?' Astrid asked.

'Well, they've got to replace her, haven't they?'

'Do they?'

'I guess . . .' She sounded less sure. 'I mean, someone's got to take her position, you know, do the job she was meant to do . . . hydroponics. We'll need to grow food still.'

'Someone will have to replace Maggie, too,' Poppy reminded them. And it was true, they would need a flight surgeon in case they were sick and to perform all the medical examinations that had already become routine. Astrid wondered if the new person would also count down, *five, four, three, two* . . . before taking their blood, but sometimes stick the needle in on *four* or *two* so it came as a surprise and was over a few seconds sooner.

'But who . . . ?' Astrid asked. 'It's not like they can train someone up in a night.' What Astrid really meant was who would have Ara's magic eyes, or smell as sweet and welcoming as Maggie?

'Someone from the backup crew, obviously.'

It always made Astrid uneasy to think about the other six candidates who had almost made it. It was a reminder of how lucky she was, because the difference between herself and her

Earthbound alternates probably had less to do with points in test scores and more with an alignment of stars.

The door creaked open and they all turned, expecting to find Eliot striding in, returning for his breakfast. But instead Professor Stenton walked briskly in, and at the sight of her they all began to stand. 'No, no, don't stand up.' She waved a hand dismissively. Dr Golinsky was in tow, and to Astrid, the two adults appeared just as tense as they had when she spied them earlier. 'Finish your breakfast in five minutes. I expect to see you all— Where's Eliot Liston?'

'He wasn't hungry, Professor,' said Harry, who had climbed out of his seat anyway and straightened his back.

'Well ... I can imagine.' She examined them all with her hawk-like eyes and then clapped her hands together and said, 'Right, right. The cars are scheduled to leave in one hundred and twenty minutes. I need you dressed and ready to go in ninety. Just a note of reminder, they are bound to ask about the tragic accident in the press conference today. We've prepared some answers for you to read over in the cars but feel free to say that you are not prepared to comment if they ask anything too personal. It's understandable – you're all grieving. Before the launch we'll have a minute of silence. But in the meantime, I expect to see you all in the council room in five minutes for an emergency meeting.'

THE BETA TOOK THE lift up to the council room together, and by the time they arrived everyone was already there. The provost and Dalton's other directors, along with the president of the British Interplanetary Society and some executives from the UKSA. Doctors, technicians and press officers too, maybe forty people in all. Astrid shuddered with something like stage fright as she and the rest of the crew entered and a silence fell over the assembled party.

Commander Solomon stood in front of the projector screen, so the interlocking rings of the Off-World Colonization Programme strobed across his cheekbone. Next to him was the flight engineer, Igor Bovarin, but Maggie Millburrow was nowhere to be seen.

'You can sit here.' One of the directors indicated five seats that had been vacated for them at the front of the room, near the podium, which was draped in the Union Jack.

Astrid felt as if she was attending a wake. Most of the people in the room were suited in black, eyes bloodshot and grief-stricken. Several of the governors patted her shoulder as she shuffled past towards her seat, and whispered consolations.

The provost took the podium. 'Thank you, thank you.' She raised her hands to silence the room. 'Lord Davidson—' she nodded towards the president of the society. 'It's been a difficult night for us all. As I'm sure you know, Dr Millburrow has asked to step down from her post.'

'You mean she's *been asked* to step down,' Harry muttered to Astrid.

'But I'm relieved to say that Doctor Friederike Golinsky, our senior medical officer, has volunteered to take her place.' A round of applause exploded across the room, and the five members of the Beta looked up to see a thin woman by the provost's side. The woman Astrid had seen crying downstairs only half an hour ago.

Although they had met Dr Golinsky many times before – overseeing medical examinations, or in the shadows during a meeting of the board of directors, her head down, drumming her long white fingers on the back of her clipboard – none of them knew very much about her. There were rumours that she used to be a ballerina but her career was cut short by an accident. She did indeed have a dancer's body. She still possessed an epicene beauty; always tied her jet hair in a tight bun at the top of her head. Underneath her security pass, which hung from her neck on a lanyard, the cage of her chest was sheer as a cliff-face. She had always frightened them a little. Because she could often be heard reprimanding junior doctors in her thick German accent, and because a long puckered scar split her face from forehead to left cheek.

Now she smiled and leant into the microphone, waiting for the clapping to die down before she said, 'Thank you. Twenty years ago, when I moved to the UK, I would never have imagined that I would be chosen to play even a small part in this historic mission. And twenty days ago I would not have imagined that I would be chosen to board the shuttle to travel to Terra-Two. But I am greatly honoured.' Another smattering of applause.

'Now, we understand that the tragic loss of our crew member Ara Shah yesterday afternoon came as a terrible shock. But the purpose of the Off-World Colonization Programme was to send six young adults to Terra-Two in 2012 to establish a permanent human settlement.

'Ara's job on the ship was to assist our hydroponics expert Dr Cai Tsang – who is currently on the International Mars Base – in growing the crops that will come to be the astronauts' primary food and oxygen source. It's a vital role. And at this late stage, as many of you may have seen on the eight o'clock news, a member of the reserve crew will be taking her place.'

When Astrid looked around, she saw that the faces of the other crew members were pale. Eliot's head was in his hands. 'Who is she ...?' Poppy whispered, as they both struggled to remember who in the reserve crew had been assigned Ara's job.

'Please welcome ...' The provost stepped back a little from the microphone to make space. Astrid could feel the blood draining from her face. The crowd parted. For a minute some part of her thought that she would find Ara standing amongst them, smiling her playful smile and flicking the river water out of her long hair. *Fooled you*, she'd say with a laugh. This entire day, this nightmare, just an elaborate joke.

A tall bronze-skinned boy stepped onto the podium dressed in a flight suit, and applause swept across the gathered crowd like rain. Cheers, whoops of relief. It was all going to be fine. The mission would go ahead. All of that work, all of their hopes, none of them wasted.

Jesse Solloway – Astrid recognized him immediately. The misfit who never made the cut. They couldn't have chosen anyone less likely than this young man, whose coal-black eyes were distant and dreamy, who braided broken shells and mantled leaves into his waist-length locks. Jesse had always radiated his own kind of lonely cool. Once, in a careers lesson, when asked what he wanted to be, he had said 'deity' and the class had tittered nervously. They only took it seriously a few months later, when he didn't make the Beta and stopped coming to school. Rumours spread that he was going to die.

'You,' Juno said, her eyes wide.

'Me,' he said with a happy lazy smile, 'I made it after all.'

ASTRID

13.05.12

T-MINUS 4 HOURS

FOUR HOURS BEFORE THE launch, Astrid found Harry standing by the window of the dormitory, staring at his reflection in the sun-silvered glass. He turned when he heard her feet on the linoleum outside. 'What is it?' he asked.

'T-minus four hours,' she said. 'I thought you'd be down already.'

'I'm coming in a minute,' he said, turning back to the window. 'Just practising my smile for the camera.' When he raked his fingers through his hair a couple of blond strands stuck to the damp on his forehead. 'You know, it's the last they'll see of us.'

Cars were pulling up outside, and Astrid could hear the rumble of helicopters overhead. It was the kind of cool spring morning with air that is bracing and sweet and promises sunshine. A bright ridge of light peered over the roof and cast across the lawn. The *Damocles* – the magnificent ship that would take them to Terra-Two – winked overhead. If Astrid squinted she thought she could see it, about 660 kilometres above London. The shuttle they were about to enter would ferry them that short distance, out of Earth's atmosphere, and to the spinning decks of the *Damocles*, their new home. From there, they would accelerate out of Earth's orbit, past Mars and the moons of Jupiter, around Saturn and then out of the solar system.

As Commander Sheppard ushered them into the cars, Astrid realized that the worst part of the wait had begun. The hours before the launch would be the longest as the seconds ticked down to take-off.

When Astrid and her sister were younger, their father made frequent trips to South America and West Africa. A certain melancholy always came over the house in his absence. The kitchen table was joyless without his laughter. His study, just opposite the twins' bedroom, was unlit and silent and still smelt of him even though a thin layer of dust had settled over his books. Astrid and Juno would come home to their mother stifling tears and wringing her hands over the sink. They were all holding their breath, waiting for his return. And all the while he crowded their dreams, trekking across open savanna, Bible in hand, or baptizing babies in the Niger. Proclaiming, *Behold the lamb of God!* in bustling marketplaces, the same way he did across their dining-room table.

Astrid and her sister would count the sleeps until his plane touched down. As the day drew nearer she would have to dig her fists into her stomach to wrestle excited butterflies, but the afternoon his plane was scheduled to land, her excitement always curdled into a strange kind of dread. She didn't know what she was afraid of: that he would come back with a different face, that he might have forgotten her name . . . that unsettling boundary where long-held dream meets incipient reality.

Waiting in the crowded arrivals lounge next to WHSmith, flowers in hand, Astrid would scan the weather-beaten faces of every man who passed. That was always the longest wait, just before she spotted a dark searching face, brow furrowed, gaze straining over heads in that sweet moment before eyes meet eyes. A smile would break across his face, and when he bent low to hug her she would inhale the familiar scent of his aftershave, and the new far-away smell of dust on his dashiki. It was always impossible, then, to remember what she had been afraid of.

It was the same that morning. As Astrid watched patches of blue break through the clouds she lifted up one of her hands to find that it was shaking. It occurred to her that they had been subjected to countless 'launch simulations' in preparation for this exact moment. The moment when her mind flailed into the future for some certainties she could hold onto.

There were a couple. They had visited the launch site seven times, so she was familiar with the way the trees fanned out along the motorway until they reached flat, open grassland, streaked with the shadows of clouds. Soon they would turn off into slip roads until all she could see up ahead were dark armoured cars, travelling in the same direction – towards the unglamorous low-rise buildings near the site.

Terminal Countdown Demonstration Tests – Maggie called them 'dress rehearsals'. Astrid wondered if Dr Golinsky was the type of person to say something as whimsical. As the technicians helped her into her spacesuit would she remember lacing up the ribbons of ballet slippers with her own nimble fingers? Or would she be thinking about what lay ahead of her? Astrid knew that when she entered the shuttle they would strap her in lying on her back, so tightly that she would only be able to move her head. This time, the eyes of the world would be on her, and after the final countdown her body would begin to rock with the vibrations of the APU, the engine and the solid rocket boosters. The shuttle would be shaking so violently that she would not hear the final snap of shackles as it exploded off the launch pad and filled the eyes of every spectator with light. Everyone who watched from a distance would look up at the trail of smoke blazing against the sky and think about what a special thing it is to be human, to be able to build machines that could soar out of the grip of gravity.

The sound of tyres crunching on the gravel woke her from her reverie. They had arrived. When Commander Sheppard opened the passenger door, a roar crested outside and rolled like thunder from the gathered crowd. The moment Astrid stepped out of the car a camera flash temporarily blinded her. She blinked the spots from her vision, looked around and was met with more people than she had ever seen in one place. A sea of sweaty faces and flailing arms that swept out as far as she could see. They were waving flags and jumping up against the barriers, brandishing phones and calling out for attention. Reporters were snapping cameras held in front of their faces like snouts.

Astrid turned around in wonder to find that there were more people nudging the barriers behind her. Many of them had camped out near to the mission control centre, sleepless but exultant, hoping to catch a glimpse of the astronauts before their feet left the ground. Off at the sides were hundreds of schoolchildren gathered in bleachers or spread out across the sun-scorched grass, craning their necks to see the countdown projected on the giant screen: T-minus 2.5 hours.

She felt as if she were standing on a football pitch during a game, disorientated by the solid wall of sound coming from the crowd. A few metres away, a group of young people were waving hand-painted signs that read, 'Go Team GB 2012' and 'Another World, Another Chance'. One teenage girl was waving a sign that read 'Harry is Hot', the A and the O replaced with bubbly pink hearts. Astrid hid a smile and turned to call Poppy's attention to it. Poppy had already slammed the car door shut behind her and turned her smiling face towards the crowd.

'It's Poppy,' someone shrieked. 'Over here!' Poppy was the favourite – that had always been clear. She was winsome and relatable and the tabloids spun her and Harry's story so they were cast as star-bound lovers. They played it up in front of the cameras; every now and then Poppy would slip her hand into his and the crowds would whoop. Ara had hated it. She thought that the only reason Poppy's face adorned the covers of every magazine from *Astronomer's Weekly* to *Seventeen* was because her skin was ivory. Her lightly freckled face was English and feminine, her eyes quietly clever and the colour of an overcast sky. Astrid herself had to admit she had felt a twinge of jealousy when Poppy was chosen to light up a screen in Piccadilly Circus, holding a chilled can of Pepsi to her painted lips.

Poppy swanned towards the grinning girls, blowing kisses. She wasn't allowed across the painted line that separated them, but she posed for pictures. Half of her fans were waving and shouting, a couple even clutching each other in tearful excitement.

'Should really have parked closer to the entrance,' Commander Sheppard said through gritted teeth to the driver. He was eyeing the crowd warily.

'Let them look,' the young man said.

Camera flashes exploded across Astrid's retinas with dizzying quickness. Juno turned to her sister in joyful disbelief and asked, 'Does it feel the same for you too? Like we'll wake up from this any second? Like the way we felt when we made it into the Beta?'

'I don't know,' Astrid said. But really, nothing in this whole adventure had ever felt more real than this moment, surrounded by people, the air electric with anticipation. The world was about to change, and she could feel the excitement sizzle in her stomach.

'Astrid!' someone shouted, and she turned to find a group of girls leaning against the barriers, their jumpers tied around their waists, patches of sweat blooming under their arms as they stood in the heat. Astrid distantly recognized their faces. She had seen them striding through the halls of Dalton in tight groups. They were a couple of years younger than her. They cheered when they caught her eye and bounced up and down on their heels. 'Ast-rid! Ast-rid! Ast-rid!' they yelled hysterically in a chant that caught on all around them, other people clapping as they picked it up: 'Ast-rid! Ast-RID, Ast-RID . . .' Her heart soared. There was nothing to be afraid of. She was loved.

'Hey, look.' Juno pointed up to the screen erected near the bleachers. Their own identical faces had just appeared on it, from a different angle. They looked bright as two bees in their flight suits and they were smiling.

After some time, Commander Sheppard ushered them away from the car and the crowd and into the shade of the mission control centre. Inside, Astrid's heart was still throbbing and her ears buzzed in the relative hush of the building. Eliot was pale, and squeezing his hands so tightly into fists that his knuckles were turning white. 'Are you okay?' Astrid asked.

'I will be in a minute,' he said quietly. 'You know I've always hated crowds.' But he was just as tense during the press conference, sweat beading on his forehead as he stared in strained silence out at the reporters, even when a question was directed at him. Harry and Commander Sheppard charmed them all, though, and smoothly diverted attention away from Eliot. Just before closing, Harry leant into the microphone and said, 'On behalf of myself and my crew I would like to say thank you to everyone on the ground for your hard work. It's in our DNA to explore, and though it will be our feet touching Terra-Two, it's the work of thousands of dedicated men and women here on the ground that made that possible.' There was a round of happy applause and then the commander initiated a minute's silence for Ara, and Astrid thought she saw Juno cry.

They came out to greet the people one final time. Astrid was glad to see that the weather forecast had been correct and during their brief period inside every cloud had blown away. The sun was high in the sky and sending limpid rays down onto the brass band. The noise of the trumpets and the rumble of the drums was still ringing in Astrid's ears when she entered the suit-up room. They were handed over to the technicians, who helped them into their spacesuits.

Once she had pushed her hands into her stiff gloves and collected her helmet, Astrid trudged to one end of the room to join the others in a pose for the final crew photographs. The six of them wore dazed smiles, the bags under their eyes illuminated in the glare of the lights. The photographer rearranged them tentatively and placed Jesse where Ara always used to stand, by Eliot's side. Jesse threw his hands up in awkward surrender. 'You can take one with just you guys,' he said, stepping back. 'I don't have to be in it.' Into the stony silence, Commander Sheppard spoke. 'It's an honour to have you on the team,' he said, patting the boy's back.

They took a picture with the junior and senior crew together – Dr Golinsky, Igor and their commander – then countless others with flight directors, operational managers and even their old teachers. Astrid began fidgeting as her mouth started to hurt from smiling. Emotions were running high by that point, everyone's eyes were glittering and it was difficult to tell whether they were saying 'good luck' or 'goodbye.'

BY THE TIME THEY drove out to the shuttle they had been in their spacesuits so long they were all beginning to sweat. They were sitting opposite each other in the van, five facing five, but were mostly quiet. Only Harry, Igor and Commander Sheppard were comfortable enough to make cheerful banter. The others avoided each other's eyes, each in their own private world of anticipation. The silence became more noticeable as they left mission control behind, along with the band and the cheering crowd and the screen that read T-minus 90 minutes, and made their way to the open stretch of land where the shuttle was chained to the Earth.

The *Congreve* was far bigger than Astrid remembered, the size of a cathedral. The orbiter, the small space where the crew would be strapped in, sat on top of propellant-filled towers which generated enough thrust to hurl them through the atmosphere. Astrid climbed out of the van at the foot of the giant, that hissed and thrummed, and from where she stood, could see steam curl off the steel surface like breath through parted lips.

Sixty metres above her the orbiter access was like the arm of a crane, and as they took the lift up to it Astrid felt the drop in her stomach. Yet she knew this thirty seconds of acceleration was nothing compared to the flight that awaited her on the other side of the shuttle's hatch, where they would soar to twenty-six times the speed of sound in eight minutes.

The elevator door slid open to a sunlit bridge and they were greeted by the close-out crew – the white-suited technicians who approached the senior astronauts with hugs and the members of the Beta with handshakes. 'Just follow the yellow-brick road,' said one of the men with a number 2 printed on his back. He was pointing to the yellow and black chevrons painted on the narrow walkway that led to the white room, the small chamber in front of the hatch. The little space was packed with people and almost as soon as Astrid entered three of them descended on her, tugging at the straps on her spacesuit and re-attaching communication lines.

'Hey. Jesse looked up from the small crowd in front of him and asked, 'You don't know how to . . .' He was fiddling with the straps on his parachute, blushing with confusion. Astrid was about to lean over to help him when one of the suit technicians brushed her hands away and attached it herself. 'You're ready,' she told him, and Jesse took a deep breath and headed into the shuttle. 'See you on the other side,' he said over his shoulder.

'How does that feel?' A man peered up at Astrid from behind his glasses, fastening the final strap on her suit. 'Too tight?'

'Not really,' she told him, and then it was her turn to step through the hatch. It was a little circular door and climbing in was an inelegant process that required Astrid to get on all fours and then to roll onto her back, every movement a struggle in her heavy suit. She felt like a diver wearing a second skeleton, but it occurred to her, as the crew fumbled to strap her in, that these were the last people she would see on Earth, and she didn't even know their names.

Once they finished, Astrid was tied down so tightly she could feel the pulse throbbing in her legs. Her ears were filled with the chatter of mission control. 'As you know: I've done this a few times,' Commander Sheppard said with a smile. 'It's over quickly. Your job is just to take it all in.'

Something strange and wonderful occurred to Astrid then. The fight was finished. For the first time in her life, even if she did nothing at all, she would be in space.

SOMETIMES HER FATHER WOULD call upon new believers to tell the story of how they came to faith. Their testimony. And this was hers. Astrid had grown up knowing that there was a distant planet outside her own solar system, a green twin of Earth orbiting dual stars. The first day that a longing to go there awoke inside her, she had been in assembly. All the children in her year group had been ushered into the school hall to watch a video, part of a presentation delivered by a team from the UKSA. 'Another habitable planet,' announced one of them across the darkened room and the screen lit up with dazzling vistas of an alien land. Astrid saw an ocean, lush mountain ranges and terracotta canyons ridged like jewel-box shells.

'They call it a "New Earth",' said the young astrobiologist with exaggerated air-quotes, 'but our findings actually suggest that Terra-Two is many millions of years older than our own Earth; truly, *we're* living on Terra-Two.'

Under the collar of her shirt, Astrid's neck prickled with goosebumps. She sat up as if she had been called by name, and in a way she had. This, they'd told her, was a place for the intrepid. The first settlers would not arrive until they were middle-aged, even if they left today. Their job would be to chart terrain, and to explore the land, to name the secret schools of fish that swept through the coral reefs, and photograph night-blooming flowers. Someone in this room, they'd said in a reverent whisper, may be the first to set foot in the crystalline caves that had formed underground. Astrid had imagined herself descending to find her own adult face reflected in the frosty mineral beams.

This is a job for the brave, they'd said, a job for dreamers, for people who, like Astrid, woke every morning longing for another world. 'Imagine it,' the recruiter had said. And Astrid had.

That week, she'd bounced around with the hyper energy of a new convert. She would get into Dalton, she would specialize in astrobiology, she would be accepted into the Beta and she would go to Terra-Two.

Astrid would remember the years after that assembly and before the launch as a single shining line of triumph. The shortest route between point A, the naming of her desire and point B, leaving Earth – its sole zenith of realization.

Later, they would ask what she had been thinking when the hatch slammed shut. Had she been contemplating what a slow labour their mission was, how many minds and hands it had taken to get her to this point, to this two-minute launch window? Or was she counting every sacrifice, every year of her life she had given and was still to give?

As the flight director commenced the countdown, she heard Professor Stenton's measured voice crackle through the headset. 'Take care of yourself,' she said, the thing she said whenever she bid them goodbye from the driveway before a school trip, or at the start of a holiday with the sun in her eyes.

They would ask Astrid if she had been afraid and she would answer 'no' every time. And if she ever looked back at the strange arc of her life and wondered if any moment had been as perfect as dreaming of it, she would say, 'that one'.

The shuttle launched. Astrid burst through the luminescent atmosphere and into the black firmament beyond. She had been longing to leave her whole life, and finally nothing was standing between her and the stars.

PART TWO

JUNO

13.05.12

LAUNCH

IT TAKES OVER A million pounds of fuel to launch a shuttle into space. A fact that occurred to Juno when the engines fired and the fear came. The shuttle pitched and rolled. Juno felt the back of her seat drop away from under her and she gasped.

This was the dangerous point. Just before the solid rocket boosters lit, the computers could still call off the launch. It could be anything that forced them to abort: an overheated pump, a broken coolant valve or something more dangerous like a tank rupture. They had practised emergency escapes, jumping out of the hatch and running back across the access arm into the metal slide-wire baskets that would release them down the 400-metre drop to a shielded bunker to take cover from an explosion.

As mission control counted down the final seconds, Juno was sure that something had gone wrong, because she felt as if the orbiter was about to roll right off the launch pad. Perhaps some bolt had ruptured too early and the shuttle had ceded to gravity at this first hurdle.

But, by the time the flight director said 'One', they were upright again and then they were flying.

'Lift-off!' came the exultant voice from mission control, the same way men shout, *'Goooooooal!'* during a football match, 'We have lift-off!' and over the headset, Juno could hear laughter and applause.

It was a brutal ride. The vibration rattled her bones and her muscles seized against the shockwaves. It felt as if the rocket was strapped right onto her back. As they shuddered up into the sky, she clenched her jaw to stop her teeth from smashing like china. Her arteries flooded with adrenaline and her heart thrashed against her sternum.

Outside the window, the ground disappeared. And then, as they cleared the cobalt stratosphere, the solid rocket boosters burned the last of their fuel. Juno sensed the instant they detached because, for a second, the shaking stopped. She pictured the two cylinders falling back on themselves through the sky and into a foreign sea. Then the next stage fired and her spine was slammed back into her seat.

It was a little like being on a rollercoaster, that quick point when the carriage swings up and the passengers are pushed down, momentarily heavier.

The crew were speeding to twenty-six times the speed of sound, and for Juno, the acceleration was terrifying. She felt it first in her arms; when she tried to lift them up they crashed back onto the armrest like felled trees. Then the force intensified. They accelerated at 3g and her eyes were pinned open. Juno felt the pull of the force in the sides of her face and around her mouth as the soft tissue peeled away from her bones.

Six minutes into the flight, she weighed almost four and a half times as much as she did on Earth, and it felt like being buried alive. Her chest was trapped in a tightening vice and drawing every breath was a struggle.

All the senior crew – the veteran astronauts – had snapped their fingers and told her that the moment of suffering would fly by, but, for Juno, it felt like hours. She couldn't think past the pressure on her lungs. How long until a bone snapped? What if her heart tore loose from the sinews holding it in her chest and collapsed like a punctured balloon? It felt possible.

She had seen a video of a pilot sitting up at 3.5g. It took only a few seconds for the blood to drain from his brain into his feet, and for his eyes to roll back as he convulsed into unconsciousness.

Juno was saved from this because she was lying on her back and because her suit was designed to grip her body and stop her blood pressure from dropping too low.

When she was finally thrust into orbit, she instantly went from weighing four times as much as she did on Earth to weighing nothing at all. Her brain tried to process the sudden change and for a while – although she was still strapped in her seat – she could not shake the dizzying sensation of tumbling forwards again and again into the control panel by her feet. She had to close her eyes to fight the tide of nausea whirling in her gut.

When she opened them again, everyone was laughing with nervous relief. The checklist in Dr Golinsky's hand had begun to float and the mad-eyed statue of St Joseph of Cupertino that Igor had affixed to the dashboard for luck had come unstuck and was hovering in the air.

Out the window, it had gone from a sunny day to complete

blackness. Over her headset, mission control said, 'Good luck and Godspeed.'

SHE WOULD PROBABLY NEVER be weightless again, Juno realized with an odd disappointment as she looked for the *Damocles* through the window. Their little shuttle was due to dock with the imposing ship in thirty minutes and as they approached Juno could start to feel the heaviness of its artificial gravity.

Like other members of the Beta, she had trained for 200 hours in the Weightless Environment Training Facility – a fifteen-metre-deep pool in which scaled-down mock-ups of the *Damocles* and the *Congreve* were sunk. Those exhausting days meant that, now, the Beta were expected to take to weightlessness as instinctively as creatures designed for the sky.

But true weightlessness was different from swimming. Although Juno's clothes clung and floated around her chest in the same way, there was no real sense of *up* or *down*. No pool floor beneath or light refracting above. After a while in the orbiter, her sense of balance disappeared. There was no need for it. She unstrapped from her seat and found that she already knew how to move around the cramped space, the exact right angles to push off surfaces, the amount of force to apply to her weightless limbs. Poppy clapped as Astrid and Jesse turned gleeful somersaults in the air.

'There she is,' Commander Sheppard said, as Juno turned to see the *Damocles* rising like a shard of glass out of the shadow of the Earth. It was a strange shape, a long shining central truss banded by three torus decks – which looked like aluminium doughnuts – with no wings or rudders, nothing to suggest flight. It was not streamlined like their shuttle, because it did not need to drill against friction to escape Earth's atmosphere. It had been assembled in orbit over the past five years – a gradual process that all astronaut candidates for the Beta had followed with hopeful interest, dreaming of making it their home, of walking the round decks or harvesting crops in the glassy greenhouse that ran through its spine.

Perhaps that was why, as she spotted the glinting vessel, Juno shivered with recognition. She herself had been excited every time a new module had been built, launched into orbit and locked by skilled engineers onto the central truss. She had bought a kit and built her own model of the *Damocles* to mount on the desk in her bedroom at Dalton, a model with real decks that spun around tiny crawl-spokes, with hollow little bridges running between them all. She had even coloured her own Union Jack with red and blue gel pens and tacked it onto the round control module that protruded from the upper deck.

However, she suspected her recognition ran a lot deeper than a scale model or simulation mock-ups. She wanted to believe that the reason she felt a twinge of closure as they locked on to the giant vessel was because it was her home.

As they edged closer to it, gravity tugged at the crew. Juno's limbs grew heavier and the fluids drained from her face. The congested flu-like feeling that being weightless induced in her sinuses began to clear. The *Damocles* was equipped with two gravity-dromes that emitted 1g of fictitious force to stop their bones from crumbling and their muscles from atrophying during the long-haul journey.

When they finally docked, Juno was one of the last to climb out and when she did she felt like a swimmer surfacing, crawling back onto land. Her bones were made of iron, her head a millstone. As she stepped out of the airlock and onto the craft the muscles in her thighs began to tremble. Her first view of the ship was glittering with stars, and then her vision blackened and the floor smacked the side of her body.

JUNO AWOKE FEELING SPACESICK, shaken to her core by an unfamiliar dread. Had she made a mistake? She had made a mistake. In the window, Earth was bright as a marble and tumbling from view.

'Do you know where you are?'

Juno looked up to see a pair of steely blue eyes. 'Dr Golinsky?' she heard herself say.

'You must have blacked out,' the doctor said. 'No, don't try to get up just yet.' It took a second for the room to come into focus. Juno lifted her head and felt the bed sway beneath her, so she lay back down.

The doctor had taken off her spacesuit and changed into uniform: navy overalls and a lab coat. Eliot was also in his uniform overalls, Juno noticed. He was eye-level with her, curled up on the opposite gurney, his face glistening with sweat.

'Are you okay?' Juno asked. Before he could reply he convulsed and retched into the bucket beside his bed. The air filled with the sharp tang of vomit.

'Spacesick,' Dr Golinsky said. 'It should wear off soon, now that we're back in 1g. I'd prefer not to give him an anti-emetic for it – it's better to let him adjust to the new acceleration. You can call me Fae from now on. Brits find it easier. Are you okay to sit up?'

Juno ignored the trembling in her biceps and made a second attempt to lift herself up onto her forearms. 'It seems like low blood sugar,' the doctor said, emptying a sachet of pink powder into a glass of water and giving it a quick stir. Juno stared at the sparkling liquid, then gulped it down.

'Mmm ... strawberry,' she murmured. The sugar was a delight on her tongue.

'Yes, that's probably it.' Fae made a quick scribble on her clipboard. 'Has this ever happened before?'

'No,' Juno lied.

'You can stay here for a while to rest,' the doctor said, 'or maybe you want to nap in your cabin?'

Juno didn't want to sleep. 'Where is Astrid?' she asked.

'Probably in the crew module,' said Fae, already ticking off notes on another page. 'There'll be a lot to do for the next few days. We've worked out a rota, we'll discuss it tonight. I'll go and tell Commander Sheppard that all his crew are nominal.'

'"Nominal",' Eliot groaned, and spat into his bucket.

'You'll be all right,' Fae said. 'You just have to find your space legs.' A joke, Juno recognized. Eliot ignored her.

'Do you know where Astrid is?' Juno asked again.

'I don't know where anyone is.' He rolled over on his back and shielded his eyes from the lights.

'Poor thing,' murmured Fae as she left the room. 'There's always one.'

'Actually, one-third of astronauts suffer from some form of space adaptation sickness,' Eliot said, 'for her information. It's not just me ... and Juno, when you see Harry tell him to go fuck himself.' Juno winced as she remembered the comments that Harry had made to him that morning over breakfast.

The small windowless room was claustrophobic and the acrid smell of sick made Juno's stomach roil. She stepped unsteadily off the bed, her head still swimmy and light, and followed Fae out.

It took a moment for Juno to figure out where she was based on the mental map she had of the vessel. She had just left the infirmary, which was on the upper deck. She had to walk all the way around the circular corridor to get her bearings. To her left were four cabins with the names of the senior crew printed on the doors:

Commander Solomon Sheppard – Commander/Pilot

Igor Bovarin – Flight Engineer/Educator

Dr Friederike Golinsky – Flight Surgeon/Educator

Dr Cai Tsang – Botanist/Hydroponics Expert

That last room was empty, and although a pile of bleached white sheets had been left on the bed, no one had taken the time to strip the plastic off the mattress yet.

The kitchen was filled with sealed boxes, and although the counters were gleaming and untouched, particles of dust glittered in the air and the place smelt unfamiliar.

'You're alive.' Harry was seated at the table, his face illuminated in the light of his personal computer.

'Fortunately,' Juno said, stepping inside.

'I hear Eliot is sick too,' Harry said, a smile curling at the edge of his mouth, 'should have listened to me.'

'Oh.' Jesse, who had been leaning on the counter at the far end of the room, looked up as if Juno was a ghost. 'It's *Juno* Juma, right?'

'Right. Most people find it hard to tell us apart at first.'

The colour rose in his cheeks, 'Well, you know – fifty per cent chance,' he admitted.

It had been more difficult when they were younger. Juno and

Astrid had dressed in identical outfits until they were fourteen. But, four years on, the differences between the twins were obvious. Astrid wore make up, lined her eyes with kohl and painted her lashes emerald or tangerine. She wore tie-dyed dresses and sandals, while Juno wore either her uniform or shapeless utilitarian clothes that looked like uniform.

'What happened to you?' Jesse asked.

'Low blood sugar, probably.'

'Right.' He reached out and offered her a bag of Fruit Pastilles. 'Well, have some of these.'

Juno looked down at the rainbow-coloured sweets.

'You sure about that?' Harry glanced knowingly at Juno from across the room.

'Sure about what?' she asked.

He shrugged. 'Don't take food from strangers.'

'Jesse's not a stranger,' Juno said, although she couldn't help but notice how different he looked from the boy they had trained with only a few months ago. His hair was long now, braided. His whole face hollowed out with a kind of gaunt beauty.

Reaching into the packet, she pulled out a yellow pastille and put it into her mouth. It was lemon flavoured, sharply sweet, and stuck like mud to the back of her teeth. 'Have the whole thing,' Jesse said, offering her the packet again. 'It's bad for me to be eating so many sweets anyway.'

'Well, by all means, give them to *her*.' Harry rolled his eyes, then pulled his headphones out of the socket on his computer. 'Come and look at this.'

Juno crossed the room to peer over Harry's shoulder. On the screen was a news segment, the headlines rolling across the bottom.

'*A historic day for Britain …*' the suited reporter said, shouting over the noise of the crowd. '*From the early morning hours thousands gathered near Sandsend Fields to catch a glimpse of the launch …*'

There was a slow montage of all their faces and Juno noticed Harry gazing out at the crowd, his hair lit up by the noon-time sun. For a second she saw what they saw. A handsome leader who exuded a cool confidence.

'*Lift-off! We have lift-off. At twelve minutes past the hour: lift-off for Expedition One.*' From the cameraman's vantage point the shuttle was as little as a toothpick, trailing ribbons of smoke as it lanced against the cloudless sky. In three seconds, it was out of sight.

It was difficult to believe that morning she had been on Earth. Already, it felt like a dream. The shouting crowds in the bleachers, the reporters, the brass band …

Juno had been so busy over the past few months that there had been no time to think. But now, a frightening notion nudged to the surface of her sleep-addled mind. What if she hadn't been brave, choosing to leave? What if she had only been blind? Trading everything she knew, everyone she loved, the rest of her life, for mere promises.

'Where is Astrid?' she asked, feeling the clench in her throat.

Harry shrugged. 'Downstairs, probably.' He rewound the clip and began to watch it again.

Juno left the kitchen and climbed through the hatch to the middle deck. 'Astrid?' She felt disorientated and bereft. Once she found her twin she might be okay. She might be able to orient herself, like a shipwrecked sailor in relation to a star.

Juno searched the large crew module, then the girls' cabin.

'Heya.' Poppy's voice was bright as the door slid open. Their cabin was small. Two bunk-beds nestled into the wall with a patterned curtain for privacy, like a Japanese capsule hotel. Juno's eyes roamed to the stacked boxes at the far end of the room, to the names written on them, to the one marked Ara. 'Yeah.' Poppy followed her gaze and sighed. 'I don't know what to do with it? And we have a spare bed as well now ... we'll have to swap one of the bunk-beds with the boys, since they have one extra. Oh hey, I forgot to ask. Are you okay?'

'Low blood sugar.'

'Right, right. Can you hold this for a moment?' Poppy thrust a box in Juno's direction and rummaged around in it for a while, before pulling out a clattering string of fairy-lights. Then she searched around for a socket before plugging them in and deactivating the main lights. The room was suffused in a warm amber glow. 'Good thing I thought to bring them.' Poppy smiled, 'And my duvet covers. Makes the room look more homey. Don't you think?' She flopped back on her floral-print quilt. Only Poppy would have thought of such details. Astrid and Juno had brought comfortable clothes and books in one box, Earth food they would never see again in another: canned peaches, cookie mix, marshmallows, hundreds and thousands.

Poppy had packed frilly throws and crepe-paper lanterns, a black and white print of Audrey Hepburn. Everything they'd packed had been sent up to the shuttle months ago and was covered now in a thin layer of dust. Other items had been launched years ago; a two-decade supply of toothpaste sponsored by Colgate, microfibre duvets from John Lewis. Heinz had donated 100,000 cartons of dehydrated soup and baked beans.

'Do you think the bed could fit two?' Poppy flopped back onto it.

'Planning on inviting anyone?' Juno asked. Poppy smiled mysteriously and tapped her nose. Juno shuddered at the thought and changed the subject. 'Have you seen my sister?'

'She was in here a minute ago,' Poppy said, making a snow angel in her duvet covers.

'Was she?'

'Like ... yeah, well maybe half an hour ago?'

'Did you see where she went?'

'I dunno, maybe she's down in the hold.'

But Astrid wasn't there either; the large gloomy room under the ship that held supplies in sealed, colour-coded boxes. She wasn't in the greenhouse, the bathroom or the boys' cabin. Juno was beginning to grow frantic, retracing her steps, calling out her sister's name as maddened thoughts began to rush through her head. What if they'd left Astrid behind somehow, and Juno was spinning out into space, away from her?

Juno felt the way she did during the nights when she was young, when she woke up in their shared bedroom groping around in the darkness, post-nightmare, for a warm body that she recognized.

'Astrid,' she cried out as she looked around this new place. It was nothing like home. It smelt bitter and synthetic, like burning polymers and heated metal. It would take her a while to adjust to the level of noise as well; the mechanical whir and hum of machines rattling under the floorboards, the whoosh of air through the vents and the constant deep-sea moan of the motors whipping around the central truss made Juno wonder if she would ever sleep soundly again. And the walls felt like ice,

Juno noticed, the metal was cold like space was cold. This was going to be her home for two decades.

Twenty-three years in this tin box the size of a townhouse. Back on Earth, twenty-three years had merely been a bridge to cross to get to Terra-Two, foreshortened by her own anticipation. In twenty-three years she would be forty-one – as old as her parents were now – and she would have lived in the darkness for more years than she had lived under a sky. *This is my new life,* she thought with a sinking in her stomach. Suddenly, it didn't matter how fast they travelled – how many fractions of the speed of light they reached – Terra-Two still seemed terribly distant.

'Astrid!' she yelled, her voice threatening tears.

'Juno?' came a muffled reply. She heard it, or she thought she heard it, from behind the heavy door of the engine room.

Juno found her twin hugging her knees in the corner, half-hidden behind a bundle of pipes and wires. 'Astrid?'

'Yeah ...' Astrid's voice was thick, drowned by the shriek of an exhaust fan. Juno fumbled for the light switch but her fingers found nothing, so when the door slammed shut behind her, she could only see by the blinking glow of the computer displays in the corner, and the quicksilver flashes of light reflected off the steel blades of a fan.

'I couldn't find you.' Juno groped around in the darkness for Astrid, until her fingers caught between the soft folds of her cardigan. 'I thought ... I thought ...' The thought was too horrible.

'I just wanted to be alone for a bit,' Astrid said. 'I'm just grateful I made it.' Juno put her head in her sister's lap. And as she did so, she felt an inward release of pressure. The feeling of being home.

Juno and Astrid had been born three and a half weeks early.

Their mother had told them the story only once, described the trauma she had suffered, the blood loss. The isolating terror of that night. And when the sun rose, their mother, delirious with exhaustion, had gazed at them – these keening blue creatures that the doctors had ripped from her – and said to their father, 'We can't undo it now.' Words that had frightened Juno for years. Her mother had been saying that she would never not be a mother. That when she laid eyes on the twins, the permanence of her new status hit her with a sudden and brutal force. She would be their mother until she died and even after.

'Did we make a mistake?' Juno asked. Astrid was making quick sharp gasping sounds, her shoulders shuddering. 'Are you crying?' Juno strained to discern her sister's face in the darkness. Her cheeks glistened. She nodded.

'Do you think we made a mistake?' Juno ventured again.

Astrid shook her head.

'Are you homesick?'

Astrid shook her head again.

JESSE

13.05.12

UNLIKE OTHER MEMBERS OF the crew, he had not spent as much time training in a mock-up of the ship. He didn't already know where everything was and no one had the patience to help him. So Jesse spent most of the afternoon exploring on his own. There were three main decks; the crew's living quarters and bathroom were in the middle, while the seniors resided on the top deck near the command module. Harry and Solomon Sheppard were already there when Jesse reached it, but he shivered with excitement nonetheless. The control deck was the glittering nucleus of the ship, it was filled with light, dazzling star-maps and spinning astrolabes, the screens of a dozen monitors reeling off endless dizzying scrolls of data. It was a fantasy just standing here. Jesse watched for a moment as Harry took it all in, stroking the leather-backed commander's chair and the pilot's seat beside it, as if he, himself, could not believe his luck.

'It begins today,' Solomon Sheppard said with a smile.

Jesse had grown up wondering how it felt to be people like Harrison Bellgrave. Surely boys like Harry believed that greatness was their birthright. Strode through life, their hands open for the Oscar, the medals, the knighthood, while people like Jesse crouched in their shadow. The awkward interloper.

'Ready to feel the burn,' Harry joked to their commander. Now that they'd arrived on the *Damocles*, Harry and Commander Sheppard would perform the engine burn that would boost them out of Earth's orbit. Jesse watched the scene now, with some bitterness.

Like Harry and a large number of students at Dalton, Jesse had fought to be accepted on the pilot stream in his fourth year, when they choose specialisms. The pilot stream students trained in a separate facility, miles from Dalton, where they could practise flying for hours a day. Perhaps because of this separation, and because it was widely understood that the deputy commander would be chosen from this gifted group, the stream took on a glittering mystique, and in reverent tones was referred to as 'Command School'. Jesse himself had spent all of two weeks in Command School. He'd fought against the teachers at every turn. He had not wanted to cut his hair short, like the rest of the Command School students with their androgynous buzzcuts – the research scientists performed EEGs while the students flew and it was easier to measure their brain's electrical activity when they didn't have long locks of hair on their heads. He'd hated the loneliness of it, twelve-hour days locked in damp simulation cubicles, flying through virtual space for so long that during his brief trips outside he became fixated by the sight of the sun as if he'd stolen a glance at the face of God.

Jesse was already behind, even that first week. Many of the students, like Harry, had already logged years of private flying lessons on their families' estates, or at their town's aerodrome. But Jesse struggled with every test and knew that if his average kept dropping he would be thrown out of Dalton by November half-term. So he placed a request to switch to the least competitive stream: hydroponics. Six months spent baking under the dome of the greenhouse, or bent over trays of static solution cultures, and his score went up. It turned out that Jesse had a knack for working with living things. But he could not stifle the sting of regret, or the shame of failure.

In the end, his defection from Command School had still only earned him a place on the backup crew.

'Jesse Solloway.' Jesse was startled by the German accent of their doctor. For a second, he wondered if he was in trouble, if he had no right to be on the control deck. 'You know,' she said, 'you are just the person I've been looking for. Can you do something for me?'

She wanted him to take a box of the dead girl's things down

to the cargo bay, and Jesse realized, from her hushed tones, that she wanted him to keep it a secret.

She was everywhere, the dead girl. Not more than twenty-four hours after it had happened and her dark presence already permeated the ship, stood between Jesse and the rest of the crew, lingered at the end of every unfinished sentence. Her name, ARA SHAH, was embossed on the door to the girls' cabin, above Astrid's. Her spacesuit was boxed up next to theirs in the equipment bay, a hard shell custom-made for her dimensions.

Jesse could think of no good reason to object, and soon he found himself hauling the crate down the hatch to the lower deck, where the whirring of machines was louder and the fluorescent lights hissed like wasps. He held the barcode on the box against the scanner and the monitor flashed green. 'EARTH CARGO', it read, 'miscellaneous/personal effects/SHAH, ARA.' Jesse knew that this box, like many of the crew's belongings, had been sent up to the *Damocles* four months ago with the final supply shuttle. She would have been alive back then. Her name on the screen sent a little thrill of curiosity through him, and as he pushed inside the dully lit room, Jesse gave in to it and pried the box open.

Although most of her clothes were vacuum-packed, the box was filled with the powdery, fresh smell that Jesse associated with the female dormitory at Dalton. The faint aroma of orange blossom and jasmine. It was like a time-capsule of a teenage girl. A box of souvenir plectrums printed with the Union Jack, a string of Mardi Gras beads, an ornate hairbrush with strands of thick black hair twisted in its teeth, crushed Chinese lanterns and Polaroids. One of Eliot Liston asleep and splayed atop a mountain range of rumpled duvets. Another one of her own young self, fingers pressed against a fretboard, sitting on the refectory table. Jesse thought he remembered the incident. One lunchtime Ara and her friends had surprised onlookers with an impromptu performance of 'Knockin' on Heaven's Door', which earned them a standing ovation. At the time, Jesse had been quietly annoyed, but now he realized that he'd only been jealous. Jealous of the self-assured way that Ara grabbed at the world, with a foolhardy optimism. Her class believed that if she was not chosen for the Beta she would rise to fame in some other way, as a musician or a striking and strange runway model. She had talent and intelligence, and the unwavering love of Eliot Liston in one of those freak school romances that survived more than a summer. To Jesse, she'd seemed to have everything.

For the first time, he wondered about the person whose destiny he'd stolen. He could not fathom the darkness of a girl who could leap to her death.

What was left of her? This feeble assortment of items, vacuum-packed clothes, a spiral-bound journal with an illustration of a half blown-out dandelion clock on the cover, little seedlings carried on an imaginary wind, off the page. Jesse opened the book and flicked through it. Scrawled dates and doodles looping through margins. Moons. Falling leaves. The rings of Saturn. Thickly-lashed asymmetrical eyes. He turned right to the last page and found a blurred satellite picture of Terra-Two. *In my dreams*, she had written, *I'm already up there.*

HARRY

13.05.12

THERE HAD BEEN NO uncertainty in this arrival. No failed viva or imperfect test score, no lost tournament, not one moment during selection when Harry had questioned if he was talented enough, hard-working enough, deserving enough to make the Beta. He had never looked around at the others and asked, *Why me?* Why not? It had been his will to succeed, and so he had succeeded. The skill of his hands and the unwavering force of his determination had propelled him towards this moment. The afternoon after the launch, the first day on the ship.

Dinner that night tasted like triumph.

They had docked their shuttle with the *Damocles* at around 4 p.m. GMT and gathered five hours later in the kitchen for a celebratory meal. The lights in the corridors and common rooms were set to cycle through twelve hours of light and dark, so by the time Harry had showered and headed to the kitchen, the lamps were dim and tinted a dusky indigo. The door slid open. Harry saw that everyone was already gathered in their flight suits. Commander Sheppard at the head of the oval table, Fae and Igor either side of him.

Harry smiled at their commander. His nerves were still

jangling from the flight earlier. The engine burn that took the *Damocles* from its orbit above London, around the globe and out on an interstellar trajectory that led first to Mars, where they would meet Cai, and finally to Terra-Two. Nothing had prepared him for the sight of the entire Earth unspooling below as they dived beneath its perimeter, beneath the jagged summits of mountain ranges, smothered in clouds, below desert and ocean, day then night then day again, faster and faster until they reached escape velocity. Harry had actually yelled in excitement as the Earth sped away, the black expanse of space enveloping them, stars brighter than they had ever been. And now in the kitchen, all of their faces were bathed in the azure glow of their planet, which hung like a pendulum in the window. Every time he glanced at it, it was smaller.

Juno was leafing through the week's itinerary. Poppy sat on the counter kicking her heels up and chatting happily to Igor Bovarin in Russian.

'Say hello.' Poppy nodded at the camera Eliot was holding and then turned to Harry. Harry saw his own eyes reflected in the black lens.

'You're filming me?' he asked, suddenly wary of his hair, which was still damp from his shower and dripping down the back of his flight suit. He ran his hands through it.

'I will be,' Eliot said.

'I thought Poppy was in charge of comms,' Harry said.

'It's a two-person job, Harry.' Poppy rolled her eyes. 'I can't hold the camera *and* present.'

'Right.' Harry nodded at Eliot, who was standing close behind him.

Although he was not actively retching, Eliot still looked a

little green, and Harry was sure he could smell the bitter scent of bile on his clothes. He noted the ambiguous brown stains around the collar of his uniform, emitting an odour that never failed to repulse. Harry had not vomited involuntarily his entire life, not after the Leavers' Ball, when he and his friends finished off a bottle of Jack Daniel's, not during simulated launches, not on the human centrifuge, where he and his classmates were whirled around its fifty-foot arm in order to experience 3, then 4g. The other astronaut candidates would pale with nausea and beg the technicians to stop, but Harry had always roared 'more,' the sensation of speed nothing but exhilarating.

Some people were born for this life.

Even now, the artificial gravity on the ship felt as familiar to him as the cockpit of a shuttle, and he took to it as if he had lived amongst the stars his entire life. Fazed by nothing; not the absolute blackness of space, nor the constant ambient noise of the ship, because he was surely right for this voyage. He took his place beside the other astronauts at the table.

'You're just in time.' Commander Sheppard beamed. 'We go live in ten minutes. Better get your camera face ready.'

The meal was rehydrated beef steak and green vegetables they had brought with them on the shuttle. It reminded Harry of Sunday lunches at Dalton, but he had eaten nothing all day and it was all he could do not to shovel the food into his mouth with grateful abandon. Halfway through the meal, Igor passed around little plastic cups of sparkling white wine and held one above his head to toast.

'Before we finish eating, I'd just like to say a few words.' Solomon stood up, and his large body cast a shadow across the table. Everyone put down their forks and waited. 'These past few months were some of the most trying of my life. I know they must have been for you too. I can tell you this now . . .' he looked down for a moment. 'We lost someone we love on Saturday, and, for a while after, I wasn't sure I would make it up here at all. Ara's death is something I know it will be difficult for us to recover from.' He paused again, swallowing. Harry watched the bubbles in his cup surge to the surface. 'I've been involved in this programme since its conception. I still remember the day I saw a couple of you walking through the school gates at age thirteen, and every time I think about it I remember how far you've come. Watching you all at the launch site, waving at the crowd, taking it all in your stride, I realized that you've not only become fine astronauts. You've become fine adults. This morning, I have to say . . . I was proud. .

'It's an honour to be your commander. It's an honour to be part of this mission. You know, in Greek, the word *Damocles* means "the glory of the people", and that's what this mission will be for our country, insh'Allah.' He held his cup higher above his head and said, 'To Britain! To all of Earth!' and they all echoed him happily, clinking their glasses together and swallowing down the sharp sweet champagne.

'Okay,' said Poppy, once Commander Sheppard sat down, 'my notes from the ground said that they want us to look as natural as possible. I'll go around the table as you eat your meal. Tell the viewers how excited you are, what a smooth journey it was, et cetera. I'll start with the Beta and then pass it around to the two seniors and then Commander Sheppard can say goodbye. Are you ready?'

They looked around at each other and nodded, Eliot counted down and then the light on the side of the camera came on and Harry could tell that he was broadcasting live to Earth, because the monitor of the computer perched on the counter said so. Poppy listened to instructions from the ground through her big headphones and then finally gave them the thumbs-up.

'Welcome aboard the *Damocles*,' she said, addressing the camera. 'I'm Poppy Lane, head of communications and in-flight correspondent for this mission, which means you'll be spending a lot of time with me and my colleague, Junior Flight Engineer Eliot Liston. It's a real privilege to serve on this mission. We're grateful to the team on the ground, who are supporting our flying, and to you at home for cheering us on.' Then, for the international audiences, she said some words hastily in French, Russian, Mandarin. '*Bienvenue à bord du* Damoclès/*Menya zovut Poppy Lane/Gǎnxiè nín de zhīchí . . .*' The selection committee had been right; like Harry, Poppy was a perfect face for their mission. '*Et maintenant, un message du restes des Bêta.*'

Poppy handed the microphone to Harry first. 'So,' she began, 'Harrison Bellgrave. As one of the youngest people in space, at the start of this historic mission can you tell the viewers back on Earth how you're feeling?' Harry smiled at his own reflection in the lens, his pupils big and dark as singularities. Although, even as he felt it, it was fading from him. That familiar feeling of pride at his accomplishment. The golden shards of sunlight on the arm of the trophy as it was handed to him, the familiar weight of it. The evanescent thrill of victory. He enjoyed the game because he always won. The sound of the crowd, of a million hands clapping just for him, swift and vanishing as a roll of thunder, and what came after this? More years of striving? For what? What now?

Harry smiled anyway.

'Tonight, I feel like . . . an astronaut.'

JESSE

13.05.12

THE SOUND OF THE siren knifed into his sleep, and Jesse awoke shivering with a primitive kind of fear. He tumbled into an awareness of his surroundings. It was his first night on the ship, and he was in danger.

His time at Dalton had conditioned him into a Pavlovian response to the master alarm – stop whatever you are doing. Get up. Find the nearest exit. So that is what he did. He shimmied down his bunk and landed on the floor in time for Harry to flip on the lights.

'Do you think it's a fire?' Harry asked, his eyes wide with terror.

Eliot squinted from his bunk. 'What?' he croaked, rubbing sleep from his eyes.

'Maybe a meteor?' Jesse said. He pictured a flying rock searing a hole through the hull of their ship, and then rapid decompression as the oxygen poured out. His back prickled with goosebumps.

'Let's go,' Harry said, flinging the door open, and they dashed out into the darkened crew module where Poppy and Astrid were already gathered, blinking in their pyjamas, their faces illuminated by warning lights.

'Maybe it's a drill,' Poppy said.

'On the first night?' said Jesse.

'Drill or not, let's just do what we're supposed to.' Harry fumbled for the hatch. Jesse cast his mind back to training, where they'd slide down the ladder so fast they sustained friction burns, bare feet smacking the lower deck. Then, they were expected to strap themselves into an escape vessel and contact the ground for recommendations.

But, just as they were about to head down the ladder, Igor's voice boomed through the speakers. *'Solar storm. This is not a drill.'* Jesse heard the words with a stab of terror. *'You have six minutes to get to the shelter.'*

The blood drained from Harry's face. 'Okay,' he said, catching himself. 'This way.' The corridors were blazing the fire-engine red of the warning lights in the ceiling. Harry led them back along the corridor and Jesse was at his heels as they sprinted across the bridge that led to the greenhouse. The gravity was lighter here, in the centre of the ship, and Jesse felt it in his knees as he raced to the radiation shelter at the far end in high, flying bounds.

Harry twisted the lock and the door slid open, revealing a room only slightly larger than the infirmary, with high shelves stacked with medical supplies and tinned food. Jesse couldn't help but think of civilians in the Second World War ducking inside Anderson shelters to wait out an attack. He sank down, exhaling in relief.

Radiation from a solar flare was the silent killer in space. Every now and then flaming whips of plasma exploded from the sun's magnetic field and sent deadly showers of high-energy particles through the blackness of space. Earth was protected from most of the impact but, outside its atmosphere, Jesse and his fellow crew members were as vulnerable as a raft in a storm.

They were safe inside the reinforced shelter, but outside the alarm was still bawling. If it hadn't been for the alarm, Jesse would have slept while showers of high-energy particles ghosted through his body. Most of them would have slipped right through but a couple would shred his DNA. Best-case scenario: he would not feel the damage until years later when cancer bloomed in his bones. The worst-case scenario involved vomiting, diarrhoea and hair loss, then death within a few days or weeks. During the early years of Disaster Training, they had been taught to fear solar storms. Unlike an explosion or a collision, this was a disaster they could not see. *So*, their instructor had said, *see this instead*. He'd shown them pictures of nuclear accidents, Chernobyl victims, children blistered and bald, black and white photos of flash burns and ulcerated skin. *If you see nothing when you hear the alarm*, he had said, *remember this*.

'Lock the door,' said Igor. 'We're looking at an X-3 solar flare.'

'Right now?' Astrid was wrapped in a towel, her hair still dripping soapy water onto her shoulders from a late-night shower.

'The ground gave us a bit of warning,' Igor said. He clapped his hands to hurry them up, but they were already in a line by their bunks, and shouting their numbers.

'One,' said Harry.

'Two,' said Astrid.

'Three,' said Eliot, who, like Harry, had had no time to change out of the running shorts he'd fallen asleep in. They both stood near the door, their forearms covered in gooseflesh.

'Four,' Poppy said.

Jesse watched them in confusion, unsure where in the line he was supposed to stand, and all the while watching the Geiger counter on the wall tick up and up. There was a moment of silence and everyone looked around in alarm.

'Five?' Jesse said, guessing that perhaps this was his turn to speak.

'Where's Juno?' Poppy asked, ignoring him.

'She wasn't in our room,' Astrid said.

'I didn't see her,' Jesse said, recalling that he had not spotted the second twin racing through the corridors behind the others.

'Oh no,' Astrid gasped in horror, 'she must be *outside*.'

'You can't go out there.' Jesse motioned towards the door as if to block it.

'She's my sister.' Astrid lunged at him.

'Well, she has five minutes,' Igor said, looking at his watch. Once the shelter sealed she would be trapped outside.

'Five minutes?' Jesse echoed, looking around at the pale faces of the crew. He pictured Juno as she had looked only a few hours ago, unconscious in the infirmary, quiet and helpless. He imagined her panic, being trapped outside the shelter, alone, and his heart jolted.

'I'll get her,' Harry said, pushing Jesse aside.

'It's against protocol,' Commander Sheppard said. 'It's too dangerous.'

'You won't have time to get back,' Eliot said, looking at his watch.

'We can't just leave her!' Astrid was frantic, her face streaked with tears. 'Go! Please!'

After her panicked imploration, Jesse heard himself say, 'I'll go.' If there was one thing he had always been good at, it was running. So he dashed out the door, glancing at the figures on his watch.

'Get back.' Harry was gaining speed behind him. 'We don't need you getting in the way right now.'

'You take the upper deck,' Jesse yelled without slowing, as he dashed barefoot across the greenhouse, 'I'll go down.'

Jesse lunged through the hatch and onto the lower deck, landing so hard that the bones in his shins rattled, before running past the rooms in which she was unlikely to be hiding; the cargo bay and the equipment locker. The sound of the alarm squealing bored into his temples like a drill, and Jesse gritted his teeth in irritation. He wondered how it was possible for Juno to ignore such a racket. And then it occurred to him that wherever Juno was, she probably couldn't hear the alarm. 'Where?' he said out loud over the noise.

He knew that Juno had found Astrid, earlier that day, crouched like a mouse in the warmth of the engine room. It seemed likely that the siren was less audible there, but Jesse could not picture Juno herself seeking out solitude amongst the dim light of Igor's devices.

His watch said he had two and a half minutes left, and so he went back on himself around the lower deck. Back up to the middle deck, where the warning lights reflected manically off the walls in a way that made his head spin. As he ran he heard the pounding of Harry's bare feet behind his.

Back into the greenhouse. At the opposite end, on the far side from the radiation shelter, was a tiny module called the Atlas. Jesse headed towards it in one last search for the missing crew member. When the hatch slid open, and he stepped in, Jesse found her. Juno was curled up on one of the chairs, and Earth was large in the window. It hung above them in a way that gave Jesse the unsettling sensation of falling. But for a moment his fear vanished, and he was transfixed. He could see the Antarctic, South Africa and the Southern Lights, iridescent curtains of red and green light rising like steam off the hot bubble of the atmosphere. He had never seen them before.

As the doors closed behind him, the sound of the alarm disappeared like water sucked out of a drain. Jesse leant over to wake Juno, but paused. Her frizzy hair wafted with static electricity, her sleeping face eerily lit by the Aurora Australis. Jesse remembered that he had seen her the night before the launch. Emerging like a shadow from a briar, wearing a thin bathrobe, which, in the dim light, made her look like a visitation. The soft edge of a breast delightfully visible. The cord of her robe cinched tightly around her waist. It was an image that lingered with him.

Jesse Solloway, she'd mouthed. It had been hard to miss the distant look of disappointment on her face. The same disappointment he'd seen in all the Betas' eyes when Professor Stenton had introduced him, as if they'd hoped for someone else.

Me. I made it after all, he'd thought.

'Juno!' Harry yelled, throwing the hatch open behind them. Juno started awake, her eyes wide and vacant as a recent dreamer. The sound of the alarm crashed like a wave into the small capsule and Jesse realized, to his horror, that they had only thirty seconds. Harry grabbed Juno's arm and half-dragged her out of her seat. 'You're hurting me,' she cried. They stumbled over each other in their rush to get out. Twenty seconds. The other end of the greenhouse had never seemed so far away.

Jesse saw Astrid's terrified face peer from behind the closing door. '*Hurry!*' she screamed, the fear in her voice sharp as a blade. Jesse bounded towards her, but even as he did the door was sliding closed, the red 'Lock' light flashing. Astrid pushed her fingers through the gap in an attempt to keep it open. Jesse's lungs were on fire. He thought he could make it, but he was a metre away when the door slammed closed and he heard the hiss of mechanics as the hatch locked. It bit Astrid's finger as it shut and she let out a howl of pain, which, in a moment, was silenced.

Jesse slowed, panting. Harry and Juno were at his heels. He had never seen Harry look so terrified. Harry reached out to Juno as if to shield her, her thin body sliding into the hollow of his chest, but Jesse knew that the gesture would do little to protect her from the invisible storm of particles that were, even then, tearing through their bodies. He almost thought he could feel the burn, on his exposed skin, in his lungs. Feel his eyes growing cloudy with cataracts.

This is how it happens, he thought with numbed disbelief. He had escaped Earth only to die here, on the first night. He dropped to the ground, his knees no longer able to hold him.

There was another susurrus of locks and hydraulics and Jesse turned to find the door of the radiation shelter slide open once more, revealing a tearful Astrid, cradling her hand. Eliot threw up his arms as if to shield himself from an explosion. Igor strode out before the group.

'What are you doing?' Harry said.

'You're all dead,' Igor said to the three of them. And Jesse looked up in confusion. He realized that Dr Golinsky's look of terror had vanished.

'What?' Harry asked.

'You're too slow,' Commander Sheppard said. Igor pressed a button on a remote he was holding and the alarms fell silent, leaving a ringing absence in Jesse's ears.

'It was just a drill,' said the doctor.

Jesse wasn't sure whether to feel relieved or angry. He'd been given his life back. His heart was still galloping in his chest, and his legs felt weak under him.

'Juno.' Sheppard turned to her, his brow furrowed. 'What were you doing? When you hear the alarm you come straight here.'

'But,' Jesse protested, 'she couldn't hear the alarm. She was sleeping in the Atlas module. It's not her fault. The speaker must be switched off in there.'

'Good to know. We need to get that repaired tomorrow,' Sheppard said. 'That's the reason we do drills. To learn about hazards like that.'

Harry clenched his fists. 'I didn't know we were scheduled a drill. I'm commander-in-training. *I* should have been informed, at least.'

'Oh?' Igor growled, marching forward. 'I'm a six-time Mars veteran. I can tell you that when there's a technical failure, a hydrazine leak that leads to a fire or when you are hit by a meteor, when the pressure goes down, there's no prior warning. No one informs anyone, even you. Disasters can happen at any time and no email is sent round in advance. You kids think that now you've made it up here you've got to the safe part. That you're in the home stretch. But I can tell you that the danger has just begun. Don't get too comfortable.'

He spat the last sentence through gritted teeth, his own fists clenched. Solomon Sheppard put his hand on Igor's shoulder and laughed into the silence.

'Okay,' he said, 'that's enough. Is everyone all right?'

Jesse looked around at the shell-shocked crew. Both Astrid and Juno had tears in their eyes. Eliot was clutching his stomach as if he was about to be sick, and Poppy was leaning against the door of the shelter as if it was all that was keeping her upright. Solomon Sheppard smiled sympathetically.

'I think we all learned a few lessons to take away. I want you to think about how we could have made that evacuation more successful and come to our tutorial tomorrow morning with three recommendations. But, for now, crew, get to bed.'

ASTRID

27.05.12

IT WASN'T THE FIRST of her Terra dreams.

When Astrid opened her eyes, her cheek was pressed against wet sand and the sunlight burned. Above her head shone one amber sun, big as a dinner plate. The other, an ivory speck, small enough to cover with a thumbnail at the end of an outstretched hand.

When she sat up, the roar of the waves filled her ears. She watched them crest and then crash against the beach, sending tepid foamy water up the backs of her calves and sucking the sand back to sea. The smell of the water and the silver light glittering across it was no surprise. She had been here before. She had swum right along this stretch of beach, wriggling in delight as colonies of red anemones recoiled from her touch. And, even this afternoon, as she climbed unsteadily to her feet, it was as if she had dug her heels into this shore before.

Across the stunning expanse of water, she could make out the rings of distant planets, arcing against the sky like crescent moons drawn in chalk. After almost a lifetime on the ship, it was a relief to see a horizon. Water vapour rose up off the surface of the sea in billowing clouds and behind her vegetation waxed.

Green and yellow plants sprang up in the shadows of alien trees, their hanging vines heavy with strange, beautiful fruits that ripened in the shade.

Even if she wanted to, she could never leave, because rising above the canopy of trees was the gleaming belly of the lander. The one they had used to tear through the atmosphere and crash onto this new and welcoming Earth.

The planet was beautiful. The air was warm, sweet and spiced with the flecks of golden pollen that blew off the blossoms. The sand gave under her feet. Hers were the very first footprints. Astrid smiled as if this brilliant stretch of land had formed just for her. And perhaps it had. She was home, and she could feel it right to the marrow of her bones.

Later in the day, she would stretch out under the mottled shade of the trees to rest. Next week, in her position as Terra's first astrobiologist, she would lead an expedition further into the forest with the hope of making it all the way to the peaks of the mountains beyond. She would slip into the healing water of the lagoons, which the ship's navigator told her lay several miles east. After a year or two, voyagers from the Gamma, Delta and Epsilon missions would people this Earth, filling the air with hybrid languages and native songs. They would invent new, thoughtful customs, celebrate their arrival, tell each other again and again the story of the journey. When her hair began to silver, Astrid would wrap the first new baby in her arms and say, 'Everything good is happening at the same time.'

There was so much ahead. There was so much to discover that Astrid would never have her fill of wonder.

Someone was calling her name.

Astrid's eyes followed the footprints along the shore and she was surprised to find her sister standing in the sand, one hand on her hip and the other shielding her eyes from the sun. She called Astrid's name again. Behind her was a hand-painted flag. It cracked in the wind and swayed on a flagpole twice her height.

'Astrid!'

The whites of Juno's eyes were visible in the darkness of the dormitory. She leant up on her elbows and scowled.

'Astrid, your alarm is ringing.' Astrid became aware of the persistent buzz of the clock on her bedside table, and the tight edge in her sister's voice.

'Switch it off.'

As she fumbled for the button, Juno wriggled back under her duvet. 'Don't set it so early if you can't wake up for it.'

'I am awake,' Astrid said, rubbing her eyes.

She thought she could still feel the sand of Terra-Two between her toes.

'Juno?'

'What?'

'Have you ever dreamt of Terra-Two?'

'Not really.' She yawned and rolled over. 'We've never been there. What would I dream about?'

'I—'

'It's five a.m., Astrid. It's too early to chat.'

Swinging her legs from under the duvet, Astrid climbed out of bed. The cycling lights in the corridor were turning the tepid amber of a sunrise. The crew module was quiet; everyone was still asleep. In an hour and a half the morning alarm would ring, the lights above her would brighten to mimic the vivid blue of a morning sky, the thunder of the crew's footsteps would roll down the halls. They had been on the ship for two weeks now, and Astrid was surprised to find that the routine was not so different from the one they had fallen into at the space centre. They would gather around the same time in the kitchen and jostle for the coffee machine or trail sticky crumbs across the counter. At 7.30 they sat together around the kitchen table for the Daily Planning Conference. Commander Sheppard would read out a list of duties for that day, and any notices that had been uplinked from ground control the night before, then they would disperse and join the senior crew for their individual tutorials before regrouping for lunch.

That morning, Astrid thought that she might make a late start on some tutorial work that Igor had set them before their lesson later that day. She headed to the upper deck and around to the kitchen.

On her way, she passed the open door to Cai's bedroom. The hydroponics expert was expected to arrive on a shuttle the following day. Whenever Astrid imagined him, she pictured his skin – would it be gun-metal grey from lack of sunlight? Would his bones be long and thin, distorted by the low gravity of Mars?

Further along the corridor she was distracted by the sound of a child's voice. It was a young boy's, filtering thinly through the open hatch by the flight deck. '... Daddy? When are you coming home?'

'Stop asking him,' said a woman.

'I told you.' Solomon Sheppard's voice was still rough from sleep, undulating the way adults tended to when speaking to a child. 'When you get a little older, you'll come up here and live with me. In the place I'm going. Everyone will.'

'Mummy too?'

'Don't put ideas into his head,' said the woman. 'Can you just sing. He won't go to sleep if ...'

Astrid stepped a little closer. The control deck was like an arcade, a wonder of maps, dials and spinning gauges, hundreds of colour-coded buttons lit up on different dashboards. A vast array of glowing monitors displaying the status of key components of the ship, close-circuit television screens, hand controls like joysticks.

She pressed her face against the glass to get a better view of the commander, speaking to his young son and wife. She had forgotten he was married. His wife was a fragile copper-skinned creature, cradling her son's head against her chest. Already, her son looked bigger than Astrid remembered him. Commander Sheppard's wife had been balancing him on her hip as she waved goodbye to the ship on launch day. Astrid had been too excited to think much of it, and Commander Sheppard rarely talked about his family. Astrid wondered, now, what Sheppard's dreams were of Terra-Two – if he pictured it as a place for his children to grow old by his side.

'I'll sing your mum's favourite,' Solomon said, winking at his wife. Then he began to sing, and Astrid gasped in recognition. It was a Smiths song she'd loved growing up. She closed her eyes, pressing her face against the doorframe. She could almost hear the tristful guitar chords under his tenor. He was still humming it when the call shut off and the room filled with the grey light of static.

'I love that song,' Astrid said, opening her eyes finally.

'Oh, really?' Commander Sheppard must have known she was standing there, because he didn't start or even turn around. He leant forward in his chair and pressed his hand against the monitor, as if it was a window to a darkened bedroom back on Earth.

'How old is your son?' Astrid asked. She felt the way she used to when they left Dalton on the weekends and spotted their teachers laughing together in the Café Nero at the train station or holding a pint at the local pub. It was like spotting a rare bird out of its habitat.

'Three. I won't be able to talk to him for much longer. There's already a bit of a lag. And by the time we pass Mars real-time conversation with the Earth will already be impossible.'

'Does your son want to be an astronaut as well?'

'What three-year-old doesn't?' Sheppard turned in his seat. 'But soon he won't have a choice. The world is about to change, Astrid. Before the end of this century, the average global sea level is expected to rise six to nine metres. Half of the world's population lives close to the sea and at about four degrees of warming, scientists are expecting the loss of *all* coastal cities. Venice, New Orleans, Tokyo, Dhaka ... countries will be rendered entirely uninhabitable, vast swathes of North Africa and the Middle East, Central America. It will cause a new kind of refugee crisis, millions and millions homeless, destitute.

'Can't you see it happening now? An increase of extreme weather events, heatwaves and food shortages. Britain may be the first nation to land on Terra-Two, but how long until everyone who can afford it will flock to the skies? One day soon, there will be no "astronauts" or "pilgrims", only "refugees", "immigrants" and "fellow travellers".' He was silent for a moment. 'My son will likely have no choice,' he finally said. 'Nor will his sons and daughters.'

Astrid nodded. She had heard talk like this before. She'd

been born in the generation where they learned about climate change in geography and science classes from age nine. Heard about it so often that Astrid regarded global warming with the same limp and abstract horror as she did when she thought about the certainty of the sun dying and engulfing the Earth. The last Christmas had been particularly mild, and Astrid had even spotted daffodils sprouting near the wire fence around the churchyard. Everyone discussed the balmy weather and acknowledged their mutual and distant concern about global warming. Astrid sometimes guiltily indulged the thought that she would not be around to see it happen.

'After being captain of this ship, my main responsibility involves writing reports about the progress and success of this mission and sending them back to Earth in the hopes that more like these will soon follow. Mass off-world colonization. For everyone. Not only the chosen few. I want to make that a reality.'

Astrid stepped further into the room and noticed with a start that Solomon was not wearing any shoes. These were the daily intimacies she'd have to get used to. Living with Solomon Sheppard, Astrid was able to witness the legend up close. To look at the bare soles of the youngest Brit on Mars, and become familiar with his daily routines. In the past two weeks of living on the ship, Astrid had noticed that he prayed five times a day on a mat he laid out in his bedroom. He didn't drink coffee, but every morning he prepared himself a pot of peppermint tea, which he drank slowly and then cleaned meticulously. He liked jazz. Instead of a morning bell, he blasted John Coltrane's *Interstellar Space* through the speakers, so that every morning the crew awoke to the crashing cymbals of 'Mars'.

'Was it hard to leave them?' she asked, changing the subject and nodding at the computer monitor. Solomon shrugged again. They were on London time on the ship but in Houston – where his family had moved to – it was six hours behind.

'It was hard,' he said. 'For Na'imah. But then she knew what she signed up for when she married me.'

Astrid was trying to figure out exactly how old Solomon was. When he'd been selected as the only Brit to fly to the Russian station on Mars, he had also been the youngest astronaut in history, at just twenty-five. Astrid had been eight or nine, then, which made him . . .

'You know what that song's about right?' she asked. He shook his head, eyes blank and tired. 'It's about hope. You know, "the light"? The light that never goes out.'

'Right.' He half smiled. 'Of course. That's what brought us up here. That's all that can keep us.'

POPPY

29.05.12

TWO WEEKS ON THE *Damocles* and Poppy was already tired of hearing Astrid talk about Terra-Two. She could not imagine the schools of silver fish that lanced through lagoons, or the periwinkle birds' eggs nested in leaves, or the mountain ranges where the suns never set.

For herself, Poppy couldn't wait to see the green prospect of Terra-Two in the window of the ship. The thought of taking the shuttle down into the atmosphere and leaving the first human footprints on white alien shores made her stomach quiver with excitement. And yet the finer details of her life on Terra-Two had always been vague. She never understood how it was possible to ache like Astrid for a land she had never travelled. Earth was enough for her.

Earth had always been enough for her, and she realized it only when it was gone.

There was a Portuguese word for it that Poppy knew: *saudade*. A longing for something that might never return.

After the launch, Poppy had witnessed her first orbital sunrise through the window of the shuttle an hour before they were due to rendezvous with the *Damocles*. They had been allowed to float out of their seats and gaze out the window at Earth below. For most of their journey the planet had been cast in shadow, a black and swollen ocean. Poppy watched as it tumbled slowly out of the way of the sun. Dawn began as an electric-blue arc of light cresting above the horizon, and when the sun appeared it was a fire-red pea on the perimeter, which burst forth, turning white and filling the porthole with brilliant rays of light. Everyone turned for just a second; even Fae and Igor stopped what they were doing, looked up from their monitors and craned their necks to gaze down at their old home.

There is a strange disassociation that comes from seeing something for the first time in real life when you have seen it thousands of times before on television or in magazines. The Eiffel Tower, the Angel of the North, a total solar eclipse. Poppy had anticipated that she would feel that same detached familiarity when she finally saw Earth. But that afternoon after the launch, in the shuttle, Poppy realized that she had been mistaken. Realized that, in the vast solar system, her planet was the greatest sight to see. Impossible not to marvel at it. To tremble in its light. Whorls of clouds, larger than mountains but delicate as breath, ivory vapour trails, so much dark sea. When she finally beheld it, with her own eyes, and not through satellite images or computer reconstructions, she began to cry. She felt like Lot's wife as she gazed at the deserts and the sea. Ripples in the sand dunes appeared as black striations against the golden ground. The coastlines were a brilliant chrome blue and the mountain ranges were like scars on the earth. Poppy felt it for the first time – a scintilla of doubt. Her own sickness, homesickness.

To her relief, in the tumult of the days that followed – when they were settling into the *Damocles* and every hour was filled with work – she would only remember that feeling whenever she awoke in the night with a jolt and saw, in the porthole of her bedroom, only darkness.

Their days on the *Damocles* were similar to their final day before the launch. They were expected to wake by 6.30 for a full day of classes, tutorials and three hours of chores required for the maintenance and upkeep of their home. The only free time that Poppy could really enjoy was after dinner, at 8 p.m. The Atlas – the observation capsule near the greenhouse – had become her favourite place to lounge. It was just big enough for two people to sit on the little bench in front of the glass. There was a telescope and a monitor displaying a star map, and when she touched the screen it answered her questions about the constellations. Poppy would climb the ladder up to the little room, look back at Earth and read about Andromeda, Cassiopeia, Fornax, Orion ... every one.

She loved watching when the planet rolled in front of the sun, and the cities began to blaze against its shadowed face. Through their telescope, she could pick out London and Lagos and the whole of the east coast of America through a recognisable lacework of roads. By day, the cities were cement-coloured smudges against the land, indistinguishable from the grey-green of suburbs and countryside, but, at night, humanity shouted its existence at the stars. Poppy could tell the population density from the sodium orange belts of light that made up roads, country borders and interstate boundaries. Japanese cities burned blue-green, and a bright sprawl of mercury vapour lamps illuminated the streets along the black hollow of Tokyo Bay. Their commander pointed out Mecca, a patch of light against a jet desert, and the interstate highway that lanced across El Paso. All the places she would never go.

'No wonder there's global warming,' Juno said that night, leaning into the window to take a photograph, 'when you look at all this. There are so many people. It's so bright.'

'I can still see London,' said Poppy.

'It looks like a neuron,' Juno said, jostling for the eyepiece. Poppy knew what she meant. The glowing nucleus branching off in glittering interlocking trails of light. The Thames slit a dark line through the city and opened like an inky mouth at the estuary.

'Do you think they can still see us?'

'Not likely,' Juno said, shrugging, 'not without a telescope.'

Viewed from the side, Poppy could see the opalescent layers of the planet's atmosphere. It looked as delicate as a bubble and yet it kept the world beneath them alive. It trapped in heat, it set fire to rogue asteroids on course for civilization and protected the life below from cosmic radiation. For a few days, their course had been on the right latitude for Poppy to see streams of charged particles sucked into the Earth's magnetic field. They smashed into atoms in the upper atmosphere and excited electrons. The Northern Lights. Whenever she gazed at them, she thought about what a great thing it was to be alive right at that moment.

There were people on Earth squinting through telescopes and following the progress of the *Damocles* through the sky. *Is my mother one of them?* Poppy wondered sometimes. Her mother was the only one she was leaving behind. Just weeks into their mission and she only communicated with her daughter in cryptic emails, hyperlinked articles that Poppy couldn't always open, photographs of horoscopes cut out from the local newspaper or screenshots from websites. Poppy never knew how to reply. She always wondered if her mother scoured the internet for the predictions she knew were relevant – perhaps that was why the most recent had read:

Virgo: Jupiter continues to transit your solar ninth house. Under this influence, you may have opportunities to travel, study abroad and expand your horizons.

Whenever she opened a link to another horoscope, Poppy couldn't figure out if she was confused or disappointed. She had been glad to leave her mother behind, and every time she was glad she was also guilty.

Dear Poppy, this year eclipses will fall into your solar fourth and tenth houses and third and ninth houses. The sun is setting fast. Take a stand against disillusion. Good things can last.

Did she think that Poppy would understand her, now that they had the stars in common?

ELIOT

03.06.12

ELIOT KEPT THINKING ABOUT Cai's life on Mars. The man had arrived in his own shuttle, a week earlier, worn out by his journey. They'd all stood by the hatch grinning, and Poppy had painted a banner saying 'Welcome'. As the hatch opened they all clapped, but Cai greeted the crew with a narrow-eyed snarl, so exhausted by the ship's gravity that he slumped against the airlock wall. He was in his fifties and had spent most of his life on Mars, talking to computer monitors and plants. He had engineered anaerobic cacti that flourished in the arid craters of that planet, tended to oxygen gardens and landscaped botanical parks. He'd spent so long on Elysium Mons that most of his equipment was still stained the haematic red of the soil. Eliot had heard Igor say that they had been lucky to recruit him for this mission. Cai had been coming to end of his tenure at the International Laboratory and was looking to discover, for himself, what alien plant life blossomed in the soil of Terra-Two.

Years spent hunched in the low gravity of Mars had altered him forever, stretched his bones long and thin. He stood, now, at almost seven feet, his femurs and spine grossly elongated but brittle as a bird's. He could barely stand in the 1g force on most of the ship and preferred to spend his time in the greenhouse, where the gravity was 60 per cent that of the Earth's.

Cai's arrival had been exciting for the Beta crew for all of five minutes. He spoke little, rarely turned up to dinner and when he did he was sullen and ornery, his mouth turned down as if he was sucking on something sour. 'Poorly socialized' was the phrase that Eliot had heard Fae whisper.

Eliot wondered what it had been like to be alone for that long. He wanted to ask him, but was nervous about approaching the older man. In between the arrival and departure of various international expeditions, Cai had manned the Mars laboratory alone, living on the same cycle of freeze-dried meals and thumbing through the same old paperbacks abandoned in the library.

The reporters on Earth had regularly posed that same question to all of the members of the Beta: how do you cope with the isolation on board the ship? They didn't know that, in some ways, this was the least alone Eliot had been his whole life. Sharing a room with other boys, the constant chatter that rumbled through the walls from morning bell until night, the regular keening of various life-support machines. Everything was shared, the one-size-fits-all jumpsuits that they all took turns scrubbing and then posting into their uniform cubbyholes on the lower deck, the bedsheets and most of the food. The board games donated by various charities and the vast library of TV shows and movies and books stored in the ship's databank.

He'd said to the reporters, 'I'm handling the loneliness just fine.' But he never mentioned the other kind of loneliness that was eating him like a cancer; the constant phantom-limb pain of grief over Ara's death. He was certain that everyone could see his suffering and was wincing at the sight of it. So most of the time Eliot communicated with the rest of the crew from behind the lens of a camera, which made them smile dumbly at him and stare straight through.

What was Mars like? he wondered. *Was the ground soft like sand underfoot, or was it cracked as skin and stone-hard?*

Some months, Cai had been the only person on the entire planet.

'How did you fight the loneliness?' Eliot finally summoned the courage to ask him one evening after dinner.

Cai did not look up. 'Are you filming me?' he asked, tipping heaped teaspoons of sugar into his coffee.

'Not yet,' Poppy said, turning to Eliot just to double check the light on the side of his camera. Then she looked back at Cai and asked, 'How can you drink that stuff? It tastes as if it was made in a lab. It tastes like lighter fluid.'

'Is lighter fluid a popular beverage in England?' Cai asked, his mouth curling a little.

Poppy and Eliot had been instructed, by a few producers at the Interplanetary Channel, to downlink more footage of the elusive new astronaut.

'Everybody has their drug of choice,' Cai said. His nervous fingers drew a circle around the rim of his cup. Eliot noticed that they were stained the acid-green of the fertilizer he handled all day. 'Though,' Cai continued, 'spend as long as I have in space and you'll discover that choice really has very little to do with it.' Finally, he turned to the camera with his grey eyes. 'Put that thing down, would you?'

Eliot obliged.

'Now, what did you ask me?' Cai asked.

'About what?'

'About the loneliness?'

Blood flooded Eliot's cheeks. He hadn't realized that he'd asked the question out loud. 'Nothing,' he said. Cai simply stared at him, his stained fingers making hollow tapping sounds on the side of his cup.

'I mean,' Poppy said, to fill the silence, looking between the two men, 'you haven't set foot on Earth for over thirty years.'

'That's correct,' Cai said.

'Is there something you miss the most?' she asked.

The scientist took a moment to think and then said, 'Nothing at all. You know, there is nothing about this life that does not suit me. There were 2.7 billion people on Earth the year I was born and now there are 7 billion. Sometimes I used to lie awake at night and think about all the people in the world. Jumbled hive of consciousness, trillions of busy multiplying cells. It was claustrophobic. There is no frontier left to discover, down there. Almost every inch of the Earth has been trodden under a million feet. Photographed hundreds of thousands of times. But,' and he closed his eyes, 'to be alone is divine. To trek through lightless craters, leave the first and sole footprints on Martian mountains. Tear through the hard vacuum of space unfettered by the sickly mass of humanity we left behind.' He leant forward and caught Eliot's gaze. 'There is only yourself, first and last. Meet him with courage, meet him with gladness. There is only one. There is love to be found. Adventure to be had.'

Eliot shifted uncomfortably, then pressed record on his camera, if only to put a barrier between himself and this man. 'I . . .' he said, 'I've been told to go around the ship and ask everyone about their first impressions of life on board. I only have you and Jesse Solloway left.'

Cai stared unsmilingly at the camera. 'Nothing to report. Progress has been good. About fifty years ago, before fictitious-force gravity-dromes were widely used, a lot of the time aboard a new craft was spent adjusting to zero gravity. That's no longer an impediment; with our feet firmly on the ground, I've spent the past week or so making the ship habitable. As the hydroponics expert, I spend a lot of my time up in the greenhouse growing the plants that in a year or two we will come to rely on as our primary food source and which will provide and filter a small percentage of our oxygen. Needless to say, this is a vital role and that is the reason I was scheduled to rendezvous with the *Damocles* so early on in the mission instead of in a month when the ship flies-by Mars.

'At the time of this recording, we have twenty-three years until we reach Terra. Twenty-one days down, approximately 8,374 to go.' Cai set his empty mug in the sink before he left the room.

'Was it good?' Poppy asked, leaning over Eliot's shoulder while he played the recording over again. She crossed the name 'Cai Tsang' off their list. 'Only one left,' she said, then brushed her fingers across her forehead with a frown. 'You know, could you do the last one alone? I think I have a bit of a headache. I might go and lie down.'

Eliot gritted his teeth and headed downstairs to find Jesse.

Jesse and Eliot had never been good friends. Their social circles did not intersect, and the only term they had lived together was in the first year of sixth form, when Eliot had been assigned Jesse as a roommate.

On the face of it, the two boys had cohabited for ten weeks in a kind of awkward peace. But Eliot, who had always been terrified of confrontation, found Jesse's strange habits deeply irritating. He despised the smell of incense, which Jesse burned whenever the dormitory was empty in flagrant disregard of the school's fire-safety regulations, so that their room smelt like a hippy curiosity shop. He hated the other boy's slovenliness. Eliot alphabetized his DVD collection; Jesse discarded his boxers like orange peels across the rug, alongside foil wrappers of cereal bars spewing stale crumbs. The odd hours he kept, waking up late and then staying awake until the early hours of the morning, his skin sickly in the wan light of his computer, googling diseases and then examining the whites of his eyes in the mirror. It was the autumn term, and, as the days diminished, so did Eliot's patience. Something about the darkness that cloaked their room, something about the cold that set in and the condensation that blinded the windows, made the situation even more claustrophobic. By the time December came, Eliot despised even the sound of the boy's footsteps, cursed the obnoxious way he cleared his throat.

A cruel joke, now, that they were sharing a room for years. Those grim weeks of annoyance and passive aggression had been a brief primer for eternity. Instead of Ara's face, he'd wake up to Jesse's. Eliot shuddered as he headed down the bridge. Once again he reminded himself that it wasn't Jesse's fault. But Eliot could not help but remember that, less than four hours after Ara died, Jesse had leapt into the light and volunteered for her place, like a vulture descending on a corpse. He hated him for that.

The boys were on the lower deck, competing on the simulator. Jesse sat in the mock commander's chair in the centre of the room, and Eliot could see that his eyes were narrowed behind virtual-reality goggles, watching the controller with white-knuckled concentration. Harry leant over the edge of it as if he was watching a football game, and when Eliot entered the room with his camera they both groaned loudly.

'Move out of the way,' Harry shouted, swatting at Eliot's thigh but missing.

'I need to get one last interview,' Eliot said. But Jesse didn't reply.

Of the many games banked on the ship's computer, this was their favourite. It was an adventure game that involved traversing some artist's schizophrenic dream of the galaxy, where cosmic background radiation shimmered like television static against an aubergine sky. Every now and then, a star burst into brilliant light, filling the screen with silver, red and gold. At each level, the computer taught the gamer new skills, which they had to manipulate and alter in the following levels. Jesse was in the middle of crash-landing on an alien planet. His craft had sustained damage and he didn't have much time, according to the dashboard. Jesse collided with the stratosphere at the wrong angle, like a belly-flopping diver. So badly that Eliot winced. Jesse swore as the screen lit up and the hull of the ship began to flake away like crepe paper, flayed by the friction of the planet's atmosphere. A virtual alien on that planet might look up and see a shooting star for a few brief moments as Jesse set fire to the sky.

Harry clapped slowly, laughter on his lips. Jesse's measly score appeared on screen.

'I'll show you how it's done,' Harry said, climbing out of his seat to grab the controller. Jesse pulled off his VR goggles and rubbed his eyes, the shame boiling in his cheeks.

Eliot suddenly remembered his purpose. 'I need an interview,' he said, nodding at Jesse.

'Right, right,' Jesse agreed. 'Wait, isn't Poppy supposed to be doing this?'

'She has a headache,' Eliot said.

'Sure.' Harry rolled his eyes. 'Anyway, can't you see that we're busy.'

'This is our job,' Eliot snapped at them, already tired, his own headache coming on like a slow drumbeat behind his skull. 'We can't all be commander-in-training.'

Harry's mouth curled into a sneer. 'I guess.' His eyes rolled down to the little pin with bronze wings attached to the side of his overalls.

'You know,' Eliot said, massaging his temples, 'guess whose photographs will make it into the history books? When we get to Terra-Two, who will capture that moment for the world?'

'And who will be in those photos?' Harry retorted. 'Some record history and others *make* history. No one remembers the cameraman.'

'Okay ...' perhaps Jesse could tell that Eliot's patience was running thin, 'let's do it.'

As Eliot switched on the camera, Harry dropped the conversation and settled onto another game.

'The questions are the same as the ones I've been asking everyone. How do you feel about the mission? Have you been settling in? What have the past two weeks been like for you? That sort of thing.'

'Right.' Jesse's eyes rolled up as he thought for a moment. 'To be honest, it's a bit of a challenge. I'm from the backup crew and so I didn't get quite the same training as the prime crew. So, a lot of things are still new to me. But, you know, it's great to be here. Sometimes I wake up in the night and forget and then remember . . .' Jesse glanced at the game Harry was playing on the screen. He was already through the first level. Harry was always winning. He flew through the easier levels with a practised ease, dodging and diving past radiant formations without a sideways glance at the star chart. It was as if he could navigate the universe by heart. Even Eliot abandoned the conversation for a few minutes to watch Harry's fingers fly across the controls, his eyes triumphant behind sheets of reflected light. He was exactly as good as he thought he was. Able to preserve his ship and crew as he soared through lightyears of imagined space. Eliot could tell that it stung Jesse a little to watch, nightly, as his rival soared unvanquished past all the others, racking up higher and higher scores every night. 'He's in a different league,' Jesse muttered to Eliot, his eyes fixed on the screen.

'So,' Jesse said, turning back to the camera, 'I remind myself to be grateful every day. I'm on a real adventure, even if the day-to-day life of being on a ship is not always thrilling. I still feel like one of the luckiest people in our solar system.'

Eliot cringed.

In the background, Harry swore loudly. They both turned.

'Watch it,' Eliot said, pausing the recording. 'You can't swear. This will be broadcast all over the world. Schoolchildren are watching this. Jesse, can you repeat what you said?'

But Jesse was again distracted, watching as Harry's small vessel came into contact with a space station. Harry was tasked with executing the complicated set of manoeuvres required to dock with its port. It was moments like this when Eliot appreciated the graphics, the elaborate detail of the imaginary station circling a phantom moon. Eliot could tell from the beads of sweat on Harry's forehead that he was struggling.

'Can you repeat what you said?' he asked Jesse.

'Sure,' but Jesse turned again at a sound from the simulator, and the screen filled with light. Harry had guessed the angle of approach wrong and lost control of his shuttle, which crashed into a wing of the space station. On the screen, it shattered like glass, one whole truss snapping off, exploding in incandescent shards that accelerated in all directions. With a groan of failing machines, the game was over. Harry let out a huff of frustration, but Jesse keeled over in hysterical laughter.

'I'd like to see you do better,' Harry said. He tossed the controller at the wall and stormed out.

In the instant the door closed behind him all hilarity evaporated, and Jesse eyed the simulator screen warily. Perhaps remembering that Harry was going to be their commander one day. 'I guess, it's not just a game, though,' he said.

'No,' Eliot said. 'Not to him, I don't think.'

'Not to me either,' Jesse said, gritting his teeth.

LATER THAT NIGHT, ELIOT re-watched the recording he had made on his laptop. He examined the scene carefully, Jesse's face in the foreground, with his eyes fixed on the projector screen. Harry, in the distance, holding the controller. And there, in the window, Eliot thought that he could see something. Ara's face, staring at him through the glass, her lips black, eyes yellow and half-open. Even then, when he gazed at it on his computer, his heart kicked in his chest and he was unable to breathe for a moment.

'*What's wrong?*' Jesse asked the screen.

'*Nothing,*' came video-Eliot's voice from behind the camera.

Eliot paused the recording, rubbed his eyes and pressed play. But staring at Ara's face was like staring at a fluorescent light. Even when he closed his eyes, the shadow of it stained his retina. 'Ara,' he said, touching the screen.

Jesse smiled from behind it. '*Hey—*' he laughed nervously. '*You looked for a second like—*' Eliot pressed the rewind button. But this time, Ara's face had vanished from the window. He rubbed his eyes again. It had just been his own startled reflection.

'*What's wrong?*' Jesse asked in the video.

'*Nothing,*' video-Eliot had lied.

'*Hey,*' Jesse said, smiling at the camera, '*you looked for a second like you'd seen a ghost.*'

POPPY

THE DAY THE EARTH disappeared, Poppy had been reading. One of the few novels she had brought with her: the first Harry Potter book, a scrappy second-hand copy she'd been sent by her father. He'd found a Latin edition, *Harrius Potter et Philosophi Lapis*, in an Oxfam bookshop. This dog-eared paperback with its coffee-stained cover was a delight to read, because it reminded her of home, of lying on her back on the carpet, feet pressed up against the caging on the radiator, transported again and again away from the tedium of her own life and down the dim halls of that dead language. Latin had not been her first, but it was her favourite. Poppy liked to believe that simply by thinking in it, she was breathing life into it. *Non est ad astra mollis e terris via*, as she had thought on the shuttle. *There is no easy way from earth to the stars.* She was like a linguistic necromancer. She might not be a medic or a robotics genius, she might not have as much to bring to Terra-Two as her clever friends, but Poppy liked to console herself with the fact that she could bring this, she could bring Japanese and German, she could teach Latin to colonist children and resurrect it.

People often asked Poppy whether or not the languages ever

became 'mixed up' inside her head, like a jumbled salad of half-formed tongues, muddled masculine and feminine, pronouns and present perfect, alif and alpha. Which was a question that Poppy always found difficult to answer because, in her head, sometimes the words *did* run together. She'd begin a thought in English and then find the perfect untranslatable word for it in French. *Dépaysement. La douleur exquise.*

How had it started? Poppy had heard about driven parents who hired nannies to teach their children four different languages, and there had been a few students at Dalton whose mothers had glamorous international jobs that required spending their summers in Myanmar, finishing off high school in Cape Town, a sabbatical in Lesotho; children who learned the languages as a matter of necessity.

Poppy had not been one of them. She'd come of age on a council estate in Liverpool, but within those concrete walls she had heard dozens of languages. Their Polish neighbours had four blond boys they'd sometimes ask Poppy's mother to babysit. One floor down lived Amira, the easily frightened Ethiopian woman whose clothes Poppy had offered to wash when her machine broke. In 9a lived the three-generation Pakistani family, Mr and Mrs Bhatia with their clever daughters and grandchildren.

One day, Poppy returned from school to find that her mother had disappeared. Absconded for a week to Ibiza with a boyfriend who disliked children. She'd pinned a pink fifty-pound note to the noticeboard by the front door and the phone number of her boyfriend's sister.

Tia, the willowy Kenyan woman who lived upstairs, horrified that her neighbour had left her nine-year-old daughter alone for so long, offered to let Poppy stay for the week. Poppy slept on the sofa. But Tia's young daughters did not like their new house guest; they called her '*muzungu*' and picked at her hair as if it had fleas in it.

'What does that mean?' Poppy had asked.

Tia had shrugged. 'It just means "white person",' she'd said with a dismissive wave, only the way that they said it, it sounded like an insult. So Poppy had worked hard that week to learn a few phrases in Swahili – *hujambo, asante sana, lugha moja haitoshi*. And the girls had accepted her words like a peace offering. Gave her others to add to her collection. Soon, the mood in the house changed, as if Poppy had crossed a threshold into their family, and by the end of the week they were singing raucously to Swahili songs, clapping their hands and braiding each other's hair.

By the time Poppy's mother returned, suntanned and exhausted, Poppy had realized that *she* had travelled somewhere too. It occurred to her, then, that there was a cure for her loneliness, that perhaps language had been the only barrier all along between herself and Amira, or the Bhatias and their blushing children. Six months later, she returned home from school and bumped into one of Tia's daughters, who had showed her the friendship bracelet she'd woven for her out of loom bands and said, '*Ninakupenda.*' *I love you*.

That was how it began for Poppy. She found that she had a knack for languages, that her tongue bent easily into unfamiliar shapes, that learning each new language felt like furnishing the mansion of her mind with new rooms through which she could wander. Soon she was asking her mother for language courses for Christmas, finding the cheapest ones she could afford, online lessons, podcasts. She requested *Harry Potter* in Japanese, Polish, Swahili. And the more she learned, she found, the more her mind was able to acquire, as if it was some impossible well that could never be filled. At first, Poppy used languages to help her to escape her mother's neglect, but later, she discovered with delight that the languages could help her to escape her whole insipid life.

She had probably been given an interview at Dalton because one local newspaper had named her the city's youngest 'hyper-polyglot'. Poppy had always suspected that something about a mind that could grasp the counter-intuitive logic of another language appealed to the directors of the space programme. It meant that Poppy had easily picked up computer coding, learned the syntax and semantics to express the algorithms.

'What are you reading?' Jesse asked, breaking into her reverie as he climbed down the ladder and squinted at the title. 'Is that *Harry Potter*?'

'Yep.' Poppy didn't look up from the dog-eared pages.

'In Italian?'

'In Latin.'

'Ha.' Jesse smiled. 'There's a version in Latin?'

'That's right. Only the first two books though. I've heard there's a version in Ancient Greek as well. It's the longest Ancient Greek text written since AD 3.'

'Children's books in Ancient Greek – pretentious much?' Harry said from across the room.

'Says the man playing chess.' Astrid rolled her eyes.

They'd gathered, as they often did after dinner, in the crew module, which after three weeks on the *Damocles* had taken on the same chaotic energy as their sixth-form common room. It was filled with the flotsam and jetsam of their confined lives. Abandoned board games, balled-up uniforms socks and UKSA-issued vests, joint property that no one felt strongly enough to lay claim to. That evening, Astrid was plaiting Juno's hair into cornrows at one end of the room, Juno cross-legged on the floor, resting a cheek on her sister's knees. Harry and Eliot were engaged in a hectic game of chess that involved moving their pieces and then hammering the timer down after each turn.

'Nice to see someone reading a real book,' Jesse said.

'What do you mean "real book"?' Juno asked, unable to turn her head as Astrid slid the oiled teeth of a comb into a tuft of her hair. 'Like paper and glue?'

'Yeah. Instead of the computer screens and tablets we always use. I know weight restrictions mean we can't bring our whole personal library up here, but nothing compares, you know, to the smell of the paper, and a book doesn't need batteries.'

Poppy flipped to the next page.

'It's not about paper and ink,' Juno said. 'What's important is data. For the next generation. When we get to Terra what will happen to all our history, all our science? If our technology dies and that's where all our information is recorded, will it take them another millennium to remember that bacteria causes disease? What happens to Sophocles and Sylvia Plath? It only takes a generation to lose all that. It's all information, stored in terabytes of data in our hard drives. Backed up, incorporeal.'

'It's not just about preserving the past, though,' Astrid said. 'We'll discover new things. Our children will write their own literature, new philosophies.'

Poppy reached the end of the chapter and stood up. Drawn, as she often was, towards the window. Up until this point in the journey she could cover Earth with a thumb pressed against the glass, watch as it diminished to the size of a blue star. But, that evening, Earth had disappeared altogether. She examined the other windows, rubbed the sleep from her eyes, wished it back into being.

'What are you looking for?' Astrid noticed her agitation.

'Have you seen it?' She was surprised to find that her stomach was suddenly tight as a fist inside her.

'What?' Astrid blinked in confusion.

'Home,' Poppy said. 'It's gone.' Eliot and Harry looked up from the chequered board.

Astrid got up off the sofa. She pressed her face to the window in silence, then said, 'So it is', her voice light with wonder.

'Don't be melodramatic,' Eliot said, without looking up. 'It's not "gone". Where would it go? It just looks like a star.' He glanced up at them then sighed, walking over to the glass wall and beckoning them over. 'Look over there—' he pressed his finger against it. 'Earth looks just like a star. A big star, and right next to it – there, can you see? – the moon. It's just smaller. In a day or two you'll need a telescope to see it.'

A wide smile spread across Astrid's face. 'It's beginning,' she said, and walked back to the sofa.

'What is?' Harry looked a little uneasy, though he'd returned to his game. Juno returned to her position under her sister's comb.

'Can you feel it in here?' Poppy asked them, touching her stomach. 'Like spacesickness . . . ?'

Astrid shook her head. 'The best part of the journey,' she said. 'Everything's ahead of us.'

Something about Astrid's words and the glee with which she delivered them made Poppy feel ill, an elevator-drop panic that she had been cast adrift in this nothingness, continually accelerating away from sky and sea and solid ground. She had to run back into the bedroom before her mouth dropped open with a cry of fear and despair in front of the others.

Sobs tore out of her, and with them everything she had been hiding for weeks, months. Her private doubts about the mission, her loneliness, her grief for home and for Ara and everything she had left behind. Then other things too, the tumult of the pre-launch days compared to the lull of space, her boredom, her impotence and wriggling insecurity. Her sobs came out in huge quaking gasps and even as they did she felt the indulgent satisfaction of them. All those years in Dalton it hadn't been okay to cry, but today . . .

Est quaedam flere voluptas. There was a certain pleasure in weeping.

Poppy only looked up a little while later, when she heard the sound of the door clicking open. She drew a hand across one eye, wiping away just enough of the tears to see Harry's outline in the light.

He observed her silently for a moment, with an expression she couldn't discern. 'You look so ugly when you cry,' he said.

And she saw him for a moment, as she sometimes did, as just a little bit mean, his mouth twisted in a cruel sort of smile. But in the next moment he leant down and kissed her. She'd seen the shampoo that he used in his bathroom cubbyhole, an expensive brand. Sicilian lemon and tangerine. The smell was heady.

'I feel it here too.' He touched his stomach in the same place she had. 'It hurts for me too.'

ASTRID

07.06.12

ASTRID WAS SURPRISED WHEN Poppy did not turn up for their lesson on Thursday. Group sessions normally took place around the kitchen table, with the senior crew member taking them standing at the head. That afternoon it was Cai, and the room was still ripe with the smell of the rehydrated chicken soup they'd had for lunch.

'There are five of you,' Cai said, looking over all of their heads as if he was not certain.

'Poppy says she's sick,' Juno said, flicking a sticky pea off the table. 'Who was on cleaning duty this week?'

'Sick with what?' Harry asked, slamming his folder down in front of him.

'I don't know.' Juno sighed. 'She says she's been having headaches.'

'Well, she's supposed to get permission from the commander to miss a group lesson. And she'll have to catch up,' Cai said, then looked down at his tablet. 'We're going to look at the article I sent you all from the *Journal of Marine Science and Ecology*—'

'Oh,' said Juno, tapping the correct page on her tablet. 'I've read it already. I think. The one about conservation genetics and coral reefs?' She saw Astrid straighten up at her words, her eyes alight with excitement.

'The reefs on Terra-Two?' she asked, and as she said it she could see them, the rainbow-coloured coral, wreathed in teal weeds. She clapped her hands together in excitement. 'We're finally going to learn about them.' But Astrid was surprised to see that everyone was looking at her quizzically.

'What are you talking about?' Harry asked. 'What reefs?'

'The coral reefs on Terra-Two,' Astrid said. Eliot raised an eyebrow.

'I'm not familiar with that,' Cai said. 'I don't think we have much evidence of the marine life on Terra-Two. Now, can you please open that page?' He turned to the whiteboard he'd wheeled from the corner. 'Does this pen work? That'll do. Right, now. Who can summarize *negative* frequency-dependent selection . . . ?' Juno and Harry raised her hands.

AS THE LESSON CONTINUED, the thought niggled at Astrid. She couldn't remember anymore where she'd come by the notion of coral reefs on Terra-Two, or why she had such a clear image of them in her mind. During dinner that evening, both Commander Sheppard and Igor confirmed that they were not even sure that coral could survive, considering the high ocean temperatures on the planet.

So, during her free time after dinner, Astrid accessed the *Damocles*' online library on her laptop. She discovered quickly that Cai had been right and there was no evidence of reefs, but Astrid followed one link after another, opening tab after tab in an encyclopaedia deep-dive that led her to a few biographies of Tessa Dalton.

Tessa Dalton had been the first person to dream of Terra-Two – although she lived and died in near obscurity. Astrid first heard the name in her second year in the programme, when a bronze statue of Tessa was erected in a red-brick quadrangle at Dalton Academy. The sculpture had been different in every way from the serene marble busts that overlooked the school assembly hall or the stern likenesses of the founders standing watch on the front lawn. A group of parents had complained when it was first donated to the school, because her naked body looked so lifelike. Tessa Dalton's eyes were protuberant and pupil-less, turned skyward. It was not a flattering likeness: the wasted muscles in her thighs, the puckered scars on her forearms, deflated breasts hanging on the cage of her chest. Astrid came across a news article, dated the first of June, stating that the statue had disappeared.

Astrid already knew that the Dalton Estate was over 400 years old. The family owned acres of land north of the River Thames, and had, for centuries, made their fortune from property developments in affluent swathes of the city. During Astrid's lifetime, they were most famous for the multinational venture capital conglomerate to which they gave their name. But she knew that their school had been named after James Dalton, a maverick nineteenth-century offshoot of their family who worked all his life as an astronomer. James Dalton had discovered that the sun's second-closest star system – after Alpha Centauri – was a binary. Two stars orbiting like dumbbells around a common centre of mass. Twins, swapping places every century, eternally eclipsing each other.

James's only daughter, Tessa, devoted her life to watching the stars for signs of another planet. In space – as on Earth – Newton's

Third Law applies. When a star tugs on an orbiting planet, the planet tugs back. From where Astrid was on the ship, the Earth already looked like a blue star in the darkness, but once they reached the edge of the solar system it would blink out of existence. The sun would grow indistinguishable from all the other stars and the only way to tell that there was a little planet spinning in the blackness around it would be a slight wobble measured in the sun's light.

Years ago, Astrid had been tasked with researching Tessa Dalton for a history paper. It had been a challenge, because history did not have much to say about her even though she had, essentially, discovered Terra-Two.

Tessa published a single paper, proposing the existence of an extrasolar planet circling Dalton's binary system. Articles supporting and disputing the notion trickled out, but interest in the stars waned until the world's first deep-space telescope broadcast low-resolution images of Terra-Two. Of course, back then, it had not been called 'Terra-Two'. It was D56A, just another extrasolar planet in a 'goldilocks zone' – an area close enough to its suns' warmth to sustain life but not so near that it couldn't thrive.

After the Second World War, UK aircraft manufacturers, like those in the USSR and the United States, had turned their efforts to aerospace engineering. Two decades later, the British Interplanetary Society launched four unmanned satellites at the sun's nearest stellar neighbours. The initial objective was to examine these solar systems for any signs of life. The project was called Daedalus, and, by all accounts, it was a success. Findings suggested that Tessa Dalton's planet was terrestrial, with a mass 0.6 that of the Earth's, and could potentially sustain life. D56A became the focus of attention from astronomical institutions worldwide. It was circled by Soviet satellites in the 80s and was the landing site of NASA and JAXA rovers by the end of that century.

The papers had dubbed D56A 'Earth-Two' or 'Terra-Two'. Some people sported bumper stickers with twin Earths locked together in a peace sign. The Beach Boys released a single titled 'Another Earth, Another Chance', which stayed at number one the entire summer and became the informal motto of the Off-World Colonization Programme.

The year that Astrid was born, the International Astronomical Union held a summit. They reviewed all the data collected in the past forty years about D56A, and after a month of consultations, they tentatively declared the planet habitable. According to most accounts, this was when the race to Terra-Two really began. Both NASA and UKSA suspended their space shuttle programmes indefinitely and swore to send a crew to Terra-Two before 2020.

Just before the 2008 financial crisis, China's National Space Administration had launched a generation ship to the nearby star system. It was slated to reach Terra-Two by 2120. And although the mission was famously unsuccessful, it spurred engineers on every continent to pioneer the fastest way to leave the solar system.

The UK's programme would not have been possible without the continual funding of the Dalton Estate, and corporations like it. In fact, it was the group's current owner, aristocratic billionaire Edmond Dalton, who had famously claimed, 'the Americans got a rock, we'll get a planet.'

During Tessa Dalton's lifetime, historians claimed, there had been no way for her to predict the presence of an extrasolar planet, let alone a habitable one. And yet, she had. Her diaries and letters home were filled with tales of 'the beautiful planet'. She described the saltwater lakes and green lagoons, the flourishing plant life and peaceful animals. The soil, she said, was untouched by human feet. Every night she felt the pull of it. She longed to die under the light of its suns but she had been born a century too soon. In 1932, her family committed her to St Augustine's psychiatric hospital in Kent.

The patients on her ward claimed that she spoke incessantly about another, better world and infected the other women with hope. The halls began to echo with their sobs. '*Fernweh*', the doctors called it, or far-sickness. The patients were sick for somewhere they had never travelled. Would never travel.

Tessa was confined to a windowless room, but she managed to escape. One February night, she made it out into the frosted grounds. She had trampled an erratic path through the long grass, footprints in the snow leading to the fountain in the middle of the garden. *What had she been thinking?* Astrid always wondered. *Was she a madwoman or a prophet?* Perhaps she believed everything she had promised those far-sick girls; that to get to Terra-Two all they needed was hope. But she died instead. The staff found her floating in the fountain the next morning, her eyes unblinking, her body blue.

By the time Astrid finished reading, the lights in the corridor had dimmed and she could tell that the other members of her crew were asleep. She shut the computer and rubbed the blue shadows the light bleached behind her eyelids. Before she fell asleep that night, she saw Dalton's empty quad as it might have looked that night, the grass bleached white as bone by the June sun. The black patch of soil where Tessa Dalton's feet had been.

ELIOT

19.06.12

YEARS AGO, WHEN ARA had been struck with appendicitis, Eliot had sat by her bedside the entire twelve hours it took for the surgeons to finally confirm the diagnosis. He'd watched the doctors come in and out of the infirmary, draw her blood, press down on her stomach and ask, 'How much does it hurt? From one to ten – ten being the worst?'

'Eight,' Ara had said each time, 'and a half . . .'

Later on, she told Eliot that she had lied. It had been the worst pain she had ever felt, but she'd been too afraid to tempt fate and say 'ten' in case it grew any worse. She said that it hurt too much to move. Hurt too much to cry. Hurt too much to breathe except for in careful shallow sips. She'd said, 'I just wanted to rip myself open and tear it out. Whatever was broken.'

Eliot hurt like that now, all the time. One part of him couldn't wait for the day he awoke and remembering that Ara was dead didn't hit him like a sick surprise. But another part of him never wanted to get used to living without her.

'That's interesting to me,' said Dr Golinsky, 'that when I asked you to describe pain, you used Ara as a reference.' Eliot was in the ship's infirmary with her. The psychological team on the ground had given him a thorough assessment before the launch, and scheduled twice-weekly counselling sessions with Dr Golinsky. Eliot dreaded the meetings.

'Eliot,' the doctor asked after a minute of silence. 'I can't help you if you don't talk at all.'

'I don't think you can help me,' he said, his eyes drifting to a poster of the human skeleton above her head. It was more artistic than anatomical, the bones delicate and beautiful as egg-shells.

'What makes you say that?'

'It's been five weeks since she died and I feel as if it's getting worse,' Eliot said.

'Are you talking about the nightmares?'

'I'm talking about everything.' Eliot gritted his teeth. 'I keep checking my emails to see if I got one from her. Look around the table for her face, waiting for her to roll her eyes every time someone says something funny.'

'Well,' Fae said, 'it might help if you think of grief like a physical injury. That it might take a long time to heal, that it will happen in small increments—'

The bell rang for dinner, and Eliot felt an answering rumble in his stomach.

'Would you look at the time,' Fae said with a theatrical gasp. She glanced at the digital face of her watch.

'Can I go?' Eliot asked, already standing.

'Yes, but it's vital that you turn up on time for our next session, otherwise I can't give you the full forty minutes. And don't forget to take your vitamin D tablets.' She indicated a blister pack of them on the counter. 'Your latest blood tests flagged a deficiency.'

When Eliot left the infirmary, he bumped into Astrid and Commander Sheppard talking in the narrow corridor as they together headed towards the kitchen, '. . . turns out the rumours were right,' Astrid was saying, 'apparently Tessa Dalton's statue was stolen.'

'It's not as dramatic as it seems, though.' Sheppard waved dismissively. 'It was just a New Creationist stunt.'

'New Creationist?'

'That's what I've heard, anyway.'

The air in the kitchen was steamy and thick with a school-dinner smell of vegetable stock cubes and rehydrated meat.

'Smells good,' Sheppard announced as he entered, nodding at Juno, who was bent over the counter island at the far end.

'Don't get too excited.' Harry slammed forks down on the table at intervals. 'It's only macro.'

Eliot's stomach was already beginning to turn at the smell of macronutrient broth, the thick, bland porridge-like substance served for either lunch or dinner every other day. They tried to improve the taste by adding spices or stock cubes, but there were only so many times Eliot could eat the same meal without growing to despise it.

'Poppy said she would cut up the leftover potatoes and make chips today,' Astrid said as she sat down.

'Well, Poppy isn't here, is she,' Harry said.

'Where is she?' Juno asked. 'This is the third time she's missed dinner this week.'

'I'd bet you a grand she's sleeping,' Harry said.

'Everyone has to eat dinner together,' Juno said. 'That's the *rule*. We weren't allowed to stay in bed at Dalton.'

'We weren't eating slime every day at Dalton,' Harry muttered.

'Every fifth meal,' Eliot corrected quietly.

'This mission is not the same as school,' Commander Sheppard said, moving to the head of the table. 'You are all adults now, professionals, and you have more freedom.'

'But,' Juno said, 'eating together is an important part of

team-building and morale. We're a family now. It's important for us to spend regular recreational time together.'

'All right; cool it, Juma.' Harry put the last glass down on the table. 'You sound like you're reading straight from a psych manual. She says she's ill.'

'She's not,' Juno said. 'Eliot was *actually* ill. For two weeks, with spacesickness, and yet he cleaned and cooked and came to tutorials just like everyone else.'

Eliot winced at the memory of those interminable days of nausea. His head still spun like a fishbowl if he stood up too quickly, his body hungover and heavy in the mornings.

'Poppy's been suffering with migraines,' Dr Golinsky said gently. 'That's real.'

'But the thing is ...' Juno continued, '*someone* has to do her chores.'

'Yeah, *us*,' Harry said, folding his arms. 'Apparently.'

'Look what I found.' Astrid held up two tin cans. 'Extra rations of peaches. We can have them for dessert. That'll make a nice change.' They sat in their usual positions around the table, the senior crew on one side and the four Betas on the other. Eliot was on the corner of the table. He stirred his broth. Their meals were carefully calculated to keep them at an optimum weight and contained the right balance of ingredients to suit their particular nutritional needs.

As Juno passed around a bowl of bread, Eliot's eyes drifted towards the window, where he thought that, for just a second, his reflection had changed.

'Who are the New Creationists?' Astrid asked over the clinking of cutlery as everyone began to eat.

'I actually thought you might know a little about them,' said Commander Sheppard.

'Why?' Astrid asked.

'Because they're some weird Christian sect,' Harry said.

'They *claim* they're Christians,' Juno said, leaning forwards and making dramatic air-quotes, 'but they're some kind of doomsday cult.'

'Sounds like the same thing to me,' Cai said. He smiled. Juno did not.

The short moment of tension was diffused by the rush of feet up the hall, and they all turned as Jesse burst into the room, his eyes wide as if he was expecting a slap. He looked quickly at Juno, then said, 'I'm sorry I'm late.'

'Only by a few minutes,' Dr Golinsky said, and gestured towards his bowl. He wavered for a moment and then came to sit between Eliot and Juno, still breathing hard.

'Where have you been?' Sheppard asked.

'The greenhouse. I lost track of time.'

'Cai tells me you've been doing great work up there.'

'Does that mean we'll be having something other than canned food and macronutrient broth soon?' Harry asked.

'In a few weeks,' Cai replied.

'Why are they a cult?' Astrid asked.

'What are you talking about?' Jesse looked up at her.

'Apparently a group called the New Creationists stole the statue of Tessa Dalton from the quad back at school.'

'The New Creationists?' Jesse repeated. 'Even their name sounds like a cult. Like a group of Bible-thumping Americans who burn copies of *On the Origin Of Species*.'

'They *are* American,' Fae said, 'and they have a point. I'm sure you'd agree, Commander. They talk about the holes being torn in the ozone layer, ice caps melting, all the bees disappearing and the extreme weather we've been having. That bit is true, you know. Climate change is taking place before our eyes and about twenty years ago was the time to do something about it. They believe it's not a coincidence that Terra-Two appeared right now, right in this century when we need it. And sometimes I'm inclined to agree.'

'Hmm.' Commander Sheppard put his spoon down. 'They do have a point, but I don't approve of their ways of getting their message out there. Stealing the statue is an act of vandalism.'

'No.' Juno shook her head. 'They don't think that Terra-Two is a second chance. They think that it's the new Eden. Like the Garden of Eden. Like in the Bible. They think that only a few chosen people are destined to go there.'

'I suppose that's quite a whimsical comparison ...' Fae said. 'One could see it that way. It's untouched. Fresh water and clean air. No war. No history. And in a way, we *have* been chosen.'

'Okay,' Harry threw his hands up in mock surrender. 'I don't see why we need to get all religious about this. We – humans – chose who would go. We—' he waved at the party sat around the table, 'were picked because we're qualified. Not because of destiny or God or anything. Think about it: there's no intelligent life on that planet, in the whole solar system, in fact. From where I'm sitting, consciousness seems like a pretty rare thing. Isn't it our job to spread our ideas, our technology, our humanity as far across this empty space as possible? I don't see why you're so caught up on making Terra better; why can't we just make it an-*other*? Another Earth, another Britain, another empire.'

Juno shuddered.

'I hope you've realized,' said Jesse, 'that the 1967 Outer Space Treaty means that no one country is allowed to own Terra-Two.

The moon doesn't belong to the Americans and the Russians don't own Mars. Assuming we are the first to land on T2, it won't belong to Britain. It will be international commons. "The province of all mankind".'

'I know. I'm just saying,' Harry continued, 'that everyone says that humans are the problem, that we destroy everything we touch, but we're creative and resourceful. We survive in the most inhospitable environments – like out here! – we build things out of nothing, we create diamonds in labs and we eradicated smallpox. We're amazing. We're fucking brilliant. We'll make Terra-Two better just by being there. We'll bring it to life. Intelligent life.'

Eliot saw it again, then. Some shape in the darkness behind the window. At first it looked like his own reflection but the second time he looked ...

'Eliot?' Dr Golinsky's eyes followed his to the window. 'What is it?'

'Oh ... I just—' he stared back at his bowl. 'I thought I saw something, that's all. '

He didn't have to raise his spoon to his mouth to know that he couldn't eat any more, and when he glanced up again he saw her. Ara. She was floating behind the glass, her lips stained black, her eyes half-open and sightless.

It was all Eliot could do not to cry out in horror. He squeezed his eyes shut, hoping the image would disappear. His heart was tight as a fist in his chest and the blood drained from his head.

'Eliot?' It was Dr Golinsky's voice, but he was too scared to look up at her, in case he might have to see that face again, that terrible face. 'Eliot, are you okay?'

He didn't remember getting up from the table, only he must

have because the next thing he knew he was running down the corridor. He made it to the bathroom just in time to vomit in the sink. Gazing at the sludge of macro broth curdled with bile as it washed down the plughole, Eliot knew that he would never be able to stomach it again.

He sank down onto the floor, his head pressed against his knees, shaking all over, his heart galloping behind his ribs.

A few minutes later, the door creaked open. Eliot dreaded looking up to find the confused face of one of his crew members. How could he explain to Juno or Harry what was wrong with him? He squeezed his eyes shut. 'Go away,' he hissed, but a cold hand touched his. For just a second, he thought it might be Ara, as cold as she had been in his arms when he'd pulled her out of the river and clung to her until the ambulance came.

When he opened his eyes, Cai was crouching down beside him. 'It's okay,' he said, his stained fingers tight on Eliot's skin. 'It's okay.' He said it again in a soft voice that Eliot had never heard him use before.

'*What* is okay?' Eliot heard himself say when he could finally speak.

Cai leant back on his feet, the bones in his thighs making a sharp line through his trousers. 'When I was eleven, my father hanged himself in the downstairs bathroom. Tied an extension cable around his neck and the exposed piping in the ceiling and then let go.'

Eliot shuddered.

'I'm sorry,' he said.

'Don't apologize,' Cai said. 'You can't hold onto these things.' He took a pen out of his pocket and pulled back a sleeve, exposing the olive skin on his wrist. He began to draw a hexagon, some bent lines, NH2, OH, OH, all the blue veins in his arm protruding. 'Do you know what this is?'

'No, it looks like some molecule ...?'

'Dopamine,' Cai said. 'And this?' He quickly sketched another molecule.

'Serotonin?' Eliot guessed.

'These are the only things that really make you happy.'

Eliot glanced up at him. 'I don't understand.'

'People will try to tell you that it was some misalignment of the stars, or that she had some sickness in her soul. Some blackness that, if you had fathomed it earlier, you could have called her out of and made her whole again.' Eliot felt a lump rise in his throat. 'But that's not true. It's just bad chemistry, mixed-up biology. Not enough monoamines to make her happy. Ara was a sick person. My dad was a sick person. There is nothing I could have done to save him.'

Eliot frowned.

'I realized that when I was twenty-four,' Cai said, 'and it freed me. So I'm telling you.'

'But what about the way I feel right now?' Eliot said quietly, lowering his gaze. 'That I loved her? Where does that all go?'

Cai pointed to the sketches on his wrist.

'It's just chemicals,' he said. 'Infatuation, love: oxytocin, dopamine and adrenaline.' He pushed his green finger hard against Eliot's temple. 'One day we'll know the molecular formula for disappointment, for despair, for grief ... it all happens in here.' He pushed harder. 'Chemical reactions. Nothing more.'

Eliot swallowed, noticing that his heart had stopped pounding, although his fingers were still trembling, the sunless skin over his arms raised up in goosebumps. 'But,' he said, feeling a little ungrateful, 'I don't understand how that makes it any less important?'

2001

HE HAD LOVED HER with everything he had. They'd met for the first time in the playground at their primary school when she had been talking to the wind. She convinced the other girls that she was a witch and that when she called the wind came rushing. They'd believed her, of course they had. Ara had been like the Pied Piper.

She'd said she was magic and for a while Eliot, too, had believed it. She'd raised an arm, and a second later a breeze kicked up, scattering leaves. But Eliot spotted the glimmer of uncertainty in her eyes, the moment of doubt that crumbled the entire illusion, like a curtain drawn back, the glimpse of the old man behind the wizard. He could not un-see it, even if he wanted to.

'I don't believe in witches,' he'd told her.

'Then I don't believe in eleven-year-old boys,' she'd said.

'You lied.'

'No.'

'You told us that you could control the wind.'

'That's not what I said,' she insisted, letting her arms fall to her sides. 'They just choose to believe me.' She glanced at the girls in the corners of the playground, giggling, braced against the gusting wind.

That was all anyone saw, Ara breezing through life, swallowing up whole days in her manic search for glee. Looking everywhere.

When they were teenagers, she wore glitter under her eyes

every Friday night, even after it was cool, even before. They went to a club night called 'How does it feel to be loved?' and she'd danced like a firecracker across the floor, the only one. He alone had caught up with her at the bus stop, and she'd been crying so hard, for no reason at all, that glitter dripped off her lips, her whole face spangled like a disco ball. 'Everything hurts,' she said, clutching her chest as if she'd been shot.

And yet he loved her like she'd lived, as if she wouldn't be around for long. Loved her to the marrow of his bones, the only way a teenager can. Hysterically, electrically, with everything he could give.

Could he have saved her?

Maybe it was a miracle that she'd ever existed at all. She had been the love child of a seventeen-year-old Indian girl and her middle-aged boyfriend. They were only together for five weeks and, seven months later, Ara was born, bringing with her nothing but shame. She'd been in the intensive-care unit for six weeks, working all day just to draw air into her underdeveloped lungs, her skin so paper-thin that her mother's touch could burn.

In Dalton, Ara had been like the best kind of soul friend. Something like a sister, but also something like a special dispensation from the universe, some creature who had entered this world solely to make it a better place for Eliot Liston to live.

They'd discovered sex early, before anybody else had even heard of it. The very first time had happened at sunset in Battersea Park, in the subtropical garden – a little fenced-off area where unlikely plants grew, giant reeds and dwarf palms, banana trees. They'd stayed out all night and the next morning the dew-covered earth was a little different.

'I feel the same,' Ara said, rolling over to him after, her cheek plastered with grass.

'Me too,' Eliot had lied. He'd kissed her before she crossed the road and took the bus in the opposite direction, her school tights scrunched up in her rucksack.

He slept until noon the next day. And, in the dream he had, he and Ara were in the subtropical garden again, snapping exotic fruits off vines that were heavy with them. In his dream, Eliot bit right into a mango and, when he opened his eyes to the kind 1 p.m. light, he felt as if his body and his heart had come alive at the exact same time.

JESSE

30.06.12

THE LONELINESS WAS BEGINNING to sting. It was the end of June, and after seven weeks on the *Damocles*, the elation of the launch had finally evaporated for Jesse. The flurry of emails, well-wishes and congratulations from friends and family members on Earth had subsided and Jesse's life on the ship had naturally settled into the ebb and flow of their routine. Waking up to Commander Sheppard's recording of Coltrane's *Interstellar Space*, queuing for the bathroom, breakfast, which happened quickly, everyone rushing about the kitchen reading the news on their tablets and squabbling over the coffee machine before they settled down for morning briefing. Then they'd disperse into their different areas of the ship to attend to their own chores and tutorials. During the week, that meant that Jesse was alone for three hours in the greenhouse, weeding and fertilizing, logging notes on the ship's computer using an arcane system of Cai's devising or reading about the biochemistry behind hydroponics. After lunch, there were medical checks and their group lessons, then dinner. Whole days sometimes went by without anyone speaking to him directly. The semi-playful banter between the seniors and the Beta never included him, and sometimes he walked past the five other junior astronauts in the crew module, huddled up on one of the sofas watching a movie, Harry's hand buried in Poppy's hair, Juno's head on Astrid's lap, Eliot nearby, all of them enjoying the cosy comfort of friendship. If they didn't fall completely silent when Jesse approached, then they lowered their gaze or greeted him with brittle formality. 'They're still grieving over Ara,' Fae had explained to him during one of their counselling sessions. 'They'll warm up to you.' But almost two months into their journey, Jesse became less and less hopeful.

That weekend, he somehow managed to sleep through the ecstatic tenor saxophone solos of 'Mars' and 'Venus' that burst through the speakers every morning, and by the time he trudged into the kitchen, breakfast was over. Poppy was watching a comedy on her laptop, the canned laughter ringing obnoxiously even through her headphones. Juno was absorbed in some task that involved poring over notes she had made during the previous day's lesson. They didn't greet him.

Jesse had been pouring sweetener into the morning's first milky cup of coffee when he heard Poppy's scream. He jolted and the hot liquid splashed over his hand.

Poppy, still attached to her laptop by her headphones, reeled backwards, knocking a plate onto the floor.

'What is it?' He turned to her in alarm and noticed that her grey eyes were wide with fear. She pointed a trembling finger towards the counter, and turned away in disgust.

'What is it?' Jesse asked again, taking a step back.

'*Look* …' she urged. Her voice had turned up an octave into a whine.

Jesse walked tentatively to the counter, edging into the shadowed corner to which Poppy was pointing.

When he spotted what had frightened her, he let out a laugh of relief and surprise. It was a spider, about the size of the base of a cup, a black thing with sharp legs, kicking at its silvery web.

'I've seen bigger,' Jesse said.

'Where?' said Poppy. 'In Mombasa?' She had calmed down a little; her mouth was twisted up in disgust, but she was no longer shaking.

'What is it?' Juno looked up from her notes.

'Just a spider. Just a little—'

'Don't touch it!' Poppy shrieked, jumping back again and rubbing her arms. 'Kill it. Oh please kill it.'

'No way.' Jesse searched around his vicinity for a cup. Killing spiders had been a crime in his household, and this was the first living, moving thing – aside from his crewmates – that he had seen for almost two months. His heart jumped with the same excitement and surprise he'd experienced the first morning he'd climbed up the ladder to the greenhouse and noticed the little green heads of his seedlings bursting through the soil.

'Hey, buddy,' he said, placing a cup over it, trying his best not to squash any of its spindly legs. Poppy moaned in horror. 'Stop being such a wimp,' he hissed.

'Don't be rude,' Juno said. 'It's a phobia.'

'Don't tell me *you're* scared of spiders too?' Jesse's mouth twitched into a smile as he caught sight of Juno in the corner of his eye, hanging back by the breakfast table.

'Spiders are scary,' Poppy said.

'I'm not scared.' Juno shuddered. 'Just disgusted. There's something about them. The legs maybe . . .'

'And their bodies,' said Poppy, 'and their webs.'

'It's the way they move.' Juno shivered again. 'I'm disgusted just thinking about it. That fast, silent way they scuttle. It's almost inherent, a quality in their step, it's repulsive. It's unnatural.'

'Nonsense.' Jesse had managed to loose it from its web and it tumbled down the smooth sides of the cup, which he covered quickly with a sheet of paper. 'There's nothing unnatural about it. You don't have to be embarrassed about saying you're just scared, you know. I read somewhere that arachnophobia may have an evolutionary advantage.'

'Yeah, because people who run away from spiders *live*,' Juno said. 'Spiders are predatory. They eat their sexual partners. They strangle their prey with silk, vomit digestive fluids into them so that they liquify before they're eaten.'

'Spiders are just misunderstood. They're survivors,' Jesse said. 'Found on every continent except Antarctica. They can establish a habitat basically anywhere. I mean – look at this.' He gestured to the glass, and the spider at the bottom of it.

'What are you going to do, name it?' Poppy was edging towards the doorway.

'Maybe,' Jesse said. 'Now I have a pet.'

'Charming.' Juno grimaced. 'So long as you keep it away from me.'

Poppy backed out the door. In the silence that followed, Jesse returned to his work, wiping up the hot water he'd spilled on the counter. He was almost finished when Juno looked up. 'Oh Jesse,' she said. When he turned her face was full of concern. 'You burned yourself.'

'Yeah …' Jesse looked down at the reddening patch on the back of his hand. It was only now beginning to sting.

'You have to put it under hot water,' Juno said, standing up. 'I mean, cold water.' She took his wrist and held his hand under the tap, examining it, the cool stream catching on the little hairs behind his fingers. The cold was a relief. So was her touch. Jesse noticed that her nails were chopped short, dotted with flecks of turquoise nail varnish. Her fingers were lightly calloused, and she ran her fingertips along the sensitive skin on the back of his hand. The constant ache of his loneliness felt like a fever that had only just broken. How wonderful, the nearness of Juno. She was like the other girls, busy and mysterious, but how many of them would have come to his aid like this?

He closed his eyes, hoping to hold onto this moment. But Juno let go suddenly. Jesse opened them again and noticed that she was peering at him quizzically. She stepped back. 'It um … doesn't look too bad.'

'Thank you,' Jesse said. Juno sat back down, brushing stray coils of her springy hair behind her small ears.

'It's my job,' she said. 'You know, Fae's training me to be the ship's medical officer.'

'Oh, right, yeah.' A flash of disappointment.

Juno looked back down at her notes, wielding a highlighter. 'We've just covered first aid and minor injuries again.'

'Right.' Jesse held his hand under the tap for a few moments longer until the numbness began to prickle up his fingers. Juno was already far away, absorbed in her notes again, her pen locked between her lips.

By then, his coffee was the sort of lukewarm he liked, and he finished it in slow drags, leaning against the counter.

'Hey.' Juno looked up at him again. 'Jess . . .'

'Yeah?'

'I forgot to tell you . . . thank you.'

'For what?'

'For saving my life that time. During the solar storm.'

Already that night felt like a year ago. While it had been terrifying at the time, Jesse could no longer remember it without a twinge of embarrassment. 'Well,' he told her, 'you weren't really going to die. None of us were.'

'You didn't know that,' Juno said, 'and you barely knew me at the time. You could have stayed in the radiation shelter, but you didn't.'

'Yeah . . .' In retrospect, he probably should have. Flouting orders on his first day had by no means endeared him to their commander.

Jesse thought about the day ahead of him, another day of bracing himself against the coolness of the rest of the crew, against homesickness.

'You know,' he took his cup to the sink to rinse it, turning his back to her, 'this is the most anyone's spoken to me since I got here.'

'Really?'

From the corner of his eye, he saw Juno flinch at his words.

'I mean, I know what it is. It's not like I don't understand it. If I had a really good friend who I thought I'd spend my life with, and then some other guy comes in at the last minute and takes her place, I guess I wouldn't be too fond of him either. But I ... I thought it would have stopped by now. It's been almost two months since the launch and I feel as if it's getting worse.'

'I don't know.' Juno leant back in her chair. 'It's not just you. None of them talk about Ara, either. Or what happened, or why it happened. Not since the launch. And I know we all think about it. You're kind of a reminder.'

Jesse hung his mug on the rack and thought for a moment. The silence was growing heavy again.

'You know ... I feel guilty about it. But sometimes I feel ... grateful. Like, this is the way it was meant to be.' He regretted it as soon as he said it. The words hadn't come out quite right. What he'd meant to say was that when he looked out at his life, he liked to think that some silent power in the universe or the shining hand of destiny had brought him to the gates of Dalton, on the eve of the launch, at just the right moment. Yes, a girl he'd never really known had died, and, yes, that was tragic. But the fact remained, as inescapable as plain subtraction: if she had made it, then he wouldn't have. Was it wrong to be glad?

When Juno looked up her eyes were brimming with tears.

'Meant to be? Meant to be that my friend jumped into a river? Meant to be that she died alone and helpless and our teachers leapt over her grave to find a replacement?'

A knife-twist of guilt. Jesse shuddered, tripping over to take back his words.

'No, I didn't mean – I didn't mean ...'

'Save it ...' Juno slammed her laptop shut and left the room.

*

LATER ON, WHEN HE was in the greenhouse, Jesse replayed the words in his head and groaned. 'What's wrong with me?' he said out loud, although there was no one to hear. He let the spider crawl up his arm and stayed there for a long while before he heard footsteps clambering up the ladder. For just a second his heart jumped, and he was sure it was Juno, come to rescue him from himself. He had already practised his apology.

Only, when he saw the blond head of hair, his spirits sank further.

'Hey,' Harry said. Jesse sat up.

'Hey.' From his vantage point, Harry looked frighteningly tall. 'I hear you want to be one of us. Part of the team.'

'I was picked. Just like you,' Jesse said. 'I *am* part of the team ... now.'

'Okay.' Harry smiled. 'I think it's time for you to try and prove it.'

HARRY

IN HARRY'S EARLIEST MEMORY, he is playing chess opposite his father in the dining room. He's so small that his feet do not yet touch the marble floor. His father is teaching him how the knight captures – in an L shape, two squares vertically and one square horizontally, or vice versa. To demonstrate this principle, his father arranges every pawn on the board in a circle around the knight and asks Harry which pieces he can capture. Each time he reaches his hand to touch the wrong one, his father smacks it back, resulting in a hideous stalemate. Harry is terrified and tired, and even when he picks the correct one, his father, rightly, accuses him of 'just guessing'.

Harry's eyes roll with sleepiness. 'I don't care anymore,' he whispers, realizing as he says it that it's true. 'Please, can I just go to bed?' The weight of his exhaustion like a millstone around him. 'Why is this important?'

Harry can't remember the exact words but his father told him then, and kept telling him, that chess was everything. That if he understood chess he'd understand life. A notion so gorgeously simple that, even now, Harry hopes it is true.

At thirteen years and eleven months, his father had been the youngest chess grandmaster in the world, a title finally snatched from him in 1999 by Bu Xiangzhi. Harry never reached anything close to his father's formidable mastery, but those early lessons in logic and strategic thinking had almost certainly contributed to his eventual success at Dalton. Harry had learned from his father about the importance of constant practice, a principle he applied even before he was streamed into Command School as a possible contender for the position of pilot of the *Damocles*. Competition had been tough, but Harry excelled because he had practised flying every day of his life from age twelve, logging hours in the winter-pale skies above the Bellgrave estate, or, when the weather did not permit, in a dank basement simulation room, VR goggles strapped to his face so long that the skin on the bridge of his nose began to peel. For Harry, it had become something of a cosy ritual, waking up in the morning, a run before breakfast, a practice flight after. One he continued throughout Dalton.

In fact, the only time in his life that Harry had failed to practise had been a Saturday morning eighteen months before the launch, when the sky above his dormitory had filled with smoke. He'd emerged from the shower to find the grounds swarming with paramedics, the police evacuating all the students. Harry heard that his roommate, Jack Redcliffe, had crashed the academy's Cessna 172. The cause, he later learned, was engine failure that, the coroner's report claimed coldly, was due to 'pilot error'.

Pilot error: words that had rattled through the bones in Harry's head every day since then. It had not been the first time someone had died at Dalton, and it would not be the last. But

Command School was closed for half a day, all flights grounded, and a few pupils were assigned a counsellor and sent home for the rest of the week to recover. Including Harry himself, against his will.

After the accident, Harry dreamt of losing control of the plane, and making a nosedive for the ground. The day after he returned home, he abandoned the hope of a good night's sleep and headed down to the TV room. There he spotted his father's head of blond and silver hair resting on the sofa. He was watching the fuzzy replay of the accident that had been looping all day on the news.

'It's a good thing it happened now, and not later,' his father said, without turning around.

'Why?' Harry asked, glancing at Jack's photo in the corner of the screen. The greasy red hair he was always shaking out of his eyes.

'Engine failure after take-off: what would you have done?' His father finally turned to him.

'If it was immediately after take-off, I'd close the throttle, attain a recommended gliding speed, pick a landing path and concentrate on a good landing . . .'

'*He* made a mistake,' Harry's father said, nodding at the television.

'A common one,' Harry said quietly. 'I think he tried to turn back and land in the aerodrome. He panicked. Maybe he wasn't thinking about the airspeed and load factor . . .'

'You see, Harrison, that is what your training is for. To make these mistakes now, to weed out the less competent. Imagine if something like this had happened up there.'

*

HARRY BEAT JESSE ON the simulator. They raced in neighbouring ships, but Harry was far more skilled than Jesse and he ascended to the end of the level, laughing as he did so.

'How often do you fly on this simulator?' Harry asked. Jesse shrugged, tugging at the elastic on the back of his goggles, which had tangled in his long hair.

'Like, every week,' he said.

'How many times a week?'

'Once or twice,' Jesse said. Harry raised an eyebrow.

There was not one thing that Harry admired about Jesse. At Dalton, Jesse had been part of the sub-class of indie kids, who sulked at the edges of the canteen and shunned team sports, as if physical exertion was somehow beneath them, not realizing that half the work of being an astronaut was physical, and that teamwork was essential. Harry had been surprised when Jesse had been sorted into the piloting stream, but unsurprised when he'd dropped out and switched to botany and hydroponics after a matter of days.

Harry had watched the video of Jesse volunteering to take Ara's place, the fervour in his eyes. If it wasn't impossible, Harry might have thought that perhaps Jesse had killed her, pushed her into the river himself, just so that he could seize her place on the team.

'Why did you switch to hydroponics?' Harry asked.

Jesse shrugged. 'Seemed a better fit, I guess.'

'Seemed easier?'

Jesse said nothing.

Harry knew the answer. Jesse was the kind of person who believed in 'destiny' and not hard work. It had taken Harry's father ten years of practising chess for six hours a day to become a grandmaster, and Harry had taken to flying with the same devotion.

Harry motioned to the sensor and the screen went blank. He stood up and clapped Jesse on the shoulder. 'Look, Jesse Solloway, I don't know whose arm you twisted to get on this ship. But I know that you don't belong here.'

'Oh, really?'

'Really,' Harry said. 'You're a lazy cheat, switching to hydro just because it's easier. Trying to play the system. And then you convinced them to take you. Don't think I haven't seen you eyeballing me when I fly. It took years of practice to get where I am, so stick to planting seeds. Piloting is real work.'

ELIOT

01.07.12

WHEN ELIOT IMAGINED LIFE on Mars he pictured scientists crouched in modest hab-labs, ticking off the days until their return. Billionaires pouring money into developing zero-g retirement homes or polar ice-hockey rinks. Immigrant workers from nameless corporations drilling down into the dust until their bones grew thin and brittle. There wasn't much on Mars, and no one went there unless they had to.

There had been a time when his grandparents were enchanted by the red planet. They pictured faces of Martians etched into the dust. People still spoke about the first manned Mars landing with a little shiver. Eliot forgot how many times he had seen the iconic black-and-white footage of the day the Soviets pushed their flag down into the rust-coloured soil, nine months before the British.

According to the history books, Igor Bovarin had been at the front end of that race. He had been one of the chief engineers whose work contributed to the VASIMR engine, the patented device that shortened the journey to Mars from around seven months to seven weeks. The joke that the USSR could make it to Mars and back before the US or the British left the launch pad was not entirely unfounded.

Igor rose to fame as the main pioneer of ion-propulsion technology. By the time Eliot was in secondary school his name slipped off anyone's tongue when asked to name a famous engineer, and, although Igor was serving prolonged missions to Mars, his sights were already set on interstellar travel. The UK Space Agency recruited him to work on their Off-World Colonization Programme. Igor had been approaching retirement age by then, but the rumour was that the UKSA had offered the old man something he could not refuse.

Thanks to Igor's invention, it took Eliot and his crew only forty-nine days to pass through Mars' orbit, and he watched the planet grow wide in the window.

Eliot had taught himself the mechanics of ion propulsion. The engine on the *Damocles* used radio waves to tear the electrons off atoms of argon to give them a positive charge. Heating the gas up to 50,000°C, turned it into a substance known as plasma, the fourth state of matter. It gave Eliot a small thrill to know that plasma – the substance created inside nuclear fusion reactors, the stuff that suns were made of – was also being produced by the engine on their ship. A magnetic field directed the plasma out of the back of the rocket like an aerosol from a pressurized can.

Igor's rocket provided them with enough thrust to accelerate constantly at less than a thousandth of a g. This had always seemed a small amount to Eliot, but it nevertheless meant that their speed was increasing all the time. It had taken them seven weeks to fly by Mars but, at the rate they were travelling, they were scheduled to reach Saturn in just over a year, even though it was much further away.

Terra-Two was three lightyears away, a figure that made

interplanetary distances seem relatively measly. Eliot knew that, at their current acceleration, it would take the crew 150 years to reach Terra-Two, but Igor and his team had engineered the ship's engine to swing by Saturn like a ribbon around a maypole, using the planet's gravity to increase their speed by a factor of 100, enough to catapult the *Damocles* from their solar system and into interstellar space.

As the red planet loomed large in the window, Eliot began to wonder what it had been like for Commander Sheppard, Cai and Igor, who had served multiple missions on Mars. Eliot didn't find it difficult to imagine Igor weathering a dust storm, his pellucid blue eyes shining behind his visor as he endured another season of sunless polar nights.

'Do you think we'll be able to see the hab-labs from here?' Astrid asked when she entered the kitchen and joined Eliot by the window. The air was bitter with the smell of coffee – Juno was behind them, scooping the black sludge of brewed grounds into the disposal unit.

'Do you think we can see the what?' Poppy asked, dusting crumbs off her overalls.

'Not from here,' Juno said. 'With a telescope maybe.' Mars was the size of a copper penny.

'Do you ever wonder what it's like down there?' Eliot asked. Juno shook her head.

'Like a desert,' said Poppy. 'That's what Commander Sheppard says.'

'Like a cold desert,' said Juno. 'Just you wait until we get to Jupiter. We'll actually get close to it.'

Eliot could not help but smile as he imagined watching the gas giant from the window of the crew module. A late but exciting addition to their mission involved helping to deliver supplies to the US station orbiting above one of Jupiter's moons. Eliot was looking forward to meeting up with the seasoned astronauts on station, but he was still curious about the surface of Mars. If he squinted he thought he could see it, pock-marked and terracotta. The dusting of ice at the poles – larger on the top than the bottom – suggested that it was winter, now, in the southern hemisphere.

'Hey.' Astrid turned to Eliot, rousing him from his reverie. 'Igor says he has something to show you. On the engineering deck.'

Eliot's ears pricked up with curiosity. 'Really?' he asked. 'What?'

Astrid beamed. 'Terra-Two,' she said, and then rushed out of the room. Eliot hurried after her and down the ladder that led to the engineering deck.

In Eliot's capacity as trainee engineer, he spent a lot of time with Igor on the windowless engineering deck, and it had quickly become one of his favourite places on the *Damocles*. When he walked, he could feel the ship's heartbeat through the soles of his feet. What little light there was on the engineering deck came from the scrolling readouts off the monitors and the orange glow of hot filaments.

The deck reminded Eliot of his uncle's studio. After his parents' death, he had been sent to live with his father's brother, a perilously thin autistic man who worked for a watchmaker in south Wales and let Eliot spend long hours in the studio with him as he built timepieces. Eliot traced his interest in engineering back to those days of flipping through user manuals, jiggling his leg on the rungs of a stool while CNC cutters buzzed in the background. He'd come to admire the machinery, the reliability of it, as he leaned over the desk as his uncle polished tiny cogs and screws. There was something impressive about the fine micro-mechanics of a wristwatch, small things, some no bigger than a two-pound coin, and yet inside was an entire whirring solar system built of golden shafts, steel springs and gearwheels. Each watch contained over 1,000 components, some barely visible to the naked eye.

That was how Eliot began with robotics. He turned his bedroom into a workshop, collecting what equipment he could from his uncle's studio and, in the dead of night, building machines straight from his dreams. A robotic finger that could twang the strings of a guitar, a hand that high-fived; then more complex machines: a sunlight sensor attached to the railing on his curtains, so they flew open when the radius of the sun at the horizon was exactly sixteen arc minutes. He designed a head for a Terran rover that performed calculations – based on the viability of water, and the partial pressure of various gasses – and yielded the probability of finding life in that region. He'd called the programme the Liston Algorithm.

His uncle had been so impressed by it that he entered the work into an engineering competition run by Imperial College London. Eliot did not understand the exact chain of circumstances that led to his work landing on the desk of Igor Bovarin, but he still remembered the day that the legendary cosmonaut had called him up on the house phone. A week later, four men in suits arrived at the house and sat in the living room, which Eliot clearly remembered was flooded with white afternoon light, gulls arcing and wheeling through the window.

'So, you're Eliot Liston,' they'd said. 'How old are you?'

'Six hundred and sixty-seven,' Eliot had said. 'Weeks. Twelve point eight years. Almost . . . thirteen.' A low whistle of surprise from one of the men.

They could not believe that the work had come from someone so young. Surely, they appealed to his uncle, he'd had some help. At least with the more complicated calculations? But his uncle had insisted he'd done it alone. Then, Igor Bovarin, the man – the legend – at the far end of the room, brought out a pen and wrote an equation on a piece of paper. Handed it to Eliot. Eliot had solved it quickly with a little laugh. Another, harder this time. Then another, in a tense back and forth exchange that ended, forty minutes later, in applause from three of the men.

They told him then about Dalton. A school on the outskirts of London where he could meet other students like himself. Had he heard of it? Of course he had! They told him about the work he could do there, the freedom he would have on the engineering stream to work with others as brilliant as himself, to be properly challenged by the best professors in the world. And, most enticing of all, if he agreed to go, his machines would be built. 'Even the wild ones?' he asked. Even the code he'd already written with a basic harmonic theory for a robot that could improvise a guitar solo.

'Eliot, those are the most important ones,' Igor had said with a smile.

There were already supply vessels heading for Terra-Two with the pre-fabricated hab-labs and equipment. But, they'd told him, once they made landfall they would need a mind like his not only to repair and update the machines, but to invent new ones. Machines that could meet the environmental challenges they were bound to face, that could drill into the land for water, that could drive for months, collect data and broadcast back the coordinates of optimal settlement locations.

They bought the patent to the Liston Algorithm and told him to pack his things. Two weeks later he was at Dalton, working under Igor on the engineering stream. Years later, he was on a ship bound for Terra-Two.

ASTRID

01.07.12

THEY CALLED IT A 'doomsday cult', but the New Creationists were the opposite. Their leaders did not rally docile crowds to keep vigils for the end of the world. Their eyes were fixed on the skies, happily heralding the arrival of a new one. The new Earth, the second chance. And wasn't that, really, what everyone believed?

After that night at the dinner table when Astrid first heard about their movement, she could not help herself. She watched all the videos she could find about them. Clips that had already garnered thousands of views in certain corners of the internet. Read comment threads and forums devoted to discussing Tessa Dalton, the unwitting founder and martyr of their movement. She'd been called out of obscurity like Mary, the mother of Jesus, like the Old Testament prophets, or the Magi who trekked across countries following portents they'd divined in the stars.

New Creationism was in perfect harmony with Astrid's religious upbringing. In Sunday school, she'd been taught about the Garden of Eden. For a whole year of her life she could not help but imagine it: eternal life, milk and honey, God walking like a giant amongst the trees. She imagined the agony of being cast

out. Tried to envision what kind of life Adam and Eve could eke
out after that. Rebels, fools, they'd lost everything.

And so Astrid was converted to New Creationism. It happened all at once, like an earthquake, a momentous shift, the
tectonic plates of her belief rearranged violently under her. It
happened the day she saw Terra-Two.

She had followed Eliot down to the engineering deck to see
the new images of the planet that had been uploaded by NASA.

Astrid had always found the engineering deck a little creepy.
As the ship's engineer, the person who spent the most time there
was Igor Bovarin. His pencilled diagrams were draped across
empty patches of wall and any careless step threatened to knock
over a wobbling tower of his dog-eared manuals. Astrid spotted
him emerging from the shadows between the machines so often
that every darkened alcove seemed to mirror the hunch of his
back. Every oil spill looked like a footprint from his boots and
the chug of the machines resembled his dry cough and heavy
breathing.

'Astrid said you wanted to see me?' Eliot asked, stepping
further into the gloom. Igor smiled, the light coming off his old
lamp illuminating his face sodium-yellow and accentuating the
lines in his liver-spotted skin. Astrid followed Eliot and ducked
into the honey-coloured light of their little workstation. It smelt
of oil and ink.

'Astrid, Eliot,' Igor said, their names still an exotic delight in
his thick accent. 'Sit. I have something to show you both.'

Astrid saw Eliot's eyes fill with the kind of rapt attention he
only ever paid the aging cosmonaut. It was no secret that Eliot
idolized the man. Astrid had been present the first time Igor
made a surprise appearance during a physics class at Dalton,

and Eliot had been struck dumb with delight. So happy that he waited behind by the Bunsen burners for everybody to leave and then asked Igor to sign a battered copy of his biography, which Astrid knew Eliot kept under his desk for inspiration. It was no surprise that Eliot had been chosen to come under Igor's tutelage. He was lucky to be learning everything Igor could teach him about engineering, physics and the ion engine in the two decades they had together, she thought.

Igor was holding a device shaped like an egg.

'It's an Albatross,' Eliot explained to Astrid as she ran her finger quizzically along the upturned base of it. 'One of the most powerful cameras in the world. If we flew this thing over London Bridge we'd probably be able to count all the greys on every head.'

'That's right,' Igor agreed.

'NASA were using one for a long-range reconnaissance mission. To retrieve high-resolution pictures and geological data of Terra-Two.'

'Today, they broadcast their findings on global television,' Igor said, and Astrid gasped with excitement. 'You want to see?'

'Please,' Astrid said, breathless. Igor tapped some buttons on his keyboard, opened up windows and then expanded one into a full-screen video.

Astrid watched open-mouthed as the pictures unfolded on the screen. The room filled with the blue light of cresting waves exploding into white foam on alien shores. The bright reflections of two suns shimmered like silver coins off the surface of the water, one huge and one small.

'Look at this.' Igor paused the video as the aerial camera swooped over the ocean. He used his mouse to zoom into the mottled navy pattern that haloed a small island. As the picture resolved, Astrid saw what he was pointing to. A strange chalk-coloured skeleton just visible under the pale water. 'Calcium-carbonate,' Igor said. 'The main compound in pearls, snail shells, egg-shells and—'

'Coral reefs.' Astrid finished the sentence for him, touching the screen. 'They're real.'

'That's right,' Igor said. 'Who would have thought?'

Astrid laughed. Terra-Two was beautiful and everything, every single thing was just the way that she had imagined.

That night was another of her Terra dreams. Astrid awoke mistaking the hum and sigh of the ship for the rhythmic lapping of water. She could feel it, the feather softness of the surf, the way it slid up her thighs and kissed her face. Only it was the rumpled peach cotton of her duvet covers, and when she'd rubbed her eyes and sat up, her mattress was rocking against ivory shores.

She woke up early for the rest of the week. And every time she did, she would climb out of bed, and type 'New Creationism' into her tablet search engine.

HARRY

14.07.12

HARRY BELLGRAVE WASN'T IN space. He was sprinting through a forest he had never seen. The vegetation was so thick underfoot that he was forced to edge closer and closer to the river. The water was like glass. Every now and then he caught sight of a fish, the sun momentarily igniting its scales red or gold or green before it slipped again into shadow.

He was glad to be outside, to catch glimpses of the sun rising through the foliage, to watch as water sloshed across the coloured rocks on the bank, and how they glittered and skittered over each other as they were drawn back into the river. It looked as if the ground was crumbling beneath his feet.

Sometimes, moss-covered branches would fly into his field of vision, as if to whack him across the face, but he would ghost through them unharmed. That was one of the problems with the simulation. He could see things but he couldn't feel the morning sun on his shins or the sharp wet rocks at his heels. These limitations stopped him from ever truly escaping the bounds of the games room.

Presently, the trees gave way and the river bulged sideways. Harry barely had time to stop running before the ground fell away and he was standing on the edge of a sheer cliff-face. River water sluiced over the side and crashed down into the glistening pools below, sending a foamy spray up into the trees.

He saw, then, how high he had climbed. Golden shafts of sunlight burst through the granite peaks of surrounding mountains. From his vantage point he felt as if he could grab the half-faced moons in the sky.

Below, a dozen waterfalls converged in misty pools or disappeared into the foliage. He could see all the way out across the bleach-green lagoon and untilled fields to the ocean, which was stained with pre-dawn pink. Goosebumps prickled up his arms. All around, the unblemished, unpeopled earth beckoned. That was where the footage ended.

It had been Eliot's idea to connect the footage from the five Albatross cameras up to the simulator. So that when the crew were running on the treadmill, it was projected before them.

Pulling off his goggles, Harry jumped off the treadmill. His thighs and arms were glistening with sweat and he was still breathing hard from the workout. He took off his shirt and slumped down on the floor, his lips salty and wet.

If he were still at Dalton, he would not be training alone. He would be tearing through the school grounds with his friends, feet battering the field, their laughter misting on the morning air as they raced to beat each other's speed. Life at Dalton had been as exciting as a war, and he missed it. He'd thought more of them would make it, the boys he called friends, but when they'd all been streamed into command school he knew that only one of them would be picked for the Beta. There could only be one commander-in-training.

After two months on the *Damocles*, Harry's battle was against boredom. The constant pain of it. So he worked to keep his mind on his job, on the simulation, on the game.

In the silence, he heard someone coming. A soft tread. He hoped for a moment it might be Poppy, but instead it was Astrid who appeared in the doorway. She was still in her nightdress, the skin on her cheeks creased from the rumples in her pillow.

'Oh, it's you.' She sounded disappointed.

'Did you want to use the treadmill?' Harry asked. 'I'm almost finished.'

'No ... actually I wanted to look at ...' Her eyes found the footage of Terra-Two, frozen on the screen, and her focus drifted for a moment. 'It's beautiful, isn't it?'

Harry shrugged. 'You came down here just to look at it?'

Astrid glanced at him, then lowered her gaze in embarrassment. 'You'll laugh at me.' She said it more to herself than to him. Harry was silent, still catching his breath from the run. 'Everyone thinks that Tessa Dalton discovered Terra-Two by accident.'

'Through calculation,' Harry corrected. They had all learned about it in their astronomy classes. She'd noticed the micro-distortion the planet had on the gravity of the primary star, and with the most powerful telescopes of her time she had seen the slight dimming of light that indicates the presence of a planet.

'I know. But the fact was, she had been dreaming about it all her life. Another planet with two suns and two moons and not a soul on it. Terra lit up her sleep at night, she painted pictures of it. So by the time she made the discovery it didn't feel like a happy accident. It felt like a homecoming.'

'Yeah,' said Harry. 'There's a whole lot of mythology surrounding the discovery of Terra-Two. Some people even think she was a prophet.' Astrid's wide-eyed gaze irritated him.

'I think *I* do,' she said. 'How else would you explain it? She spends her whole life writing about Terra, claiming it's habitable when they didn't have the technology to know that then. Claiming there's life somewhere else in the universe and years later we find that everything she said was correct. How do *you* explain that?'

'I don't know.' Harry sighed. He hadn't had breakfast yet and his blood sugar was low. 'I think if you're crazy – and she actually *was* sent to an asylum – you find what you're looking for.' Astrid's face fell. 'Besides,' he added, 'she wasn't right about everything. Have you read her papers? She says that Terra is like the Garden of Eden or something.' Astrid was still staring at him in wounded disbelief. 'Astrid? You know that's just some New Creationist crap. That there are some people on this ship chosen by God who will make it to Terra. You can't honestly believe it.'

'I don't know why I thought I could tell you anything,' Astrid hissed, her face growing dark with fury.

'Yeah,' Harry said. 'Why *did* you tell me? You know I don't believe in any of that stuff.'

'I don't know. I came downstairs and you were here. I just wanted to talk to someone. Anyone.'

'To tell someone that you're part of some cult now? Because I think you should probably keep that stuff to yourself.'

'*I* dream about it too.' She waved a hand at the frozen projection of Terra-Two, which was casting a dull light on the side of her face. 'Every single night.' She stepped back. 'For months

I've been dreaming about the beach and the trees and the types of birds that land on them without knowing what it was. Then this footage from the cameras arrives, and it's exactly the same as my dreams.' Her voice had dropped to a whisper. 'I know how it sounds, okay. But I also know how the sand bakes under the suns so at midday it's too hot to walk on. The bittersweet fruits that grow in the forest: there's one that's bright red and hangs low on the trees. It's the size and shape of a human heart. Tough as a mango but when you bite ...' Astrid closed her eyes for a half-second, her chest rising in silent rapture. 'Juice bursts out, sweet and thick as blood that dries black in the sun. On the footage. You can see it on the footage – the fruits, just in the corner and just for half a frame, but they're there. And the reefs, Harry. Don't you remember, a couple of weeks ago in Cai's lesson, I said that I was sure there were reefs. And now there's evidence.'

'I don't know what that proves.' Harry wondered if Astrid's delusion was something he should mention to Commander Sheppard.

'That I'm not making this up.' Her voice was raised now, her cheeks flushed again.

Harry was still staring at her in amused scepticism. Astrid exhaled in fury and pushed him aside, striding towards the door.

'Fine then,' she said. 'Ignore me.' Her voice echoed down the corridor.

Harry pulled his goggles back on and returned to the simulation. He was running again on the treadmill, though on a lower speed because – though he didn't consciously admit it – he was looking for something. He replayed the footage from the beginning, running through the forest, ankles rustling through the thick undergrowth. Most of the trees were tall, letting only slivers of light down into the forest floor. Harry ran past the ancient trees that lined the edges of the river, their roots bulging up from the soil, then he noted something. He paused the simulation, rewound, zoomed in. Blood-red fruit, the size and shape of a human heart.

POPPY

2005

LATER, THEY WOULD TELL her that sadness was a sickness. Poppy suspected that she'd caught it from her mother. She imagined that it had passed like poison from her breast milk, or had been woven into her genes from conception. Perhaps it filled the air in their flat like a miasma, and drove everyone away, all the boyfriends Poppy's mother invited into their home.

Poppy's best memories were from those moments in between the boyfriends and the bouts of her mother's teary-eyed self-loathing and depression. When they would watch *Fresh Prince* together while eating butter sandwiches and stuffing the crusts down the side of the sofa. Or staying up all night toasting marshmallows on the stove, and turning unpaid bills into origami boats that they sent racing across the bathtub.

The boyfriend who stayed the longest was Stephen. Stephen was one of those men who never stopped looking like a teenager. His facial hair still grew in patches, he was tall and thin and almost imperceptibly out of proportion. Everything he did was ironic, like the way he wore Reebok jumpers and dungarees. He was an artist, apparently. Poppy caught a glimpse of his art one afternoon when they were driving home in his shabby Ford and the wheels juddered as if they'd hit a speed bump. Poppy's mother took in a sharp breath.

'What?' Poppy asked. They'd stopped.

'I think you've run something over, Steve,' her mother said, her face pale. Poppy imagined a tiny person curled up under their car.

'Probably just a fox,' he said.

'Go have a look.'

'What do you want me to do, bury the thing?'

'Steve . . .'

He climbed out of the car.

Poppy scrambled after him, slamming the door shut behind her. 'What is it?' she asked.

It was only a dead bird. She saw it when she walked around to the front. Stephen had crushed its little bones under the wheel of the car and he stood staring at the carcass with wide, curious eyes, as if he could see colours in it that she couldn't.

'It looks like fireworks,' he said quietly. Poppy tried to pretend that she didn't know what he was talking about: the way the blood sprayed the dusty tarmac, bits of feather, flesh and indistinguishable strands of sinew bloomed on the road.

'It's the same colour as your hair,' he said, then knelt down and pressed a thumb into the blood before touching her forehead, as if it was Ash Wednesday. Poppy felt something grow in her stomach. She felt proud and special.

'*Adieu pour toujours*,' she said. She'd been reading *Bonjour Tristesse* in the car.

Stephen pulled a camera out of his pocket to take a picture.

'What are you doing?' she asked, the spell suddenly broken.

He looked at her and spoke slowly. 'You're right, of course, a picture won't do it. I need to take it with me. I need the real thing, right?'

'For what?'

'For art,' he said.

Which began their life on the road. Stephen was so captivated by his new idea – driving up and down high roads in search of roadkill – that Poppy's mother didn't attempt to stop him. Instead, they all came along. They made a family outing of it, every Saturday waking up early to pile into the increasingly foul-smelling car and drive up and down the roads until the sun slipped off the horizon. Poppy downloaded language podcasts, and mouthed the words silently at the window – *Il mio nome è Poppy, Come ti chiami? Mi annoio. Annoiato. Annoiato* – looking at the open fields, the power lines and houses with the adolescent certainty that something immensely fun was happening elsewhere.

She could hear Stephen and her mother arguing some nights, through the wall beside her bed. She'd bury her face into her pillow and fight to sleep.

One night she opened her eyes and saw a small flickering light in the darkness. 'No, don't move,' said the shadow at the end of her bed. He was holding up a video camera.

'What are you doing?' Poppy asked, her voice still thick with sleep.

'It's got to be natural.'

He'd come most nights after that. Poppy didn't always know because it was always after she was asleep, although sometimes she would wake from a dream and see the flashing light of the camera at the foot of her bed. The most he would ever do was raise a finger to his lips to *shh* her, and in the morning he would be gone.

When she was older and she thought about it an uneasy feeling would settle in the pit of her stomach. She could never figure out why she'd never simply locked her door.

THE ARGUMENTS ESCALATED, AND when the house wasn't filled with her mother's stony silence, she and Stephen were screaming at each other across the kitchen table, smashing glasses no one swept up, so they would all have to tiptoe around the debris for a week. Poppy had become an expert at using tweezers to pull sharp little splinters from the balls of her feet.

One day, from the living room, Poppy heard her mother call him 'a shit artist' and the shouting stopped.

She listened out for a little while but then she heard the door click open and the sound of a car horn outside. Another few moments of stillness before she pressed mute on the remote and listened for the growl of the engine revving up.

'*Poppy*,' a voice called, and she stiffened. 'Poppy!'

'I'm coming.'

It was Stephen's shout from the open door of the purring car. Poppy was still in her pyjamas but she slipped into a pair of old slippers and ran outside.

Stephen and her mother were sitting in the front, her mother's face wet with tears. 'Get in,' he said. Poppy bit her lip in hesitation, but Stephen was starting up the car and the wheels were already beginning to push off the tarmac when Poppy jumped in and slammed the door behind her.

The car accelerated so quickly she was thrown back against her seat. 'What are you doing?' her mother gasped. They rounded a sharp bend in the road and Poppy was thrown against the window. 'Put on your seatbelt,' her mother shouted. 'Steve, what are you doing? Stop the car. Stop the car.'

'You think you know about art?' he roared, pushing on the accelerator. The car flew over a speed bump, almost knocking them out of their seats and causing Poppy's spine to slam back down again. 'You don't know a thing about art.'

Another speed bump and, though she'd braced herself, it tore a cry of terror from her as she lifted off the seat.

When they turned the next corner they narrowly missed another car, which swerved past, horn blaring. Poppy felt the air evaporate from her throat.

'You're driving like a madman, Ste—*Watch out!*' They'd driven right off the road, juddered up onto the pavement and burst through the picket fence surrounding the common. Stephen was charging towards the pond and, for a horrifying moment, Poppy thought they were heading right into the cold water, but he turned them around at the last second with a shout of delight and trundled over the grass.

The car accelerated again, heading for a group of ducks, and both Poppy and her mother screamed as something rolled under the tyres. Feathers flew up by the window and the air filled with the squeal of birds, the crunch of branches and bone. 'Stephen!' Poppy's mother shoved his hands off the steering wheel and Poppy squeezed her eyes shut as the car lurched back towards the pond. They were going to plunge in, she was sure of it, but she was too scared to unbuckle her seatbelt.

Then, she felt the car slow under her and come to a sudden stop. Scrambling to open the door, Poppy made it out just in time to throw up on the grass.

When she finished and wiped the side of her mouth, she was surprised to find that she was crying. Heat spread across her face as more sobs came and she did nothing to wipe them away. She walked away from the car for a while, sat on the bench overlooking the scummy pond.

The sky was a disgusting colour, and she was shivering in her thin pyjamas. She wished she'd brought a coat in addition to her now-soiled slippers. There were Coke cans floating in the pond, and when her tears finally subsided she could see across the water to Stephen's car, and the feathers smeared into the tyres. She wondered if her mother was okay, and knew that she had to go back. When she did, she couldn't spot either of the adults behind the windscreen and wondered if they had walked off and left her. Then she saw her mother in the back seat. She was being attacked. Poppy pressed her face against the window but then wished she hadn't. Understanding came to her all at once; her mother squeezing Stephen's hair in a wet fist, the knife-bright slice of thigh, a jet spray of hair at the base of Stephen's spine, his bottom waxing over the edge of his loosened belt.

She ran.

As the wind stung her eyes she thought that she heard her mother's voice calling out behind her, but she didn't look back.

A WEEK LATER, STEPHEN finally left for good. Poppy was called out of her class by the school's receptionist and driven to the hospital. For the rest of her life, whenever Poppy recalled the way her mother looked that day – tiny and helpless, folded in on herself, her eyes closed, still connected to a drip – it was with a twist of pain. 'Has she done this before?' the social worker asked.

Poppy had nodded. 'A couple of times.'

Poppy was filled, then, with an urgent terror that if she spent another year in that flat she would die there.

So she applied to Dalton, applied to everywhere that would take her, and only thought about how she might pay for it when the acceptances slipped through the letter box.

Even after she was accepted by Dalton Academy, and most of her time was spent with her new friends in the grounds of the school, the dread rose up in her whenever the holidays approached.

There was only so long she could survive in that flat in Liverpool, breathing air that was stale with her mother's misery. And, although there was a nostalgic tether that tugged at her every time she left, although the cracked roads rose up to meet her, although her mother begged her not to leave when the term began – the tide of dread and self-preservation was always stronger, beckoning Poppy further and further out again.

JUNO

15.07.12

BY SUNDAY, JUNO WAS convinced she had not seen Poppy leave their cabin all week. Poppy had tried to convince the senior astronauts that she was too ill to attend lessons or group mealtimes. And, as the days went by, the senior crew were getting more and more concerned. Every time Fae or Commander Sheppard attempted to talk to her about it, Poppy would burst into tears. Sheppard had suggested that they give her 'some space,' that perhaps she needed more time to adjust to their new environment, but by mid-July Juno was sure that they should try another form of intervention.

She woke up early that morning and went for a run. Once she'd showered she headed up to the comms deck, where Poppy was supposed to be running software updates. Instead, she found Eliot and Astrid hunched over the keyboard, both their ears covered with headphones.

'What are you doing?' Juno asked, looking down at her watch. Astrid and Eliot stared unflinchingly at the display, her face cast in pale light, his eyes far away.

When Juno tapped her sister on the shoulder, she jolted, then looked up with a startled intake of breath.

'I can't hear you,' she shouted, even as she pulled her headphones off her ears.

'Where's Poppy?' Juno asked.

'Where she always is,' Astrid said with a shrug, 'our bedroom.' She touched her headphones, already threatening to put them back on, then she turned to her sister with a frown. 'What were you doing?'

'I just went for a run.'

Astrid stared at her. 'It's not your day,' she said, her voice spiked with suspicion. 'You don't do cardio on Sundays.'

'You don't do comms ever,' Juno said, gesturing towards the monitors.

Astrid's eyes brightened with excitement. 'Eliot's showing me how to use the new communications software. Want to have a look?' She gestured toward a little navigation display. 'See, that's us.' She pointed to a little blip just under the amber disc of Mars. Jupiter was cut off in the corner of the screen, so Juno could only see the pale arc of its edge in the schematic. In the dotted path of their ship's trajectory was an ivory bubble, which represented Europa. 'That's the *Orlando*.' Astrid pointed to a tiny flashing light on the moon's perimeter. 'Though you can't really see it, and we won't be able to until we get a bit closer. But we're getting near enough to tune in to them. In a week we'll be able to have a conversation in real time.'

The thought filled Juno with excitement. The rendezvous with the American space station had been added relatively late to their itinerary, so soon before the launch that Juno had all but forgotten about it. She and her crewmates had been about ten years old when the first expedition launched, so young that

Juno had grown up with the distant sense that there had *always* been people orbiting Jupiter's icy moon.

The first astronauts to go had been Captain Omar Briggs and Dr Sie Yan, a married couple who specialized in xenobiology. It made Juno's mind reel when she realized that for over a decade the two of them had been staring down the lens of a microscope, working to genetically engineer a crop of plants capable of thriving in the ocean that was hidden under the frozen surface of Europa. 'A decade alone in a box is enough to test any marriage,' Commander Sheppard often said with a laugh. He'd been the best man at their wedding, and he and Briggs had shared a tent for seven months when they scaled Olympus Mons.

The second expedition to the *Orlando* had launched years later. The astronauts involved were young recruits who'd emerged from the USA's space academy system: Kennedy, James and Cal, the smiling, suntanned forerunners of the Beta. Juno couldn't wait to meet them.

'Can you talk to *anyone* on that?' she asked, nodding at the computer.

'Sure. If they're within range,' Eliot said, then he rolled his eyes up in thought. 'We can always send messages. But, obviously, the further out we go the further the signal has to travel. And the longer we have to wait for a response. By the time we reach Saturn it will take about eighty minutes for Earth to get our messages, and the same amount of time for us to hear a response. So, you know, no kind of real-time conversation will really be possible. But, we don't have to think about that for a while ...'

'And the *Orlando* is the furthest human outpost,' Astrid finished. 'The furthest humans have travelled in our solar system.'

'Except for the *Shēngmìng*,' Juno said.

'Well, not really.' Eliot took his hands off the control deck. 'No one knows where that ship is. Or if it's even still out there.'

'Of course it's *out there*,' Juno replied. Although the Chinese generation ship had gone radio silent around two years ago, Juno still imagined it floating like a shadow through the solar system, making its slow way to Terra-Two. The Chinese government had launched it four years ago – a bright vessel with 100 passengers, on a trip expected to last a century. Sometimes Juno wondered what it would be like to leave Earth behind, and – unlike the crew of the *Damocles*, who had access to Igor's technology – to know for certain that only her grandchildren or great-grandchildren would ever set foot on Terra-Two. What would they be like by the time they arrived? The children of another century, whose parents and grandparents had lived and died in the void? It had seemed inhumane to Juno, to raise children in the sanitized air of a spaceship, who would live and die without ever seeing a cloud or touching a lake. By the time they reached their promised destination, would they even remember what they were looking for?

Two years ago, the crew on the *Shēngmìng* had filed for the right to be recognized as a separate state, which led to an inquiry into life on the ship. Their commander, Zhang Wei, had died and been replaced by the scientist Xiao Lin, whose voice crowded the airwaves for a while. They had painted a new flag, changed their name and written up a constitution. The astronauts refused to be considered employees of the Chinese National Space Administration and proudly presented themselves as citizens of a new country.

They had debated it in school. Some argued that the Outer

Space Treaty meant that a spacecraft could not be considered an independent country. To many, the idea was ridiculous. And yet there was no denying that the citizens of the *Shēngmìng* appeared to have adopted their own set of laws and system of government, and lived in harmony under its jurisdiction.

'We have built a beautiful country,' Xiao Lin had said.

And now Juno could imagine how it happened; of course the tightly knit group of astronauts, sharing space, sharing food, united against the hostile environment outside, would come to identify with each other, come to rely on and love one another to the exclusion of everything else in the universe. 'For all we know, they could all be dead,' said the cynical spokespeople when the ship went silent. But this speculation was squashed once the government picked up video feeds of smiling people in flight suits, their faces reflected in the glassy torus of the deck. At their feet were bouncing children with free access to education, healthcare, food, everyone working to give back to each other. It sounded like a utopia to Juno.

'But we could find them, theoretically,' she pushed, not prepared to abandon the notion.

'I don't know,' Eliot said. 'The mission was suspended after they declared independence.'

'And in a year or so, their space agency will probably try again. Maybe with a faster engine this time,' Astrid said. 'One that might reach Terra-Two sooner.'

'But not faster than us,' Eliot said with a gap-toothed smile. 'This is a "race" after all. We have to get there first. And anyway, if the *Shēngmìng* is out there somewhere, if they're still on the course set by their flight engineers, they'd be somewhere just beyond Jupiter by now. Maybe.'

So, theoretically, we could see them? Juno thought, but she didn't have time to voice her question before the sound of feet came thudding up the ladder. When she turned around she was face to face with Harry, who smelt like coffee and menthol.

'Hey there,' he said. 'Having a little party on the comms deck?'

'I'm doing the software update,' Astrid said. 'Eliot's teaching me.'

Juno remembered why she'd come to the comms deck in the first place. 'Poppy's supposed to be doing that.' She frowned.

'Can't you leave off it today, at least?' Harry said.

'I'm just saying—'

'Today is her birthday. So she probably wants to lie in bed and cry or something.'

'Oh,' Juno said, guiltily.

Astrid smacked her hands over her eyes and groaned. 'I forgot!'

They all had. They'd been on the ship for two months and already the lightless days had taken on a strange uniformity. Juno found it difficult to believe that on Earth it was summer. In London, the sun was rising at 5 a.m. and setting at 10 p.m. In just under two weeks the Olympic games would begin. But here there was no change in temperature to mark the passing of the seasons, no marigold leaves or humid, impossibly long twilight.

They gathered a few minutes later with the senior crew in the kitchen for Sunday breakfast, which was normally an hour later, and began the one day they did not have to attend lessons or do many chores.

The calendar next to the fridge was divided into ten columns. Juno ran her finger down Poppy's, found that day's date. The words '*Poppy is twenty*' burst from its borders, the tails of the Ys trailing into curlicues.

Juno left the kitchen and headed back into the dormitory, where Poppy was drowning in duvet covers. When Juno called her name she cracked open an eye laced with sleep-grit. She wore a night-slip that she had not taken off for a week, pale-pink cotton that was grey around the edges. Her ginger hair was matted, skin white as bone.

'Hey, Poppy . . . ?' Juno stepped tentatively over to the side of the bed and felt the metallic crunch of a chocolate wrapper under her heel. Poppy grunted in acknowledgement.

'You need to get out of bed.' Juno had not seen Poppy at a single meal in the past week – although Fae came downstairs twice a day with a tray to try to coax her into taking a few bites. Juno was not sure she had even spotted Poppy stepping in or out of the shower. Her corner of the room was ripe with the smell of an unwashed body.

'I'm tired,' she sighed. 'Gimme an hour.'

'When did you last get up?' Juno asked.

The radio was on low. Poppy had tuned it to whatever channel she could find, and at that moment two men were conversing in a guttural language Juno did not recognize. Every now and then their voices were washed out by a sea of static.

'Poppy.' Juno's voice tightened in irritation. 'What day is it?'

'Thursday . . . ?'

'No.'

On Earth, Poppy had been the type of person to send out calligraphed 'Save the Date' cards two months before her birthday parties.

'You know. You must know what day it is,' Juno pressed.

'Saturday . . . ?'

'*Poppy!*'

Poppy moaned, reached out a pale arm from under the duvet and swatted Juno lazily away as if she were a fly.

'Go away,' she said, and rolled over to face the wall. 'It's not like days even exist up here. Only night.'

Juno left the room, her stomach knotting up inside her. When she entered the kitchen Commander Sheppard and Fae were standing at the head of the table. Eliot and Astrid were on breakfast duty, adding water to dried milk and measuring out rations of cereal, while the others were seated opposite each other, Jesse playing Solitaire, the cards organized in neat black and red rows, Harry watching a recording of the news on his computer.

'Juno.' Fae exhaled slightly.'You're here.' She kept an eye on the door, and after it slid shut she continued. 'We're concerned about Poppy.'

Commander Sheppard nodded in agreement. 'This can't go on for much longer,' he said. 'This is an important mission and she has duties to fulfil. The team on the ground are furious. She hasn't sent a video update in two weeks.'

'I've been covering it,' Eliot said.

'I know you have.' Commander Sheppard nodded at him. 'But you have your own duties and it should not be necessary.'

'But she's sick,' Jesse said, placing a seven of diamonds atop an eight, 'it's not her fault.' Fae and Commander Sheppard exchanged a look.

'I've been visiting her for extra counselling sessions. She says that she's suffering from migraines, but I'm inclined to believe at this point that there is nothing physically wrong with her.'

'Physically,' Harry muttered.

'So now we're faced with two options,' Commander Sheppard said, making a steeple of his fingers. 'Sanctions, or—'

'Sanctions?' Astrid turned with a gasp. 'It's her *birthday*.'

'July the fifteenth,' Fae said with a grimace, 'Yes. Of course.' They stood in silence for a moment before the microwave dinged and Eliot started.

'We can get her a gift ... or something,' Astrid suggested tentatively. 'We could make a cake.'

'A party,' Jesse said, throwing his arms up theatrically. 'Let's make it a party.'

'I know how to make cake,' Astrid said.

Fae's face brightened a little. 'That's a lovely idea. That might really cheer her up.'

'Okay!' Astrid clapped her hands together and grinned. 'What do we need? Sugar, flour rations ...' She was counting on her fingers. 'Some decorations, party games, a gift ...'

'I can find something,' Jesse said.

Astrid nodded towards him and Juno. 'Great. You guys look for a gift. Eliot and I can make a start on a cake.'

'Great,' Fae said. 'A party at five o'clock. What a delightful idea.' Commander Sheppard gave a sceptical smile.

Juno followed Jesse down to the crew module, but stopped when she reached the threshold of the boys' cabin.

'You can come in, you know,' he said, and she stepped inside uncertainly.

The boys' cabin was like the girls', only a little smaller. The bunks were oblong alcoves in the walls with a net curtain for privacy. They had done little to decorate their space. Eliot's was the only bed that was draped in a hand-knitted patchwork quilt and not the UKSA-issued navy duvet covers that reminded

Juno of the spartan dormitories they had left behind at the space centre. All their beds were neatly made, the duvets folded under the mattress the way they had been taught. Only Jesse's bunk was a mess. He had never properly unpacked, and his things spilled from his trunk. Tie-dyed scarves were draped over the curtain rails, old documents had been folded up into paper cranes that hung from threads above his bed. He was growing an ivy plant above his bed, the spidery arms of it pinned to the wall. It was beautiful to see this little bit of nature staking claim to a corner of their ship. 'That's cool,' Juno said, gesturing to it.

'Yeah, thanks,' Jesse said. 'I'm hoping that eventually all the walls around the bed will be covered in it, so I'll feel as if I'm sleeping in a treehouse.'

'You haven't unpacked yet?' Juno said, glancing at a pile of books atop a maroon rug.

'Oh,' Jesse said, and began to rummage through his things, 'I never unpack. By the time I unpack I almost always have to re-pack a month later.' He grinned. 'Sorry. I might have cleaned up a little if I known I'd have company.'

'I'm fine.' Blushing, Juno stepped back to sit on Eliot's pristine bed.

The bunk above Jesse's belonged to Harry. He'd pinned up a few school ties, the full and half colours he'd received for academic achievements. Brass and silver tankards glistened on the shelf by his head.

'Right.' Jesse recovered a box from under a pile of crumpled clothes. 'I think … in here …' He was rummaging through it, chucking out books, sachets of coffee and bags of beads. Juno watched him. She had never been able to guess where exactly Jesse was from, and now it seemed too late to ask. His voice had a slightly Irish lilt but his skin was a kind of bronze that appeared coppery in the right light. Around his temples and under his braids his jet black hair was loosely curled. It occurred to Juno that she actually knew very little about this boy who she had lived with since the launch.

Jesse's brow was furrowed in concentration as he rifled through his things, and Juno thought about how keen he had seemed to give Poppy a gift, how often he asked after her, the way he stared at her across the kitchen table. Then it occurred to her that he must *like* her. *How obvious*, she thought, *and how uninspired. Everyone* liked Poppy, with her delicate limbs and thick russet locks. Even now, unwashed as she was, Juno knew she would emerge from her bedroom, after much coaxing, and everyone would still look at her like she'd just walked off the pages of *Vanity Fair*. Juno stood up, caught off-guard by her own disappointment.

'Aha!' Jesse held something up in his hands like a trophy, then handed it to her. It was a conch, the most beautiful one Juno had ever seen, pearly orange with a hard spiralled shell and a flared slit along its length. Inside it was smooth and cool to the touch, pink as the wet skin inside lips.

'Don't you want to hear the sea?' Jesse asked. Juno was puzzled for a moment before she remembered and held the conch to her ear to listen to the sigh of the waves inside its body. Such things didn't excite her anymore. When she was younger she really had believed that sea shells remembered the sea as old women remembered their youth. The swansong of a domestic object that had once known the majesty of an ocean. 'Seashell resonance,' she said. Any curious child knew that the same sound was audible in mugs and empty jam jars or a pair of cupped hands held up against an ear. 'Where did you get this from?'

'I think … that was Mombasa. My sister saw it under the water and she dove right down and gave it to me.'

'Oh, Kenya?' She looked up.

'Yeah, my mum's Kenyan.'

'Really? And your dad too?'

'No, he's from Dublin. But we lived in Nairobi for a while when I was little.' He pointed to a picture pinned to his noticeboard of a smiling family. Jesse, younger, with springy shoulder-length black locks. Their faces blurred by candle light. 'That's my tenth birthday. That morning we went to Nakumatt supermarket and tried to buy a cake, but they were like "a *ready-made* cake?"' He mimicked their surprise. 'So my mum bought a tart instead and then, just as I was blowing out the candles, the lights went out.'

'Power cut?' Juno asked, remembering her own child-hood home.

'Yeah.' Jesse smiled. Juno examined some of the other photographs. Jesse's sister smiling at a market stall. 'Where's that?' she asked.

'Istanbul,' Jesse said casually.

'Is that New York?' Juno pointed at a picture of a white man and a dark woman standing in front of a yellow taxi.

'Vancouver,' Jesse corrected. 'My family travel around a lot.'

'I gathered that much. Why?'

'Well – my dad's a journalist, sort of. He does this documentary series called *Undiscovered Earth*, maybe you've heard of it?' Juno nodded. She had come across a few episodes on the BBC. The kind of Sunday-night viewing that was comfortable to fall asleep in front of, as surprising vistas of far-flung places lit up the screen. It was difficult to imagine that the gaunt presenter was related to the handsome golden-skinned boy standing before her.

'And he travels around a lot to research disparate communities and the effects of climate change, and my mum's an author so she can work anywhere. Wanderlust, my parents are sick with it. They took me and my sister out of school for eighteen months to travel across East Africa. My dad taught my sister most of GCSE chemistry. For Christmas, we took a cruise down the Nile.'

His braided hair reminded Juno of the overly tanned white boys she'd seen at Kenyatta airport, sunburnt and peeling, blond locks in cornrows. 'That sounds . . . amazing,' she said. 'My dad is a missionary, he travels a lot too. But we didn't really get to go with him so often.' She paused. 'I feel bad, actually. I don't think I've asked you anything about yourself. You sound like you've had an interesting life.'

'So have you,' Jesse said. 'You're an *astronaut*.'

Juno rolled her eyes. 'We're all *astronauts*,' she said, mimicking his tone. 'But you've been to all these places. Places I'll never get to go.'

Jesse shrugged. 'It had up- and downsides – travelling so much. When I was younger it seemed like a lot more downsides, if I'm honest. But I got to pick some things up along the way; a suntan, some passing phrases in Arabic, this shell . . .'

Juno ran her fingers along its blunt spines. 'You must like Poppy a lot, since you're giving this to her.'

'I dunno. I've been wanting to give it away ever since Morrigan gave it to me. I mean, it's pretty and all, and it made me feel like Ralph from *Lord of the Flies* but – you're going to think this is so dumb – when it was on my shelf I kept thinking about how big it was, and how big the thing that used to live inside it must have been. I felt a little guilty because it was once something's home, and I also got a bit grossed out.' He seemed to shudder at the thought of the soft slimy animal that made its home in the shell.

'Maybe it's evolution,' Juno said, trying to hide a smile.

'People frightened of invertebrates live longer?' Jesse teased.

'I'm sure I heard that somewhere,' she replied, and they both laughed.

'I don't even know how this ended up in my box,' Jesse said. 'It's kind of spooky actually. I feel as if I'm being followed.'

'Imagine if we got to Terra and there were hundreds of them all over the beach.'

'Exactly. So I'm glad I'm giving it to Poppy. Does that make it bad? Like, not really a gift?'

Juno thought. 'Sometimes, for Lent, I'd give up tomatoes. But I've always hated tomatoes.' He looked puzzled for a moment, so she continued. 'It's supposed to be a sacrifice.'

Someone coughed behind them and they turned to find Astrid standing at the door. 'I found something,' she said, and opened her hand to show Juno the bejewelled hair slide that looked worth more than the six pounds she'd paid for it in Camden. Now, it probably was.

'Jesse's got something too.' She showed her sister the conch.

'Wow.' Astrid grinned, taking it from her sister and holding it up to her ear. Her eyes glazed over as if she could already see the crashing waves.

POPPY

15.07.12

SHE HAD NOT BEEN ready for the darkness of space. Other astronauts had warned her that it came as a real shock, the complete unilluminated blackness. But, at the time, Poppy had been looking backwards and not ahead. She had been looking back down at Earth at everything she was glad to leave behind, not ahead into the vacuum.

Sometimes she felt as if the blackness was actually inside her. As if space itself yawned inside her, and the cold of it had leeched into her bones.

Two weeks after they'd arrived on the *Damocles*, Poppy had come down with a cold – a mild fever, airways stuffed with cotton wool, a head that felt like a fish tank – and Fae allowed her to take a day off work on the condition that she catch up with her chores over the weekend. Poppy had spent the next three days in bed, and sleep came so easily, submerged her again and again like warm water. Even when Poppy tried to get up, a few days later, her bones were heavy. Suddenly everything seemed like an awful lot of work and she no longer had it in her to do it. She couldn't see the point. As the days passed more and more things fell away. She realized that she had spent her entire life blindly beating back against a tide of futility, performing tasks she would only have to do again and again: changing filters, cleaning rooms, updating software, scraping away the black dirt that aggregated under her fingernails. The others could not see with her keen eyes; they were still fighting, they were still working as if they had forgotten that one day their eyes would shut and maggots would wriggle into their stomachs and the marrow in their bones would turn to dust.

That was happening to Poppy already, only slowly.

The day of her birthday, Poppy opened her eyes and saw Harry's face. He had twisted a sheet of coloured paper into a cone and tied it on top of his head like a party hat. 'It's your birthday,' he said with a smile.

'Is it?' Her mouth was sour, her teeth furry and unbrushed.

'You're twenty.'

'I'm twenty.' The words came as a hollow surprise and made Poppy's stomach twist.

'Hey, don't cry,' he said, although she hadn't realized that she was. Harry leant down, wiped a tear away with his thumb and then licked it.

Twenty, she had heard, was young in the scheme of things. And yet it was the oldest she had ever been.

'We have a surprise for you,' Harry said.

'You do?'

He nodded. 'Outside.'

When Poppy stepped outside, everyone shouted 'Happy Birthday!' They had cut strips of paper into ribbons and hung them from the beams in the crew module, made a banner with a red Sharpie and printer paper so the Ps in 'HAPPY' and 'Poppy' looked like candy-canes. They'd made her a cake, substituted apple sauce for the eggs they didn't have and covered it with icing and hundreds and thousands. Commander Sheppard sang as Eliot thrashed out lively chords on his guitar. Fae, Igor and Cai clapped, while Juno, Astrid and Jesse gesticulated wildly, with all the glad energy of a circus troupe.

Poppy looked at all their smiling faces and felt the love. She smiled back, because these people didn't know that it hurt inside her, and why should they have to? Their singing, peppy and discordant as it was, came to her as if from behind a pane of glass. She smiled numbly the whole way through and when they were finished she ate the cake with her fingers. It was good, the way the sugar entered her veins, and she closed her eyes and said, 'This is good.' It was the first thing she had eaten all day and she could feel it sizzling in the emptiness inside her. 'I could eat the whole thing. I could eat several, every day for the rest of my life.'

'Well, just a little for me,' said Juno, leaning over Astrid's shoulder as she held the cake knife. 'No . . . No, less than that. Half – I said *half* – of that . . .'

'Shame we don't have any candles,' Astrid said. 'Fire hazard.'

'Twenty's a lot of candles,' Harry teased.

'It'll be you in a few months,' Juno reminded him.

'Yeah . . .' He was thoughtful for a moment. 'You're right.'

'Twenty's okay,' said Astrid. 'It's eighteen or nineteen that's the problem. When you have to buy two packs of candles and they come in these weird sets of, like, seven or eleven or prime numbers and you always have loads spare.'

'Oh yeah . . .' Poppy laughed at a memory. 'Remember when we had to buy something like four packs of five for—' She cut off suddenly and her eyes darted to Eliot in alarm.

He looked up from the ground. 'You can say her name, you know.' Everyone ducked their heads. 'That was Ara's birthday. I remember.'

'Well,' Fae said, nibbling at a spoonful of her cake, 'just wait until you get to fifty-six, that's all I can say.'

'Or seventy-eight.' Igor laughed.

After they finished eating, the adults politely absented themselves, leaving the Betas to continue the party without them.

Poppy stuffed the rest of the cake in her mouth then ran a finger around her plate, licking off the remainder of the icing. 'Well,' she said finally, 'it was always Ara who had the best birthdays.'

'No,' Harry said quickly, 'there was Sebastian Branwell's eighteenth.'

For a moment the name drew a blank, but then Poppy remembered the thin boy with the living room the size of her mother's flat. She remembered being happily drunk and looking up at all her faces reflected back in the crystal teardrops on the chandelier. 'There must have been about three hundred people,' she said. The rooms were packed, and students she knew distantly from the local schools were smoking weed in the garden, daring each other to leap topless into the marble fountain.

'More than that, for sure.'

'And that cake ... it was like a wedding cake.'

Harry started laughing. 'Yeah, Oliver Tammon and I played that game to see how far we could hit the ball out and I got it all the way across that field. Like four hundred feet.'

Poppy was still smiling when she looked at him quizzically and asked, 'You did?'

'Course I did. You were there,' Harry said. '*You were*. And Oli bet you and Kate fifty pounds that you wouldn't be able to get it back.' Poppy shook her head with a shrug. 'How could you forget that? It was so fucking awesome. Everyone was talking about it the whole night.'

'Maybe I wasn't there for that bit?'

'You were!' Harry shouted loud enough to make everyone start.

'Okay,' said Jesse, cutting another piece of cake from the plate in the middle. 'Cool it. It's not like it matters anymore.'

'Right,' said Harry, turning on him, 'that's your philosophy, isn't it, nothing matters. I bet it makes you feel so cool. But something's got to matter.'

'Well, you know,' Jesse stretched his legs out in front of him, 'nothing really matters. I mean, Earth stuff. Think about how famous you guys were when we launched – all those people and all those magazines – for a while you were the most famous people on the planet. And what use is it to any of us up here? It's not like it makes a difference anymore, not like we can take it with us. Even other things, like school, being popular or being rich . . .' He trailed off with a shrug.

'Some of it's got to matter,' Harry said, quietly, more to himself.

'I suppose we can decide,' Juno said. 'Hey, when you think about it, we're sort of like a community or a society, right here, the six of us. We get to choose what's important to us.'

'That's weird.' Poppy shuddered.

'Why?'

'I don't know, like we're . . . on our own . . .'

Astrid looked up. 'Is it though? Look around.' And Poppy did for a moment, glancing at the others, who were seated cross-legged in a circle around the half-eaten cake. 'Can you imagine what it will be like the day we look out the window of the Atlas module and we see Terra-Two the way we used to be able to see Earth? Can you picture us all swooping down into the atmosphere on the lander and standing there, feeling like we've come to an end but also a sunlit beginning. Picture it, for a moment,' Astrid continued, her voice strong. 'I do, every day. When you think about it, we're like pioneers. We're the first, and after us, if we're lucky, there will be a whole country. Countries.'

'It's kind of a big responsibility,' Jesse said.

Poppy leant forward in the silence and took another fat slice of cake. Dessert was such a luxury in this world where they survived on macronutrient broth.

'It's a little childish,' Astrid said, 'but I thought of a few games we could play.'

Harry smiled. 'It's not a party without a game.'

JUNO

15.07.12

THEY HAD USED THREE rations of sugar and cocoa powder to make the cake, so it was sickly sweet and black as sin. Juno had been so distracted by the hot feeling of it in her stomach that she missed the count and was out of it until everyone was running to find a hiding place.

Harry closed his eyes and Poppy spun around, her heels flashing pink as she shimmied between a gap in the bookcases, a finger pressed against her lips as she disappeared. In half a second Eliot and Jesse were gone, racing down the corridor, thrilled by the competition. Astrid dashed through the hatch, down to the lower deck, flicking off the lights as she went, the sound of her stifled giggle audible in the sudden darkness. Everyone was trying not to trip over things as they ran, their blood thick with sugar, the air chiming with laughter or bated breath.

Juno didn't want to get in the way of the fun, but she had no real appetite for another game. Over the past few weeks, she had watched both Eliot and Jesse grit their teeth as Harry's high score on the simulator tripled and their progress stalled. She'd witnessed the competition spill out from the games room into the crew module, where Jesse beat Harry and Eliot in a four-hour chess tournament, to the kitchen – the setting for red-eyed staring contests – and Igor's lessons, where Harry and Eliot argued over formulae and scribbled convoluted equations on the whiteboard. Card games and arm-wrestling matches almost resulted in blows. The air between the three boys prickled with the static of imminent combustion.

'Juno, quick,' came a voice from the shadows. Juno strained her eyes in the gloom, searching for the source, but, as Eliot slammed the door to the boys' cabin, she remembered that time was running out. If she didn't find a place to hide, she'd risk the embarrassment of being caught first, standing gormlessly in the middle of the crew module.

'Ten seconds,' Harry said. Juno's heart quickened and she looked around for a place to hide. She could crouch in one of the darkened alcoves, but as soon as Harry flicked the light on he was sure to find her. The girls' cabin struck her as an obvious choice, but she had no time now to run across the crew module.

So she lunged in the opposite direction, to the bathroom, tore open the door and dived in. As it closed behind her, she heard Harry count down, '. . . six, five . . .'

The room smelt of damp and detergent. Juno's eyes were not accustomed to the darkness so she groped around for a few seconds to get her bearings. It was a decent place to hide, she supposed, surely the last place Harry might look. Fumbling for the latch, Juno pulled the shower door open and stepped in.

'What the—'

Her hands flew to her mouth too late to catch a startled whimper.

'Shh,' Jesse hissed savagely. He was standing in the shower too, only a shadow in the gloom.

'Sorry.'

'Get your own spot,' he said, but his mouth clamped shut mid-sentence as Harry's voice rumbled on the other side of the door. 'I know you're in there,' he said. The creak of footsteps.

Juno's heart skipped and she leapt into the shower.

'I thought you said this game was stupid,' Jesse said in a whisper.

'Of course it's stupid. But I don't want to lose first.'

Juno knew that they were all trying to be cheerful in the face of Poppy's melancholy, which was probably why Astrid suggested the first game that came to mind. It had been a while since they had allowed themselves to do something silly.

Both Juno and Jesse swallowed back a gasp when the bathroom door flew open. Juno held her breath, her chest full, her heart skipping.

Harry's silhouette was projected across the tiled floor, outlined by the illumination from the crew module. Could he see them? Juno peeled open her eyes and glanced sideways. If Harry switched the light on, he would find them straight away.

When she looked up she realized that Jesse had been staring at her the whole time. His pupils were dilated, his face illuminated oddly in the rose light that filtered through the door. His moist lips were half-open, as if in surprise. Their heads were so close that Juno thought she could feel the static buzz off his hair.

'Hello!' Harry boomed, trying to startle whoever might be hiding in the bathroom. Adrenaline flooded Juno's veins, but she bit her tongue and hoped that he would not find the two of them pressed against each other in this small space. There was a long moment of silence, and she wondered if Jesse could feel her heart hammering against her ribs. She held his gaze. Then, finally, the door slammed shut. Light flashed against Jesse's retinas and then they were in darkness again. They both exhaled involuntarily. Jesse's breath was warm on the bridge of Juno's nose, his molars black with chocolate cake. She was painfully aware of the closeness of this other body. She caught the chemical whiff of the plant fertilizer he handled, the scent of birch leaves and sweat and long grass. For a minute, she forgot about the game. Heat radiated through the thin cotton of his shirt and his forehead glistened.

'Are we okay?' he asked, trying to smile.

'I think so,' Juno whispered, stepping back. But Jesse's breath was still quick and irregular, Juno's hands were shaking and, in the unilluminated air between them, there was a shift.

JESSE

29.07.12

THERE WAS SOMETHING BETWEEN them. Was there? Even two weeks later, Jesse thought he could feel it. A frisson of nerves whenever she was near or caught his eye across the table.

Could she sense it too?

Everything reminded him of her. That afternoon in the greenhouse it was the freshly watered earth, which was the same dark brown as her lips.

Jesse knew it had something to do with proximity. The fact that he saw Juno every day, in the kitchen measuring out rations, or scratching the nape of her neck with the edge of her pencil during Igor's classes. But that was nothing new. Jesse had trained with Juno for years at Dalton. Back then, she had simply been the 'other' twin. The one who never turned up to parties, and whose grades were so high they were the bar that everyone furtively measured themselves against. The one on the Christian Union's committee and the debating team. Her name was listed on every other page in the school newsletter. There had been something unattractive to him about this overachiever, the girl he would sometimes spot from his window running laps around the frozen hockey pitch before the bell rang for breakfast.

So why now? Why did he desire her now?

Jesse didn't want to think that it had anything to do with being pressed up against her body in the shower three weeks earlier at Poppy's party. That it was something as simple as the fluttering of her heart and the smell of coffee beans and chocolate on her breath that had reminded him what a fine and foreign thing a girl was. So he mustered his self-control and banished the thought of her in order to focus on his chores.

He had a lot of work to do in the greenhouse, which was fine, because he enjoyed it. He loved the huge transparent dome and, beyond it, the conflagration of stars. After fitness checks and scheduled exercise sessions, Jesse spent his free time on his back, lounging under the fluorescent lights between the tall vats of algae and the soil that promised fruit.

A couple of weeks post-launch, he had swapped almost all of his on-ship chores for weeding and watering in the garden. The work was repetitive but it gave him time to think. His only company was Cai, who had a little lab set up in a corner of the greenhouse where he performed experiments and continued his research. He'd explained some of his research to Jesse early on: it involved studying the development of plants in below-Earth gravity. While the ship was provided with 100 per cent gravity by the dromes surrounding the hull, in the greenhouse it was only 60 per cent. Which took some getting used to. The effect made half the crew horribly spacesick and dizzy in the early days, but for Jesse it was magical, like he was walking in water. Fallen leaves drifted across the ground as if skimming over the settled surface of a pond, English ivy curled up around the cords of hanging lamps. Whenever he climbed the ladder and entered through the hatch, his stomach flipped as if in pleasant surprise.

The garden was growing every day. He liked to imagine it in two months, when the foliage would be splashed with the bright reds and blacks of tomatoes and berries. He liked to picture the faces of his crew when he presented them with baskets of runner beans, potatoes and apples, fresh vegetables and fruits that they had not eaten in months.

Most importantly, the greenhouse reminded him of Earth. Under the antiseptic smell of their fertilizer was the familiar scent of leaves and soil, and if he closed his eyes a little, the light from the 20 kilowatt xenon lamps nestled like silver coins of sunlight in his lashes.

'What is it you're meant to be doing exactly?' Jesse was startled by Cai's voice.

'Errr . . .' Jesse scrambled to his feet.

'That grass is just beginning to grow. The last thing I need is you rolling over it like a puppy.' Jesse climbed to his feet and dusted some of the soil off his trousers. 'You're supposed to be pouring fertilizer into the spires.'

'Right, I was just about to—'

'Get on with it. And keep off the grass.'

Cai skulked off, back to whichever corner of the greenhouse he had been lurking in, and Jesse picked up one of the buckets he'd left near the spire, his mind once again occupied with the task at hand.

Arguably, his job was the most important on the ship. While Harry might help pilot the *Damocles* and Eliot worked with Igor to keep it running, Jesse and Cai took care of the most important part of the ship's life support system.

During shorter missions, a crew could survive on supplies shipped from Earth, but on a long-haul mission such as theirs, survival was only possible if they created a closed ecosystem – or as closed as possible. Nothing could go to waste and the most important aspect of that was the oxygen supply. Each time Jesse exhaled, he added to the partial pressure of CO_2, which was being constantly mopped up by the filters and dissolved into the carbonated water that bubbled through the spires in the greenhouse. The greenhouse was filled with these tall green columns, which were bunched together and ran from floor to ceiling like the interior of a cathedral. The light from the buzzing fluorescent lamps provided energy to their unicellular chlorella, an algae that mopped up the CO_2 and pumped out breathable air around the clock. When drained and dried, the algae was also an efficient source of protein, and was part of the reason that their macronutrient broth had a slightly green tinge.

Jesse was always careful to pull on a fresh pair of gloves whenever he poured the foul-smelling fertilizer into the bioreactor, so as to avoid contaminating their algae. But somehow, when he climbed down from the step ladder and tugged the rubber off his fingers, his skin was sometimes stained acid green and smelt like bleach.

He got through his supply of fertilizer quickly, and still there were two dozen more spires to go. More fertilizer needed to be mixed up from the stock solution, a task that Cai still didn't trust Jesse to do himself. He was about to call out to the scientist when he spotted Juno on the grass.

The sight of her in his sanctuary sent a jolt through him. She couldn't see him. He could tell because she was walking differently, leaning down to touch the grass, which stood on end at her fingertips. She took off her shoes and took a few tentative steps. It was early afternoon, but for some reason she was still wearing her pyjamas. Jesse spent a lot of time trying to imagine what Juno wore to bed. How could he not, with only a wall separating their bedrooms, and the girls breathing right next door? He'd seen Poppy in the corridors in her lace camisoles and mini-shorts, and Astrid in her floaty nightdresses, but Juno never walked around in anything other than her navy uniform, the cuffs of her overalls rolled up around her ankles.

It seemed just like her, he supposed, to shrug off the fantasies of men and sleep in an oversized T-shirt and shorts. Jesse could see her bare legs, the golden brown skin, her shins dotted with stubby black hairs. Even her high-arching feet were a thrill.

Jesse kept watching as she took a clumsy step out on the grass, flung an arm up and did a playful pirouette, her laughter ringing through the air as she twirled gracelessly. It was wonderful to see this personal exuberance. He considered revealing himself but thought better of it. How could he face seeing her expression harden, as he knew it would? Her arms fall by her sides, all traces of her careless abandon vanishing in a second?

He slid back a little behind the spire and took a deep breath. Why was he reacting this way? For five years they had schooled together. She'd hung around with a small group of serious friends who *shh*-ed students like him in the library.

Juno looked up suddenly and stiffened. She turned her gaze in his direction. To avoid risking the shame of being caught half-crouched behind the leaves, Jesse stepped out and revealed himself.

'He-y.' His voice cracked; he had been silent too long. 'Hey.'

'What are you doing up here?' she asked. Jesse swung his empty bucket in answer.

'Oh right.' Juno nodded. 'Of course, you're Cai's pupil.'

'Servant, more like,' Jesse muttered. But then he felt a flash of annoyance that he'd had to explain himself to her, as if *he* was the trespasser.

'What are *you* doing?' he asked.

Juno looked at her feet, a little embarrassed,

'Oh, I just felt like seeing grass. I was taking a nap before dinner and I had a bad dream about— I mean, it's just what I do sometimes. Come up here when I feel homesick. When I want something familiar.'

'You're not really supposed to stand on the grass,' Jesse said, and then regretted it as soon as she jumped off the soil and onto the tiled ground. He sounded like Cai.

Impulsively, he kicked off his own shoes and leapt onto the grass. Juno watched him in silent confusion.

'Actually . . . it's fine,' he said, but she didn't move.

He could feel the weight of her gaze as she examined him, and suddenly he wished he was a little better dressed. The arms of his overalls were tied around his waist, revealing an unwashed Bob Marley T-shirt.

'You're up here all the time,' Juno observed.

'Yeah.' Jesse smiled and looked around, at the reservoir just opposite and the lilypads bobbing on the surface, at the English ivy beginning to grow into curved arbours.

'It's kind of magical, you know,' Juno said. 'You guys are doing a good job.'

Jesse smiled, ducking his head modestly.

Sleep softened her somehow. Her eyes were still far away, not so unnervingly penetrating. A few strands of curly hair were coming loose from the fat braids in which she tied them.

'It's pretty lucky that your specialization is the same as Ara's,' Juno said.

'Not lucky, it's the reason I was picked from the backup crew to take her place.'

'I mean—' Juno blushed. 'I know that. What would you do if you could do anything?'

Pilot the ship, Jesse thought, instantly. Imagining himself in the second-in-command seat next to Sheppard, Harry's bronze wings pinned to the lapel of his own flight suit. But he banished the thought.

'I don't know, but I like it here,' he said. 'What about you?'

'I wanted to be a scientist, actually. Before I was selected for the Beta.'

'Really?'

'Yes,' Juno said, and her lips tightened. 'I wanted to be a bio-chemist. When I was eleven or something, a man came to our school to tell us about gap proteins. He said memory is a chemical reaction. He told us that the smell of cut grass – my mother's favourite – was due to hexenol. A bent line with a double bond that he drew on the board and then made – *made!* –in a test tube. I can still remember the thrill of it. This clear liquid that actually smelt like grass. It was like magic, only better, because it was real. The smell that reminded my mother of her girlhood home and sunning herself out on the lawn by the tennis courts could be made in a test tube. I wish everything was that simple.' She smiled wistfully. 'I wish we could go, "Oh look, here is regret", draw it on a board, make it in a test tube. "Fear of the passing of time". "This is a nightmare, right here in this flask."'

Jesse loved the thought too. He grinned. 'Maybe one day we will.'

'We sort of have,' Juno said. 'Think of how far we've come in understanding already. Take the sun. It's nuclear fusion. Atoms of hydrogen smashing into each other and making helium and pure energy. It's the simplest reaction ever, the smallest elements, and yet people worship the sun, have worshiped it for millennia, squinted at and shied away from it as if it was the hand of God. I mean, maybe it *is* that, as well.

'So when I picked advanced chemistry in Dalton, I thought I'd spend my life pursuing that kind of order. I'd specialize in neurochemistry. And live my whole life reading loads of books and being an academic at Darwin College, Cambridge – same as my dad was for a bit – punting and thinking about the chemicals that make us *us*.'

Jesse was transfixed by the peach wrinkle of her bottom lip, so he couldn't hear the hurt in her reply when he asked, 'What happened with that?'

'I came here, obviously.'

'Why?'

Juno lowered her gaze. 'You know I ask myself that more often now. I'm scared that ... that I chose to come because my sister wanted to come. Because I was scared of being the one left behind.'

She came to sit beside him, and then lay back on the grass. Jesse could see right into her dark eyes. The lamps, the vaulted ceiling, her long eyelashes all reflected into them.

'You said you had a bad dream, and that's why you came up here,' he said, leaning back on his elbow next to her. Juno nodded, and closed her eyes. He could tell from the sound of her voice that her tongue was growing thick with tiredness.

'Not bad exactly. Just, you know, homesickness. Lots of

memories ... me and my sister playing with a hosepipe in the front garden. This day when Ara and I went up to Wandsworth Common and took Polaroids with a camera she got for her birthday. In all the pictures we're squinting because the sun is in our eyes. That was the last day before our training for the Beta began. Everything is sun-bleached and we're smiling.'

Jesse guessed she must be quite homesick, because he'd never heard any of the others speak about their dead friend around him.

'I still have the pictures somewhere. I brought them with me. Most of the photos I have are on my phone, but you know the box we were allowed to put our belongings in?'

'Yeah.'

'I kept thinking ... if I was really brave, that I'd bring nothing at all.'

'Up here?'

'Yeah, to Terra-Two. Just leave everything behind.'

When her eyes were closed Jesse couldn't help staring at her, the soft slope of her nose, her full brown lips. If he looked carefully he could see a few freckles dotted in the skin just under her eyes.

'Do you dream of Earth?' she asked.

'Course.'

'What do you dream of?'

'Silly things, I guess, like gasoline rainbows and mallards and sunburn.'

'Astrid says she never dreams of Earth. Just Terra-Two and space and grass she's never seen before and what the sky looks like with two moons and two suns.' Juno exhaled heavily.

'Well,' said Jesse, 'we can't all be prophets.'

Juno giggled. 'It's nice up here,' she said, softly.

'It is?' Jesse didn't know why it came out sounding like a question.

He wanted to kiss her. And lying next to her on the grass, with the fresh soapy smell of her, it felt suddenly and wonderfully possible. He sat up a little, leant over her face so that his shadow cast across her flickering eyelids. She didn't stir, so Jesse bent down and pressed his mouth against hers. Her lips were slightly parted and he squeezed his eyes shut, feeling her body tense up. She didn't pull away. For just a second, Jesse was sure she was kissing him back, but then he felt something wet and cold seep into the gap between their cheeks, and she was pushing him away with a cry of pain and despair.

When he fell back onto the grass, his heart was pounding. First with excitement, and then with fear. Her face was wet with tears. His stomach dropped, as if he'd just misjudged the depth of freezing water and felt it now lapping over his head as he sank down.

'Juno . . . ?'

She didn't say anything. She simply stared at him for half a minute, her eyes shining with hurt. 'I'm sorry . . .'

It only occurred to him to chase after her a moment later, by which time she was already scrambling down the ladder that led out of the garden.

JESSE

29.08.12

AFTER WHAT HAPPENED IN the greenhouse, Jesse was almost convinced he'd deserved what Harry did to him a month later. They had been alone in the games room, Jesse watching Harry play on the simulator. He watched so long, leaning back on one of the beanbags, that the game took on a pattern, and he really began to notice Harry's strengths and weaknesses. He was fast – it was a thrill to watch his lightning-quick reflexes as he dived past every obstacle that swung into his path. And he was a quick study, picking up the manoeuvres that the computer taught him with such uncanny ease that Jesse understood why Commander Sheppard had selected him to co-pilot their ship. But Harry's greatest strength was his determination. Hours of tackling the game had given him a formidable knowledge of the simulation, and he ascended the levels with a practised ease, even at the complex higher levels. There the computer anticipated his next moves and blocked his way, pitched surprises and forced him to combine or alter the various manoeuvres he'd learned on the easier levels.

But, Jesse observed, Harry couldn't tolerate surprises. When a fuel tank exploded, his sudden impulsive jerk of the controller sent him veering off in the wrong direction, losing power too soon to complete his mission. When a rogue ship careened past, Harry was too surprised to prevent a collision. He seemed to lack the cunning or creativity to improvise at higher levels.

After the fuel tank explosion, Jesse said, 'Hey, you know if you switch from the damaged fuel tanks to the *secondary* rocket boosters you'll be able to land without too much excess drag.' Harry had said nothing. 'Also, it's all about the angle of entry,' Jesse added, 'right now you're going in too steep. That's why you keep—'

Harry interrupted by switching off the simulator and yanking off his goggles.

'Hey, Jesse,' he said, 'do you want to see something?'

'See what?'

Harry spun round in his seat and leapt off with a little chuckle. 'I can't tell you,' he said. 'That would ruin the fun.'

'No, I'm fine here I think.'

'Really? You don't have a minute or two for a little competition?'

Jesse's immediate desire was to shrug his shoulders and remain in the comfort of the games room. But it was the way Harry always said the word 'competition' that piqued something inside Jesse, something like curiosity and determination.

So he followed him into the half-lit corridor where, instead of climbing up the ladder as Jesse had expected, Harry slid towards the store rooms. Jesse had only ever gone down that way a few times, during that first night when they were all moving in, or when Cai requested extra cartons of stock solutions to mix more fertilizer.

Further down the hall was the round door he'd never touched.

'The airlock,' Jesse said.

'That's right. So they taught you something about the ship during your midnight astronaut crash course.'

A quick flame of annoyance sparked inside Jesse, but he didn't want to give Harry the satisfaction of seeing him ruffled. 'I'm just as trained as you,' he said.

'Actually, you're about *half* as trained as me.'

Jesse had expected this, sooner or later. Each time he asked a question in their tutorials about something he had not been taught he could almost feel the sneer on Harry's lips. It made him sheepish and embarrassed, keen to hide his deficiencies but certain everyone was taking note of them. Jesse said what Commander Sheppard kept repeating to him: 'Everything else I need to know I can learn on this ship.'

'Exactly.' Harry's eyes glittered. 'Like how the airlock works.'

'I know how the airlock works. It allows entry or exit without compromising the environment inside the ship.'

'Good. How does it do that?'

'Why are you asking me?'

'How does it do that, Jesse?'

'Two doors – well, two pressure-sealed hatches – and a space in between; one opens out into space, the other into the ship. If someone is leaving, the compartment between depressurizes. The opposite if they are entering.'

They were standing before it; the round door with the fat metal latches. Jesse peered at his reflection in the airlock's porthole as Harry found the gearbox mounted on the side of the wall and twisted the handle. The hinge mechanism groaned and then, with a low hiss of air, the hatch swung open.

The airlock was about the size of their tiny bathroom. Two spacesuits were charging, hooked to either wall, and they stared out at Jesse like astronauts with darkness for eyes. On the far end was a window to space.

'You scared?' Harry asked,

'There's nothing to be scared of.'

'Exactly. Though that's hard to remember sometimes.' He stepped a little closer and Jesse followed behind him. 'Have you heard of a sensory deprivation chamber?'

'Yes—' Jesse began, but Harry continued as if he hadn't spoken.

'During training they put us in one to see how long we could stand it. No light, no sound. Most people can't last fifteen minutes before they begin to see things, begin to panic. They don't even know what they're afraid of. Themselves, maybe. In the darkness every fear finds a face. You imagine being buried alive, being paralyzed, and some people can't handle it.' Jesse shuddered as he, too, imagined it. He was silently glad this ordeal had been omitted from his training. He tried to picture Harry in the darkness.

'Do you know how long I managed it?' Harry was still talking. 'Seven hours, forty-three minutes. Sounds impossible. Especially for someone like you, who's afraid of the dark.'

'I'm not afraid of the dark,' Jesse said. 'What kind of astronaut is?'

'Prove it.' Harry folded his arms and smiled. Jesse could only see part of Harry's face in the half-light of the corridor. He was dressed in his uniform, as he usually was during the daytime, clean-shaven, his straight blond hair slicked back from his forehead.

Jesse swallowed, a lie suddenly on his lips. 'I have a fit-check in five minutes, so maybe another time.'

'This will only take five minutes.'

Jesse's heart sank. He had no choice but to step inside the air-lock. Harry's silhouette was backlit on the threshold behind him.

'Igor will probably tell you that when Russian cosmonauts train they're put in isolation chambers, for weeks sometimes,' Harry said. 'Some of them call it the Chamber of Silence. Can you imagine it, Jesse? Can you imagine what thoughts would be going through your nervous head. There's more to being an astronaut than just *wanting* it, you know. You have to *prove* you can do it.'

He paused, and the dread in Jesse's stomach grew.

'The astronaut can't fear enclosed spaces,' Harry said, his fingers on the handle. Jesse's nerves panged. In another moment, Harry would close the hatch and he would be left alone there.

'No, don't—'

'The astronaut can't fear the darkness.'

Jesse saw Harry's silhouetted hand lift and realized, too late, that he was letting the airlock close.

'Harry!' Jesse rushed towards the door as it shut. 'No!'

'The astronaut can't fear death.'

A hiss of air as the door sealed closed, and Jesse was left alone in the almost total blackness. All sound from the noisy ship disappeared, and he could hear only his own heavy breathing and the sweat prickling on his back. The air was stale and unmoving. How long until it ran out?

'Harry,' he called, 'this isn't funny.'

I won't panic, he thought to himself, but still he remained pressed up against the door. Sinister shapes were already beginning to encroach upon him in the darkness. He blinked them away.

'You said five minutes.' Five minutes. How long had it been already? One? Thirty seconds? He just had to keep calm for five minutes and then Harry would free him. He tried to distract himself by taking deep breaths, but inhaling the still air only made him more nervous.

Jesse had often thought about what it might feel like to suffocate: the agony of oxygen deprivation and the clenching full body panic that came with it. Getting trapped under ice and drowning. A silent final scream of desperation as he fought to suck air into deflating lungs and instead felt the violation of freezing water rushing into his mouth. His throat sealing shut.

'Harry!'

Harry's smiling face lit up the porthole. His voice audible through the intercom on the side. 'Scared *already*?' he asked. What little light there was glinted off his retinas. 'You're not much of an astronaut, are you? I knew there was a reason you didn't make it first time round.'

'This isn't funny,' Jesse called, slamming his hand against the window. It was so thick, two sheets of bolted polycarbonate, that he wasn't sure that Harry could hear him.

'Being in the airlock is not half as scary as being in space. While the six of us were cramming for physiology exams, you were probably out smoking weed and contemplating cloud formations, or whatever else it is you did with your abundant free time, so let me fill you in. There is one door separating you from the hard vacuum of space, the void between astronomical bodies, the possibly infinite ocean of mostly nothing-ness. It's a bit like death. But do you know what would be more like death? Me, out here, turning this handle and watching you float out into space. What would a place like that do to a body like yours?'

Jesse's mouth went dry as he imagined it. The latches unbuckling, the airlock depressurizing, the door swinging open. This was the closest to the emptiness of space he had ever been. If he pressed his hand against the icy surface of the hatch he might even feel it, something of the coldness of space – around -270°C – but instead he was running his trembling fingers along the edges of the door, looking for an emergency button or loose seal – an escape.

'Want to know a little something about surviving in space?' Harry asked. 'When I open the airlock and all the oxygen rushes out, try not to hold your breath. If you do, the air in your chest expands, your lungs will rupture and bubbles will spill out into your bloodstream, so your girlish scream of terror might just be the thing that saves your life. For a minute. And, out there – of course – no one will be able to hear you.

'You'll collapse after about fifteen seconds and begin to turn blue, although you look pretty blue to me already. No pressure in space means that, despite the sub-zero temperatures, all the water in your eyes and mouth will actually *boil*. Oh, and your body will swell to twice the size. Are you listening?'

Jesse was screaming for help now, banging his sweaty palms against the door hoping that someone, anyone, might hear him. His heart kicked against his chest. The air in the room was smothering.

'One comforting thought is that a human can survive over a minute out in space before he dies. So if Dr G hauled your bloated body back inside the ship and injected you with pressurized oxygen before your heart gave up entirely, you might just make it. I mean, you'd be in excruciating pain, but you'd be alive. Let's see for ourselves, shall we?'

The moment Jesse saw Harry's face in the window, he knew that he was actually going to do it. Harry reached out and twisted the equalization valve. As he did so, Jesse heard the hiss as the airlock depressurized by venting air out into space. He almost thought he could see white plumes of gas bulge out into the blackness.

'Five seconds,' Harry called out. The little hand of the pressure gauge slid down.

Jesse clawed at the inner hatch. In four seconds the outer airlock would unlatch and he would be ripped out of the safety of the ship. This was it, he realized with a dizzying rush of dread. He was going to die.

'Stop, please!' Jesse screamed. He wasn't ashamed to beg for his life. *'Please!'*

Harry's eyes flashed, his blond lashes translucent.

'Three . . .'

'No—' Tears filled Jesse's eyes, and he scraped at the solid metal of the door so hard that blood bubbled under his fingernails.

'Two . . .'

The edges of his vision blackened, and the muscles in his legs crumpled. He had escaped the gravity of Earth only to die in the darkness here.

'One . . .'

JUNO

29.08.12

WHEN JUNO AND ELIOT climbed down to the lower deck, the first thing Juno heard was Harry's laughter echoing along the narrow corridors. Perhaps that was the reason she chose to head towards the store rooms, instead of the simulation room where she had expected to find the two boys.

Over the sound of Harry's laughter, Juno thought she could hear the high-pitched whistle of air escaping vents. A terrifying noise that turned her blood to ice. Without a backwards glance at Eliot she began to run. The ceilings were low nearer the airlock, and she had to crouch down a little to save from knocking her head. At the end of the corridor, Harry was bent in front of the gearbox, shaking with laughter. The window into the airlock was dark, but the digital readout on the side of the wall was ticking down.

'*Five...*' Harry shouted.

'What are you doing?' Juno yelled. Although as she said it she knew that the airlock was decompressing. Harry was laughing so much he had to suck in air just to speak.

He said, '*Four...* It's just some fun, Juma.'

'Is someone in there?' Juno yelled. A hand smacked against the porthole – from inside the airlock. Juno screamed.

'*Three* ...' Harry continued. Juno lunged for the gearbox, knocking Harry out of the way with strength that surprised even her, and grabbed the handle of the equalization control. The gauge was sliding down as oxygen hissed out of the vents. If the pressure reached zero, whoever was inside would suffocate – or worse, once the doors opened they would be dragged out into the hard vacuum of space. Juno heaved the handle in the opposite direction and watched as the pressure began, again, to climb.

'*Two* ...' Harry shouted, his face flushed. Juno grabbed the lever that controlled the inner hatch door and yanked it towards her, just in time to hear the locking mechanism release.

'*One* ...' The hatch swung open, sucking air in such a violent slipstream that both Juno and Harry were almost knocked off their feet, and two displays tore off the wall.

The lights in the airlock activated.

'Where is he?' Harry's face fell as they looked around the small compartment. Juno had never entered this airlock chamber. It was set up for spacewalks, with spacesuits plugged into ports on the walls. It was a tangle of wires and equipment, with only enough space to comfortably fit two astronauts at any one time.

Jesse was curled in a dark heap in the corner. When Juno approached him, his lips were blue and he was gaping like a fish, sweat soaking his shirt. 'Jesse?'

Instead of replying, Jesse clutched at his chest as if he was choking, knocking one of the boneless spacesuits mounted on the wall hard enough to detach it. Juno's heart pounded with panic. She turned on Harry. 'What did you do to him?'

'I-I ...' Harry stammered, all traces of hilarity draining from his face as he leant into the airlock chamber, holding the hatch open like a car boot. 'I don't know.'

When Juno pressed a palm against Jesse's chest, she felt that his heart was fluttering shallowly.

'Jess . . .' She squeezed his damp hand and peered into his tiny pupils. 'It's okay . . . you're safe.' She tested his pulse, counted his staccato breaths.

'Is it asthma or something?' Harry asked.

'No, you idiot,' Juno snapped. 'He's having a panic attack.' Juno remembered what she had been taught the afternoon their instructors had hauled Poppy's shaking body out of the sensory deprivation tank. She instructed Jesse to take deep breaths.

Eliot's pale face appeared in the doorway. 'Should I get Fae?' he asked quietly.

'Yeah, do that.'

'Don't!' Jesse managed to gasp, but Eliot had already disappeared. Jesse dropped his head into his hands. Juno was pleased to see he was breathing more evenly now. 'I'm fine. Jesus Christ . . .' he gasped. 'I feel so stupid.' His hands were still shaking. He clenched them into fists. 'I really am fine. Don't tell anyone.'

'You're okay,' Juno said, trying to comfort him with a smile, smoothing the sweat-soaked baby hairs from his forehead. 'You will be.'

A few minutes later, Eliot and Dr Golinsky appeared in the corridor, and they helped Jesse up to the infirmary. Although some of the colour had returned to his face, he still needed to lean on both of them to stand, the muscles in his thighs twitching uncontrollably.

Harry stood silently the whole time, pressed up against the

wall near the gearbox, his face blank. Once Juno heard the sound of their footsteps fade away, she climbed to her feet and faced him. As she did, she noticed the spots of blood on the inside of the porthole where Jesse had tried to claw his way out, a greasy handprint against the polycarbonate. Rage boiled up inside her so suddenly that she flew at Harry before she could calm herself and slammed him against the wall.

'You *sadist*. What were you thinking?' Although she'd taken Harry by surprise, he was a lot stronger than she was and even in that moment Juno could feel the bulk of his muscles flex beneath his flight suit.

'It was just a game, you know ... I didn't know he would freak out like that.'

'You were going to throw him out of the airlock. You were going to kill him. Of course he "freaked out".'

'I wouldn't actually have done it.' Harry shrugged Juno off easily. He was twice her size, and – not for the first time – Juno resented his power over her and the rest of the Beta. The authority he'd been given under Sheppard.

'I guess we'll never know that,' she said, stepping back.

'Never know if I'm capable of killing a person?' Harry smiled wryly. 'Don't be dramatic, Juma. I was just teaching him a lesson, that's all.'

'What lesson?' she asked, her body still tight with fury.

'That it takes some nerve to do what we have to do. That you have to deserve to be here.'

'He *does* deserve to be here,' Juno said. 'And what gives you the right to—'

'I'm the commander. Or have you forgotten?' They stood in silence for a moment, Juno's fists clenched.

'Commander-in-*training*.'

'Have a sense of humour,' Harry said finally. 'It was only a game.' He ruffled her hair, then made to walk off.

'You're not fit to be commander,' Juno shouted after him. 'You're not fit to be behind the wheel of a car, let alone a spaceship, if this is all just a game to you.'

Harry didn't even turn, just spoke over his shoulder as he strode down the corridor. 'That's all there is up here, though. Games. And everyone chooses to play because we're all bored out of our fucking minds.'

JESSE

29.08.12

WHEN JESSE OPENED HIS eyes in the infirmary, Juno was standing over him. 'You're okay,' she said softly.

'I guess so . . .' he began, but as soon as he said it, the memories flooded back. The cardiac plunge he'd experienced when he'd looked in Harry's eyes and realized that he really was about to die at his hands. The violence of his final moments, thrashing at the sealed door, the bruises around his elbows where pinpricks of blood had burst out of his capillaries. Juno had been the one to save him. He recalled, with a visceral shame, his own begging howls, the tears that had come to his eyes, the way she had looked when the airlock opened, a floodlit nimbus about her face, the fleeting moment of wonder at her touch. All of a sudden, Jesse wished she would leave.

'I'm fine. I'm really fine,' he said, trying with some effort to sit up. 'You can go. You probably have something to be doing.'

She shrugged. 'I have an excuse to miss dinner, which, today, I'm glad about. I think if I see Harry again today there's a real danger I might stab him with my fork. Eliot and I are going to tell Sheppard tonight.'

For a moment Jesse was sick with fear and embarrassment.

He imagined trying to explain what had happened. 'Don't,' he said. 'Please. It'll only make things worse.'

Juno shook her head doubtfully. 'Sheppard should know. Fae already knows you had a panic attack—' Jesse grimaced at the word. 'But she doesn't know what Harry did to you. The senior crew should know that Harry's dangerous. Possibly insane.'

'Don't be dramatic. It just got out of hand, that's all.' Jesse tried to swallow, though his throat was tight. A flash of Harry's grinning face came to him and he turned cold with rage. 'I don't want to talk about it again. To anyone.'

'Are you sure?'

'Yes,' Jesse said darkly.

'That was a terrible thing he did. I can't actually believe ...' Juno trailed off, shaking her head in puzzlement.

'Can't you?' Jesse asked. 'Everyone acts like it's a surprise whenever Harry does a bad thing.'

'What do you mean?'

'Just because he's been *chosen* to be here and is a good pilot doesn't mean that he's a good person. He's going to be our commander when Sheppard is gone but he's nothing like Solomon Sheppard. He's not quiet and humble, or wise and good. He's cruel. Just because he's a talented pilot, just because he's good at sports and handsome and shagged half the girls in our year, doesn't make him a leader.'

'I guess you're right.' Juno looked down. 'There were always those things he did, like pranks and mean jokes that I thought he just did because, I don't know, he's a teenage boy. But now I wonder if that's just the person he is. The person he's become.'

They sat in silence for a moment. Then Jesse revealed

something he hadn't admitted before. 'You know . . .' He searched Juno's face for a sign she would understand. 'I've been think-ing . . . I think I, kind of, *hate* Harry.'

'Don't say that.' Juno frowned. 'You're just angry, that's all. I am too. But we're a team. And we're supposed to be a family.'

'A family.' Jesse snorted. 'Some dysfunctional family that I'm sure as hell not part of.'

'Don't *say* that.' Juno was getting upset. 'You know,' she said, 'you don't actually have to do everything that Harry says.'

'Of course I *know* that,' Jesse snapped.

'Then why do you always go along with his games? You follow him around like—' she paused. 'Like you admire him. Almost like you want to *be* him. You watch him at dinner, you laugh at his jokes, you sit in the games room and just watch him while he plays on the simulator. For *hours*.'

'You don't understand,' Jesse said.

'No, I don't.'

For a moment he hated them all. All the members of the Beta. They were grossly entitled and self-absorbed. He hated the way they had swanned through the school in the final days, crowds parting in awed enchanted waves before them. The way they had emerged before the entire world, that day before the launch, as if they were crowned in laurel, the whole coun-try chanting their names when only a week later they'd been absorbed again in their little problems.

Most of all he hated them for hating him, for the way they had all closed ranks against him as if he had pushed Ara into the river and then slung her ghost like an albatross around his neck. He needed to be alone.

'Get lost,' he said to Juno.

She looked stung for just a moment but then stood up. 'Whatever.' She pushed her chair back under the desk. 'You think you have it so much harder than everyone else, don't you?'

'*You* don't have to apologize for being here,' he shouted.

'Neither do you.' She headed for the door and before she slammed it behind her she said, 'And – when you're not feeling so damned sorry for yourself – I'm glad you *are* here.'

AS SOON AS JESSE was feeling better, he headed down to the games room and spent the rest of the evening using the flight simulator. Harry was already at the ninth level, and his high score glittered on the screen every time Jesse loaded the programme.

Jesse started well, making it easily through the first and second levels, then, with less ease, to the fifth. By the time he reached level six his ship had sustained too much damage to hold up against the high temperatures, and when he tried to land in the thick Venusian atmosphere, sulphuric acid clouds flayed the already battered hull. He never made it down to the troposphere, and every member of his crew died.

After a while, the sound of feet and the low rumble of voices on the floors above faded. He checked the numbers on his watch and guessed that most of the crew would be asleep. He headed back to the boys' cabin but found that Harry was still awake, lamplit at the desk, watching something on his laptop. It was a boat race. Jesse was unsurprised to see the interlocking Olympic rings in the corner of the screen. Jesse guessed it was the coxless fours, as there were four men in lime-yellow boats, oars cutting the water in unison as they lanced down the wide lake.

The voice of the commentator was barely audible over

the crackly cheering of the crowd coming through the laptop speaker ... *'Can the British team retain this rhythm and concentration? Their training up in the Alps, is it going to pay off for them? They've had so much disruption this year, when they were beaten in Munich by the Australians ... and here come the Australians now ...'*

Harry's eyes were unblinking and filled with light. He had been watching the television recordings every night since the games began, on longer and longer delays.

'They're upping it now ...'

He was actually holding his breath.

Jesse already knew that the UK had won. His father had sent him the results a week ago, but Harry had wanted to watch all the games and tally them up himself.

Jesse had always enjoyed watching the Olympics at home, everything from fencing to synchronized swimming. But he'd never understood rowing the way that Harry did. He'd been told that when you got it right it felt like flying. It never did for Jesse, who had been drafted into the rowing class at Dalton for all of one term. Every Wednesday afternoon he'd have to take the train down to the boathouse with the laughing boys who never spoke to him. It wasn't for him, hoisting the jauntily named boats out onto the brown water. The miserable weather. The cold. When he'd complained about the sub-zero temperatures, the others had whispered that of course 'black men don't row' – a sentiment that had made him all the more determined to stick it out for the term. He stayed behind in the tank just to practise again and again on the stagnant water, in the rotting boat that was nailed to the floor. It wasn't until he'd burned calluses into the palms of his hand – and scraped the sculls over his knuckles so often that he'd ripped the delicate skin clean off – that he got the rhythm right. And, even then, he never flew. One day it was so cold that he lost sensation in his fingers for hours, and he realized that he hated every boy in his boat. He'd been in too much pain to help haul it back out of the water and the coach had rolled his eyes. It had rained, foul-smelling Thames water had flooded over the gunwales and Jesse discovered a hole in his boot. He never came back after that. He switched to running, the only one in his class, around and around their school's grassy track. Somehow that had still been less lonely.

'... *towards the finishing line. It looks as though they're gonna do it! It is gold for Great Britain!*' Harry let out a breath he'd been holding in ... *Silver, Australia, and bronze United States of America* ....

It was a sunlit day on the screen and a blond rower in the Team GB boat was blowing kisses at the crowd.

'*This is a truly magnificent moment ...*'

Jesse wondered if Harry was imagining how it felt. He had always wondered why Harry had chosen space over some sunlit river in early summer, slicing through the water on a boat while his round-bellied relatives raised glasses of Dom Pérignon. Perhaps Harry wanted something different from his older brothers, twins who had won silver for rowing in the Beijing Olympics and were competing again that year in London. Perhaps Harry had lurked in their shadow his entire life, in silent wait for the day the entire world would cheer for him as he ascended the sky on a jet of flames.

JUNO

19.09.12

THE SUMMER JUNO AND her sister turned fifteen, their uncle had died. Juno remembered waking up to her mother's wailing, the unnatural quiet of the funeral home, poking her finger at the coffin lining. It was softer than her own bed. Her mother's mascara left gritty charcoal tracks down her cheeks.

She hadn't grasped the reality of their uncle's absence until the next week, when she noticed that no one had taken out the rubbish bags. He usually did the job, hauling them out into the front garden on Wednesday nights, but the black sacks were still out in the garden, baking in the sun. She'd tiptoed out in her socks and picked up two of the heavier ones, carrying them through the kitchen and then out the front. She was halfway across the tiled floor when she'd noticed a grain of rice on her hand, on the boneless stretch of skin between her finger and thumb. But, just before she could flick it off, it had moved, shrunk and then engorged, slithered on her wrist. She'd gasped and dropped the bags to flick the maggot off her hand. As she did so one of the slimy rubbish bags had burst open, spilling thousands of maggots everywhere. They'd surged across the tiles in a seething wave. It was something about the way they'd moved their fat white bodies, the horrific stench, the surprise of suddenly being surrounded by living wriggling things, that had made her scream.

Astrid had heard her and run downstairs. 'What is it?' she'd asked, but Juno had looked down at the tiles just in time to watch the maggots writhe into the shadows under the dining table. They'd slipped into the dusty slits of darkness under the fridge and the dishwasher, they'd slid into the unreachable warmth behind the radiator. Before she could squish even one of them, they had all vanished. Juno kept rubbing the skin on her arms to check that nothing was nibbling at them. She'd asked her mother to check her hair for bugs. No matter how much she scrubbed that evening, she could not feel clean. She'd never walked barefoot in the kitchen again.

That was the first day that she really missed him, her uncle. The man who performed a thankless task with faithful regularity. She had relied on him and she didn't know it. Without her uncle this might have happened earlier – the bags rotting in the sun – but every week he'd kept her safe from it. And it was strange, his absence came only then as a sickening surprise to her, like finding maggots twitching on the tiles, like sunlight pouring on the unmade bed that still smelt of him.

The memory of that summer flashed across Juno's mind when she opened the disposal unit to find that someone had stacked plates in it and they had gathered a fluffy green layer of mould. The macronutrient broth had separated in the unwashed bowls into an acrid brown liquid, with soft green clumps floating like curds across the top. The smell was overpowering, and even when Juno slammed the door shut she still had to fight the urge to vomit in the sink.

'Whose turn was it to do the washing up last week?'

Jesse shrugged. He was sitting at the kitchen table, his mouth full.

'It wasn't me,' Astrid said, looking up from her book.

Juno swallowed back nausea and headed for the fridge, where the cleaning rota – written in her own hand, and colour-coded with her own fine-liners – was displayed. Under 'Washing up' and 'Disposal', Poppy's name was printed in red.

'Poppy,' Juno said, stabbing a finger at the name and gritting her teeth. Of course it was. Poppy had not only neglected the washing up, but she had stowed the dishes away in the darkness to fester. A cup of milk had spilled down the side of one of the walls in the disposal unit and a green scum clung to it. Juno shuddered at the recollection. Seven days. Poppy had shirked her duties for *seven days*, hiding the plates away like a thief. It was not only lazy, it was dishonest.

This could not go on.

Juno stormed down to the bedroom, her gut hungry for justice.

Poppy was bundled up in her yellowing bedsheets, face down, her back rising slowly. 'Poppy,' Juno said, reaching out to touch the other girl's back. When Juno touched her, her skin was damp with sweat. 'Poppy, wake up.'

When Poppy finally rolled over, her eyes were sticky with sleep. She squinted up at Juno and moaned something incoherent.

'Poppy, it was your turn to do the washing up last week.'

'Juno,' Astrid said, standing in the doorway behind her sister, 'just leave it alone will you.'

'No – this affects all of us,' Juno said. She turned again to Poppy. 'You are impossible to live with.'

They had been tiptoeing around her for weeks. Her misery seemed to suck all the air out of every room. She lay in bed, if not sleeping then quietly crying. When had she last taken a shower? Looking at her greasy hair, the black dirt under her fingernails, the sour smell of Poppy's doughy body, Juno felt something of the disgust she'd experienced when she'd opened the disposal.

'When did you last get out of bed?' Juno demanded. Poppy rolled on to her back like a creature washed onto the shore, her face tear-stained and swollen. She shrugged.

'Can't you see she's—' Astrid began.

'—sick.' Juno finished Astrid's sentence for her. 'I know. Everyone knows. You're missing Earth. We're all missing Earth. Ara died but you don't see Eliot skipping chores, and she was basically his soulmate.'

'Juno,' Poppy said softly, her voice a rasp from weeping, 'don't you ever just wake up and want a different life?'

'*Of course* I do. I could have been a contemporary dancer or some person who drives along windswept roads and takes pictures of rare cloud formations. Or I could have stayed in London with my parents, who love me, and gone to Imperial with Noah, who loves me, and become a scientist and discovered a cure for myasthenia gravis. Before the age of thirteen we decided to be astronauts, and here we are. You made a choice when you applied to Dalton, and when you agreed to be a Beta, and now is too late to quit. Think about it practically, Poppy. You don't have a lot of options. Either you can lie in bed until your muscles waste, leaving our food to rot and waiting out the next two decades, or you can put your head down and work as hard as you can and do your best to make everyone's life a little bit easier.'

'I'm glad you think it's so simple,' Poppy said. 'I wish we could all just will ourselves out of sadness.'

'I only need you to will yourself out of bed. I'll write a list of all the chores you've skipped. And you need to catch up this afternoon and for the rest of this week.'

'Juno,' Poppy hissed, a tight edge in her voice, 'you're not my mum. You're not the commander. Stop thinking you can boss everyone around.'

'I don't want to have to get Commander Sheppard involved again,' Juno said, already sensing she had played the wrong card and too early. Now she sounded like a whiny toddler, threatening to snitch.

'Go away,' Poppy said, rolling back into her duvet. 'You can't make me do anything.' The words stung with unavoidable truth. Poppy was an adult, Juno's crewmate, over whom she wielded no authority. Astrid turned to her sister with a sympathetic shrug of surrender as she stalked out.

LATER, JUNO SAT STIFFLY on one of the chairs in the crew module, grinding her teeth. She would not go to the kitchen and clear up Poppy's mess, and yet the thought of leaving the food there to gather more mould – the thought of living with the smell for another hour – made her stomach turn.

Two months had passed since Poppy's birthday. Sheppard and Fae had confronted Poppy about her behaviour. Each time, she would make an effort to work for a week or two, film her educational videos, but then her enthusiasm would lapse again. She'd complain of symptomless illness, retire to bed early, do the bare minimum so the rest of the crew would have to work hard to finish her chores or do the communications work that she had neglected.

The damage had already been done. Poppy's behaviour was beginning to affect the other members of the crew. They were reluctant to come to meals, they complained far more about chores and grew sullen and argumentative at the slightest provocation.

Juno imagined the next year, and then the next twenty after that. Years of her crew members abandoning their duties, sunk low in the self-absorbed pit of their own despair and unwilling to help each other. What a hateful place their home could become if they thought only of themselves, of avoiding work, of ignoring justice.

Juno stood up.

When she imagined life on Terra-Two she pictured unity. Their little colony working joyfully to tame the land, to set up a base. There would be no arguments about chores because everyone would work to ease the others' burden. There would be no fighting, there would be no more of the juvenile competition that had spread amongst the boys. But that needed to begin now. They had to train themselves to work together now, not two decades from now.

'We need to start again,' she said. Eliot, who had been nodding to music on his headphones, looked up quizzically.

'We're supposed to make things *better*,' she said, heading towards the ladder. 'We're supposed to build a beautiful new world. No violence. No arguing. No selfishness.'

Juno rushed up to the kitchen and grabbed a bucket from the sink. She shovelled handfuls of ice into it from one of the storage units and then filled the rest with water. It was almost spilling over as she climbed back down to the crew module, her stomach burning with passion. 'We need to do it *right* this time.'

Juno stormed into the girls' cabin and heaved the contents of the bucket onto Poppy.

Poppy screamed, first a high shriek of shock and discomfort but then, as the burn of the cold set in and she wiped her eyes to see Juno's stern face, a roar of fury.

'You monster,' she yelled, her eyes blazing. 'This is why no one likes you.'

'I don't care who *likes* me, Poppy,' Juno said calmly. 'And now you have to get out of bed, at least to have a shower and wash your bedsheets. And when you get back into bed, I'll do this again. And again until you clean out the disposal unit and catch up with your work.'

Poppy peeled off her saturated duvet and wiped the wet hair from her eyes. Her pale thighs were covered in goosebumps and she started to shiver. 'I won't forgive you for this,' she said, getting unsteadily to her feet.

'Hey,' Astrid said, from the corner of the room. 'That was really harsh.'

Juno turned to her sister, her brow knitted in fury. 'Whose side are you on?'

'No one's,' Astrid insisted, then glanced at Poppy's dripping bedsheets. 'She's just sad.'

Juno kicked the empty bucket to the opposite wall and shouted, 'What does that have to do with anything?'

POPPY

21.09.12

TWO DAYS LATER, POPPY was still reeling from the fight with Juno. Her nerves still zinged with rage whenever she heard Juno's clipped voice through the corridors of the ship. It had escalated, turned into a screaming match, Poppy's heart still pounding from the shock of the cold and the other girl's rage. She'd said every vicious thing she could think up, slinging curses and hurts at Juno, but her words had seemed to glance off her. Juno had simply stared back, her eyes so narrow they were nothing but darkness. She'd fired insults at Poppy like well-aimed darts, right into her ribs. Juno had always had a way with words and every blow stung. Even two days later, Juno's accusations tormented Poppy. She had been forced to cede the battle, to leave the bed and catch up on the chores she had missed, as well as turn up for dinner promptly, choking down every bite of food she had no stomach for. Juno oversaw each task, mentally ticking off debts in her head: the dusty corners, unchanged filters, broken lightbulbs and the filthy disposal unit. Poppy had spent the time since the fight tending to them all.

By the time she was finished scrubbing the grease-blackened

tiles by the side of the stove, she was full of hate and in need of a shower.

She entered the bathroom. Taking a shower on the *Damocles* was problematic. When the water didn't surge out boiling hot, it was icy cold and, no matter how many knobs Poppy twisted, she could never seem to get the balance right. Climbing out of her clothes, she switched it on and reached a hand out to test it. The water spattered out with a hiss, then roared to full pressure, searing the skin on her forearm. She fought the urge to tug it out of the steaming jet and instead let the pain grow more intense, the stab of the burn radiating to her elbow.

It was a relief to feel something. This pain was something. Her anger with Juno was something. Better, she had to admit, than the hollowed-out numbness that had ached inside her for months.

'Pops?' came a voice.

She started, and snatched her arm out of the water. Steam curled off it, and the skin flamed red.

Someone was banging on the door. 'Let me in.'

Picking up the towel with her nametag on it, Poppy covered her nakedness and opened the door.

Harry was standing on the threshold, grinning. 'Hey, dirty girl. Figured you were taking a shower. Mind if I join you?' He entered and closed the door behind him before Poppy replied.

'You did a good job out there,' he said. Poppy shrugged, looking down at her black fingernails. She knew what Harry wanted before he asked, and she dropped her towel and tried to smile, hoping it would feel good, like holding her hand under the hot water felt good.

Harry had been Poppy's first. It happened only once before the launch, during a club night in East London called 'How does it feel to be loved?' The Smashing Pumpkins, The Kings of Convenience and, predominantly, The Smiths played on the loudspeakers. Clever songs that were not easy to dance to. By midnight, all of Poppy's friends were slumping on the edges of the room in serious little female huddles of conversation – growing maudlin and slipping out into the brisk night air to give the sweat on their shins a chance to dry.

Harry was famous at Dalton. In the dining hall, on one of the oak-panelled walls, was a list of names, winners of various school tournaments and awards. Under the provost's annual award for sporting attainment, the name Harrison Bellgrave blazed against the dark wood three years running. Poppy was star-struck by him. She liked to imagine what it was like to *be* him, crowned in his mother's famous gold curls, surrounded always by friends whose names were printed on the backs of their jackets, friends who sat on the tables in the canteen and shouted to each other across the narrow hallways as if the school was too small for them.

He could have chosen anyone but that night he chose her. She had been feeling so rotten, so keen not to be left alone in her own skin, nursing a drink while she skulked near the bar, too self-aware to dance alone.

When he'd asked her to dance, she'd asked herself why not. When he'd kissed her under the disco ball, his mouth had tasted of grenadine syrup and rum. He'd hailed a taxi back to his empty townhouse and when Poppy had slipped her shoes off in the entrance hall the marble beneath her heels felt glacial.

When he brought the condom out between his fingers, pink and shiny and cheap as toffee, she said it out loud: 'Why not? Why the hell not?'

Harry had been tipsy and slurring his words, his eyes bright, his face flushed.

It's happening, Poppy had thought, waiting for the explosion inside of her.

It was nothing like she'd imagined. She'd hoped that sex would be the opposite of loneliness. Perhaps during all those nights spent staring into the gloom at Dalton or watching her mother sob into her coffee, perhaps what her empty body had yearned for was another body. Despite the bathroom stall chatter, Poppy hadn't really believed that it could hurt. Not as much as it did. She would tell her dorm-mate later that, 'it was like shoving a fist in your mouth.' But even more of a surprise was that, otherwise, sex felt exactly the way she had feared it would. Like getting drunk for the first time, the giggly numbness, the sickening lack of control, the uneasy topple back to consciousness and the 'is that all?' Like turning thirteen, like turning twenty. It was a surprise that it wasn't a surprise.

He could have chosen any girl but he chose her. This beautiful boy. This rich boy. The only part she'd liked had been the end, Harry's eyes squeezing shut and then the sound he made, like a child almost, plaintive and soft.

When he'd rolled over afterwards she'd found that a barrier had dissolved between them. They talked about 'How does it feel to be loved?' and laughed about it.

They had both been disappointed by fragile mothers, and ignored by their fathers. They were filled with the caution that children of single-parent homes are heir to. If you ever watch the pavement yawn open and swallow whole all the idle pedestrians on the street, you might never stride along it with the same careless ease ever again. You'd never be certain it would hold you. Hungover and sleepy, they'd talked about that as the night slipped by. 'How does it feel to be loved?' They agreed they would never be sure.

She knew that it would end, but not as suddenly as it had. At school the following week he could barely look at her, and then he told the boys in her class that, inside, she felt like sandpaper.

It was only a year later, when they were both accepted into the Beta, that Harry approached her at the bus stop and suggested the arrangement. He'd tiptoed around the exact words, his lips hiding a smile in the twilight. 'Twenty-three years is a long time,' he'd said. 'It'll look good to the public. And since we're both going, and we've done it before, and you won't be able to get pregnant...'

WHEN THEY WERE FINISHED, Harry helped to wash her hair. It grew so fast and thick it was already halfway down her back, and the feeling of his fingers on her scalp, the sweet kiss of the suds slipping down her shoulders, was so good that she began to cry. Harry stopped what he was doing, swept her hair aside like a curtain and kissed her neck. She could feel his nose pressing along the side of her spine; his lips brushed the little hairs that grew there. She longed more than anything to fall asleep in his arms as he stroked her hair, but instead he stepped back, pulling his lovely bare skin away from her, and the cold stung.

'You need to talk to someone,' he said. 'Maybe there's something wrong.'

'With me?' she asked, and was ashamed to feel more tears welling up in her eyes.

'No. Yes.' Harry switched off the shower and reached for his briefs. 'With your head maybe.'

'Maybe.'

'When my mum stopped acting she cried for months and months. All the time. She drew the curtains and slept all day and they said she was ill. Like, mentally ... so, maybe talk to Fae.' He shrugged and towelled himself off, flipping his hair back from his chiselled face. He was shrugging off her sadness as if it was still hanging on him, and when he left the bathroom Poppy felt like skin that had been shed.

LATER ON, WHEN SHE talked to Fae, the doctor offered, again, the silver-sided blister pack of pills she had been recommending for some time. 'Try them,' she said. 'You have to give it a few weeks to start working. Don't give up.'

Poppy finally accepted them. 'Do you think I caught it from my mother?' she asked.

Fae smiled sadly, 'It doesn't work that way, Poppy. I know it feels serious, but this happens to lots of astronauts on long-duration missions. It's completely normal.'

'Will these make me feel happy again?'

'Hopefully,' Fae said, brushing a strand of hair from her sunken eyes. But hers was not the face of a hopeful person. Poppy saw it, then. The distraction in Fae's face, a glimmer of pain. She gritted her teeth against it. *Does she have it too?* Poppy wondered. And, if so, how could she help Poppy if she could not help herself?

Later, Juno posted a list of rules in the crew module. There were only a couple at first, written in her neat hand. Things like *No one is exempt from chores* – from now on skipping chores required finding a willing replacement amongst the crew to complete the task. *Everyone attends dinner* – which, she usefully expanded, was vital for crew bonding and team-building. *Use the ship's equipment maturely and responsibly (that includes the airlock!)*

Juno didn't know that it was already escaping from them, the hope they would need to survive up here.

'You did a great job catching up,' Juno said, breezing past Poppy with a smile as she read them. She glanced at the list she had pinned up and Poppy thought she could see Juno's shoulders relax. As if she truly believed that, in the vacuum, the firm hand of order was all they needed to keep themselves from harm.

JUNO

JUPITER WAS SPECTACULAR. THE first time Juno saw it through the window on the control deck she said, 'It almost looks like another sun from this distance.'

'Well,' said Eliot, 'it's about ten times smaller than the sun. But I see your point. It's big. Bigger than 1,300 Earths, and it has more than sixty moons. Imagine if our planet had that many moons.'

'The night would look like the fifth of November,' Commander Sheppard said with a smile, his eyes reflecting the sky.

The atmosphere of Jupiter was comparable to that of the sun. It was composed of hydrogen and helium, with so many moons in orbit that it was like its own solar system. From their vantage point Juno could only just discern the vermillion belts that circled the planet. She could not yet see any hurricanes, or surging clouds of ammonia crystals. She could not even find the Great Red Spot, the storm that had swirled in the Jovian atmosphere for over 300 years, big enough to engulf Earth twice.

'Is this really a good time for an astronomy lecture?' Harry said through gritted teeth. He was in the pilot's seat.

'It's not for him,' Poppy said as Eliot held the camera up

before his eye. 'I can't just show our audience Jupiter in the window. I have to teach them about it.'

'I know,' Commander Sheppard said. 'Tell them that Uranus has twenty-seven moons and they are all named after characters in Shakespeare plays.'

'Do you mind repeating that,' Poppy asked, 'but to the camera?' Sheppard obliged, turning to the lens with a smile.

'Uranus,' he said, as if it had just occurred to him a second ago, 'has twenty-seven moons and they're all named after characters in Shakespeare's plays. The largest are Titania and Oberon.' Eliot gave him a thumbs-up and turned back to the sight in the window.

'We're filming this on 29 September.' Poppy's voice always chimed with synthetic glee whenever she spoke to her increasingly large following of schoolchildren back on Earth, all keen to be the next cohort to leave for Terra-Two. But Juno was glad to see her back doing her job after two weeks of absence. 'A quick shout-out to all our viewers who are going back to school this month. Good luck!

'It has taken us almost five months to travel 5.8 AU, or 540,000,000 miles from Earth.' She gave a low whistle at the figure. 'And this is just the *start* of our journey. It will still be a couple of days before we're close enough to Europa to safely dock with the American space station *Orlando*. In the meantime, our ship is in the capable hands of Harrison Bellgrave, our commander-in-training.' Harry's eyes brightened and he smiled for the camera.

'Switch it off,' Igor growled from the communication deck, motioning to Harry. 'This is a serious job. How can he concentrate with all this talk?'

'Igor's right.' Commander Sheppard turned to Eliot, Poppy and Juno. 'I think you both have tutorials to get to. And it will be a while before we'll be able to see Europa. Longer still before we spot the American station, and you'll get a better view of it from the observation deck.'

Juno sighed and drifted towards the door. She wanted to stay in the control room – seeing the planet in the window reminded her that they were really going somewhere, instead of suspended in the darkness of space. In a few weeks, they would meet other astronauts – she smiled at the thought – and in just over a year they would be the first humans to leave the solar system entirely.

Fae was kneeling in front of the monitor on the communications deck, cursing in German.

'Still not working?' Juno asked as she walked past, glancing at the flickering static. Fae turned to Juno, her eyes red-rimmed and narrow. She let out a growl of frustration that made everyone jump, her voice a soprano knife-edge over the low buzzing of machines. She stormed from the room, the hatch hissing shut behind her.

'Wow.' Juno let out a whistle of surprise.

'Maybe she can't get through to Ground?' said Eliot.

'Or Moritz,' Sheppard mumbled.

'Who?' Juno asked.

'Her husband or boyfriend or something,' Poppy said. 'He works for the European Space Agency.'

Juno had never even asked about Fae Golinsky's family.

'You're still talking!' Igor grunted, and Juno left the room.

It was past time for her tutorial with Fae and she was dreading it. Increasingly, she felt, it had been her tedious job to navigate the hostile and ever-changing landscapes of everyone's moods.

When they were alone together during lessons, Fae seemed to simmer constantly with a quiet rage. Whenever she spoke it was through gritted teeth. She left dinner early to be alone or to tune and retune the communication channels on deck, trying to reach home. Poppy wasn't much better. The previous week she had caught up on her chores but whenever Juno entered the room she would fall silent and narrow her eyes. There was no companionship to be found with the boys, who had fallen out since the airlock incident. Harry and Jesse rarely came within a metre of each other. And Astrid only wanted to discuss New Creationist theories.

As Juno headed towards the infirmary, she noticed Jesse walking towards her. She still couldn't look at him without her pulse thumping in her ears; without thinking of the afternoon in the greenhouse when he'd tried to kiss her. 'Hey,' he said, averting his gaze. The corridor was narrow and he had to stop and stand aside to let her pass. Juno nodded and dived into the infirmary, where Fae sat with her head in her hands. Juno had entered so quickly that it took a second for her to take in the scene; Fae hunched over her desk with the heels of her palms pressed into the hollows of her eyes. Music filled the room, Tchaikovsky pealing from the little speaker in the corner. Some nights, Juno walked past the infirmary and heard *The Sleeping Beauty* seeping under the door, and she imagined that when the crew were asleep, Fae emerged like a night-blooming flower, tearing off her lab coat to cabriole across the floor. But when Astrid had asked Fae over dinner if she ever kept up with her ballet and if she could teach them a few steps, Fae had said, 'I never dance now' with such miserable finality that all Juno's whimsical imaginings evaporated.

She slammed the door shut behind her and said, 'Doctor? I mean, Fae ...' Fae's head flew up, she lunged towards the radio and jabbed the *off* button so the music cut out.

Wiping her eyes, she turned to Juno and asked, 'What now?'

'Um ...' Juno straightened her back and glanced again at her watch. 'It's time for our lesson?' She noticed that none of their books had been set out, and the board had not been wiped clean after yesterday's lesson on the endocrine system. Juno chewed her lip and looked around awkwardly. 'Should I come back at a better time?' And then she added – for courtesy's sake, 'Are you okay?'

'Um ...' Fae's voice was tight, '*no*.'

'What is it?' Juno asked. She was not sure which was better; the gift of comfort or the gift of privacy.

'Do you care?' Fae asked.

'Of course ...' Juno said. 'Of course I do.'

Fae exhaled heavily and then reached up to pull the pins out of her hair. In one swift movement, her hair spilled down her back like a stream of molten rock. She was thin as a prepubescent girl, with light little bones, but when she let her hair down the skin around her forehead sank, revealing the lines etched there. Under the V-neck of her jumper her grey skin puckered like crepe paper over the rungs of her sternum.

'Who's Moritz?' Juno asked on an impulse. Fae turned to her, eyes narrowed as if she suspected a trick.

'You don't know?' she said with a frown, then, more to herself, 'Of course you don't know.' She rubbed her liver-spotted hands and said, 'Moritz is my fiancé.'

Juno's eyes were drawn to the ring on the doctor's third finger. Art deco, with a pale topaz set in silver filigree. It glinted in the light, the clinical blue of the doctor's eyes. Had she always worn it? Juno wondered how she had never noticed such an extravagant piece of jewellry.

'Y-you're engaged?' Juno stammered. She could feel the colour rising in her cheeks. Why had she never asked?

'Yes,' Fae said. 'It happened a week before the launch. Ten days, actually.'

'Oh,' said Juno, with dawning realization. 'When Ara died you had to take Maggie's place.' Juno, too, had said goodbye to a boy she thought she might spend her life with, but Fae only had the space of an evening to say her goodbyes, to make her arrangements. Juno wondered if the doctor awoke every morning with regret for the life she chose.

'Why did you agree to come?' Juno asked.

'I don't know,' Fae said. 'I knew there would be a chance I might have to go. That was always the plan if Dr Millburrow couldn't launch. But as time went on ... you all loved Maggie so much ... but it was the night before the launch and ... I don't know. There were so many people, so much pressure and they were all looking for someone to blame. I didn't want it to be my fault if we failed. When we had come so far ...' She shrugged. Juno didn't think she had ever heard Fae say so many words. 'And we already knew that Moritz couldn't join the UKSA. He's not a dual citizen like me. So he joined the running to be part of the Vierzig and we thought—'

'The Vierzig?'

'*Die Ersten Vierzig,*' Fae said, her accent curling around the words. 'The First Forty.'

Juno recognized the translation, of course. A German-speaking group who were part of the European Space Agency.

For a long time they had been tipped to launch first and to reach Terra before the British. Forty men and women, all post-docs and older than the Beta. Juno guessed that Fae had thought they might reach Terra-Two within a decade of each other and be reunited there. It was a romantic thought, a wedding on the shores of a new planet. 'It could still happen,' Juno said, and she could see it herself, for a second; Fae, aged but dressed in white, her hand in his, making promises that were swept up by the wind.

'No,' Fae said. 'It won't. He didn't make it into the forty. It looked like he might but . . . I found out today, they released the list of the finalists and his name is not on it.'

Juno's stomach twisted. 'I'm sorry,' she said. 'I'm really sorry.'

A few things made sense to Juno now: photographs she'd seen in the back of Fae's binder, her frequent calls to Earth, the way she presided over the crew with a cold resentment as if they were children she'd never wanted. A swell of silent sympathy came over her, but she fought against it. 'Maybe something good has come out of this. Surely it has,' she said. 'Not everyone made it onto the *Damocles*. Not everyone has this chance to make history.'

Fae's shoulders began to shake with suppressed sobs. 'Don't you see,' she said, 'that it doesn't matter?'

'What doesn't matter?'

'We're alone out here. You're a child.' The word grated on Juno, but she let it go. '*I* know, though. I know that our chances are slim.'

'What are you talking about?'

Fae shook her head, drawn again into her own sorrow. She turned away and said to herself, 'What am I doing here?'

'Don't say that.' Juno's voice was firmer. She'd had enough self-pity on this voyage. Everyone has their moment of despair.'

'*Moment?*' Fae stood up suddenly, and her chair tipped to the ground. Juno jumped backwards, buzzing with surprise. 'My whole life is despair.' Lunging forward, she threw an arm across the table and sent the books flying. Juno jumped back to avoid a glass paperweight, which shattered against the wall. 'Why did I choose *this?*' the doctor asked over the clattering of stationery at their feet. 'This graveyard voyage. This suicide mission?'

Juno's heart was pounding. She couldn't tell if she should comfort Fae or abandon her. Her feet chose for her. She darted from the room, shaking with dread. She didn't stop running until she reached the crew module and the sound of Fae's wild sobs was no longer ringing in her ears.

JUNO FINISHED READING THE final chapter on the endocrine system alone, with grim determination. The crew module was deserted – everyone was either in their bedroom or working and, behind the door of the girls' cabin, Poppy's radio had hitched onto a station that played melancholy jazz tracks all afternoon.

When Juno finished her work she caught sight of Jupiter again, a little larger in the window, a claret flurry of storms now faintly visible in its atmosphere. A long note rose from a clarinet, echoed across the crew module, and in that moment Juno realized that she was lonely. She had continued – in the only way she knew how – through the tutorials, through the weeks and months, as the excitement of space travel flaked away and living in a confined space with her crewmates began to feel like a bad marriage. *Twenty years more of this*, Juno thought wearily.

Twenty years of Fae's resentment and Poppy's self-centred sorrow. Eliot's broken heart. Harry's competitiveness. Jesse's desire. Astrid's dreams, which no one could share. And the cold, and this loneliness.

She was almost relieved when the bell rang for dinner. But only Harry, Astrid and Commander Sheppard turned up. On the menu that night was one of Juno's least favourite meals, bitter beef stew and rice with vacuum-packed crackers.

'You're not eating,' Commander Sheppard said.

'Sorry.' Juno pushed her sticky rice around the bowl.

'Well, don't play with it like that or we can't recycle it.'

The thought of recycling it for another dinner rotation – which meant that in ten days Juno would be faced with this very same meal again – made her stomach turn. She imagined what might happen if she never ate her beef stew. Would it just pile up and up?

'Not many people are at dinner,' she said, in an attempt to change the subject. Harry feigned surprise, looking around at the seats between them as if he'd only just noticed that they were empty.

'It does begin happening around this stage of the trip,' Sheppard said. 'In my experience, by the time we'd been on Mars three, maybe four, months … the crew start to get restless and some people get sad. The Russians call it "asthenia". Low mood, tiredness, you know … it's best just to wait it out. Happens all the time.'

'But in the meantime,' said Astrid, 'they're making everyone else miserable.'

'Yes,' Juno agreed. 'Can't we *make* them come to dinner? I'm sure they'll feel cheered up once they're here.'

'That might be true.' Sheppard put down his knife and fork and exhaled slowly before speaking. 'You see, Juno, that's a good suggestion. At Dalton you and your crew might have received sanctions for missing a meal or chores. Or worse, of course, some people were excluded from the programme. But that's not the type of punitive environment I'm looking to cultivate up here. I'm aware, on one hand, that you are the youngest crew I have ever worked with, which poses a few ... challenges. But on the other hand, you need to learn to build up the good habits and a caring culture between yourselves of your own volition. That's one of the most important lessons you will learn during this mission. And I'm not sure that I want to stand around trying to *make* you.'

'You want us to want to,' Astrid said, leaning over Juno's tray to stab her fork into a lump of meat.

Harry looked distracted for a moment, his gaze distant and unfocused. Finally he spoke. 'Poppy's party was kind of nice. Doing something together. Maybe we could do more things like that, as a group.'

'Like a crew meeting?' Juno suggested.

'Has no one taught you the meaning of "fun", lady?' Harry said.

Commander Sheppard chuckled. 'Thank you for your suggestion, Harry. I think something recreational might be more enjoyable.'

'Jesse and I thought that we could have a harvest lunch at Christmas time. By then, a lot of the fruits and veg from the greenhouse will be ready to cook and eat.' Astrid licked her lips in excitement.

'Or the Olympics,' Harry suggested. 'None of you watched

the Olympic opening ceremony with me. It was amazing. James Bond, J. K. Rowling, The Beatles, the NHS.'

'Oh, yes.' Juno felt a pang of regret. 'I missed that.'

'Well, I have it recorded,' Harry said. 'We could all watch it together.'

'That's another good idea.' Sheppard smiled, and then took a long drag from his glass. 'The thing you have to remember, Juno, is that it helps to be a little forgiving. No one has done this before. With some things, we'll just have to see how it goes.'

SHEPPARD'S WORDS BOTHERED JUNO even after dinner was over and they had all retired for the evening. She wasn't sure she liked the thought of venturing out into the void with no role models, nothing to anchor herself.

That evening, she ended up scouring the ship's data bank on her personal computer, looking for files. She came across the Xiao Lin papers, articles published by the scientist on the Chinese generation ship. Xiao Lin had laid out her ideas about the importance of living in harmony on a closed system like the *Shēngmìng*. Fellowship and justice, she had written, came above all else. Juno was captivated by the idea. And by Xiao Lin, who seemed to embody a cold brilliance. She'd managed to distil 'fellowship' into a few simple rules of human behaviour, and Juno read and reread them so intently that she didn't notice time passing.

'You're still awake.' Astrid sauntered in a while later, in her pyjamas.

'It's not like I have anything else to do,' Juno muttered, looking up from her screen. The indigo light outside the door indicated night-time and it was a surprise to see.

'No, not since everyone is angry with you.' Astrid said it in jest but Juno flinched. Poppy still wasn't talking to her, and she had not seen Fae all evening.

'Did you know that Dr Golinsky is engaged?' she asked.

'Yeah.' Astrid turned to Juno. 'Everyone knows that. She had to leave Earth really suddenly and she didn't even have a chance to say goodbye.'

Juno chewed on her lip for a moment. Something about Fae's breakdown had ruffled her, made her suddenly aware of her own friendlessness. It reminded her of those days during primary school when Astrid was ill and she found herself alone in the playground, the harsh wind licking at her calves, carrying the sounds of other people's laughter.

'Do you think all the senior crew are like Golinsky?' she asked.

'Like what?'

'I guess I always imagined that they came on this mission because they had nothing to leave behind. Well, except for Sheppard.'

'Everyone has something to leave behind. They probably came along for some of the reasons we did, because it would be amazing. Because maybe it's worth gambling all we have for the promise of a better life.'

'They must get lonely. Like Cai, spending all day up in the greenhouse, or Igor – I know he left a wife and children and grandchildren behind on Earth,' Juno said.

'I never understood why they couldn't just pair up with each other,' Astrid said. Juno cringed at the thought, picturing Fae's stiff body in Commander Sheppard's arms.

'Like – what's his name? – that captain on *Orlando*, his wife lives on station with him. They've been married for thirty years or something.'

'I guess that's just luck,' Juno said. 'Being put on a mission with someone you grow to love.'

'Or destiny,' Astrid said gently.

Juno looked down.

'You know,' Astrid said, 'you act as if we're all still crew, like we're all work colleagues doing a job together, but it's not like that anymore. We're a family now.'

'Yes,' said Juno, looking down at the highlighted pages of the Xiao Lin papers. 'That's exactly what I've been thinking about. Fellowship. We need to engage in team-building—'

'I don't know if we need more plans. More rules.' Astrid rolled her eyes. 'Maybe we need more friendship.'

Juno thought for a moment. Pictured again the photos she had seen downlinked from the *Shēngmìng*, three generations in some of them, smiling scientists and their young children, the first hundred, their faces lined but quietly joyful. Juno had found candid shots of the crew gathered in the *Shēngmìng*'s greenhouse to celebrate the Duanwu Festival, racing mini motorized dragon boats across the reservoir, faces lantern-lit, crew members toasting each other with realgar wine, toddlers on tiptoes grabbing at cherry blossoms.

'Juno,' Astrid came to sit beside her, a mischievous smile on her face. 'Can you do something for me?'

'Depends,' she said. 'What?'

'I want ... some tuck.'

'Astrid—'

'Just a little. I know you don't let anyone touch it but I haven't eaten chocolate in weeks. We all know you have real chocolate hidden away in that cupboard with all the rest of the junk food you were too disciplined to eat. Share some with me? Please . . .' Her eyes grew wide and pleading.

'Just a little?'

'Just a tiny bit,' Astrid promised, squeezing her finger and thumb together to indicate just how small. Juno sighed.

Her tuck locker was the cupboard full of perishable food from Earth that she'd been allowed to bring with her: hot chocolate, marshmallows, Mars Bars and Pringles all stacked neatly in the kitchen. By their third week in space, the others had eaten through most of their food and were busy trading the dregs. Juno had arranged the food from the back of the cupboard in order of expiry date and written up a timetable in order to preserve it for as long as possible. Commander Sheppard told them tales of the Mars mission where they ran out of coffee and traded favours for sachets of the stuff. 'You'd be a rich girl,' he said, 'if only you'd swap your food for chores.'

Juno opened her locked cupboard. It smelt of preserved sugar, tall stacks of tin cans glinting in the low light. She had only a few chocolate bars left, and didn't want to spare a whole one, so she picked up a large half-opened Galaxy bar, pushed her finger under the creased gold paper, broke off four squares and surrendered them reluctantly.

Astrid was already licking her lips. 'Can I eat it now?' she asked breathlessly.

'Eat it when you like,' Juno replied, feigning indifference, although, in her position, Juno knew that she would draw the experience out over four days, letting one square each morning melt in her mouth.

Astrid took a bite, then smiled, her front teeth slicked brown with chocolate. 'I don't know how you have the control to stare at all that food and not eat it.'

'Years of practice.' Juno laughed. 'Anyway, I'd feel bad if I ate it all. I'd probably be sick.' Juno remembered what they had been talking about before. 'The thing is . . .' she began, retrieving the thread of the conversation, 'I think that if we just learn from the mistakes we made on Earth, and dedicate ourselves to—'

'You know, you're not the boss here, Juno, and you can't keep telling people how to live their lives. That's why Poppy still hasn't forgiven you.' Juno was taken aback by her sister's harsh tone. 'You know what Dad would say . . . what happened to your faith?'

'Faith in what?'

'In our destiny. In Terra-Two. You haven't seen it, like I have. But, Juno, once we get there, all of this,' she indicated the books Juno had laid out on the table, 'will be trivial.'

Juno felt her hairs prickle with a flash of irritation. 'Your dreams, your stupid dreams. A dream is not evidence!'

'But how can you explain Tessa Dalton and—'

'Tessa Dalton?' Juno said. 'The crazy woman?'

Astrid stared at Juno in furious shock. 'Take that back!'

'No,' said Juno, raising her voice to match her sister's. 'I think this whole New Creationist thing is just another way for you to convince yourself that you're special.'

The blood rose in Astrid's face as if Juno had just slapped her. 'You know what? Poppy's right. You're bossy and judgemental. *You're* impossible to live with. And if you want to spend the next two decades miserable and alone, you're going about it the right way.'

*

THE SHAME OF SURRENDER was as familiar to Juno as the cool pride of self-control. That night, she went back to the kitchen when everyone was asleep and half the lights in the ship were off. In the darkness, the smell of dust and preserved sugar set her heart racing.

Then, afterwards, she tortured herself by counting and recounting how much she had consumed. The chocolate melting over her tongue, the jelly babies that stuck to the sides of her teeth and left her mouth sour and furry, the juvenile delight of glacé cherries, which she loved because, when she was much younger, she would steal them from her mother's baking cupboard. Seduced by the sight of them, Juno had grabbed one when her mother's back had been turned. Then, again, that same night she crept down the stairs and ate another, then another, tortured by the sight of them, gleaming like marbles in the box, within her reach. Soon, she was stealing six or seven at a time, her fingers sticky and syrupy sweet, a delight to lick clean. She would lie restlessly in bed, waiting for her parents' door to close, just so she could slip like a shadow into the kitchen and spoon icing sugar into her mouth, chocolates and ladyfingers, Swiss rolls and digestive biscuits. Then she would lie awake in the darkness, tasting the insides of her mouth and the low ebb of guilt.

The first time her mother caught her had also been the first time she'd ever given her a smack with a wooden spoon, on the palm of her left hand. It took Juno too long to realize that the slap had not been for the sweetness she could still taste behind her lips, but for the lies.

That night on the ship, it was no surprise when the sickness came. She felt it rise up from the base of her stomach and heard herself cry out before it filled her mouth. She bolted out the door and made it to the bathroom just in time to heave over the edge of the toilet bowl. Every time she thought it was over, a muscle under her solar plexus contracted, with the brutal force of an elastic band pinging back, and a hot flood of half-eaten junk food surged back up between her teeth.

She'd forgotten to lock the door in her rush to the bathroom, and though she knew that the sounds of her gagging would be audible outside, she did not have the energy to stand and close it. Juno pressed her cheek against the ground. She felt as if all the bones in her body had dissolved.

She didn't know how long it was until she became aware of the sound of movement outside. The soft slap of bare feet.

'Go away,' she moaned, her voice an ugly rasp. Then another hot flood of bitter food erupted from her throat.

'Juno?' Jesse's voice was edged with fear. Juno became more aware of her surroundings; the bathroom was filled with the acrid smell of vomit and her cheek was wet with it.

'Just leave me alone,' she said more forcefully, trying to get up. She couldn't think of anyone she was more ashamed to be found by. 'Please—' she gasped, and to her horror her mouth filled up again. She found the energy to sit up and lean over the edge of the toilet bowl. 'Please stay outside,' she said when she'd finished. 'I don't want you to see this.'

'I don't mind,' Jesse said. 'I've been out on a Friday night too, you know.'

'Please?'

'Okay, fine. I'll stand outside.' His shadow disappeared but she could still hear his voice. 'Hey, are you spacesick?'

'Yeah,' she muttered, wiping her mouth with the back

of her hand. 'Sick of space.' He chuckled. 'I don't think so,' she admitted.

'Then maybe it's something you ate?'

Juno's face burned. 'Maybe,' she managed to say.

'Should I go and get Fae?'

'*No*, I don't want you to wake her. I'll be fine in a few minutes.'

They were silent for a while. Juno's head clouded over with sleep, pinpricks of imaginary light stippling the darkness. The room was illuminated only by the glow from the crew module through the open door. She tried to imagine Jesse on the other side of the wall, in nothing but a T-shirt and boxers. Imagined the straight line his thigh made all the way down to his ankle, and his feet that were stained green with fertilizer from walking barefoot in the greenhouse.

Her eyes dropped closed as she began to drift into sleep, but she bit awake abruptly when her head flopped down on her neck. In panic and semi-conscious confusion she called out, 'Jesssseee . . . ,' her voice a plaintive whimper. He was by her side in the next moment.

There were tears in her eyes. 'It's okay,' he said softly, pushing them away with a thumb. 'You'll feel better soon. You're okay.'

''mnotokay,' she slurred as tears fell freely from her eyes. 'I'm alone.'

'No, you're not,' he said and pulled her close to him, though her face was sticky. 'You're okay.' He stroked her hair. She realized that this was the closest she'd been to a human body since Noah had held her in the Garden of Flight back on Earth. Such a long time ago. Nestled against Jesse's large chest, she felt slight and safe. She would drift into sleep a couple of times, only to jerk awake in a body filled with pain and retch over the toilet bowl. Each time Jesse would wake too and tug the hair out of her face, and wipe her forehead and smile lazily and promise her that she would soon be fine.

She supposed he carried her out of the bathroom a while later, and onto the sofa where she woke to find herself in his arms. By then, the worst of the sickness had passed. She felt light and tired and wonderfully clean, as if she'd been baptized in flames. She opened her eyes to discover a body without stomach cramps or tremors. Jesse was still asleep beside her, his lips slightly parted, head rolled back on the sofa, breathing softly.

JUNO

BY THE TIME DECEMBER came, everything was different. Jesse and Juno slid into an intimacy born of constant proximity. Cosy habits emerged: watching recordings of *University Challenge* and shouting out the answers or marathons of *Buffy the Vampire Slayer*. Juno discovered that they shared the same cynical sense of humour. Every new thing she learned about him was a delight. They stayed up late talking most nights, sometimes until the hallway sky simulation turned lemon-yellow with 'dawn'.

Everyone had closed ranks by the end of that year: Harry and Eliot stayed up late playing insomniac chess marathons on the control deck; Poppy and Astrid paired rations of sugar and evaporated milk to make wild saccharine confections and curled up together in Poppy's bed, discussing star signs.

A couple of weeks after they began their approach to Jupiter, an email from Noah arrived. The subject line was 'Juno?', nothing in the body of the message but a photograph of her house, and a video attachment. The photograph had clearly been taken a couple of months ago, because the leaves on the apple tree in the front garden were the colour of fire and rust. Juno touched the screen. He had given her the end of the summer. The short-ening days, Cox apples growing fat. For a moment, she was there too. Beyond the reinforced walls of their vessel. Home.

Juno clicked on the video attachment, which loaded slowly, and as it did, she shuddered with excitement and dread. Finally, Noah's face appeared on her screen. His curly blond hair had grown out so that he looked like a young Robert Plant, his chin shadowed with patches of stubble. Noah fiddled with the camera, setting it on the desk in front of him, before staring straight into the lens. '*Hey, Juno.*' He waved. '*So I was thinking about a gift to give you and your mum suggested I make a video so you get to feel like you're here with me. It's September right now but I probably won't get up the courage to send this to you until after Christmas so ... happy Christmas?*' He was in a bedroom she didn't recognize, sparsely decorated with a fire-safety notice stuck to the back of the door. '*I could see you for a while, you know. In the sky and on the news. I wish you could have been here. I don't know if they told you how crazy it got down here for a while. The Beta was on the news every day ... but I don't watch it so much anymore.*' He paused, and swallowed. '*So anyway, here is my room in uni!*' He twisted the camera around to show a rather bare room. Juno recognized some of the posters from his old bedroom. The periodic table, an old Coldplay poster, a little postcard that said 'if you're not part of the solution you're part of the precipitate', which never really stopped being funny even after GCSE chemistry.

'*My bookshelf...*' He pointed the camera towards three fitted shelves, with a couple of fat textbooks. '*We had to buy all of these books. Most of mine are second-hand. We started lectures a week ago and it's not so hard ... Mostly A-level stuff. I've probably covered half of the content at Dalton already but I kinda can't wait for it to start getting harder. Oh also, this is the view from my window –'* he pointed the camera towards a courtyard that reminded Juno a little of the space centre, only there was a group of people slouching under a smoking shelter – *'and all my photos . . .'* Stuck to the pin-board, mainly photos of the two of them, a school trip to Devon, their Leavers' Ball, Juno giving a dorky thumbs-up in the first spacesuit she ever wore.

The camera wobbled again and Noah held it close to his face, so that his eyes filled her screen. Juno had forgotten the details so quickly – forgotten how striking his eyes were. The frosty lines in his iris sparkled like cut glass. *'I still love you Juno. I know you're not coming back, but sometimes I wish you were here with me. Also . . . I'm sorry about what I said. You know . . . Please forgive me?'* The screen went blank too soon.

Juno re-watched it, and each time the video seemed shorter. Only two minutes. Juno felt as if it was only the window of her computer screen separating them. She could be in university too, reading fat expensive textbooks and wondering what to do with the abundant free time she was trusted to organize herself. University would be filled with new, exciting people, and Juno took a moment to imagine what they would be like. What she would be like. As she did, she saw, all too clearly, a different avenue her life could have taken. Why did it hurt? She had chosen this path and yet she was distracted by the distant ache of injustice. The notion that she'd been robbed of something too soon.

She flopped back on the bed, clutching her stomach. When the others asked what was wrong she'd tell them she was spacesick.

POPPY

25.12.12

SOMEHOW, BY DECEMBER, HER mind had changed. Poppy would never know if it was the antidepressants Fae had given her or finally getting used to the new rhythm of her life on the *Damocles* or Juno's determination to pursue order, but by Christmas Poppy found it easier to keep from being mired in hopelessness. On Christmas morning, she awoke with a hard knot of excitement unspooling in her stomach. She looked around in the darkness at the sleeping heaps of Astrid and Juno in their bunks and smiled. For years, at Christmas, Poppy had woken alone in her bedroom and longed for sisters.

The crew module was festooned with the decorations she and Astrid had made the night before, delicate snowflakes cut out of silver and grey crepe paper and sellotaped to the windows. Paper chains, and a sign Jesse had drawn that said 'Happy Christmas', so that the 'I' of Christmas looked like mistletoe.

'Hey.' When Poppy turned, Harry was leaning against the door of the boys' cabin, his eyes still half-lidded from sleep, his hair tousled and flopping into his eyes. Cute and dewy-skinned.

'I have a present for you,' she blurted out.

'Oh?'

'Yeah, I made it.'

'I have a present for you too,' he said, flicking his hair out of his eyes. Poppy's stomach flipped with excitement. This was the day. She replayed a familiar fantasy in her head: Harry, handing her a powder-blue box crowned in a white ribbon, she pulling out a silver charm bracelet or a rose gold pendant, his eyes twinkling with adoration.

'Don't you find it a little weird?' Poppy asked. 'Christmas without family?'

'Only a little.' Harry shrugged. 'Meet me in the engine room and I'll give it to you.'

'Okay!' Poppy chirped, and she headed back into her room to fetch his gift.

For Poppy, Christmas had never been a joyful time. Over the years they had fallen into a tradition of watching reruns of *ER* on satellite, bingeing on ready meals and chocolate in the fizzy light of the television. Sometimes, Poppy would take the old tree out of the cleaning cupboard, set it up by the window with fairy-lights. Every year the decorations were fewer and fewer, dusted baubles from Pound-Stretcher that dropped off and cracked like eggs underfoot. When she was young Poppy would push her face right into the plastic pine needles of their tree and breathe in the smell of dust and PVC. She would stare at the lights nestled in it and imagine a happy world bathed in the golden glow of Christmas-tree-light.

That was how she imagined Harry's whole life. She'd heard that his family owned a few properties across the UK, although she'd only been to his North London house once. It had been an imposing Edwardian house at the end of a leafy lane in Hampstead. She remembered being dazzled by the chandeliers, the sweeping marble staircase. She'd said, foolishly, 'I thought only people on TV lived in places like this.' He'd shrugged, and tossed an apple core at the dustbin, missed.

His Christmases were probably around a huge oak dining table, all his blond siblings laughing in the candlelight, a honey-glazed pig in the middle of the table, a seven-foot tree his burly older brothers hauled in from the garden. Poppy liked to imagine snapshots of his old life and was filled with shivers of pleasure when she remembered that, now, she was a little part of it too.

She'd knitted him a scarf, his initials messily embroidered into the corner. A labour of quiet love, and when she handed it to him later in the engine room he said, 'Wow ... good effort.' Twisted it around his neck and grinned.

'Mine's not so fancy,' he said, and then handed her a bottle of mouthwash.

'Um ...' Poppy held it up quizzically. 'Thanks ...?'

'Taste it, silly,' he said.

'Listerine?' She couldn't help that her heart sank.

Harry grabbed it back off her, unscrewed the top and took a swig, wiped his mouth noisily and smiled, his teeth bright like a wolf's in the half-light of the engine room. Poppy copied him, and she noticed the burn, the oaky aftertaste, the rush of blood to her head and neck. 'Whiskey?'

He nodded. She held the blue liquid up to the light and eyed it suspiciously.

'Food colouring,' Harry said. 'An old trick from the Dalton days.' Poppy laughed and took another sip. It burned going down, and she smiled.

JUNO

25.12.12

JUNO WAS GLAD TO see Poppy so gleeful again, giggling and pulling Santa hats over everyone's ears, smiling for the camera as if her teeth were bright pearls she'd been hiding. They wore the hats to record a video for the BBC, stood in two rows in front of the camera as if they were posing for a school photo. Eliot had forced them to practise saying 'Merry Christmas' in unison a couple of times, so by the time they were on-air their voices chimed 'Merry Christmas' after his signal with the mechanical hollowness of a music box. By that point, it took radio signals from the *Damocles* almost forty minutes to reach Earth, so they had been instructed to downlink their video early enough for it to be replayed on national television half an hour after the Queen's Christmas Message.

Igor said '*S Rozhdestvom*' to his family in Russia, most of whom, he explained, actually celebrated Christmas in January, according to the Orthodox calendar. He looked different, some-how, in the light of the control room. His voice was hoarse, and when he thought the rest of the crew weren't looking Juno caught him wincing in pain, his face pale.

'Are you okay?' she asked. Igor waved a dismissive hand at her and walked carefully over to the door.

Lunch was spectacular. Poppy had done a beautiful job with the decorating. She had plastered silver paper-cuts snowflakes all along the windows, written 'Merry Christmas' on a large roll of paper. On the table, Juno's name was on a place card, next to Jesse's. It had a fat little drawing of Santa making a peace sign.

The table was a cornucopia of food. It was Cai and Jesse's first harvest in the greenhouse; there were beets, Brussels sprouts, cabbages and carrots as well as fresh rocket, rosemary and sage. Poppy had laid out their rations in sweetly decorated bowls and plates. Sticky slices of canned peaches and pineapples floated on a lake of syrup, Jesse's lentil and cashew nut loaf was sprinkled with the watercress that had been growing in the greenhouse and some of them had donated the last of their tuck, so gold and purple packets of fudge and chocolate eclairs glittered amongst the dishes.

Sipping at her glass of water, Juno nudged at the peas, then dropped her fork with a small sigh. Jesse rested his hand on the table next to hers, rolling it over slightly so that his palm was facing up and the little brown hairs along his forearm brushed against hers. She could see the green veins in his wrists, the steel rings on his fingers, the little black infinity symbol tattooed along the wrinkled edge of his thumb where his light-brown skin turned white. When she looked up, he was smiling at her, his lips stained black with wine.

'What about presents?' Poppy said. She'd built a little card-board Christmas tree in the middle of the counter, to lay the presents under.

'Actually,' said Jesse. 'Cai and I have a present for all of you.'

'Is it under the tree?'

'No, it's a surprise. We'll show it to you after dinner.'

'Awww ...' Astrid said. 'I'm excited already.' She nudged Cai, who had touched little of his food. 'You're getting into the Christmas spirit too.'

'It was Jesse's idea,' he said.

'Don't spoil it.' Jesse pressed a finger to his lips.

Juno spooned a couple of ice cubes into her cup and listened to them clatter against the glass. She wasn't sure what was wrong with her. Jesse's proximity, next to her at the table, made her stomach twist with excitement. It was as if she'd never seen him before.

Everyone cheered, startling Juno out of her reverie. Igor had entered with two bottles of champagne. Solomon stood up at the head of the table. 'I would just like to say that I could not have picked a better crew to spend Christmas with. Sure, there have been a few growing pains. But I feel really privileged to watch you all mature, so here's to the first of many great Christmases.' He raised his glass, and so did everyone else. They whooped and swallowed down the sweet cold wine. Juno thought that she could feel the bubbles rush straight to her head.

Then they tore through their presents at the same time, in a silence that was punctuated by shouts of surprise or gratitude. Juno's was a heavy edition of *Gray's Anatomy*. She gasped, running her fingers along the bent spine.

'It's second-hand,' said Fae, apologetically. On the first page, Juno found a name written in exquisite handwriting, Fae Golinsky, and the date, thirty years ago. In the margin next to the contents page, she had practised writing her name again and again, with the title she'd studied for. 'DOCTOR Friederike Golinsky', 'DOCTOR Friederike Golinsky', she'd scribbled over and over, and Juno imagined a time she had been hunched over her books, Juno's age, in medical school.

'Thank you . . .' she said in breathless surprise, and Fae's lips tightened into something like a smile.

There were other lovely gifts too. Juno knew that Poppy had given Harry a scarf. Cai had given Jesse a couple of tiny paper bags of seeds. 'You can have a plot, only a metre or two, I cleared one for you. You can grow whatever you like there,' he'd said brusquely.

Astrid had given Solomon a dream catcher, a delicate, feathered thing she'd bought on holiday once. 'Now you can dream of Terra as well,' she told him, and he smiled graciously.

'Off we go,' Poppy called out at the end of the meal. Everyone piled out of the room and up the ladder to the greenhouse, where Cai had dimmed the halogen bulbs. The garden had begun to flourish, patches of once sterile ground now covered in bright-green plants, with leaves that seemed to float in the lower gravity. Vines curled up the glass spires, waxy leaves shivering as they passed. Wicker baskets hung along the paths, vivid and lush flowers spilling over the edges.

They followed Jesse and Cai to the centre of the greenhouse, past Cai's office, to stand before the cleared patch of land where the tallest tree had been planted. A spruce tree. Jesse had covered it in fairy-lights and some of Poppy's paper snowflakes. Juno looked around at the faces of the crew bathed in the soft light, everyone clutching their champagne and smiling.

At the top of the tree was no plastic star or gaudy angel. Jesse had painted over a bauble with the blue of seas and lime patches of land. Their gaze was drawn up the makeshift Christmas tree to the little replica of one Earth, or another, that floated above it.

JESSE

25.12.12

AFTER CHRISTMAS LUNCH, JESSE and the rest of the Beta gathered in the crew module to watch movies. They were halfway through the opening credits of an action film when Juno strode in and pressed the pause button on the monitor screen.

'I've been thinking,' she said. Harry groaned and folded his arms.

'If you're going to demand that we do chores today of all days —'

'Nothing like that.' Juno stepped in front of the screen so that her hair buzzed with static.

'I've been thinking for a while, actually, about what we're going to do when we land. You see, all the training that we've received has been focused on the technical aspect of our role as pioneers. Gathering data, finding water sources, building the settlement in preparation for the next set of astronauts. But it occurs to me now that there has been one gaping hole in our education.

'What kind of society do we want to be? What will our name be? What will our flag look like? What kind of leadership model will we adhere to? Will we have a monarchy, a president? '

'A monarchy.' Harry smiled. 'I like the sound of that.'

'King Harry?' Poppy said, rolling her eyes. 'Ruler of five people?'

'It will only be five people at first. Then more will land, and we'll tell them what's what. If you're good you can be a concubine.'

Juno did not look amused.

'There are laws already. This debate has already been settled by the British Interplanetary Society and the government,' Jesse said. 'I mean, as far as I understand it, we're sort of governed by British laws, conventions and acts of parliament. Like a colony. Like America was.'

'Because that turned out so well,' Juno said.

'I guess we do need a name, at least,' Astrid agreed. 'Surely *we* can decide that. New … something that already exists?'

'That's too obvious,' said Eliot, but Astrid continued to list them anyway.

'Like, New Earth or New London or New— wait, no, that already exists. New-New-something-or-other … New-New-England. New Paris—'

Poppy giggled. 'That just sounds silly.'

'Anyway,' Juno said. 'I don't want a new version of an old place. I want a better place, a—'

'— utopia.' Jesse finished her sentence, and Juno's face lit up.

'You can't be serious,' Eliot said.

'But it *will* be a utopia,' Astrid said. 'I believe it. Freedom. Peace. Lands flowing with milk and honey, caves glutted with diamonds. Just talking about it makes me excited.'

'To that end,' Juno said, tapping a button on her tablet, 'I've been doing some research. Commander Sheppard said something interesting – that there's no working model of this little civilization we have now. So I thought I'd look to the past for some examples. Take America—' she tapped another button on her tablet – 'I took the liberty of drafting a constitution, and I'd be grateful for your feedback.'

'A constitution,' Astrid said, laughing. 'It's so like you to focus on rules and laws. Do you want to go ahead and draft a friendship agreement for us all to sign? Do we need a sisterhood treaty?'

'I thought Britain had a constitution?' Poppy said. 'Why can't we use that one?'

Harry smacked his head. 'Poppy, this is fundamental. We don't have one.'

'We kind of do,' Eliot said. 'It's just not written down.'

'Yeah, it's been eight hundred years since Magna Carta,' said Harry. 'And that whole time we've just been waiting for Juno to draft one for us.'

'You laugh now,' Juno said, 'but imagine this scenario: we land on Terra-Two, in our great patch of land. We live happily for a while, with each other, with our way of doing things. But then another group lands. A group with their own leaders and social structure – likely bigger than ours. Then the birth mothers, young women brought over in cryogenic transporters, and everyone will have a different idea about how things should be. They want our land. They want our resources – how do we divide things fairly? How do we settle disputes? How do we punish wrong-doers, people who murder or rape?'

Poppy shuddered. 'Way to turn that into a horror story.'

'It's not a story,' Juno said, the volume of her voice rising with passion. 'It's history. This is how wars start. So I think we should decide now on our rules of law, our underlying philosophies. I've drafted a start. It's called the Damocles Document. *"We, the foremothers and forefathers, the first on Terra-Two. Have penned this document in the gladsome hope of the city we are to build . . ."*'

'The Damocles Document,' Jesse said, and heard the admiration in his own voice.

'Yes ...' Juno smiled, clearly pleased to find an ally. 'In future generations, we might be tempted to forget this time. This time that we spent labouring in the darkness. We might forget that the land beneath our feet, the sky, the trees, the whole of the Earth that we've discovered is a gift. Is sacred. So one of the fundamental tenets of our society will be to take care of it.'

'To live sustainably,' Jesse said and Juno nodded.

'We also need to remember that we left our family and country behind on the old Earth. When we arrive on Terra-two, we are all brothers and sisters. Including all the settlers who will come after us. I've realized on this ship that we can only live happily if we're all committed to a common aim—'

'But—' Harry began to interrupt, but Jesse shh-ed him violently.

'In the spirit of fellowship and charity I think that everyone in our country should have enough resources to flourish. By that I mean that no one should ever be homeless. Education, healthcare and free food. We will be a society that cares for the sick and for the disabled – although for a few generations only the healthy will be selected by the UKSA for colonization. Money is only for the practical purposes of sharing resources and cannot be hoarded. Every three years, all debts are cleared. And no one can own the land. We are simply jointly responsible custodians of the new world we've been given. We have to take care of it.'

'So where will we live?' Harry asked.

'In hab-labs, of course. At first.' Juno replied.

'But we don't own them?'

'Of course we don't own them. They were built by space agencies on Earth, we just look after—'

'No.' Harry shook his head. 'I'm not sure I like this at all. What if we find our nice patch of land, you know, water, good view etcetera, and the next group of people land, the Gamma or the European group, and try to take it from us?'

'That's exactly the point I'm making here,' Juno said. 'They will have to adhere to the law of the country they have entered.'

'And the law says that nothing belongs to anyone,' Harry said.

'The law says that we will allocate according to need. And then reallocate. No inheritance. No property.'

'"To each, according to his needs"?' Eliot said. 'So we're Marxists?'

Juno was beginning to get flustered. Jesse could tell by the way that she kept switching her weight from foot to foot, taking deep breaths.

'Don't you see, you guys,' she implored, 'don't you realize what a gift we have here? All the way through human history our behaviour falls into predictable patterns. Civil war, tribal divides, deforestation. We have a chance. Think about all the times on Earth when you thought, *What would I do, if I could do things differently?* What if we could start again, learning from all those mistakes? The experiment of Earth has been tried and failed. Now is the time for Earth 2.0.'

'Maybe,' said Eliot.

'Can I just say,' said Poppy, 'that I never *do* think that.'

'I think that we're not about to elect Juno the fascist dictator of our society,' said Harry.

Jesse could see that his words had stung. 'Hey,' he said, 'leave her alone.'

'Oh, come on,' said Harry. 'You're going to paint me as the bad guy this time too? We already have a Bill of Rights and *British* laws.

You're telling me we're just going to abandon eight hundred years of progress for her nutjob idea?'

'Yes!' Jesse surprised even himself with his fervour. 'This *is* progress. Moving forwards. I think that Juno's a genius. She's going to make history.' Juno's face softened, and she blushed.

'Okay,' said Harry, 'you're clearly saying that because you want to get into her pants.'

'I knew it,' said Poppy smugly.

A wave of shame and embarrassment came over Jesse and he saw the mortified look on Juno's face too.

'N-no . . .' she began.

'Well,' said Harry, 'I don't think he's much of a catch either. Must have been a real turn-off finding him in the airlock, wetting his pants.'

He'd had enough. Something inside Jesse, a taut wire of patience and self-control, snapped. He flew at Harry. He couldn't even tell where he'd hit him, just that he felt the impacts in his wrists, heard the soft pounding of flesh. He got about three blows in before Harry turned on him with the full force of his weight and threw him onto the ground, so hard that Jesse saw stars. Then came a punch to the solar plexus that left Jesse retching violently in pain. Another to his stomach that made his throat close, turned his lungs into a vacuum. Jesse suddenly became aware that Harry could kill him. He could taste his own blood in his mouth, hear distant screams of horror.

Harry grabbed the lamp off the stand nearby and Poppy lunged in front of him, snatching his arm. Harry was panting. He froze as if he'd woken from a dream. He dropped the lamp, letting the bulb shatter on the floor. Jesse scrambled back, his head spinning, hands sliding through a pool of blood and saliva.

JUNO

26.12.12

WHEN JUNO WOKE UP on Boxing Day, her head was pounding. She rolled out of bed, pulled on her dressing gown and climbed up to the infirmary to see if she could find some aspirin. Her nerves were frayed from the night before, horrifying flashes of Harry's face and Jesse's cries of pain. Underneath it, the sour taste of guilt. It was her fault. The argument had erupted over her Damocles Document. And Jesse had been injured defending her.

Juno found Fae seated at her desk in the infirmary, poring over a pile of documents, her reading glasses glinting in the lamplight. She pulled them off and rubbed her eyes.

'Good morning, Doctor,' said Juno.

'Good *afternoon*, Juno,' Fae said, then she lifted up a chart. 'You are just the person I wanted to talk to. Did you know that you seem to be losing weight?' Even in her stern voice, the words gave Juno a thrill. 'Are you eating all your rations?'

'Of course,' she lied.

Fae frowned. 'I'm going to recalculate your calorie requirements. You have been doing a lot of exercise.' That meant more food. Juno tried not to shudder. She normally drank at least a litre of water before the weigh-ins but she suspected that Fae was catching on – perhaps that was why she had scheduled this medical check so early in the morning.

Eating disorders had been a problem at Dalton. Despite the rigorous psychological testing and careful monitoring the students underwent, they were almost primed to develop them. Dalton was a perfect storm of stress and competition, intense exercise and emphasis on healthy eating. The young Type-A perfectionists who were likely to be selected for the programme lived in close quarters, girls and boys casting razor-sharp teenage eyes into each other's flesh. They had monthly weigh-ins and meetings with the psychological teams that were supposed to identify those suffering, but Juno had learned years ago how to get around them, rehearsed answers, water before weigh-ins, socks filled with rice, weights sewn into the lining of her knickers.

'Hey,' she said, rubbing her forehead. 'I have kind of a headache ...'

'It's not good.' Fae ignored her diversion. 'Your sister weighs two and a half stone more than you.'

'Astrid's always weighed more than me.'

'You need to eat more.' Fae said it like an order, her cool eyes unblinking. 'If you keep losing weight like this we will need to begin supervised mealtimes.' Juno had heard about this, students who were not allowed to leave the table until they'd eaten all of their food. 'And you may be relieved of some of your duties if you are not able to physically handle—'

'I can handle them,' Juno interrupted.

'I have a nutrition guide around here, actually ...' Fae turned around to open a drawer and began rifling through her things, sifting through paper-clipped sheets of paper and files. 'I know I have it somewhere. You were probably given one when you arrived, but maybe you need a quick reminder; about what artificial gravity does to your joints, about the importance of protein and fish oils . . .' She huffed out a frustrated breath, and scratched her head. 'I was sure it was here. I was meaning to put it up in the kitchen, actually. Perhaps I left it in my room.' Opening a final drawer, then slamming it shut, Fae said, 'I might go see if I can find it. Wait here a moment,' and then walked out.

Juno sat alone on the gurney, swinging her legs, when her eyes caught a pile of laminated folders Fae had left splayed across her desk. Juno glanced at the closed door and then, on a surprising impulse, slid off the gurney and grabbed one. Names were printed across them in Fae's neat hand. Juno's fingers found the thickest one, the one with Igor's name written atop most of the sheets. There were dense pages of text, letters signed off by several different doctors, charts, measurements, blood pressure readings. A glossy leaf slipped out onto the desk in front of her, and she caught it. A chest x-ray. She recognized the ivory cage of his lungs, the pale mass of a heart on the right-hand side, and held it up to the fluorescent light.

Something had been circled in green marker and, leaning in to examine it, she noticed a chalky smudge of white that filled the top left corner of the image of his lungs.

The sound of footsteps in the corridor made her heart leap. If Fae caught her looking over someone else's notes she would be furious. She might even dismiss Juno from training with her. As the door flew open, she jumped back and the papers fluttered across the desk.

'You?' Harry stood on the threshold, looking just as startled. Juno exhaled, scrabbling to put the files back in order.

'What are you doing?' he asked as she pushed the x-ray back into the folder and tucked the whole thing under the file marked Jesse Solloway.

'None of your business.' She could tell that her flushing cheeks had given her away, so she added, 'Fae asked me to find something for her, that's all.'

When she turned again, she realized that Harry wasn't really listening. He was looking back at the door in alarm. 'Hey ... er—' he lowered his voice. 'You know, I'm glad you're here actually.' As he stepped further from the shadow of the doorway, she saw how terrible he looked. A brown crust of dried blood was still visible under his nose and the skin on his face was starting to swell. The colour and texture of butchered meat.

Juno opened her mouth but Harry held up a hand, quickly. 'Look, I know what you're going to say.' Her impulse had been to tell him to go away but his shoulders slumped.

'Look, about what happened ... I didn't mean to – I mean – I didn't – I didn't ... I'd had a lot to drink, okay.' His voice had been a little slurred in Juno's memory. Juno raised an eyebrow. 'It went too far. It was a mistake. I'm sorry.'

'Have you said that to Jesse?' Juno asked.

'I will,' he promised. They stood in silence for a moment. Finally, Harry said, 'I have a lesson tomorrow. With Commander Sheppard on the simulator. He's finally going to teach me how to dock with *Orlando*.' He lowered his eyes. 'And I don't want to look like a mess.'

'You want my help?' Juno said.

'Please? I promise not to mock your Damocles Document.'

'Really?'

'Even if you drive us all into a communist dystopia. I'll say, "Heil, Juno."'

'There are so many things wrong with that statement.'

'Do I have to beg?'

Juno sighed. Her job as the ship's trainee medical officer forbade her from actually denying treatment, so she pulled the first aid kit off the shelf, glad to have an excuse to avoid Fae's nutrition chart.

They walked over the bridge and entered the upstairs bathroom. Harry pushed down the lid of the toilet seat and then sat down, the single hanging light shining between them and into his bloodshot blue eyes.

Juno worked in silence, wiping his skin, examining the cuts. Harry closed his eyes, slowly breathing in the disinfectant smell of the cubicle. His translucent skin was stretched tight across the freckled ridge of his nose. A bruise was just coming up on his cheekbone.

Two years ago, Harry'd been on the cover of *Seventeen* magazine. His skin had been sprayed bronze so that the blond hairs all over his body were like threads of silver. Throughout his adolescence, he had always looked three years older than he actually was, and the pages had been torn out and stuck to the backs of doors in the girls' locker room, biro-ed with hearts and names, and moustaches. Then there were the girls who arched their backs for him behind the iron walls of the sports shed as he pushed his fingers under the waistbands of their netball skirts. Juno had never understood the attraction.

Harry jolted upright as Juno touched the disinfectant to the torn skin on his lower lip. Opened his eyes and sucked air through gritted teeth.

'Does it hurt?' she asked. Harry nodded.

'Good,' she said. 'I'm glad it hurts.'

SHE FOUND JESSE A couple of hours later in the games room. She tried not to shudder at the sight of him. He was still in the Christmas jumper he'd worn the day before, only patches of blood matted the wool at his collar. His lip was purple and swollen like a plum. Behind the translucent display on his goggles she could see that one of his corneas was bleeding, and his eyes had a wild insomniac glint in them.

'Jesse,' she said, 'you look terrible.' Her heart filled with tenderness for him.

'Not now,' he said, with a frown of concentration.

'This is what you've been doing?' Juno said, incredulous. 'Playing a game?' Coagulated blood flaked at his knuckles and the fists in which he held the controller were swollen. The computer whined and the words GAME OVER appeared on the screen.

'You distracted me,' Jesse said, pulling off his VR goggles and tossing them aside in fury.

'You look—'

'Stop looking at me, then,' Jesse snapped.

'Have you been doing this all night?' she asked, pointing to the simulator.

'Yes.'

'Why?' Jesse gritted his teeth. When Juno realized that he wasn't going to tell her, she knelt down in front of him. 'Will you let me help you?'

'How?'

'I'm a medic.' She indicated her first aid kit.

'I need to keep trying,' Jesse said, picking up the controller again. She watched him in silent concentration: he was stuck on the eighth level, a twin player where he was co-piloting with a virtual commander. They kept losing control of the ship, running out of fuel before they entered interstellar space.

Juno watched him quietly for a while, although she suspected that her presence was making him even more self-conscious, unsteady and faltering, constantly pushing the wrong buttons.

'You know something,' said Juno, after two more failed attempts. 'Once my piano teacher told me—'

'You can play piano?' Jesse asked, rubbing at the marks carved into his face by the tight edge of his VR goggles.

'Well … now, I can only play "Chopsticks" and "Clair de Lune". But back when I used to play, my piano teacher said— have you ever heard of painting by numbers?' Jesse shook his head. 'It's a canvas with numbers for the colour of the paint. Kind of like colouring-in.' She rolled her eyes and waved a hand. 'Well, anyway. He said that my piano playing was like "painting by numbers" – I was playing the notes in the right order and the right way but with no overarching understanding of the piece that I was playing.'

Jesse frowned in confusion.

'Well, maybe you're doing that here.' She nodded at the simulator screen.

'Piloting by numbers?' Jesse smiled.

Juno shrugged. 'I mean, maybe think of the commander as your dance partner. Be more intuitive. Don't fixate on your manoeuvres, or on pressing the right combination of buttons at the same time. Let the computer lead, and keep your eyes on the goal.'

'Maybe.' Jesse rubbed his wrists, which were clearly sore from clutching the controller, and started the simulation again. This time, he let the commander lead and executed complementary manoeuvres. At first she thought Jesse was responding too slowly, but soon he relaxed and began to move more fluidly in response to the duck and shudder of the shuttle. Juno watched his ship flying on the screen, the shuttle gliding smoothly as a kite, dodging asteroids and slicing through interstellar space. By the time he was halfway through the level Jesse had sustained very little damage. She had been right. It was like a dance, and she could see that some part of his body had begun to finally understand the underlying logic of the game. The clock on the corner counted down the seconds. *Five . . . four . . . three . . .*

Jesse had almost made it to the goal – Tau Centauri. *Two . . .* sweat began to bead at the back of his neck and his arms trembled . . . *one . . .* Juno watched as Jesse let out a roar of triumph, and collapsed back in his seat.

'*Level completed,*' said the computer.

His score materialized on the screen. 185,342.

'Is that good?' Juno asked.

'It's better than Harry's,' he said. And she saw that he was smiling. 'I'm going to play his game. And I'm going to win.'

Juno looked down at his hands and saw the swelling at his knuckles, the skin scraped clean off them. He must be in pain, she thought, and she took the controller from him and placed it on the floor. Jesse relaxed.

Juno wiped the blood carefully away. Applied disinfectant. His fingers were trembling a little, and she turned his hands around in hers, traced the lines of his palms, noticed the pale-green spiral patterns at his fingertips from the fertilizer. 'You literally have green fingers—' she laughed. 'Like Cai.' And as she did, she thought about the morning she'd seen him alone in the greenhouse, and through his faded T-shirt she had seen the muscles he'd built over hours of labour. But she'd been moved by his tenderness, the gentle way he handled seedlings, the way he sang as he worked. The time he had tried to kiss her she'd run away, and Juno was sorry for it now because she craved his touch. Some nights she imagined what might have happened if she'd stayed, if she'd kissed him back.

'Are you in pain?' she asked.

'It hurts when I breathe,' Jesse said.

'Can I see?' Juno asked, worried he might have broken a rib. Jesse nodded, and pulled his T-shirt over his head. Juno took in the sight of him, the purple bruises like spilled wine down one side of his ribcage, a constellation of burst capillaries under his skin. She touched him gently, running her fingers along his collarbone, where she brushed the frayed cord of his necklaces, the ones he had collected on his travels – an eight-spoked wheel, a punctured scallop shell, a bronze 'Ohm'. She touched the hard wall of his sternum. She could tell he was in pain, because with every breath the muscles in his stomach rippled, and he gritted his teeth. When she laid her hand on his chest, she noticed that his heart was beating wildly.

Her eyes met his, and they shared a look of quiet understanding.

'I love you,' he said as if he'd only just realised.

A fierce rush of joy. Her skin prickled with goosebumps, and she smiled.

'Please, can I kiss you?' he asked.

And they kissed.

JESSE

02.01.13

THE NIGHT AFTER NEW Year's, Jesse was startled from sleep by the crash of breaking glass. The room was dark, save the glow of his reading lamp, and when he twisted around in bed he saw a thin shadow. Eliot in his pyjamas, glass glittering at his feet and blood dripping off his fingers.

For a minute, Jesse was sure it was a vision his sleep-addled brain had conjured up. But as his eyes adjusted to the gloom, the image grew clearer. 'Hey.' His voice was a rasp, and he coughed. 'Eliot?'

Eliot looked up at Jesse in surprise, staring around the room as if he had never seen it before. 'What happened?' he asked, panic rising in his voice.

'That's what I want to know,' Jesse said.

'My hands feel like they're on fire.'

Eliot moved to stand, but Jesse said, 'No, no', climbing down from his bunk as he did so. 'Don't move. There's glass every-where. You're bleeding.'

'Am I . . . ?'

Jesse tiptoed across the room and then switched the light on. Dark shadows stretched under Eliot's eyes. He was reflected a hundred times in the shards that littered the floor and bleeding so heavily it looked like tar. Dark rivulets coursing down his fingers. A hand-print like blackcurrant jam smeared across his gingham duvet cover. Jesse's stomach churned.

'That's a lot of blood,' he said. 'Maybe you need stitches.'

When Eliot looked up his eyes were full of horror. 'Jesse,' he whispered, his voice thick and low, 'I don't know what happened.'

'You broke a mirror.' Jesse nodded to the twisted frame on the edge of the bed.

'But I don't remember doing it.' Eliot began to shake.

'It's okay, Liston. You know, you were probably sleepwalking.'

'Did you see me?'

'No, I was sleeping too.'

They both looked around the room. Harry's bed was empty. Jesse supposed he might be in the control room still. It wasn't so late; the figures on the clock read 23.40.

'Come on, I'll help you get to Fae.'

But Eliot flinched at Jesse's touch. 'Can I tell you something?'

'Sure.'

'You won't tell anyone?' Jesse shook his head. Eliot bit his lip, his eyes wandering the room, then re-examining the door as if he was afraid that someone was about to burst in. Finally, he leant forward and said so quietly that Jesse had to strain to hear him, 'I think something's happening to me. I'm seeing things. And forgetting things, whole hours of time and—'

'Seeing things?' Jesse said. Eliot nodded slowly. 'Like what things?' But Eliot just shook his head. 'You know,' Jesse continued finally, 'astronauts travelling to Mars kept seeing white flashes of light, and no one knew why, for ages. Until, finally, scientists discovered that it was actually cosmic rays going through their optic nerves. Cosmic Ray Visual Phenomenon.'

Eliot didn't look comforted.

'Come on.' Jesse was careful not to step on any splinters of glass, and helped Eliot to his feet. The boy was unsteady, and shivering. They headed out of the room and into the infirmary.

When Fae asked them what happened Eliot told her that he had tripped and fallen against the mirror.

JESSE WOKE UP LATE the next morning and breakfast was almost over, the sound of chairs grinding against the floor as everyone left the kitchen to commence chores echoing up the corridor. There had been troubling news from NASA that night: the MMACS – the Mechanical, Maintenance, Arm and Crew Systems flight controller – had detected a problem on *Orlando*. Igor explained to them that they were worried there had been a hydrazine leak somewhere on the ship. Jesse saw the disappointment in everyone's eyes when they heard that their rendezvous with the *Orlando* might be delayed by a few days.

After breakfast, Jesse headed to the infirmary to check on Eliot, and found him playing his guitar, leaning over the instrument, strumming softly and singing.

'Hey.'

Eliot stopped mid-lyric and looked up, his mouth open, revealing his gappy teeth. 'You,' he said.

'I came to check on you. To see if you're all right and all.'

'I'm all right.' Eliot looked away. His hand was bandaged. Jesse had heard his cries of pain the previous night as Dr Golinsky picked glass from his flesh with tweezers. Jagged flaps of torn skin hung loosely from his knuckles in a way that made Jesse wince.

He came to sit beside Eliot on the gurney. 'You're pretty good,' he said, glancing at the silver strings of his guitar.

'I'm kind of rusty. Haven't practised in a while.' He tapped his fingertips with his thumb. 'I can feel my fingers have gone all soft. Your callouses go if you don't play for a while, but never completely.' He dropped his plectrum on the bed beside him, and Jesse picked it up. A black piece of plastic the size of a coin with the Union Jack stamped on it.

'It's not really the same without her. Singing, I mean.'

'Yeah, you and Ara were in a band together, right?' Jesse vaguely recalled a school concert at Dalton where Eliot and his skinny friends covered a song by Muse, their greasy hair in their eyes. Ara had fronted the band in stonewashed jeans, her brown thighs shining through the ripped denim. She sang like a siren, her eyes closed the whole time.

'They're not going to let me fly this mission. I don't think,' Eliot said, looking away.

'What do you mean?' Jesse asked. Harry and Commander Sheppard were going to pilot the shuttle to *Orlando*, then bus the crew back to the *Damocles*. A journey Jesse knew Harry was looking forward to, because Sheppard was allowing him to lead. In the passenger seat would be Poppy – a UKSA/NASA joint mission was big news, and of course ground control wanted Poppy to cover it. Eliot had also been selected to travel with them as the engineer.

'I'm not going. Ground control haven't cleared me.'

'Really?' Jesse asked, surprised.

'I've missed a couple of psych sessions.'

'Why?' Jesse had actually caught Eliot a few times hiding out in the engine room when he was supposed to meet with Fae.

'I think there's something wrong with me,' Eliot said in a

whisper. He ran the soft edge of his thumb along the thinnest string so it made a keening twang.

Jesse remembered what he had mentioned the night before, about seeing things.

'Do you think . . .' Eliot began, 'do you think that maybe it's possible there's someone outside?'

'Outside?' Jesse frowned in confusion, then nodded at the black window. 'You mean, out *there*?'

'Yeah,' said Eliot. 'And maybe we don't know about it.'

'Eliot . . .' Jesse wasn't sure whether or not to laugh, 'if there was someone out there, then they would be dead.'

'Maybe they are. Or, like, drowning.'

'I'm not sure what to say,' said Jesse. 'I think that's impossible.'

They were silent for a moment. Through the gap in the door they could hear the busyness of the ship. Someone was replacing a valve, and Jesse could hear the hollow clang of metal rattle behind the wall. Juno or Astrid dictating numbers from a machine readout. Commander Sheppard's voice, a comforting rumble in the distance.

'Maybe this is something you should be talking to Fae about.'

Eliot snorted. 'Forget I said anything.'

'Okay, sorry.' Jesse let his eyes wander for another moment. 'Do you think this has something to do with—'

'Ara?'

'Yeah.'

'Everyone thinks that everything has to do with her. That's all everyone wants to talk about. Her and why she did it. That note. That horrible note that she left on my phone. That I'll see until the day I die. And underneath it all I feel like . . .' He looked down at his bandaged hand.

'Like you can't remember who you are anymore?' Jesse asked.

Eliot nodded. 'My life before I met Ara is a blur, I can't remember, properly, who I even was or how I ever made myself happy. But then, my life with Ara was all about ... Ara. I feel okay telling *you* this because it's not as if you really knew her, like the others. They love her. We all do. Did. It hurts like hell, missing her. So much that I haven't been able to focus much on the work I'm supposed to do with Igor lately. I haven't even sketched up any ideas for an invention.

'I thought I'd spend my life with her, on Earth, on Terra-Two. I hoped that we'd die at the same time. I thought there was only one way that my life could turn out. But now ...' He lowered his gaze and stopped himself.

'But now ... ?" Jesse asked.

JESSE

29.01.13

THE FIRST MONTH OF the New Year hurtled by and from then on, whenever Jesse slept, he'd dreamt of flight. The control panel illuminated before him, navigating the constellations with the ease of light across water. For five weeks, he made a habit of running the simulator every single day. Once he finished his chores in the greenhouse, he would march down to the games room and play until late into the night. Sometimes, he awoke to the sound of the morning bell, tangerine sunrise-light from the hall bleeding under the door. Flying goggles still strapped to his face, etching tender creases beneath his eyes and across his brow.

As he ascended the levels, the games became more beautiful. Jesse took more time to notice the grandeur of the sky, the exquisite detail of the virtual cockpit. In the intermediate levels, planetary nebulae and the remnants of supernovae unspooled in the foreground in vivid conflagrations of light.

Even with his new, more intuitive, understanding of the games, Jesse would still get stalled for a week on a single level, unable to master the delicate manoeuvres required to steer through a cloud of accelerating space junk, or to rendezvous with another craft. During those times, the task would plague him. His frazzled mind projected planets, darkly visible in the foreground, particles of dust suddenly and momentarily iridescent before a careening asteroid knocked him abruptly back into consciousness.

One fine night, by some miracle of dexterity, Jesse managed to skate through every challenge. Though the hull of his ship was fairly dented, it remained unbreached. He dodged debris and space junk and avoided sudden death by decompression. His heart pounding and palms sweating, Jesse's mind narrowed into a corridor of exhausted focus. But he stayed true. He met every challenge with triumph, the sticky frustrating levels – eight, eleven, thirteen – he ascended them all.

How had it happened? Was it that keen blinkered attention which arose from weeks of sleep deprivation and determination? Was it that his exhaustion made him reckless and bold? Perhaps he had run the simulation so many times that something of the computer's underlying logic had seeped into his consciousness.

Experts said it took around 200 hours of flying to become a

space pilot, and, at five- or six-hour stretches every night, Jesse had managed at least that since Christmas.

Finally, here he was, on the last level, at the final leg of the challenge. Landing. He reached a half-familiar green and blue planet. Lapis coastlines and snow-white whorls of gorgeous sky. *Home?* was the message that flickered on his screen. 'I hope so,' he said to himself out loud. Hands shaking as his cockpit filled with cobalt light from the little planet. The challenge was to land at just the right angle, at just the right speed, in the thick atmosphere. But Jesse had an intuition for it now; he'd decelerated through atmospheres as thick as Venus's – ninety times thicker than Earth's and obscured by sulphuric acid clouds – and survived. This was easy. This was joyful. He slid down into the temperate embrace of the troposphere and brought his lander shuddering to solid ground. He climbed out, his avatar stumbling in the gravity, and stared, for the first time, at an ocean.

The screen went blank.

Jesse had been gripping the controllers so tightly that he could feel the blood throbbing in his fingertips. The words SIMULATION COMPLETE dazzled against the static.

Jesse had finished the game at 6 a.m., just as the alarm in his bunk would be going off. He'd played since dinner ended the night before, at 8 p.m. In game time, he had travelled for half a century.

As he sat back in the mock commander's chair, Jesse realized that this was the moment he had been waiting for. He had spent almost a year struggling to catch up with the other members of the Beta. He had been cowed and intimidated by their learning and by Harry's formidable skill as a pilot. But, according to this single metric, he had far surpassed them all. He knew everything there was to know about flying. Everything the computer could teach him. Peeling his hands off the controller, he shouted in delight. He had beaten Harry, at last, in the only game that really mattered.

WHEN JESSE AWOKE, HIS heart still full of his victory, he was not surprised to see Juno standing above him. In his half-dreaming haze, he was like a gladiator. A hero. Odysseus returning to claim Penelope. He could have kissed her she was so beautiful, crowned in fluorescent light. But she was clearly upset. 'Oh,' she said, wiping one eye, tears dripping off her thick lashes, 'you're here.' She sounded a little disappointed.

'I'm always here,' Jesse said, sitting up from the semi-recumbent commander's chair. His muscles were stiff, eyes itchy with sleep-grit, and he pulled his sweaty goggles off and snapped them like a rubber band against the floor.

'You are,' she said. Juno sat opposite him and exhaled. She looked as if she'd only just woken up. Dressed in blue paisley pyjamas, her hair still tucked under a satin scarf.

'What's the matter?' Jesse felt miserably inclined to ask, although what he wanted to do was to show her his high score.

'Solomon says he's calling a meeting in the next twenty minutes, and I think . . . I think he's going to tell us that Igor is sick.'

'What?' Jesse asked.

Juno nodded, and rubbed her red eyes. 'I think he has cancer.' Even the word gave Jesse goosebumps.

'How do you know?' he asked.

'I saw it on an x-ray. A mass in his lungs.'

'We have an x-ray machine here?'

'No.' Juno rolled her eyes. 'It was taken on Earth.'

'So, you mean that Igor had cancer on Earth and he didn't tell us.'

'Yes.'

Jesse swore under his breath. 'How long have you known?'

'A little while,' Juno admitted, lowering her gaze. 'Since Christmas, actually. But I'm not the only one. I mean, I saw it in his file, so the seniors, Fae at least and probably Commander Sheppard too, must have known since before the launch.'

'What?'

'Yes.' Juno leant forward. 'They lied to us, Jesse.'

'I don't understand.' Jesse was already beginning to feel his sleepless night. 'How could they let a dying man come to space?'

'That's what I want to know,' Juno said. 'Especially when you consider that some candidates were excluded from the programme because they were flat-footed.'

'They're planning to tell us now?'

'I think they were planning to tell us after we reached Saturn. Once they know we can't decide to come back.'

'So why is Solomon telling us today?'

'Because of Astrid.' Juno gritted her teeth with the anger she reserved for her sister. 'Astrid and her stupid dreams. She said she's been having dreams that Igor is dying. She told Fae, who accused her of accessing restricted medical files. Fae was furious, that's what all the shouting over breakfast was about.'

Jesse hadn't heard it.

'Astrid looked at private files? That doesn't sound like her.'

'I don't know ... I never know how Astrid knows the things she knows.' Juno's eyes drifted away for a moment at a memory. 'You know people in our old church used to say that she had the gift of prophecy.'

Jesse frowned. 'Like Moses and Ezekiel?'

'Kind of,' Juno said. 'But we grew up in a charismatic church.' She caught his blank look. 'You know. Groups of people speaking in tongues and laying hands on each other.'

Jesse imagined it something like the humid churches his parents had visited in India, young girls speaking in tongues, hot airless rooms, hectic crowds trembling and singing. 'Do you believe in that stuff?' Jesse asked. 'Prophecies, miracles, that kind of thing?'

Juno shrugged. 'I believe that my sister is an attention-seeker. She'd swoon during worship and everyone would treat her like a movie star. I thought it might be different, going to a school where there wasn't much of a place for that – you know, Dalton was not religious at all – but, in some ways, she's worse now. You know that she really believes in the New Creationists. I used to think the best thing was not to encourage her.' She turned to Jesse. 'Does that make me sound mean?'

Jesse shook his head.

'Do *you* believe in that stuff?' she asked. 'I mean, I know you don't believe in God, but prophecies and miracles and stuff.' Jesse gazed at the leaping static on the simulator screen. He thought about the prophecy spoken over his life almost a decade ago, the man who told him he wouldn't reach twenty. The prophecy that had led him here, into the belly of a ship soaring through space. Thought about his own sister, who had defied all expectations and survived malaria. The head-scratching doctors who had never been able to explain it. The way her heart had really stopped for a minute and then begun again. And even the mystery of space itself, the vast ocean of things interstellar bodies could never explore or explain. But instead of saying any of that, he said, 'No.'

Juno held out her hand to him and pulled him out of the commander's seat. 'Come on,' she said. 'We don't want to be late for the meeting.'

30.01.13

IT WAS WORSE THAN any of them had imagined. Fae told them that Igor was sick. An aggressive form of cancer that had begun in his lungs but had spread into his bones, his spinal cord. Fae didn't say that he was dying, but it was in everything that she said. Astrid and Poppy began to cry. Commander Sheppard looked away. Eliot twisted in his seat, cracking his knuckles and fidgeting. Harry was bone-white. The seniors were in their own kind of pain, because this announcement somehow made the dismal diagnosis more true. They had all known Igor for years. Commander Sheppard shared his dry sense of humour and called him, jokingly, comrade. And now not only was Igor facing death, but the crew had to watch him die. Even sitting across from the old cosmonaut, Jesse could hear the wet rasp of mucus in his lungs, the shuddery way that every breath came, a quiet struggle. The thought of losing a teacher and mentor, the most vital link to the past and the life they were leaving behind, made Jesse feel strangely orphaned.

'I don't understand why any of us weren't told this before,' Juno said, gritting her teeth.

'We're telling you now,' Commander Sheppard replied with a curt nod. He was the only one standing, at the far end of the table.

'And frankly,' said Fae, 'if it was only my decision I would have waited until a better time.'

'A better time?' Juno snorted. 'What would be a good time to tell us our crewmate is dying? After the funeral?' Everyone's eyes flitted to the other end of the room, where Igor was perched on a stool near the breakfast counter.

Jesse stared at him, noticing, only then, the skeletal lines of his hands, the slight quiver in his thumbs. He broke the silence by asking, sheepishly, 'How far along are you? Is it – I mean – stage . . . ?'

'Stage three,' Igor said.

'I don't remember what that means,' Poppy said, 'Does that mean it's too late for treatment? Radiation or chemotherapy? Our neighbour downstairs got breast cancer but they operated on her and she got better. That happens right? Cancer's not an automatic death-sentence.'

'True . . .' Fae lowered her gaze.

Jesse remembered something he'd read in a textbook. 'Survival rates with lung cancer are amongst the lowest of all cancers.' He lay awake at nights imagining metastasis, little fingerlings of cancer burrowing into his chest like worms in the cool flesh of an apple. 'Lung cancer is the most common cause of cancer-related deaths.' By the time you had a cough, there was rarely anything anyone could do.

'Would you shut up?' said Harry, his knuckles white.

'What Jesse says is true,' said Igor. 'It's one of the reasons I have chosen not to seek treatment, and opted only for palliative care.' There was a soft intake of breath across the table. Juno sat up suddenly, almost sending a cold mug of black coffee toppling.

'But, I'm not dead yet!' Igor continued, cheerfully. 'For the most part my symptoms have not affected my ability to do my job. Just a cough, loss of appetite.' He shrugged as if it was a small thing, as if none of them had noticed the yellow tinge of his anaemic skin. The way he leant heavily against the wall sometimes to catch his breath. 'With pain control, I will make it to Saturn and launch the drive, and then . . .'

'And then . . . ?' Astrid's eyes were glassy and she was shaking.

'And then my mission will be complete,' said Igor. 'It took the hard work and sacrifice of thousands of people to get you this far. I'm just honoured to be one of them.'

The statement made Jesse feel a little queasy. His stomach ached with pity.

'How long have you known?' Juno asked.

'A long time now.'

'There was concern amongst the leadership team,' said Commander Sheppard, 'and the psychological support team on the ground, that this news could negatively impact crew morale.'

'That was undesirable considering the upcoming mission to Europa,' Fae said. 'So we decided to share the news after we passed by Saturn.'

Poppy stifled another sob, burying her face in the scuffed sleeve of her dressing gown.

'But we found out,' Juno said. 'We found out because we're not children. You can't keep things like this from us. We're teammates, crewmates. We have to trust each other. That's what you always say, and now, once Igor is . . . once we're past Saturn, the most qualified engineer on this ship will be Eliot. What happens if something goes wrong?'

'We'll still be receiving some messages from our highly competent team of engineers. They can provide additional support.'

'Yeah, through email,' Juno said. 'What about when we lose contact with Ground completely?'

'Commander Sheppard worked on several Mars missions as an engineer,' Fae said.

'Don't you understand?' Eliot's voice was tight, his eyes glistening from behind his mop of black hair. 'They don't tell us anything. No one talks about anything, they just watch and stare and wait to see what we'll do. There's someone out there.' He threw an arm out to indicate the darkness behind the window. 'Someone is dying out there. We all know it, and no one is talking about it.'

Everyone glanced around in confusion.

'Okay.' Commander Sheppard held up his hands. 'We need to calm down. We know this is difficult news to hear – everyone needs time to take it all in. I am cancelling tutorials today – everyone take the day to reflect, absorb this news and think about how we can support each other moving forward.'

Eliot let out a howl of frustration and kicked his chair over, causing Astrid to leap back in surprise. 'That's exactly what I mean,' he said, before racing from the room, leaving the others in a shocked silence.

Fae exhaled heavily and put her head in her hands.

'Don't you think he's been acting … erratically?' Harry asked.

'Leave him alone,' said Cai. 'He's been through a lot.'

Solomon dropped a soggy teabag into the disposal and set his mug down firmly. He turned to address the Beta. 'If you have any questions don't hesitate to speak to any one of us about what's happening and how you're feeling. The senior crew have been aware of Igor's prognosis since before we left Earth. We're prepared and the mission to Terra-Two will continue uninterrupted.

'I know this is very upsetting to consider, but the reason we have such high expectations of all of you is because this mission is actually about you and not us. None of us really wants to think about it, but the UKSA opted to begin this colonization mission with young people because Fae, Cai and I will also not live as long as the six of you. And some day in the future you will have to deal with all of us passing away. But you'll be lucky to have each other to rely on.'

Jesse's stomach twisted at the thought of it. Commander Sheppard folded his arms. 'The best thing to do when you receive troubling news is to put your head down, work hard, focus on the future. And when you're finished you'll feel a lot better. I promise.'

IN THE FOLLOWING DAYS, Jesse watched as the news of Igor's sickness affected the Beta members differently. Both Harry and Eliot seemed to become acutely aware of how much they still needed to learn from the senior crew. Harry spent sleepless nights on the control deck or on the simulator, practising manoeuvres again and again. Eliot took to furiously recording everything that Igor said during their tutorials, always interrogating his responses further: 'But how will I know when there's a problem with the injector ...?' Trailing off without adding what they were all thinking, *How will I know when you're gone?*

Poppy volunteered to take over most of Igor's chores in addition to her own. An act that endeared her to Juno who, in her spare time, requested every document in the ship's database about cancer and could be found in the kitchen reading them. Jesse discovered her furiously underlining passages in *The Emperor of All Maladies*, her nails bitten to the quick.

'Cancer is just a word,' Astrid told them once over lunch.

'Right, a word that describes a biological reality,' Juno said.

Astrid rolled her eyes. 'You think everything is so simple.' Astrid was suddenly full of stories about people whose conditions defeated medical understanding but had recovered: the friend of a friend or the daughter of a pastor whose tumours disappeared, who defied death for decades in spite of a terminal diagnosis. She looked around the table and announced, 'We will, all of us, make it to Terra-Two.'

Jesse threw himself into work, as their commander had suggested. Pruning the long weeds that curled around the spires in the greenhouse, documenting the new shoots that seemed to be sprouting curly heads overnight, everywhere, as if the garden had suddenly chosen to wake up. Jesse had been delighted to find that the fruits were finally growing. His heart leapt with excitement when he noticed the first head of a tomato bursting from a vine, and fat strawberries, still sour. It felt like springtime, everything lush and blossoming. Jesse and Cai had toiled over long vats of hydroponic liquids and the shallow trays of soil for almost a year and now here they were, coming to their reward. In only a few weeks they would have harvested enough crops for the crew to subsist almost solely on fruits and vegetables reared in the darkness of space and yet tasting deliciously of home. Jesse could not wait.

Even as he worked, Jupiter cast its eerie amber light through the domed ceiling. He'd orbited it before; in the game, narrowly avoiding being tugged into the planet's fierce gravity a hundred times. It was more dazzling in real life, of course. Those furious red rings, whorls and flurries surging and descending on convection currents across its gaseous surface.

What would it be like to see Saturn from this vantage? When he'd been young, Jesse had imagined the texture of each of Saturn's rings was spiral-grooved, like a vinyl record. That he could roller-skate across their flat surface, taking in the heavens. In Dalton, he'd learned that the rings were actually made of millions of shards of ice and rock, some of them small as a grain of sand and others large as a car.

They were accelerating every second, and in eight months they would be the first humans to see the planet and its giant moons close up. But the thought of reaching it frightened Jesse a little. He'd once heard Sheppard refer to it as 'the Rubicon' – the point of no return. Once they approached the planet, Igor would launch the gravity-assist drive. An engine that would push them through the gravitational field of Saturn at the right trajectory to pick up some of its gravitational energy. They would begin to travel at about one seventh the speed of light, fast enough to soar into interstellar space and towards James Dalton's binary stars. Once they'd reached their neighbouring solar system, they would swing by the planets in the opposite direction, at the right angles, to slow their speed and allow the *Damocles* to finally be captured in the orbit of Terra-Two. By then, both Eliot and Harry would be in their forties, skilled enough to steer the ship and perform the engine burn entirely without the senior crew. And Igor would not be there to see it.

It was this fact that upset Jesse the most. Igor would never see Terra-Two. Finally, one evening, Jesse mustered the courage to talk to the old man about it. 'Doesn't it bother you?' he asked, lingering behind in the kitchen once their group lesson was over for that afternoon. 'I heard that the reason you defected from the USSR, the reason you agreed to work on this mission, was because you knew you would be old by the time the project was over but the UK Space Agency promised that no matter what, you could fly with us. '

'You heard right,' Igor said.

'But I don't understand why,' Jesse said, 'when you …' He didn't want to say it out loud. He looked down and fiddled with a loose thread on his overalls.

'I will have completed my own mission,' Igor said. 'We all have a different mission, Jesse. We're all compelled by different gods, fleeing different demons. Shall I tell you something?'

Jesse leant across the table and nodded.

'You know, I was one of the first men to set foot on Mars.' Jesse nodded again. Everyone had seen the historic picture of the Soviets pushing their flag into the surface of Mars. Four astronauts. Igor had been the youngest man on the team. 'I returned like a man in love,' Igor said. 'Once I was back on Earth, I longed for the flight, for the sight of my planet from a vast distance, for a vision of the stars unobscured by atmosphere, for the sensation of weightlessness that was so natural to me it was as if I'd been waiting for flight the entirety of my life.'

He spoke with such fervour his eyes lit up. He spoke about how he'd gone on to serve longer and longer missions in spartan hab-labs on the surface of the red planet, digging trenches to shelter from solar storms, performing experiments and broadcasting his results back to Earth. It was not an easy or glamorous life, but it was everything he had ever wanted. When Earthbound, he'd slump into a depression, slip out of the bed where his wife slept, pass his children's bedrooms to stand outside and behold the sky. Aching like a lovesick mariner.

'When I learned about my sickness,' Igor said, touching the

bony hollow of his chest, 'I knew what I had to do.' He left his wife, his children and grandchildren behind in Norilsk and smuggled with him the plans for the gravity-assist drive — the key to interstellar travel.

'So,' he said to Jesse, 'I try my best. I kept myself healthy as possible until launch. When we reach Saturn, my work will be done.'

His wish was for his body to be launched naked into the vacuum of space, where his cells would not decay and he'd drift for eternity by icy moons and elliptic galaxies, the Eagle Nebulae and the Pillars of Creation, by star nurseries and the resplendent remnants of supernovae. Some part of him would be an eternal witness to the collapse and creation.

'There are worse things,' he told Jesse, 'than death.' And, for the first time, Jesse believed it.

JESSE

07.02.13

A NEW DATE FOR the *Orlando* mission was selected by the NASA and UKSA directors in London and Houston. This time, it happened to fall on Jesse's twentieth birthday.

The morning of the mission, piano music skittered into his dreams, and Jesse ascended into consciousness picturing David Bowie's mismatched eyes. 'You know how it goes,' Eliot said with a smile, turning the volume dial up on his speakers. '"Is there life on Maaaaaaars?"' he shouted as the cellos began to play. Jesse laughed, rolling out of bed and rubbing his eyes. Eliot was already dressed in his flight suit, although a dried crust of toothpaste flaked around the left side of his mouth.

'You must know the song?' he said as the strings reached their first buzzy crescendo.

'Of course I know the song,' Jesse said, getting to his feet. And they caught the chorus again; this time they shouted it.

'Happy birthday, man.' Harry said, clapping Jesse on the shoulder. 'Old man.'

'Thanks,' Jesse couldn't help but remember waking up in his bedroom one year ago. It had been a miserable day, overcast and threatening snow. He'd just returned from months of training for the backup crew and abandoned all hope that he would ever set foot on this ship.

They all sang the chorus again, one final time, at the top of their lungs. Jesse was so happy to be alive, to be on the *Damocles*, with these people that he almost cried.

'Do you feel any older?" Eliot asked as the string arrangement began its glissando slide into the song's finale.

'I feel years older,' he said. And then there was silence.

'Hey,' Harry said, and raised his eyes to the window, 'look.'

Europa loomed large in their view. Jesse had seen the moon so many times in the piloting simulation that the sight of it gave him an odd sense of homecoming. He had sacrificed two weeks of nights to level eight on the simulator, trying to lock a new module onto a docking port. A Sisyphean task that required the most delicate manoeuvres he had ever mastered, shifting the module an inch a minute, only to crash at the final moment when the muscles in his wrist seized with cramp.

In the window, that morning, Europa's surface looked brittle and delicate as the edge of an egg, shining with so much reflected light.

Suddenly, Jesse gleaned something of the enormity of the *Orlando* mission. The American crew were hoping to make the moon habitable. It had an oxygen atmosphere, and an ocean roiled metres beneath the frozen crust of the planet, two ingredients necessary for life. But it was still far from hospitable. It was around -160°C at the equator, a temperature at which cell membranes crystallize and fracture. It was pelted daily by radiation and nothing could grow. The *Orlando*'s crew had nevertheless progressed in leaps and bounds, engineering single-celled organisms that were now able to multiply in sub-zero temperatures. Their hope was to eventually terraform the planet. Atom by atom, they planned to bend it into submission. To cover the crust with mutant lichen and moss, to one day fill the sea with alien plants. It would be decades before Europa was terraformed, if ever. Long before that happened, Jesse and his crew would be on Terra-Two, breathing the temperate air and leaping into lagoons.

When he was dressed, Jesse stepped into the crew module to a chorus of 'Happy Birthday' from the crew. Commander Solomon told him that as a reward for gaining such a high score on the simulator – and because Eliot's injured hand had still not healed – Jesse would be joining them in the shuttle. Jesse was so overjoyed to hear it that he shouted and punched the air.

The crew on *Orlando* had also recorded a message.

'Happy birthday!' yelled Dr Sie Yan.

'We're wishing Jesse Solloway of the *Damocles* a very happy birthday,' said her husband, Captain Omar Briggs, by her side. 'We're looking forward to seeing you folks soon, and eating dinner with you on the *Damocles*.'

In five hours, Poppy, Harry and Jesse would accompany Sheppard as he docked their shuttle onto the *Orlando* and met this couple who'd lived in Jupiter's orbit for a decade. And in just over twenty-four hours, they would ferry them and the rest of the *Orlando*'s crew to the *Damocles* for dinner.

Jesse tried to imagine five other people in their kitchen, seated around the table, passing on gifts and letters from Earth and tucking into a meal. How different would it feel? Five other people who also knew what it took to build a life under LED lamps. He was looking forward to the week they would spend together, and felt as if he knew them already, especially the three younger astronauts: sullen but brilliant Kennedy, the xeno-biologist, who liked the same synth-heavy glam-rock as Eliot; Cal and James, who looked as if they could be Harry's brothers. Both MIT graduates, engineers, boisterous and competitive but friendly, their laughter booming down the hall whenever they greeted the others on the video calls. Kennedy, James and Cal had trained at the Armstrong Astronaut Academy in Houston, an imposing rival of Dalton. At the age of twenty, the three of them had left the Earth to join Omar and his wife on the *Orlando*, and they would not return until the year 2020.

Because of their age, Jesse felt that the Beta had the most in common with these three astronauts, but he knew that Commander Sheppard and Captain Omar were old friends. Omar was the godfather of Solomon's son, and even though he had never met the boy in person he downlinked videos of himself reading bedtime stories, all the way to Earth.

'Can you see us?' Jesse asked over the video feed.

'Of course we can,' Captain Briggs said. 'I could spot the *Damocles* a lightyear away. She's a real beauty.'

'We should be docking with *Orlando* in ten hours,' said Solomon.

A shiver ran down Jesse's spine. That morning he attributed it to excitement.

THEY DEPARTED FOR THE *Orlando* with an air of jubilation, jostling and bouncing in their seats like children on a school trip. It was strange to find themselves in the shuttle again, the same vehicle in which they had left Earth months ago. Only this goodbye had been through an airlock, with no cheering crowds. Before she'd said goodbye, Juno had kissed Jesse. Strapped in the cramped shuttle, he was distracted by the thought of her – he could still taste the sweetness of her in the corner of his mouth.

As they sped towards the *Orlando* and away from the *Damocles*' gravity, Jesse could feel every metre by the lightness in his stomach. He had always enjoyed the feeling of weightlessness.

'I want you to remember,' Commander Sheppard said from his chair beside Harry in front of the control panel, 'that this is a lesson as well as a mission. It's the first time you three will have to practise a real-life scenario that you have been training for. Different equipment, a smaller environment than the *Damocles*. I'm looking forward to taking a back seat. You've all been working hard, and I'm proud of you.'

Poppy lifted up her camera and handed it to Jesse. 'Press this button to start recording,' she instructed, and he did what she asked. A minute later she was smiling at the screen. '*Dobriy den*, *Bon soir*, or good afternoon to you all. Welcome aboard the *Congreve*,' she said voice taut with excitement. 'It's about 1 p.m. here and we've finally set off for the *Orlando*, orbiting Europa – Jesse, hold it up a little higher – my job is to work on the communication. On a mission like this it's vital that we remain in constant contact—' she indicated the mass of wires and monitors behind her, and pointed to where Commander Sheppard and Harry were strapped into the pilot seats, '—with the crew on *Orlando* station and the crew back on the *Damocles*. Information and readouts about *Orlando* and the position of the shuttle will be downlinked to me on these computers. Which is important for us as we dock, a very delicate operation.'

'And how's it going now?' Jesse had been instructed to ask.

'I can happily say that all systems are nominal.' She winked at the camera. 'Which is space jargon for "operating as planned".'

Could she imagine the people watching? The young students from Dalton, or in classrooms in Shanghai, the constant replay on the Space Channel. All those distant eyes on her.

Poppy took the camera and turned it on Jesse, who saw his own black eyes reflected in the lens.

'Can you briefly explain your job on this mission?' Jesse hated this part, reciting, in a chipper voice, a watered-down version of their various responsibilities.

'I'm acting in place of the ship's usual engineer, Igor Bovarin, and Junior Flight Engineer Eliot Liston, who unfortunately is still recovering from his minor hand injury.'

'Most of your job doesn't really start until we get close to *Orlando*, right?' Poppy pushed.

'Right.' Jesse pointed to the computer in front of him, which displayed a digital image from the shuttle's external camera with a grid overlaid. 'This system uses radar and information from the *Damocles* to determine exactly where *Orlando* is. If we looked out the window right now, we couldn't tell it from another star in the sky. But, in an hour or two, when we get closer, the system will spot it, lock on and we'll know we're getting close.'

'That's when your job really begins,' Poppy encouraged. 'Can you explain it?'

Jesse shifted in his seat; the force of gravity was halving every minute and he was beginning to feel the stretch in his spine. Astronauts grew a few inches in microgravity – a change that was accompanied, at least in Jesse's case, by almost constant back pain.

'*Orlando* is in a very low orbit above Europa. Every ninety minutes it does one rotation of the moon – which means it's actually moving quite fast. Our job is to catch up with it and dock with it while we're both moving.'

'Well, actually – that's my job.' Harry's sharp eyes appeared in the lens and he waved for the camera. 'I'm the pilot for this mission. I ...'

Jesse leant back as he listened to Harry continue. It was difficult to watch him in the pilot's seat. Jesse's fingers tingled with longing. He wanted to be seated before the controls. He wanted to feel the hum of them beneath his palms.

As most of his job began when they got close to station, so he had several hours yet to sit and twiddle his thumbs. Every time he looked out the window his home, the *Damocles*, was smaller. It looked like a beetle, the command module a glassy head bolted to the fat steel thorax of the living modules, the kitchen and bedrooms. Most spectacular was the enormous vaulted abdomen of the greenhouse, a space garden reflecting the stars. Jesse imagined Cai watching them depart in his lab, amongst the long grass. Was Juno watching him too? Were the other young astronauts, Kennedy, Cal and James on the *Orlando*, watching them approach? Perhaps they were sitting on a sofa in their own living modules, their feet tucked under them, searching the sky for the shuttle.

After an hour of flying he didn't need to look out the small porthole of a window to know how far they had come. The *Damocles* was only a round speck in the sky and they were in microgravity. Jesse's face had begun to swell and his back ached.

'You're moon-faced,' Poppy said, her auburn hair floating up around her ears, her cheeks doughy and pink, the veins in her neck bulging. She unstrapped her seatbelt and grabbed her knees, turning a slow somersault in the cramped space of the shuttle. She finished upside-down and waved to the camera with a swollen grin. Jesse swallowed an anti-nausea pill, tightened his seatbelt and tried to sleep.

4 P.M.

HIS COMPUTER WOKE HIM when it detected the station. The words 'LOCKED ON' flashed in red letters in the corner of his screen. From this distance, *Orlando* was like a white spider in the sky, although it looked larger on his display.

The space station resembled the *Damocles* – a hulking mass of solar panels, pressurized modules and trusses, assembled in space. The American flag painted on its side spanned ten metres. It was far more spacious than *Damocles*, built for circling in low orbit over the pale moon and not for interstellar travel. At the time, the *Orlando* was the single most expensive item ever constructed in human history – that was before the Off-World Colonization Programme.

'*Can you hear me* Damocles*? Congreve? Comm check.*'

It was Juno's voice in his headset, and it startled him into alertness.

'I'm here,' Jesse told her.

'*Is it beautiful?*' she asked, breathless. Jesse nodded at the internal camera feeding back to the ship. He was captivated by the prospect, the lovely light radiating off the frozen moon. The orbiting station looked small in comparison.

'*All right,*' came Igor's gruff voice through the line. '*Plenty of time for daydreaming and chit-chat when we're all on station. Now it's time for the real work to begin. Jesse, are you ready?'*

It was a game of cat and mouse. As their shuttle slowed they would enter into Europa's orbit, just above the station in what was called a 'phasing orbit'. Jesse's job was to monitor the engine burn as they made their first orbital transfer. Suddenly the *Congreve* was a hive of activity, Harry and Commander Sheppard issuing commands and talking into their headsets with Omar Briggs, while Igor instructed Jesse over the headset and Poppy kept the channels operating. Jesse could see Captain Briggs' face on the screen, examining the incoming data from the *Damocles*.

'All systems nominal,' Commander Sheppard said over the intercom.

'I didn't catch that?' came the captain's voice. Commander Sheppard groaned and unlatched his helmet, fiddled for a moment with his mic. 'Can you hear me now?'

'Loud and clear,' Omar confirmed.

'Having a bit of trouble with my helmet and mic.' Sheppard exhaled. 'Ready for rendezvous in ninety minutes. Harry, issue the command for docking probe extension.'

They were close, and it was a great feeling. Jesse had watched the videos of docking procedures, seen the probe lock onto the port on a space station and then, once the hatch opened, all the hugs and laughter as the crew on the shuttle greeted the crew on the station. He remembered the air of exhilaration. After the long journey, to be united. The crew on one station had lined the walls with banners and balloons. It had been like a party. That was what awaited them in under two hours.

*

BY THAT POINT, THE shuttle was so cold that Jesse could see his breath in the air, and ice condensing and cracking on the inside of the little portholes, forming spidery white veins along the edges. He pulled a pair of gloves on and shuddered. His lips and chin had grown numb while he slept, and he wondered how Harry had retained his mobility in the sub-zero temperatures.

'The crew on *Orlando* have performed an orbital boost that puts us in almost the same orbit. Now, as we descend to dock with them,' Poppy was saying into her microphone, 'we're being captured by the moon's gravity. Which is about a tenth of Earth's. We're flying just above station now.' She pushed out of her seat and held the camera near the frosted window. Jesse could just make out the tiny shadow that their shuttle cast over the station's hulking frame.

'It's a very tense moment now, as we reach the space station,' she said in a shallow whisper. 'If the thrusters fail to slow down the shuttle could crash into the station—'

'Harry's about to perform a side-burn so that doesn't happen,' Solomon reassured them, with a relaxed smile at the camera.

That had happened to Jesse a few times on the simulator. He'd come close to the station but failed to slow down in time and crashed into a solar array or, worse, an entire module. At the speed the *Congreve* and the *Orlando* were travelling, even a small collision would be enough to tear through both hulls. He felt a brief flicker of relief that it was Harry behind the controls, not him.

'Is that a docking probe you've extended or are you just pleased to see me?' Captain Briggs chuckled over the intercom.

'That's the first time I've heard that one,' Commander Sheppard replied, rolling his eyes.

'You boys.' Jesse saw Sie Yan laugh and nudge her husband on the monitor. It was nice to see the easy intimacy between the three of them.

Jesse leant forward in his seat. This was the hardest part. With the docking probe extended, Harry had to bring it in for 'the kiss', as Solomon called it, where it would push into the port. Jesse realized he was holding his breath – they all were. There were two hand-controllers to pilot the shuttle; one that controlled lateral movement and another that controlled rotation. Though he ached to watch his own hands steer, Jesse admired Harry's precision, the exact angles he turned, and he watched through the window and on the monitor's schematic as they moved into the perfect docking position.

'Hang in there,' said Captain Briggs. 'You've got a skilled pilot there, Shepp.'

'Trained him up myself.' Sheppard's voice was humming with pride.

They were about 100 metres from *Orlando* when it happened. Harry had been about to issue the final command. Jesse had been staring so intently at his display that his memory of it came not from witnessing the incident himself, but from the video that survived on Poppy's camera.

There was a flash of blinding light, like a star collapsing, but no sound at all.

The *Orlando*'s central module burst open, metal exploding into the darkness of space.

THERE WAS NO TIME to scream. The shockwave flung their shuttle away from Europa. Jesse's neck snapped back in his seat. There were a few seconds of pure terror during which he was certain he was about to die. He pushed down hard in his seat to fight the blackness clouding his vision as all his blood was washed into his feet. For a moment, the acceleration was so great that the pressure on his chest and lungs meant that he could not take a breath. By the time Harry and Commander Sheppard had regained some degree of control over the *Congreve* and they began to slow, Jesse was nauseous and balancing on the dizzying fringe of consciousness.

'Is everyone okay?' Commander Sheppard asked. They had been plunged into darkness – the interior lights had gone out, and nothing but the buttons on the control panel and the ghostly light of Europa illuminated their vessel.

Poppy let out a gasp of pain, and Jesse opened his eyes to find that she had been thrown against one of the steel walls. She had unbuckled her belt to film the approach, he remembered – she must not have strapped herself back in. Her eyes were squeezed together, blood trickling from her nose.

'What just happened?' Jesse asked, working hard to catch his breath. His voice trembling.

Poppy crawled to her seat and pushed the button on her dashboard's intercom.

'*Orlando?*' she called, throat thick with swallowed tears. '*Orlando. Congreve.* Comm check.'

When Jesse turned to Commander Sheppard, he noticed the eerie fact that Captain Omar Briggs, with his softly lined face, was still smiling out at them. Holding his rough hands up at the camera in a final thumbs-up before the frozen picture splintered into hissing static.

Commander Sheppard stared at the screen, then began stabbing the intercom. 'Omar?' he called. '*Orlando* – do you read?'

Jesse turned his gaze painfully to the window. He must have lost his bearings. He couldn't find the station. But it had to be there.

'Are you there?' A voice crackled through his headphones. The *Damocles*.

'Juno?' he whispered.

'Oh, thank God.' Her voice was crackling, indistinct. 'You're alive. *Orlando* has exploded.'

'I think we saw it.'

'It looked like—' Her voice cracked. 'Jess, it's just gone.'

'Watch out!' Poppy screamed behind him. Jesse whipped around, saw it long after it was too late to do anything, something careening towards them, reflecting light like a knife. If anything pierced the hull of their shuttle moving at a high speed, it could tear through it like a missile. The air would explode out and, in a few seconds, they would all be dead.

They were hit.

Jesse felt the force of it through his seat, thought he could smell the burn, the scorch of metal. The O_2 alarm began to whine.

'This is an emergency,' Commander Sheppard said. 'We need to get out of the moon's orbit as fast as we can.' The shattered space station was throwing off debris. Another hit could cripple the ship, or kill them, and if they wanted to avoid it they would have to get out of the range of the explosion.

'Up, Harry,' Sheppard cried. 'Open it up; thrusters at full speed. Burn all the fuel you need to get us out of here.'

Poppy cried out again, and when Jesse lifted his head to look out the front window, he saw that another object was lancing towards them. A piece of machinery, unrecognizable after the explosion, something with sheer edges moving at terrible speed. Sheppard and Harry were ready this time, grabbing the controllers, they forced the shuttle out of its path.

Jesse's head spun as the blood rushed down his neck. He squeezed his eyes shut against the tilting wave of nausea, and when he opened them again he could see the space station – or what was left of it. What had moments ago been a majestic feat of design and engineering was now no more than rubble. It had been torn open like carrion; blackened truss, seared metal and hanging machinery all accelerating away from it at different speeds. It was a sickening sight – solar panels, switchboards and smashed components tore towards them, glittering in the light like shattered glass.

Commander Sheppard's face was a mask of dread. 'Okay . . .' he said, shakily at first but his voice steadied as he continued. 'Okay, Harrison, we'll navigate through this together. Follow my instructions. We can get out of this debris field and maybe we can make it out of here with our lives.'

Harry's face, reflected in the window, was chalk white. His eyes seemed fixed on a shadow in the distance. Jesse followed his gaze and realized it was a body: bloated and pumpkin-orange in a regulation flight suit. It spun through the wreckage, one half of it burnt black, chalky hints of charred bone glinting beneath a flayed skull. Bile rose in Jesse's stomach. There was another body close by, missing an arm, drifting through the blackness, its helmet visor reflecting the gutted station below.

'Harry?' Sheppard said. Jesse had never seen Harry look so frightened. Commander Sheppard clicked his fingers, hoping to rouse the boy. 'Harrison? Harrison, we need you.'

But perhaps Harry was thinking, *Those are people we know.*

He'd blinked and they'd turned into corpses. Kennedy, perhaps, or James. Captain Briggs with his gentle voice and quiet, constant hope. People just like him, astronauts, vain souls who knew that space did not care for them – but hoped against hope that it would not be their burial ground. Jesse was thinking those things, certainly.

'Out of the way!' Solomon shouted – the kind of howl that shattered the nerves. Jesse saw something coming for them in the window, a gas tank, a huge boulder of metal. Harry lunged for the controls and, at the same time, Commander Sheppard leapt to protect him.

The impact they felt was so hard that Jesse's skull slammed back against his headrest, stars exploding behind his eyelids. When he came to, four different pressure alarms were roaring and Harry's gloved hands were covered in blood.

'Shepp?' Harry said. Their commander's body was slumped forward in his seat, limp. 'Commander Sheppard?'

'What's happened?' Poppy asked. Harry twisted around in his seat to face them.

'I think he hit his head, just now. Trying to save me.' He shook the commander again, but Sheppard rolled across the dashboard. 'He's not conscious, I don't think.'

'Is he dead?' Poppy asked.

'Oh God. I don't know.'

'Check!'

'We don't have time,' Jesse said. Consciousness was rolling back to him on waves of panic.

'We're dead,' Poppy said, her breathing coming fast and irregular. 'Dead.'

Jesse knew that it was true. It was as if they'd driven a car into an ocean and the sea was bursting in with constant and deadly force. Time was running out with the same speed.

His heart was thundering so hard that he was sure it would burst in his ribs. He was terrified, paralyzed. He squeezed his eyes shut, forced himself to breathe, to work the problem as they had been taught in school, to think of a solution. And as he did, it began to resolve before him. Jesse had been here before. He had been on this ship a thousand times, looking out at a sky that blazed destruction. During the game, Jesse had piloted his vir-tual crew through dusty asteroid belts when they were running low on oxygen. He'd navigated his way through space junk and landed in deserts without his ship burning up like a firecracker in the atmosphere. At least – not every time.

Jesse saw, again, that his time had come. As adrenaline roared through his veins, he started to unbuckle his seatbelt. 'I can do it,' he said, lunging forward, just as he had the night of Ara's death. 'I can get us through this, Harry.'

'But—' Harry turned to Jesse to protest, but then realized he had no choice. 'If you can, you're a genius.'

Jesse fought hard against the dizziness and the acid boil of nausea in his stomach. 'I can do this. I've done it before.' Together they pulled their commander's body from the front seat and then Jesse strapped himself into Sheppard's chair. Pulling off his gloves, he worked to keep his trembling hands from slip-ping off the controls. Before him, in the window, huge chunks of delicate, brutalized machinery were crashing into each other and erupting into splinters of white hot metal. In space, a little acceleration went a long way, so by the time he was ready to fly, the wreckage was coming at the shuttle from all directions. Jesse fought the urge to abandon the controls and cover his eyes.

He took a deep breath and mustered his courage, determined to believe that this was not the day he would die. That a burnt-out canister would not crash through the window of the cockpit and suck him silently screaming into the hard vacuum of space. He and Harry could save themselves, and the rest of the crew. They would burn the engines until they were free. They would make it back to *Damocles*. They would make it to the sun-warmed earth of Terra-Two.

So he flew. He was playing the game then, the simulator. Working in harmony with Harry to execute joint commands, his fingers flying across the control panel as if it was a fretboard.

Something hit the shuttle and it shuddered. Jesse heard the scream of torn metal and his heart crashed beneath his sternum. Was death coming? Harry ignored it and kept yelling commands, his face red, veins bulging from his neck. They dived out of the way of a swinging truss. If he could conquer the game, he could conquer this – the asteroid belt of destruction. The sky flinging splinters of sparkling metal at them.

'This is not how we die,' Jesse declared as they soared.

'Damn right!' Harry said with an ecstatic howl of relief. And then he and Jesse were aware only of the flight. They ducked and weaved through the debris, Jesse's subconscious drawing trajectories, calculating where the junk was flying, following Harry's lead and then indicating where to go next, their hands listening as they dived and careened left, then right, but always up, up. Soon, the remains of the station were only blips on the radar and their shuttle rose out of its orbit and into the clear open space beyond.

It was then that Jesse became aware of the whine of the oxygen alarm. 'I said, put your mask on,' Harry barked at him.

Jesse's fingers were too stiff with cold to find it above his seat. The O_2 was dropping, the monitor on the dashboard reading 60 per cent, 55 per cent, 40 . . . ticking down. Jesse's vision began to tunnel and he slipped down in his seat. Harry swore, scrabbled around, then found the mask and pressed it to Jesse's face. He felt the relief of it in his lungs, and Harry laughed. 'We better not lose you now,' his voice came over the com. 'You crazy fucking genius. You – we . . . did it.' He collapsed back in the pilot's seat, his hands shaking violently, and Jesse thought he could see tears in his eyes.

Europa's icy surface was receding from view when Jesse finally allowed himself to believe that they were out of danger. His body was gripped in a vice of pain. Whiplash, concussion, exhaustion. The weight of his limbs in this gravity was almost more than he could bear. But in a few hours, he knew, they would return to the *Damocles*. As he and Harry flew back, Jesse imagined them all. In his mind, Fae, Jesse, Cai and the twins were all bathed in the cool light of the monitors and when he emerged, they were all clapping. Clapping for him.

HARRY

5 P.M.

HARRY HAD ALMOST DIED once before. During a joyride with Jack Redcliffe, his roommate. They had been friends for years, had attended the same exclusive prep school before they'd both been selected for Dalton. They shared the same birthday and, the night before they both turned seventeen, Jack had convinced Harry to sneak off the grounds for the first and only time during his school career. Harry would have said no if Jack had not showed him the new car his Californian uncle had bought as a birthday gift. A dark green Cadillac, the most beautiful piece of machinery Harry had ever seen.

Command School was situated far out of London, past the M25, in the middle of open fields with not even a post office for miles. He and Jack pushed the car to its limits along the deserted roads, unlit tarmac curving before them like a black river. Jack turned the radio up and screamed under the vibrato trill of a rock guitar. It felt almost as good as flying: the solitude, the speed, the strange exhilaration that came from breaking the rules. Where were they going? He had no idea. In his mind, they would just keep driving, the road as infinite and inviting as space; they could skate right off the flat edge of the Earth and he'd still be laughing so much that his face hurt.

They didn't see the truck until it swung around the corner. Headlights exploded in Harry's face. 'Jack! Watch out!' he screamed, thinking *This is how I die.* His friend lunged at the steering wheel, throwing them off the road. Burning smell of rubber. Roar of brakes. Pain. *This is how it happens. I die like this. Now I know.* Harry hit his head so hard that he blacked out.

When he came to, his face was covered in blood. The driver's seat was deserted. Jack had crawled from the car and was lying on his back beside the road.

Is this how it feels? Everything hurt. When Harry pulled himself out of the car, his mouth tasted of metal. Jack was grinning like a maniac, his nose twisted – later they would discover that the airbag had broken it – lips and teeth brown with blood.

'I thought we were going to die,' Harry said, his voice trembling.

'No shit!' Jack laughed, sitting up with some difficulty. Harry knelt down so that they were eye-level.

'Hey,' Harry said. 'You idiot. Get off the road.'

'Haha!' Jack turned to him. 'You're *crying.*' Harry touched his face to find that it was wet. Not with blood. 'You're alive.'

Harry nodded. He could not remember the last time he had cried, but even as he rested on his knees by the side of the road, more tears blurred his vision, seared his corneas. Soon his breath was ragged with sobs. 'We're alive.' The blood was like fire in his veins, his heartbeat a battle cry. *You're alive*, it thundered in his chest. He thought he would never feel this way again. That the stars would never be this bright again. He would never be this young again. *You're alive.* Never so alive again.

*

THE *ORLANDO* HAD EXPLODED and Harry had never been so terrified. He did not believe in God or destiny. He had only ever believed in himself and in hard work, and that this life – this life as an astronaut – had always been his to snatch. But, the second of the explosion, Harry really did think he saw his life flash before his eyes. Saw Jack Redcliffe in his car, moonlight glittering on blood-spattered asphalt. The swing-set his grandfather had built in the Bellgrave orchard. Himself and his brothers barefoot on the sun-warmed deck of their uncle's boat. London. Dalton. Whatever other life he could have had with his feet on solid ground, the world below him.

Harry and Jesse had flown, like men possessed, out of danger, to the only home they had, back to the *Damocles*. And the whole while Jack's words beat in Harry's eardrums: *You're alive. Alive. Alive.*

PART THREE

JUNO

07.02.13

4 P.M.

'OH, THANK GOD. YOU'RE alive. *Orlando* has exploded,' she said to Jesse over the CAPCOM. Juno had seen it with her own eyes, a splinter of light in Europa's dark perimeter, then a supernova.

'*I -hink ... saw it ...*' came Jesse's distorted voice over the headset.

'It looked like—' Juno felt her voice crack. 'Jess, it's just gone.'

'Jesse—' Juno cried out, but then there was a scream in the background. It sounded like Poppy's voice. 'Watch out!' she shouted before a howl of static poured through the headset, loud enough to tear Juno's eardrums. She yanked her headset off and looked up to find that all readouts had dissolved from the screens on the communication deck, where Fae was frantically stabbing at buttons and pulling dials.

'*Damocles*, *Congreve*, comm check,' Astrid shouted down her mic.

Silence. Juno couldn't breathe.

'*Congreve*? *Congreve*? Commander Sheppard ...? Harry? Poppy? Jesse?' Astrid pulled off her headset and stood up. 'It could be us. A problem with our transceiver. Maybe we're not receiving their response.' Juno saw the desperate hope in her sister's eyes.

'You go check,' Fae commanded, and Astrid shot out of the control room.

'There's no point,' Eliot said, pulling away from the display where both the *Congreve* and *Orlando* had disappeared. He raked trembling fingers through the greasy strings of his hair. 'I knew this was going to happen.'

'You what?' Juno looked up at his face, the reflected light of a star chart making silver freckles along his jaw. Igor too, leant over from the commander's chair on the raised platform of the control deck.

'A hydrazine leak,' said Eliot. Hydrazine was the highly explosive fuel found inside *Orlando*'s auxiliary power units. Juno knew that APUs were extra engines used for functions other than propulsion. On *Orlando*, the APUs provided the energy to kick-start the engines that boosted the station into a higher orbit, pushing it further away from Europa and in this case allowing it to more easily dock with the *Congreve*.

'The crew on *Orlando* reported a lower than expected tank pressure a couple of days ago,' Eliot said. Juno remembered that. Because hydrazine was so dangerous – highly flammable and toxic to humans – the news of a possible leak, almost a month ago, had been alarming.

'But no leak was detected,' Igor reminded him. 'It was a machine error.'

'Happens all the time,' Fae said.

'Then what caused this explosion?' Juno cried, her voice hysterical to her own ears, pointing out the window to the blurred mass of metal where, a few minutes ago, there had been a space station.

'I have a theory,' Eliot said, biting his lip, Orion's Belt projected by the computer across the bridge of his nose. 'The melting point of hydrazine is minus two degrees, and the surface temperature around Europa is more than one hundred times lower than that, so . . .'

'You think the hydrazine leaked and then froze, blocking the hole. Of course.' Igor's face fell.

Eliot nodded. 'Fuel leak, maybe it happened a while ago, weeks or months or years. Sometime between now and the last time they used the APU. The lower pressure is registered during a routine check, they shut it down and examine it but don't detect any hydrazine because it has frozen, blocking the hole. We get the all clear, the *Congreve* moves to dock with it. The APU is used to perform an orbital boost, and during the engine burn –'

'– hydrazine melts, the leak begins again –' Igor continued.

'– spills maybe, on a hot surface and –'

'*Bang.*' Igor said it loud enough to startle Juno.

'I mean, hydrazine's highly flammable and the atmosphere on Europa is basically pure oxygen.'

'The worst-case scenario,' said Fae.

Eliot's words rolled over Juno in a sickening blur of white noise. She was still having trouble absorbing the implications. 'Everyone on *Orlando* is . . . ?'

'Dead,' said Eliot. 'Most likely.' The blood rushed from Juno's head and she sat down again, heavily. 'I saw this coming.'

'What?' Juno frowned. 'When?'

'Just after the *Congreve* left it occurred to me but—'

'Why didn't you say anything?'

'I don't know!'

'Okay,' said Igor, throwing his hands up. 'Now is not the time for a post-mortem. It wasn't Eliot's job to recognize a fault. It was the MMACs' and the senior engineers'. Aberrant machine readings happen often, so it's a conclusion that mission control are often too quick to jump to. It's called "normalization of deviance", and sometimes it takes a pair of fresh eyes, like Eliot's, to spot the problem.'

'But if Eliot knew—' Juno began, anger bubbling inside her.

'He didn't *know*,' Fae said. 'He had a hunch.'

'He should have said.'

'I didn't trust myself.' Eliot hit his head hard with a closed fist. 'It's my fault, I killed them. Like I killed her.'

'Eliot Liston,' Igor barked, 'control yourself. Now is not the time.' For the duration of the mission, while Sheppard was on the *Congreve*, Igor was their commander. 'We're not out of danger. The explosion means that the sky above Europa will be filled with debris. Some objects will be moving faster than bullets, fast enough to escape the moon's gravity.'

'No,' Juno pleaded, 'they're in danger. Jesse, Commander Sheppard, Harry and Poppy. We can't leave them. The further we travel, the more fuel they'll have to burn trying to reach us ... they might not make it.' But, as she said it, the ground shuddered. Dropped from under her feet with a hard shockwave that felt like an earthquake. Juno had the sudden, sickening thought that this must have been what it felt like when the *Titanic* scraped against the keen edge of an iceberg. Everyone on the control deck froze.

Then the lights went out and the sirens began to howl.

ASTRID

THE FIRST HIT CAME with a loud bang, as the air inside the ship exploded into the vacuum outside. There was a sudden loss of pressure, which made Astrid's ears pop as they sometimes did in the first few minutes after a plane take-off.

Air was escaping through a crack in the porthole window between the equipment bay and the hatch that led to the service module, at the far end of the corridor where Astrid stood. The porthole was narrow, only a little larger than a splayed hand, and through it Europa's silver light cut like a scythe. Astrid edged towards it, and as she did felt the thin but insistent suction of oxygen through the deadly crack in the borosilicate glass.

A micrometeoroid, Astrid supposed – they were too far from the explosion for debris to have reached them yet. It was just bad luck that this had happened at the same time. Micrometeoroid strikes were something they had been trained for. The ship's tracking system was sophisticated enough to anticipate a hit from most medium and large asteroids, giving Harry or Commander Sheppard enough warning to perform a side-burn that took the *Damocles* out of the object's path and out of danger. But micrometeoroids were smaller, scraps of metal or rock as old as the solar system speeding through space. Tiny particles small as a fleck of paint had been known to blast like a bullet through a window. A larger object could cause enough damage to result in decompression. In which event, Astrid might have as little as eighteen seconds of useful consciousness before her brain was starved of oxygen.

Her training came back to her at the moment of the hit, overriding her natural instincts to run for cover. She had been taught to respond methodically to disasters, to assess the situation and to come up with solutions. She listened to the pitch of the air escaping and deduced that their atmosphere was leaving the module slowly enough for her to attempt to patch the hole. Astrid examined the sliver of broken glass and pressed her palm against it. The hissing stopped instantly, suggesting that this was the only hole. On the other side of the window was space, and the suction felt like a knife slice along her palm as blood burst from the capillaries under her skin. Stepping back, Astrid looked around for something she could use to plug the hole. She grabbed a first aid kit from a wall fixture, tore it open and found a hydrocolloid wound dressing, the jelly-like plaster they were meant to apply to burns and stitches. It would do for now. A short-term measure before she could go to the engine room and find some proper sealant. Peeling the plastic backing away, she applied it to the crack in the window. For a moment she wasn't sure if it would stick. She watched as crystals formed quickly in the gel as it was exposed to the vacuum outside. Then she registered the equalizing in pressure in her inner ear.

Success! Astrid thought, with a flush of joy. In her training she'd been taught that the big three disasters an astronaut could face were fire, ammonia leaks and decompression. She had stayed calm and fixed the problem on her own.

She would have to let Igor know immediately, so she headed away from the site of the accident and back up to the crew module. But, just as she reached up to open the hatch, the *Damocles* was hit again.

The impact threw Astrid off her feet and into the air. The lights shut off and, for a disorientating half-second, so did the gravity-dromes. Astrid's stomach swooped upwards along with her entire body for a sickening moment of soaring weightlessness that felt like a cliff dive. Adrenaline poured through her like rocket fuel before the dromes sent the deck spinning again and she crashed to the ground. She shouted in pain and surprise, her knee bent awkwardly under her with a knife-twist of pain, and stars throbbed behind her eyes.

The corridor was still dark and the master alarm sounded with the kind of urgent wail that told Astrid exactly what danger she was in. They were losing pressure fast this time, but she could not figure out where from. Her amateur dressing had been torn off the porthole, and cracks spread like spiders' webs across the borosilicate. She thought that she could see the air pouring out, oxygen illuminated by the sinister light of Europa.

'Astrid!' Juno scrambled down the hatch and hit the floor with a thud that she must have felt in her shins. 'We have decompression.'

Astrid's gaze was still fixed on the porthole. The pressure inside the corridor was slamming like a battering ram against its cracked surface. How long until it shattered?

'Astrid, get up.' Juno was above her now, her face a rictus of panic. Astrid grabbed her hand and struggled to her feet, although every bone in her battered body protested against her weight.

'We should try to fix it,' Astrid gasped, gesturing at the porthole.

'There's no time,' Juno yelled, dragging Astrid in the opposite direction from the way she had come, away from the hatch that would lead them to the middle deck and the crew module, past the porthole, down the corridor towards the bridge that led to the greenhouse.

'The other way's faster,' Astrid said.

'We need to get to the radiation shelter,' said Juno. 'It's the safest place right now.' Astrid knew that the radiation shelter, which was tucked in at the far end of the greenhouse, had a reinforced shell and twenty-four hours of oxygen – buying them enough time to wait for the rest of the crew to arrive. But then what?

The illumination of the flashing emergency lights was dizzying, sending their shadows spiralling up and down the walls in a way that made the floor feel as if it was rocking under them. Under the caterwaul of the alarm, Astrid thought she could hear the most terrifying sound – the tea-kettle whistle of the air escaping into space, a sound that few astronauts had lived through to describe.

A faulty hab-lab on a Mars mission had caused such sudden decompression of the crew module that all the astronauts died instantaneously. Their remains were discovered six months later, computers still running, feet and hands covered in the red dust of that planet. They had smiles on their faces. Apparently, death had come too suddenly for them to tremble at the sight of it.

'This way.' Juno hurried Astrid along, towards the shelter.

Everything that was not sealed down was whipping through the air: medical wipes, vacuum-packed bandages, eye dressings and a bag of safety pins from the first aid box, flying as if propelled by a strong gust of wind. A coldpack shot at Juno's head but she ducked and turned to find it shatter against a wall panel. They had about thirty seconds.

'Hurry up!' Juno screamed, but her voice had taken on a strange distant wail as the air between them vanished.

Astrid's awareness split as she looked around at the water vapour condensing into mist, and the crack spreading across the window, and she came to a dark understanding of the danger they were in. But some part of her was light with euphoria. She felt laughter bubble up in her diaphragm. *Why run?* she wondered.

'Astrid,' Juno shouted. 'Concentrate!' Her sister dragged her down the corridor towards the emergency hatch that led to the bridge – the narrow passageway that connected the lower and the upper deck. Eliot was standing in it with an O_2 mask strapped to his face. He motioned for them to hurry, but by the time they reached the hatch, Astrid couldn't feel her feet, her vision was narrowing into a tunnel and once they were through the hatch she collapsed on the ground inside the bridge.

Behind her, Juno was struggling to close the hatch, her body illuminated only in the red of the emergency light. 'It's not closing,' she cried, but Astrid could barely hear over the pain in her head. Her eardrums were expanding out like balloons as the pressure fell. The pain was more than she could bear, starbursts of agony through her head and jaw. Voices around her fluted into a distant whine. 'There's something caught in

the door. Wires, I think. I need you to get something to cut
them with ... Astrid?'

Astrid heard her name through the fog of pain and light-
headedness. Juno and Eliot were struggling with the hatch,
which was blocked by a dozen ventilation tubes and cables. Eliot
scrambled to unplug every wire he could find; all the while his
shaggy hair was whipping around his head as if in a hurricane.
Astrid knew she only had a few seconds of useful consciousness
left. She crawled through the bridge, where the ground under
her palms was cold as ice, blood pounding behind her eyes. On
the other side was the greenhouse, where leaves were being torn
off their vines. She forced herself to focus, looked around for
something to cut the wire with. Something sharp.

On the other side of the hatch, Juno screamed. There was a
sound like a thunderclap as the air inside the greenhouse bull-
dozed through the bridge. Glass spires near the service module
ruptured and chlorella burst out, clumps of algae suspended in
acid green slime. Astrid cried out as splinters flew at her face,
though she only realized she'd been cut when she felt the blood
dripping down her cheek.

Shunted by the pain back into her body, Astrid grabbed a
dripping shard of glass in her trembling hands and scrambled
back to the bridge. Juno took it and worked immediately on the
wires. The first one she cut filled the air with a lightning-bright
shower of sparks and the sickly smell of electrical fire.

'Careful,' Eliot screamed. He had disconnected two of the
plugs, and Juno severed a third. Together they kicked the snak-
ing chords over the threshold, but discovered, to their horror,
that the hatch still would not close.

The air was rushing out with such force that the internal

mechanism had likely jammed, a safety precaution that prevented it from closing if someone was caught in it. It would close once the pressure on the inside and the outside equalized, but by then, of course, Eliot, Juno and Astrid would be dead.

Astrid slumped against the wall, waves of pain spasming through her, the saliva on her tongue fizzing as the pressure dropped and it began to boil. Soon the oxygen in her chest would split her lungs open and spill into her arteries, but, by then, her mind would have happily disconnected from her body. The brain was kind that way, sending dizzy waves of euphoria through the dying body in the seconds before oblivion.

Eliot, the only one who had grabbed a mask from the control room, still had the presence of mind to snatch at salvation. He yanked the medical officer badge from the lapel of Juno's flight suit, his fingers stiff with cold, and jammed it into the hatch's locking mechanism. With a hiss of hydraulics the hatch slammed closed and they collapsed on the bridge, shaking in the cold. The temperature felt as if it had dropped by about thirty degrees.

Astrid felt the change of pressure a second time, like a wind that had suddenly fallen dead. 'Here you are.' Fae's silhouette came into focus by the door. She'd opened an oxygen canister and Juno was gasping, her eyes bright with tears. 'That should help for the moment. But the ship's been breached. It's not safe here.'

'Look,' Eliot pointed to the door at the far end of the bridge. Through its porthole they could see the corridor, where the window that Astrid had patched a few minutes ago had exploded under the pressure. The module on the other side of the door had turned into a vacuum and the first aid kit, Juno's shoe, the earpiece of a crew phone and everything not attached to the ground or the wall had been sucked out into the nothingness. 'It could have been us,' Eliot said.

'I think I'm going to be sick,' Juno said. She'd changed colour, looked grey and waxy and was shaking violently.

'We need to go to the radiation shelter,' Fae said. 'Now pull yourselves together and get up. You've trained for this.'

Astrid barely remembered the short journey into the radiation shelter. The pain in her ears came in keening waves and by the time she sat down on the bench, she noticed that the collar of her flight suit was wet with blood, although, between her frozen fingers, it felt like jelly.

Fae attached an oxygen mask to her face, and some of the pain subsided, giving way to an awareness of her aching body, the bloody space-hickey on her palm where she'd pressed it against the window. Astrid stared down at it in horror and disbelief.

For marooned sailors, the ocean might never be the same after they'd watched it devour another crew. It could come to seem like death personified, death with a will, death with splendid terrifying power. And so it was for Astrid, that day, as she looked down at her hand. Here was death, again, calling their names, and she had touched it.

JUNO

6 P.M.

TRAPPED IN THE DIMLY lit radiation shelter, Juno was terrified. In the wake of the loss of *Orlando*, their own mission seemed like such vain folly. 'What are we doing here?' she asked the darkness, her head spinning with fatigue. 'How did I get here?' The air was thin, and she could feel it in the tightness in her chest. Her voice roused Astrid from sleep.

'What?' her sister asked.

'Do you think they're dead?' Juno knew that Astrid would guess that she was talking about Harry and Poppy, Jesse and Commander Sheppard, the crew on the *Congreve*. It was likely that they'd been hit by flying debris. Juno imagined a solar array slicing like an axe through their shuttle. Explosive decompression, everyone inside dying with their eyes open.

Juno and Astrid were lying together on a bunk. Igor, Cai and Fae were on the beds opposite, silent, too cold to sleep, although Fae's face was buried in the crook of her elbow and Juno could see her chest rising and falling slowly.

'I don't know,' Astrid admitted. 'But they were far enough away to escape. And Commander Sheppard's a good pilot. If anyone can get them home safe ...'

'And then what?' Juno asked.

'We lick our wounds,' Cai said, 'and keep going.' He kept glancing at the door. Juno knew that he was thinking about his garden, about the shattered spires and uprooted plants, mentally tallying the weeks of work it would take to repair.

'And we were hit,' Eliot said, rubbing his hands together to try to warm them, huffing out air on his frozen fingers. 'We'll have to repair the ship before Saturn.'

'It might take an EVA or two to fix,' Igor said.

'But the thing we do right now,' Fae told her, 'is wait.'

Juno nodded, grateful for the body of her sister that she could curl into.

Two hours later, the sensors alerted them: the *Congreve* was on approach.

9.30 P.M.

WHEN JESSE AND HARRY climbed out of the airlock and back on board the *Damocles*, Juno realized that they looked oddly similar. Side by side, she noticed for the first time that they were the same height. Their faces twisted with the same desperate fear. For a moment, overwhelmed by their miraculous homecoming, Juno leapt forward and threw her arms around Jesse. 'You're safe,' she gasped. But Jesse pushed her away, shaking his head.

'No,' he said, and raised his hands up to the light. Juno saw that they were smeared in blood, a livid red, almost too bright to belong to a human. 'It's not mine,' he said before Juno could ask.

Harry nodded to the open door of the airlock and said, 'It's his.'

They all fell silent when they leant over the threshold and

saw the body of their commander slumped against one of the walls, barely recognizable, blood soaking his flight suit, eyes white and rolled back in his head.

It seemed absurd to consider now, but Juno had never seen Solomon Sheppard sleep before. Fae she'd caught a couple of times, stretched out on the gurney in the infirmary, pillow etching crease-lines into the side of her face. And even Cai, whom Jesse had once spotted napping at his desk. But not Commander Sheppard. His heart was like the beating heart of their ship. There was something reassuring about the quiet vigil he seemed to keep in the control room.

'How long has he been like this?' Fae asked, already unbuckling the collar of his flight suit to check his pulse and breathing. Juno leaned in; she thought she could hear irregular gasps coming from his throat.

'Hours,' said Poppy. 'As long as it took for us to get back here.'

'He was answering to his name for a while,' Jesse told them. 'But now . . .'

'What am I doing?' Fae asked Juno, who blinked in confusion. But, then, her training came back to her.

'An A to E assessment?' she said.

'What does that mean?'

'Airways, then breathing.'

Fae had already finished checking both. 'His airways are at risk,' she said. 'I need you to help me get him to the infirmary.'

Harry and Jesse came to her aid, clearly glad to be told what to do. Harry linked his arms under their commander's, supporting his head, and Jesse grabbed his legs. In that fashion, they followed Juno and Dr Golinsky down the corridor, pulled him up the ladder, along the bridge and into the little room.

'What are we going to do?' Harry asked, staring at the body of their commander on the gurney. Solomon Sheppard was a frightening sight, lips and fingers already purple, mouth hanging open.

'I don't know,' Jesse said.

'For the duration of this mission and for the foreseeable future, Igor is commander,' Fae said. Then her voice took on an authoritarian edge. 'But, in this room, I'm in charge, and it's too small for any non-essential persons.'

'Harry's injured too,' Poppy said. She was in shadow by the door. 'His arm.'

'It can wait,' Harry said. Although, now Juno looked at him, she could see he was gritting his teeth against the pain. 'I can come back.'

'You, sit there,' Fae ordered. 'Jesse, Poppy, report to Commander Bovarin. Juno Juma, tell me, what is C?'

'Circulation,' Juno said, watching Jesse and Poppy disappear.

'Good.' Juno watched as Fae pushed a tube into their commander's throat and connected him to a ventilator. Colour slowly began to return to his lips and nail-beds. 'You know what to do. Heart, BP, capillary refill.'

Juno nodded. She pulled her stethoscope off the wall, placed the cold chest-piece to his sternum and listened to the hollow drum of their captain's heart. She reported the number, then repeated the process for his blood pressure, oxygen saturation and capillary refill – which she tested by pressing a finger against his skin and counting the seconds it took for his skin to flush pink with blood again. It was difficult to tell in the cold.

During that time, Fae was examining his head wound. 'It's quite deep,' she told Juno, reaching for the antiseptic wipes.

'Might need stitches and a dose of flucloxacillin; they're in the cabinet by the—'

'Why is he not waking up?' Harry asked.

'That's what we're trying to find out. Juno, what do we do next?' Juno's mind flailed for a moment. It was difficult to reconcile the sterile pages of her textbooks, the mnemonics she had memorized, with the scene before her. 'Um ...'

'This is basic!'

'Glasgow Coma Scale.'

'Go on.'

Juno counted the categories off on her fingers. 'Eyes, verbal ... motion? I mean *motor*. Motor.'

Fae peeled open an eye, and Juno watched Solomon's brown iris roll under her thumb. The kind gaze Juno was so used to had vanished completely, and when Fae waggled a light above him his pupils did not constrict. The doctor swore quietly in German.

'Is that bad?' Harry asked, acutely tuned to their panic. Juno knew that unresponsive pupils were a bad sign.

Fae squeezed one of Solomon's fingers hard. His eyes didn't open. 'One,' she said. The lowest score. 'Commander Sheppard?'

The man did not move or make a sound.

'One.' Fae said. She rubbed hard on his sternum with her knuckles. Juno thought she saw his arm twitch, just slightly.

'Some motor response to pain.' Fae exhaled and then turned to Juno. 'Can you attend to Harry?' Juno knew that Fae was keen to get him out of the room, so she did as she was told and examined Harry's arm.

He'd been hurt badly. Some accident on the shuttle, Juno

imagined, a broken instrument or monitor screen, had left splinters of glass buried in his forearm. She took a pair of scissors and cut the arm off his flight suit. Harry paled at the sight of his own blood, swallowed and looked away. 'This is going to hurt,' Juno warned him. She'd have to remove the glass with tweezers. Give him a shot of antibiotics in case he developed a skin infection. He'd need a few stitches, too.

'How did it happen?' Juno asked, opening a cabinet to gather supplies.

'Commander Sheppard?' Harry's eyes were still fixed on the man. 'Our shuttle was hit. He must have seen it before I did. He banged his head against the dashboard, really hard.'

Attending to Harry took her what felt like a long time, and when she was finished Fae pushed a cannula under his skin, began the process of examining his blood. 'What for?' she asked Juno.

'Blood gasses, we can do that now. Also FBC, U and E, CRP, glucose, lactate—' Juno reeled off a page of her notes but then she paused. Solomon Sheppard had not woken up yet, even though his heart rate and blood pressure were stable.

'What, now, are our main concerns?' asked Fae.

That he'll die, Juno thought, the ground listing under her. 'Two concerns,' she said, leaning back against the desk to steady herself. 'He could be having a seizure.' Her neuroscience module had taught her that seizures were not always limb-thrashing violent affairs. 'But we'd need an EEG to tell. It's more likely – considering the severity of the head injury – that he is bleeding into his brain.'

'How can we tell?' Fae asked her.

'How can we?' Juno snorted at the absurdity of the question.

'We'd need to do a CT scan. But since this is a tiny room and not a hospital, there's nothing more we can do. Nothing.' Suddenly, the inadequacy of their medical resources was not a theoretical fact, but a physical horror. They'd reached the end of their capacity to help their captain. While on Earth he'd be rushed into a trauma unit, examined, taken for brain surgery, here on the ship all they could do was cross their fingers.

'We could do a lumbar puncture,' Fae said.

'What's that?' Harry asked.

'We put a needle into his spine and drain some of the fluid,' Juno explained, but even as she did she remembered a warning their lecturer had hammered into their little class of second-year physiologists. 'But if we do that, we could reduce the pressure in such a way that it forces his brain through the hole in the bottom of his skull and kills him.' A sound of horror escaped Harry's lips and it was gratifying to hear, because it was how Juno felt.

'So . . .' Fae crumpled onto her office chair, head dropping into her hands, 'we have a dilemma.'

'What will you do?' Harry asked.

'Juno's a Christian.' Fae didn't look up. 'She can pray.'

In the silence, Juno listened to the rumble of the machines. It was getting late now, close to 1 a.m. She was bone-tired and terrified. The ship's main lights had still not switched on, and Juno's head ached from straining under the dim glow of the single desk lamp.

'I'm done,' she said, stepping back from Harry's arm. Fae glanced over. His arm was in a sling and blood crusted below his fingernails. He still wore the skullcap he'd been wearing when the shuttle launched, so he looked like a bald, wild-eyed alien, eyebrows and eyelashes invisible in the shadow.

'Go to bed,' Fae told them. Juno hesitated. 'You don't have to stay here all night,' Fae said more gently. 'I can take it from here.'

Juno tried to hide her relief.

'Get a little sleep,' Fae said. 'I'll need you tomorrow. You did a good job tonight. All the right things.'

Juno and Harry wandered dazedly into the darkness of the corridor. The only illumination came from the yellow glow of the caution lights.

'It could have been us. Not *Orlando*.' Harry stopped walking for a moment, leant against a wall.

'I know,' she said.

'Why wasn't it?' He looked at Juno as if he really believed that she might have an answer.

'I don't know.'

'I mean . . . it just seems so random. So random and so fucking stupid. I can think of all the different ways it might have not happened. All the times to turn around. To tell them to check the fuel tank again. To . . .' Harry slammed his fist against a wall, and Juno saw that his eyes were wet. 'He saved my life, you know.'

'Who?'

'Commander Sheppard.' Harry swallowed. There were bloody smears on the wall-panelling behind him. 'It could have been me. It should have been.'

Juno was startled by this show of emotion. She reached out to put her hand on his arm, but he pushed her away, 'Don't touch me,' he said, then jabbed a finger at the door of the infirmary. 'You better do everything you can.'

'I will.'

'You better not let him die.'

'I won't,' said Juno foolishly. 'I promise.'

IGOR AND ELIOT SAT on the control deck while Astrid paced. Poppy was jabbing at buttons on the communications panel, tear stains making dirty tracks under her tired eyes. All over the room monitors were flashing with warnings and error messages. On the dashboard, instrument gauges were spinning. They barely noticed Juno as she entered.

'Umm ... hi.' Her voice was soft.

Astrid spun around. 'How is he doing?'

'Badly,' Juno said. 'Fae did what she could but he's probably bleeding into his brain. He's stable now. Sort of. We might just have to wait and see if he wakes up. There's not much we can do. It's not like there's a neurosurgeon on board.'

'Neurosurgeon?' Astrid's voice was weak with horror.

Juno stepped further onto the flight deck. 'So, the lights aren't back on.'

'No.' Poppy shook her head. 'We're asking Ground for their recommendation but – as you know – past Europa, communication's pretty patchy. Our telemetry systems constantly broadcast information about the *Damocles* back to mission control, so by now I'm sure they know something's wrong with the ship. Though they might not know the extent of the damage.'

'And what is it?' Juno asked. 'The extent.'

'We're looking at a real four-point failure,' Igor said. 'We were hardest hit in quadrant three. That whole area is depressurized, which means we've lost access to – amongst other things – the equipment bay. There was a collision in the service module as well.' Fear ripped through Juno's stomach. The service modules were the uninhabited modules that contained most of their life support equipment, the fuel cells and oxygen storage tanks, the main computer, the thermal control systems.

'There's been quite extensive damage to the greenhouse and the breathing equipment too.' Juno thought about the shattered spires and the algae sloshing across the ground. Igor said it all slowly. 'Until we find a way to fix the fuel cells, we'll be relying on storage batteries.'

'Which will last how long?' Juno asked.

'Two days,' Astrid replied. 'Two and a half maybe.'

'Why can't we just hurry up and fix the broken fuel cells?' Juno asked.

'That's the plan. It's not so simple, though,' Astrid said. 'There's a hole in the hull. Both those quadrants have depressurized. To go in to fix it we'd have to do a full EVA.' Juno tried to imagine Eliot and Igor outside the ship, struggling to fix the broken fuel cells with the clumsy gloves of their spacesuits.

'Should Igor perform a spacewalk?' Juno asked. She wanted to add *in his condition*, but the rest of the crew guessed her meaning.

'We'd need another pair of hands,' Igor agreed. 'Harry's injured. So Astrid, probably.'

'So, we'll fix the fuel cells and everything will be okay,' Juno said. 'I mean, we'll get back on track?'

Igor lowered his gaze. 'As Commander Sheppard would say, *insh'allah*. We'll try tomorrow. Get some sleep tonight.'

'How can we sleep?' Poppy asked, the static on the monitor shining a grey light on her pale skin. 'We sent out a distress signal hours ago. But I'm not getting a response.'

'Give it some time,' Igor said.

'We don't have time,' Poppy muttered. Juno knew that Poppy was thinking about the fifty hours of power they had left, or the thirty hours of oxygen. Juno was, too.

'Waiting here and worrying won't get us a response any faster.' Igor's voice was firm now. 'I want you to all go to bed.' He climbed with wincing effort out of the commander's chair. 'Besides,' he added as if on second thought, 'Sleep will save oxygen.'

JUNO WANDERED THE SHIP dazed as a sleepwalker. Everything looked different in the dim illumination of the emergency LEDs. She reached out an arm to get her bearings as her eyes adjusted to the gloom. But the walls of the middle deck were so cold already that tendrils of pain shot up to her knuckles and she recoiled.

They were running out of air.

Her mind reversed back over the same anxious tracks. It had been easy – it had been essential – to forget that the *Damocles* was delicate as a bubble, that she had ventured into the arid vacuum of space with nothing but a few metres of mylar and aluminium to protect her. She'd never forget again.

Both the Beta's cabins were empty. Poppy's radio crackled under her bed, spitting out a few bars of music, the limpid rise of a melody audible for just a moment before being consumed by static. She was not in her bed and neither was Astrid.

Juno headed to the greenhouse, and when she opened the hatch the sound of her footsteps echoed in the gloom. It was like a darkened cathedral. Through the vaulted glass ceiling she could see the spinning rings of the other decks and, beyond them, the stars cast a cold constant light.

They were running out of air.

Bright splinters of pain had begun to burst behind her temples. When mountain climbers ventured too high into the upper atmosphere, and altitude sickness set in, it felt like a hangover, then like carbon-monoxide poisoning. If they continued to climb, the partial pressure of oxygen in their lungs would decrease. They experienced fatigue, dizziness, headaches, a gradual loss of consciousness, and then ...

'Jesse?' Juno's voice reverberated off the shattered spires. The temperature had already dropped so low that her breath misted on the air. Frozen branches of trees were like twisted fingers, catching at loose strands of her hair. Every now and then a halogen lamp would flicker on and light would spear through the icy foliage, making the leaves knife-edged and the creeping undergrowth a steely silver.

When she found Jesse, he was crying. He was lying on his back on a grassy platform near the radiation shelter, on the little mound of pillows and bedsheets he'd gathered there a few weeks ago in order to sleep in the garden. It was quite beautiful, Juno realized now, a bamboo skeleton of a roof above, hung with fairy-lights and wind chimes. They tinkled as she approached.

'Jesse?' Juno flicked on a little pen-light she'd found in a first aid kit. It gave her his face in tiny snatches, flashed off his retinas and his lips, which were blue as bruises. His skin was frozen. Juno bit back a scream. She had been surprised to tumble over the still weight of his body and for a horrible instant she thought that he was dead.

But the sound roused him and he opened his dark eyes.

'Juno,' he said, his breath like smoke.

'You're crying,' she said, and he nodded. The side of his face was covered in dirt, and glass glittered in his hair.

Juno wasn't sure if he was crying because of the shock, because of all that he had endured, or out of fear and grief or because – in the greenhouse – he could see that his months of work had come to almost nothing. His seedlings torn from the ground in a quick blast, their oxygen system crippled.

'T-the air is *here*,' he stammered, the words thick on his frozen lips.

Juno took off her jumper and wrapped it around him. She had learned about hypothermia before, so she already knew about the confusion that set in after core body temperature began to drop.

'Come on. Let's go back to the crew module. You need to warm up.' He wouldn't move, so Juno tried to roll him, but her own limbs were so heavy with exhaustion that she sighed and stopped. 'Please. I'm not strong enough to carry you. You've got to help me. What are you doing?'

'P-practising,' he said.

'Practising what?'

Jesse opened his hand. In the dim light it was difficult to see what he was holding. At first it looked as if he was bleeding, as if he'd squeezed a broken piece of glass, but then she realized that the shredded skin clumping in the lines of his palm was the slick flesh of crushed berries. The pulp ran down his wrists like blood. Near his head was the thin seedling. Half the stems had snapped off and around the roots, the water had frozen into silver veins of ice.

'Dying,' he said. 'When it happens it won't be so bad. It'll be quick. Once the oxygen's low enough.' Juno pictured it, the trauma of suffocation, the tide of black horror that came with it, and suddenly the walls felt as if they were closing in on her. She had to lean back to steady herself. 'There's no alarm response,' he continued. 'You just fall asleep. It's okay, apparently, it's ... euphoric.'

'Jesse—' she was shaking. 'Please stop.'

His eyes rolled up to find hers.

'Anyway,' she knelt down beside him, 'it's all going to be okay. Tomorrow Igor and Eliot and maybe Astrid – since Sheppard is still sick – will do a spacewalk and fix the broken service module. Then we'll be okay.'

'You really think that?' Jesse asked.

'You don't?'

'What about all this?' He looked around at the garden. 'How will we fix this?'

'It will take a while but ... we'll find a way,' Juno said, although the words rang hollow in her ears.

'I thought I was going to die out there,' Jesse said.

'But you didn't. Apparently your flying was amazing, that's what Harry says.'

'Yeah. I don't know how I did it. At first I thought it was all that practising that I did on the simulator, but just now I realized what happened to me: I'm not frightened anymore. It happened when Harry pushed me into the airlock.'

'It took Harry's stupid prank to teach you that?' Juno said.

'Yes, because when I stepped out of it, all I felt was grateful for every damned thing that's ever happened to me. I've seen an orbital sunrise, I've seen the curvature of the Earth, I've been close enough to touch Jupiter's moons, I've lived for months in this garden in the stars ... and I realized that if I only get to live one life, then I'm glad it's been this one.'

When Juno opened her mouth the sobs came out. 'Jesse,' she said, '*I'm* afraid.'

He took her into his arms then and it was a good feeling, his beating heart, the smell of him.

'You know,' said Jesse, 'I don't think I've ever seen you cry.'

'I try not to,' Juno said. Her eyes were still hot with tears, falling fast. She didn't wipe them away.

He looked gentle in the dim light. His pupils flamed amber, and his lashes cast long shadows on his cheeks. 'What would you do?' she asked. 'If you *could* go back?'

Jesse thought for a moment. 'Say goodbye to my sister, Morrigan. The last night I talked to her she was trying to comfort me, about the launch and . . . I wasn't in a great place then . . . I don't think I ever properly said goodbye to her. I just ran out of the house. I think about her all the time, still sitting cross-legged in her pyjamas, where she was when I left her almost a year ago.'

Juno had never seen Jesse's sister but she liked to imagine she had the same sharp features, the same full lips and easy smile, only she was bald and beautiful. Juno had heard that since the launch she'd dropped out of university to run a vegan crêperie in Camden. Maybe when people asked she told them, 'I used to have a brother, but he went to space.'

'I don't know if you remember,' said Juno, 'but after your fight with Harry, when I met you in the games room and helped you with your wounds . . . you said—'

'That I loved you.' Juno felt her stomach leap, just hearing the words again.

'That was the first time,' she said.

'Yeah . . .' His voice was thoughtful. 'I guess it must have been.'

'Why?' she asked, and then, annoyed by how pathetic that sounded, 'I mean, why do you love me?'

'I can't give you reasons. What do you want, a list?'

'Maybe.'

'I can't do that, Juno. I can't tell you if you deserve it. Just like no one can tell me if I deserved to make it here or why Ara died. Or why an accident means that the lives of the crew on *Orlando* were snuffed out in an instant but *our* hearts are still beating. Do we deserve any of it? To live? To be loved? It's a gift, Juno. Don't you see that? You don't earn it or lose it.'

'Can I tell you a secret?' Juno asked.

'Okay.'

'I don't deserve to be here either,' she said. 'I've been thinking recently about whether or not I was ever even supposed to go to Terra-Two. It's Astrid who's always wanted to. It's Astrid who's dreamt about it. I did well in the tests but she scored more highly in the interviews and the personality quizzes when we were back in Dalton. I realized, one night, that it was very possible that one of us could make it into the Beta while the other one . . . was left behind. So we made a pact. We cheated.'

'What?' said Jesse. 'How?'

'Well, Astrid took my personality tests, and she went to the interviews with my name badge on. I did all the academics, the engineering, computing and astrophysics. We did that for a whole year.' Jesse exhaled as if the wind had been knocked from him.

'I wish you'd told me that earlier,' he said.

'Why?'

'Because I've spent almost a year here, feeling guilty. Feeling as if I have stolen my seat on this shuttle from a dead girl.'

'I couldn't,' said Juno. 'I guess I was ashamed. I think that's why I worked so hard on the Damocles Document and on being a good member of the crew. Maybe I thought I could carve out a purpose for myself, and really earn it. Deserve it.'

'Well,' said Jesse, 'I guess everyone makes mistakes.'

'But that's the other thing,' said Juno. 'It wasn't really a mistake. I'm glad I'm here. With you.'

There was a laid-back joy that came with letting go of her secret. It had been easy. Easy like letting her feet go limp on the pedals of her bike, speeding down a hill just to feel how good it was, her heart in her throat, the wind in her ears.

She leant over and kissed him. He was the sweetest thing she had ever tasted. All night, fear and starvation had filled her mouth with the bitter taste of blood and metal, but Jesse was like glacé cherries. It was as if he had never kissed a girl before. He pulled away from her in surprise, tiny beads of sweat erupting from his fingertips.

'Your heart is beating so fast,' she said, laughing, although she could feel her own pulse throbbing in her veins. They smiled at each other, Jesse's tooth caught on his bottom lip. Juno leant in to kiss him again, this time savouring everything, the warmth that spread through her, the way his hair felt through her fingers, like spiders' silk. For the first time in a while, she was joyfully grateful for her whole body.

He told her that he thought she was beautiful and even before it happened, Juno could tell that he was already picturing it; the caution lights splashing her skin amber and rose, strands of her hair fluoresced chrome green, the arc of her spine and the backs of her thighs a study in electric blue.

'Tell me when to stop,' he said, taking off his top. Juno

gazed for a moment at his skin, at the muscles he'd formed over months of labour in the greenhouse, jet hair in baby curls around his temples. She leant forward, and then her body was a warm weight on top of his. She saw, then, what an uncomplicated thing this was.

When she rolled onto her back he was slow unzipping her flight suit because his hands were shaking. He found a bleached cotton vest underneath, the same as his, and when she pulled it over her head, her breasts were like sandalwood moons, nipples like black coins. He kissed her stomach in a way that made her muscles jolt. His breath was hot on the little downy hairs that sprang up around her navel and he ran his fingers in circles along her hipbones, then lower down. Under the lace-trimmed edge of her knickers, the private warmth between her legs. It was a shock to feel someone else there, but Juno didn't tell him to stop. His fingers were like ice, but she stared up at him, and his familiar face was all she could see, circled by a dark nimbus of stars.

'I love you,' he said again, and then the rest was easy.

It was a strange mix of intuitive and utterly alien. After a little embarrassed fumbling, he was inside her and she closed her eyes. They stopped, then started, then smiled at each other. Each time she felt herself clench against him with anxiety, Jesse stroked her and told her it was okay, to relax, and finally her mind was centred in her own body, drawn back the way it was sometimes when she was running, and her flesh became a Roman candle, her nerves electric. After a few minutes, their breathing grew heavy and irregular. Finally, the jolt came. She bit down hard on her bottom lip. It happened, quickly, almost accidentally, like skidding down a sloping street of black ice, one moment of terrible wonderful weight-lessness and then the slap of hitting ground she forgot was there. Jesse tumbled with her with a sigh of gladness, and as soon as they finished they remembered the cold. It descended upon them like a net, the sweat on the nape of Juno's neck freezing. Jesse had already begun shivering again.

Everything washed back on a low tide of despair. Jesse's hair still smelt of smoke, and there was a smattering of bruises spreading across the tight ridges of his stomach.

They were running out of air.

She wondered if they could try again, and if her body would welcome her back into oblivion.

The heavy material of her flight suit was cool as a tomb when she climbed back into it, and as she did up the zip again she could tell that Jesse was still staring at her.

'Hey,' he whispered, and Juno was glad that when she lay back beside him he couldn't see her. 'Are you okay?'

She examined herself for a moment. Here were the famil-iar pricklings of trepidation and embarrassment – as she had expected – but then, gazing up at the stars, she realized she could feel something else too, something kinder and new.

ASTRID

08.02.13

THE FIRST AMERICAN TO perform a spacewalk was Lieutenant Colonel Ed White, on a mission for *Gemini IV*. Unlike modern spacewalks, which could last for hours, he had only twenty minutes until he ran out of oxygen.

What had it been like? Astrid always wondered. The first American to behold his home from low earth orbit: the California coast, the unobscured sun. People said that those were the shortest twenty minutes of his whole life.

Right at the end, when his time was running out, he found he didn't want to leave. He stalled, staring back at the Earth. The beauty of it cut him to the bone, but he was running out of time. His crewmates told him to turn away and hurry, that he was running out of oxygen. But what strength it took, to turn away from this gift he had been given – he, a mere mortal – gazing through the eyes of God. Mission control screamed at him to return, and when he finally did he said, 'It's the saddest moment of my life.'

6 A.M.

ASTRID WOKE TO THE sound of the O_2 alarm, and her mind was jolted back into her body. She had fallen asleep in one of the large chairs on the flight deck and the readout on the dashboards showed that their oxygen levels were close to critical. They had about thirty hours left.

'Astrid.' Eliot turned to her, his eyes red with sleeplessness.

'What's the time?' she asked. He glanced at his watch.

'Our EVA's in about forty minutes or so,' he said.

'Right.' Astrid nodded. Her head was still full of sleep, but she stood up slowly. 'Any news about Sheppard?"

'No,' said Eliot.

'I'll be watching all the time,' Poppy said from the comms deck.

'Right.'

'Don't be too nervous.'

'It's fine,' Astrid assured her. 'I've never done one before.'

It was true, there was a small thrill that came from being the first to do a spacewalk, even if it was only inside the ship. Astrid had spent more than 200 hours underwater in her bulky spacesuit in the Weightless Environment Training Facility at the space centre in London, so many days running through scripted procedures in the submerged mock-up of the ship that it was difficult to believe that finally she was going to do it for real.

She had always imagined that the day she donned a spacesuit it would be to step out into the darkness of space. But during this EVA she, Eliot and Commander Bovarin would only be stepping down into the vacuum of the lower deck to try to repair the damaged service module. Astrid's stomach fluttered.

If they were unable to fix it, they would not have enough oxygen or power left to perform a second EVA. Not only were her life and the lives of her crew dependent on their success, but if the mission was aborted it was possible that none of them would ever see the clear sky of Terra-Two, and the thought was too horrible to contemplate.

The ship was dark as the ocean floor. The emergency lights flared amber and red at intervals down the corridor, and the acrid smell of smoke clung to the fibres of her T-shirt. Astrid rubbed her arms – she was already beginning to feel the chill in the air. The *Damocles* was radiating heat into space. If they didn't fix the temperature controls soon it was going to get a lot colder, and quickly.

Astrid climbed down the hatch and onto the middle deck, where she found their commander. '*Dobroe utro*,' Commander Bovarin said. *Good morning*. He had already unpacked their spacesuits. 'Ready to begin?'

DESCENDING INTO AN AIRLESS vacuum required a strict set of preparations. Astrid followed Igor's lead, moving almost mechanically as they checked their EMU systems, held masks silently to their faces to pre-breathe. Then they donned their suits, a tedious process that took almost forty minutes, then more checks, examining the rubber seals in the spacesuits for leaks, then pre-breathing again. Although Astrid had long ago learned the entire process off by heart, she sometimes found herself hard pressed to remember exactly what every step was for. She knew that pre-breathing – which eliminated all the nitrogen from the body – was to avoid the bends. The bends happen when the nitrogen in an astronaut's bloodstream does what the carbon dioxide in a shaken Coke can does after it's opened. Only, inside her. The thought of bubbles itching and creeping under her skin made her shudder.

'I can't count how many hours of EVA I've logged during my years,' Igor said. 'But it's always humbling to think that there's only this—' he pressed his fingers together – 'a few millimetres of fabric and metal between you and nothing.'

'Is it true what they say?' Eliot asked, grabbing his helmet.

'What do they say?' Astrid asked.

'That space smells like gunpowder?'

'You'll find out for yourself soon,' Igor said, lacing up a boot. 'When we come back.'

'I've heard it leaves a smell on the suits,' Eliot said, looking down. 'A smell on our spacesuits and gloves. Like burning. Smoky. Sweet.'

Astrid pulled her visor down and said, 'I've heard it's because of all the combustion going on in the stars.'

Fifteen minutes later they were finally ready to leave, and headed down to the lower deck.

The darkness was unnerving. Astrid had only the lights of her helmet to penetrate the blackness. What lightbulbs there had been had broken, or blown.

A little further along the corridor she spotted the shattered porthole window she had tried to repair the previous day. She shuddered. In the hull of the ship was a scorched hole where they'd been hit. It looked as if a missile had blasted through the metal, a black starburst of soot radiating away from the hole.

'*Heading to the first quadrant.*' Commander Bovarin's voice crackled through her headset. Astrid followed him. Although she was breathing the clean oxygen in her suit, she could almost imagine the smell of the corridor, of charred plastic and electricity, and as she passed, she was careful to avoid the glinting fingers of exposed wires, the sliced ventilation tubes that Juno and Eliot had tossed aside to close the door to the bridge.

Commander Bovarin was heading around the corner towards the service modules. She and Eliot trudged after him, heavy in their suits.

The service modules were in uninhabited parts of the ship. Beneath the crew module, on the lowest deck, sandwiched between the equipment rooms and the escape shuttle. The service module was the compartment that contained the fuel cells and batteries that provided power to the spacecraft, as well as essential computer systems like guidance and thermal control. Igor pulled open the aft fuselage access door to reach it and when Astrid peered inside, her heart sank. The entire module was a tangle of melted copper wiring. She felt a sickening swoop in her stomach. The service module was their lifeline. Without it, they had no hope of powering the ship, and without power, there was no way to continue the mission.

The prospect of making it to Terra-Two was receding from them. Astrid's eyes began to sting.

As Igor pulled through the wreckage, she heard his groan of despair over the headset. But his words came to her as if from a vast distance. 'We've lost three essential buses, ESS1BC, ESS2CA and ESS3AB. . . . And a power surge in the fuel cells means two of them are unserviceable . . . The LiOH is . . .'

In the end, they settled for doing the only thing that they could do and patched up the holes in the wall, so that the crew would be able to access the lower deck without having to climb into spacesuits. Then they returned to the middle deck in silent misery, running through the motions of shutting down the EMU systems and other components, changing out batteries and cartridges.

'We don't have much time left,' Eliot said. The entire EVA had taken six hours.

'Yes …' said Igor quietly. 'The service module is just too damaged to support this crew. We don't have the spare parts we need, not on this ship.'

'We can't just give up,' Astrid said.

'No. We can't just give up. But we have to face the fact that the mission has changed now. My job now is to get the crew home safely.'

'You mean … abandon the mission?'

'We still have one serviceable escape shuttle.' Igor was taking apart his EMU as he spoke. 'It's enough to get six people back home.'

A chill ran through her. 'Six people,' she said softly. And behind both their words, the grim understanding that four people would have to stay behind. Astrid didn't know what would be worse; suffocating in their crippled ship or heading back to Earth in the cramped shuttle, heavy with failure and regret. There would be no gravity on the shuttle, and with each passing day, during the months it would take to return, their bones would begin to turn to dust. Even as Astrid imagined it she knew it wouldn't be her. She knew she would not abandon the *Damocles* or any hope of completing their mission.

'We've fought a good battle,' Igor said.

'No,' Eliot and Astrid said in unison.

She remembered what Poppy had told her, about watching Harry and Jesse steer the *Congreve* to safety. Astrid had tried to imagine the strength it had taken to keep flying even when the sky was on fire and death was at the end of any careless turn. She knew that her father would say that their God had not brought them this far to fail. Astrid had to believe that too. She had to believe that her destiny was not to die amongst the stars but to bring her crew to rest on the still shores of Terra-Two. She had to hold on to it, and even as she did an idea crystallized in her mind.

'Is there no chance we can be rescued? Couldn't a resupply rocket arrive with a new service module attached, or one with all the spare parts we need?'

Such things had happened on previous missions. Two years earlier a centrifugal module had broken on *Orlando*, and the crew had relied on a two-person resupply shuttle from Mars, whose technicians made the repair in two months.

'Even if the communications come back online and we request rescue,' Igor said, 'our nearest port of call would have been *Orlando*, but obviously it's no longer possible for them to fly here and repair the damage. The next closest manned human outpost is currently the Russian expedition on Phobos. Even if they agreed to send any technicians they could spare it would take around eight to fourteen weeks. And we're looking at a matter of hours.'

'Because of the oxygen supply,' Astrid said, biting her lip.

'What if we take apart the service module in the escape shuttle?' Eliot suggested. 'We could fix the lithium dioxide to our filters and scrub out the excess CO_2. And then ...' he was breathless with excitement, 'if we take apart the fuel cells and use them as an auxiliary power supply we would have enough power and oxygen to last us six months.'

'Three months,' Igor said. 'There are enough consumables on the escape shuttle to last a crew of five for twenty-four weeks. With a crew twice the size it would last half that time, or possibly a lot less; if you consider the volume of this ship compared to the shuttle, the pressure of oxygen would be lower.'

'Three months,' Astrid said, hope filling her like wind in sails. 'That's still enough time for a service shuttle from Mars – I mean, Phobos – to reach us.'

'Just enough ... assuming the comms are fixed and that Roscocosmos have the resources to spare. And the inclination.'

'Ig— Commander Bovarin,' Astrid said, 'it's a chance, at least ... it's a *chance*.'

'We've had our chance,' Igor said. 'I'm not gambling anymore with the lives of young people now in my care.'

'But—'

'Taking apart the one working escape vessel would be like burning a life raft.'

'It would be like *using* a life raft,' Astrid implored.

'There is no guarantee. I would rather be sure you can get back to your family alive than gamble on a chance only for us all to die here.'

'Or for us all to *live*,' Astrid said. 'For us all to live and make it to Terra-Two.'

'Astrid.' His voice was harsh. 'You just saw the damage in the service module. It's irreparable. Short of a full replacement there is no way we're going anywhere anytime soon. Commander Sheppard is badly injured. Dr Golinsky seems to think that he might be dying, and so am I.' He looked away from her for a moment as if he could see it, the space station like a bright satellite above the milky surface of Europa. 'I know what it feels like to lose a whole crew. You think you're safe, but things change like this—' He snapped his fingers. 'One moment they were talking to us, smiling at us, and then . . . at least *I* get some time.'

Astrid shuddered at the thought of the way death had snatched the crew on *Orlando*, the suddenness.

'It could have been like that for us too,' Eliot said, his blue eyes drifting to the hatch.

'That's right. I'm not a religious man but thanks to some act of fate or the universe or I don't know . . . I had a chance to save my crew. This ship didn't turn into a coffin. Astrid, I'm not throwing that away.'

By then, her throat was thick with tears; she pleaded, pushing her hands together. 'Just *think* about it?'

Igor opened and shut his mouth. 'I'll think about it,' he said finally. 'In the meantime, you have work to do.'

Astrid nodded and got on with it. But all the while she was thinking about how it could happen, the machinery, the tools she would require. She thought about the different ports she would need adaptors for and then cast her mind to rescue.

She often considered all the chance events that had led her to this point; that she had come into the world screaming in a decade when interstellar travel had become possible. She had been chosen from millions, plucked from oblivion to be the glory of the people. There were other miracles too; the fact of life, of the sun rising above an ancient habitable planet, somewhere close by, waiting for her. So why give up hope today?

JESSE

1 P.M.

JESSE SLEPT IN THE greenhouse until noon. Sunk low in the dreamless oblivion of the sleep-deprived. For the first time in months, he was plagued by no visions of the buzzing simulator or the prickling static of the controls or the cockpit splayed before him.

When he awoke, the flight simulating game was like a sickness he'd been cured of. His body was so stiff with cold that he couldn't feel his own legs. His fingers were numb, his nail-beds blue, icy needles of pain prickling up his arms all the way to his elbows. He was alone.

He sat up with some difficulty and looked around, expecting to find Juno's shadow flitting like a sylph through the trees. But she was gone, and overnight the algae spills had frozen into green floes, and water dripping from the automated sprinklers had hardened like stalactites. Everywhere, new buds were strangled by ice. Near the bridge, the blast had ripped sturdy roots right out of the ground.

'Juno?' He listened to his voice echo in the darkness, then stood with great difficulty. His feet were like blocks, his toes felt as if they had swollen in his boots and pain spiked up the back of his leg. He limped to the hatch and slid down the ladder.

On the middle deck, the alarm thundered in his ears. He looked up and down the half-lit corridor, calling out the names of his crew.

He knew that Astrid, Eliot and Commander Bovarin were probably coming to the end of their spacewalk by this time of the afternoon, and so he headed to the control room, expecting to find everyone chatting triumphantly, giving each other high-fives and crying joyful tears because they had repaired the ship. But when he arrived, he found that the control room was empty.

Jesse finally discovered Poppy, Fae and Juno gathered in the kitchen like mourners at a wake. Poppy was bent over the table, her hands clasped together, sobbing uncontrollably. Fae was putting cans of food in boxes. 'We're going home,' Juno said. She appeared like the sun from the corner of the room, and Jesse smiled in spite of himself at the sight of her.

'You need to pack,' Fae told him. 'You don't have long. Please get your personal effects together in a box,' she handed him one, a metal container twice the size of a shoebox, 'and then come back here for further instructions. I would prefer if you packed within half an hour.'

'Wait, what?' Jesse asked. 'Why?'

'The service module can't be fixed,' Juno told him. 'Didn't you hear it over the headset?'

'I was up in the greenhouse,' Jesse told her.

'They're making us leave,' Poppy said, her voice thick with despair. 'They're making us leave them.'

Jesse looked at Fae in disbelief. The doctor's hands were shaking a little and she lowered her eyes. His gut twisted with grief at Poppy's words. 'Is this true?' he asked Fae, desperate to believe that it wasn't. If they left now, she and Cai, Commander Sheppard and Commander Bovarin, would only have a few more hours to live.

Before Jesse could speak, Commander Bovarin entered and they all looked up, straightening their backs. Astrid stood in his shadow, her hair still tied up under a skullcap, which made her flint-black eyes curve up like a cat's. 'The shuttle will depart in T-minus six hours,' Igor said, looking at his watch, then at Fae. 'You've already begun the preparations?'

Jesse simply stared wordlessly at the man, his mind reeling. He could hardly begin to accept what Igor was saying, what it meant.

'No.' Astrid stepped in front of the commander, but he waved her words away.

'The decision has been made,' he said.

'And that's it: you're just giving up?' Astrid's voice was loud in the hush of the kitchen and her shadow stretched across the table.

'The decision has been made,' he repeated stiffly.

'Aren't you going to at least tell them?'

'Astrid.' Fae's voice was full of reproach. It was rare for any one of them to deliberately disobey a senior's orders.

'Tell us what?' Poppy asked.

'That there's a chance to save the mission.'

'Astrid, would you please—'

'What is she talking about?' Poppy asked.

'Eliot worked it out.' Astrid grabbed a marker from the middle of the desk, flipped over a discarded document and began writing. 'Look here. We need to survive about two months for a rescue from Phobos.' Poppy leant over to watch her write. 'That means we need oxygen.' She wrote 'O_2' next to a bullet point. 'And enough power to get and keep the comms online. We already have more than enough food to last us, and water if we ration it, and use the rest made from the fuel cells—'

'But the service module's not working,' Poppy said, as if anyone could forget.

'Yes, the main one, the one that is supposed to last us the two decades of this journey. But the escape shuttle can support a crew for six months. If we rewired the shuttle and used it as an auxiliary life support system, it could keep us alive – all of us – for at least twelve weeks. That's more than enough time for us to be rescued. Enough time for a team from Phobos to come with spare parts and a new module.'

'But—' Poppy rubbed her head in confusion. 'It took us months to get from Mars to Europa.'

'But Mars is closer to Jupiter in its orbit now than it was in July,' Astrid explained. 'And the Russian shuttle is lighter than us. It could take them only two months, even hauling a service module.'

'If they launched this week,' Juno said, staring down at the page.

'And that still doesn't solve the problem with the computers,' Cai said. 'The thermal control system has shut down; we're radiating all our excess heat out into space.'

Astrid smiled as if Cai had asked the exact right question. 'So our engine and all the electrical systems we keep running mean that we are making excess heat from electrical energy all the time, and the job of the thermal controls are to get rid of the heat, to cool us and all the equipment down—'

'Only when all systems are nominal,' Cai said. 'Right now, the thermal controls are overcompensating, so we're losing more heat than we're making.'

'After we follow my plan we might even have enough oxygen to schedule a second EVA and fix that manually,' Astrid said. 'Thermal control is pretty basic engineering, at least on the hardware side. Eliot could do it. If we just take off some of the radiators that are absorbing the heat from the ship and pouring it out into space.'

'That sounds risky,' said Poppy. 'What if rescue doesn't come, or comes too late?'

'We'll be in the exact same situation we are now,' said Jesse. 'Only without a lifeboat.'

'Exactly!' Igor's voice was startling. 'I would rather half of you made it home safely than—'

'Take a chance to make it to Terra-Two?' Astrid interrupted. 'Who's to say that, after us, there will be another mission anytime soon? What if this is our only chance for the next couple of generations? If we come back, will people want to sign up for the Off-World Colonization Programme? What if governments decide it was not worth the money – everything that was sacrificed to get us just this far. There was talk that the *Orlando* mission might be discontinued entirely even before we left.'

'Astrid!' Igor slammed his hand down on the table and Astrid dropped her pen in surprise. 'I don't want to hear any more of this. The decision has been made.' Tears sprang to Astrid's eyes but she fought to stay strong. She had been trained to listen to the captain's orders and yet Jesse could see her entire body was shaking with anger.

'You're just giving up,' she said. 'The shuttle can leave without me. I'm staying here.' She knocked the papers off the table so they scattered on the floor and stormed out of the room. In the silence that followed, Jesse heard the heavy sound of her boots as she climbed down the hatch.

For a moment, Jesse allowed himself to imagine Astrid's plan. If they were rescued, then this time next year they could be in interstellar space. But, during training, Jesse had been taught that there was no disaster worse than mutiny. That the crew in a spacecraft needed to operate like one body, with the commander as the head. Jesse had not truly believed it until he and Harry had steered the shuttle out of danger. The two of them had abandoned their disagreements and navigated the shuttle together in a ballet of technical skill, Harry taking the lead and Jesse anticipating his movements. So he swallowed his objections and kept quiet.

After the meeting, he headed down to the crew module. It was baffling to him that the ship was already a hive of activity. Eliot was on the lower deck, packing up their spacesuits for the flight home. Poppy was helping Fae to pick out the rations they required for the coming months. Harry was helping Juno download files from the ship's computer. Jesse watched her for the seconds it took her to notice him. If he had not been chosen for the mission he would not have been given the chance to love her – and for a moment fate seemed kind. But then she spotted him, and Jesse remembered that yesterday they'd had more than twenty years together and now they had only a few months. The loss was devastating.

'It seems crazy to me,' he said, rubbing his eyes, as if he still believed that perhaps this afternoon was a terrible dream, 'that we're just leaving like this. Without them.'

'I know.' Juno twisted a cable around in her hands and bundled it into a storage box. The whole ship was like a music festival an hour after the headline act, grim industrious stage hands working to take the whole show down and pack it up, no time for sentiment.

'What will happen?' he asked her.

'We'll board in two hours,' she said.

'I mean, when we get back?'

'I don't know,' she admitted, and they gazed at each other in silence.

Jesse had already pictured an alternate life for them. Imagined Juno switching from biochemistry to politics, trekking the globe to negotiate treaties, conversing in six different tongues, penning laws that were like her Damocles Document writ large. Jesse imagined himself kneading the land, working with long-haired men and women on permaculture, building compost heaps and saving rainforests. They were different people, he realized with a sinking in his chest, going different places.

He left without saying anything.

In their cabin, Jesse found that Eliot had already stripped his bed of its sheets and peeled his posters off the walls, and even Harry had taken down a few of his things. The room pulsed with the same aching vacancy as their dormitories in Dalton at the end of term. Belongings packed up, the light glaring off naked walls stripped clumsily of posters and notices. A sorry sight, the nicked metal bedframes, the plastic mattress covers, the suddenly silent halls.

Jesse looked at his untidy bed, at the draped pashminas he had used instead of curtains, the glittering dream catchers, the bamboo wind chimes that only ever sang in the morning when he leapt to his feet or when someone slammed the door. He decided, then, that if he was going to leave, he would take nothing with him.

ELIOT

2 P.M.

AFTER COMMANDER BOVARIN DISMISSED them from the kitchen, Eliot headed down to the lower deck to pack up the spacesuits the Beta would take with them on the shuttle back to Earth. Their spacewalk that morning seemed like a terribly long time ago, now.

Taking apart his spacesuit, Eliot considered, as he often did, what a marvel of engineering it was; eleven layers of material, ortho-fabric, aluminized mylar, neoprene and stainless steel. If Eliot alone possessed all the skills and equipment, it would take him around two and a half years to build himself one, and would cost him about £9 million.

The ripped and bloodied shell of Commander Sheppard's old suit was slumped in the corridor outside, and it hurt Eliot to see it.

In the same way, during the spacewalk that morning, he had seen the damage that the service module had sustained with his own eyes. It had been torn like a limb, shot right through the middle by some speeding object, wires and severed piping spilling out like organs, condensation frozen in uneven bubbles of ice all over the blackened metal. The sight of it almost induced a sympathetic ache inside Eliot, and he guessed that Igor had felt the same way too.

The *Damocles* wasn't just a machine; it was a work of art. When Eliot looked at diagrams of its engine he saw years of love, the dedication of dozens of minds, the loyal work of a thousand hands.

Igor had told them that they would have to return home, but as soon as Astrid had suggested his plan to the crew – dismantling the service module on the escape shuttle and rewiring it to the *Damocles* – Eliot was imagining it. How it could be done, which valves to switch, which wires to reroute.

It came as no surprise to him when, almost thirty minutes into his work, he heard someone coming down the hatch, stepping carefully. It was Astrid, still dressed in her flight suit, holding two of Igor's manuals and a box of tools. When she spotted him she looked up and down the corridor just to make sure they were alone.

'Hey,' she said. 'I need your help.' She glanced over her shoulder again and then looked at the work that Eliot was doing. 'Is Igor helping you with that?'

'I don't need his help,' Eliot said. 'He's on the control deck.'

'Good. I need to get into the escape shuttle.'

'Right now?' Eliot put down the helmet he was holding.

'This can't have been the plan, can it?' Astrid asked. She looked more like Juno in the half-light. Her eyes were wet, her lashes pearly and sticking together. 'For us to fail like this?'

'I don't know,' Eliot said.

'I feel like nothing good can ever happen to me if I let this dream go,' Astrid said. 'I don't want to die like Tessa Dalton, just looking and looking at the stars. I dream about Terra-Two so vividly that this ship sometimes feels like the dream. I can feel the rain, on my face.' She closed her eyes and Eliot thought he could see it too, the salty drops from Terran clouds rolling down her cheeks. 'I'd rather die than let go.'

Eliot felt an inkling of it too. But for him it was about the machines. Inside Eliot, there were robots longing to be built, and the only thing more tragic than never using them was never building them. He thought about Igor's machines, about the most spectacular one of all: the gravity-assist drive. Igor had sacrificed his life for his work, and if they left now it would amount to nothing. Eliot wanted to see how it felt to slingshot around the resplendent rings of Saturn, to soar through interstellar space.

'My whole life has been about this mission.' Astrid's voice was low.

'Mine too,' he said.

'So,' she said, looking up at him, 'will you help me to save it? I need to get into the escape shuttle, but Igor has locked me out. I need an engineer-authorized ID badge to get in. And you're the only one who can help me.' With his help, the plan could work. They didn't have to leave Igor, Cai, Sheppard and Fae to die on the *Damocles*.

'Don't you want to see what it's like?' she asked. 'If it was all worth it?'

Eliot said yes because, even after all that had happened, even after watching the crew on *Orlando* disappear, even after losing the girl he loved, this remained. He needed to know.

JESSE

4 P.M.

BEFORE THE LIGHTS CAME back on, Jesse gathered with the rest of the Beta in the crew module to say goodbye to the seniors. Poppy was sobbing quietly, wiping tears away with the sleeve of the old Dalton leavers' hoodie that she wore on top of her flight suit. It said 'Class of '12' on the back, with the names of the school's 'Final Fifty' printed inside the numbers. She and Juno were searching under cushions and chairs in the crew module as Juno ticked items off an inventory. As they'd had so little time to pack, the room looked as if it had been in the path of a hurricane, blankets slipping off sofas, wires hanging from open equipment panels and trailing out of drawers. Chess pieces toppled, three knights rolled under the spine of a book, Harry Potter in Korean, a rook mired in a puddle of baked beans.

Fae emerged from the infirmary still wearing what she had been yesterday, hair falling loose of her bun. When Jesse asked how their commander was doing she simply shook her head sadly.

Cai and Igor were helping Harry gather the equipment needed for their flight, piling it up near the hatch. Juno looked up from her clipboard and said, 'Astrid should be here by now.'

'I haven't seen Astrid,' Poppy said, her arms full of books. 'Not for the past few hours. Or Eliot, for that matter.'

Fae hissed, and glanced at her watch. 'Now is not the time for them to be wandering around.'

'I'll look for them in the engine room,' Igor said, heading back in that direction.

'And I'll do a quick sweep of the greenhouse,' Cai said.

They stood in silence for a moment. Everyone absorbed by their own thoughts of the trip ahead. The small cabin in which they would live for six months was nothing compared to the spacious beauty of the *Damocles*. It broke Jesse's heart to say goodbye, but as the hours approached a shameful, secret excitement began to dawn inside him as he contemplated Earth, his sister and his parents. Returning a kind of hero.

Fae broke the silence. 'So, as there are no members of the senior crew on this last mission home, Harrison Bellgrave is now acting commander.'

Harry looked up, his watery eyes strangely vacant. 'Me ...' He fingered the badge on his lapel, the bronze pin that he'd fought for years to wear. Then he glanced up at Jesse. 'You know what, Jesse Solloway? I don't know how or where you learned to fly like that but ... it was the greatest thing I've seen in all my years of Command School. We wouldn't be here if it wasn't for him.' Tearing off his badge, he turned to the others and said, 'I'd be dead if it wasn't for Commander Sheppard ... and Jesse.'

Then he did something Jesse had never imagined he would: he handed over the badge. It glinted in the low light, cold to the touch. 'I know it's not worth much, now that we're going back to Earth, but ...'

Jesse didn't know what to say.

'You *did* save us,' Poppy said, and she flung her arm over his shoulder and kissed his cheek with a loud smack of her lips.

'I'm proud of you,' Fae said, putting her hand on Jesse's shoulder.

'And glad you came with us,' Juno said, her eyes warm. She embraced him too, and Jesse's chest swelled with gladness.

'All of us are,' Harry said.

It was all he'd ever wanted. Their acceptance, their warm embrace, and it had come too late.

As Fae reached for Jesse the main lights came on. For a moment they appeared so bright they bleached his vision.

'What's happening?' Harry rubbed his eyes as if he'd just woken up.

'I don't know,' Poppy said with a gasp. In the same moment, the vents along the sides of the room activated, and air whooshed out like smoke. 'Maybe everything is fixed?'

'That doesn't make sense,' Fae said, running over to examine a booting-up monitor on one of the walls.

Juno clenched her fists. She already knew the answer.

'It's Astrid.'

POPPY

4.30 P.M.

POPPY HAD ALWAYS HATED arguments in her own house. One morning at breakfast her mother had told her boyfriend at the time that she would be home late, words that – from their facial expressions – clearly sent shockwaves down through some unseen well of domestic resentment. He'd reached across the table and slapped her mother with such a hard whack that blood sprang from her nose, and she looked around, her eyes whirling in surprise. Poppy had stared between the adults in horror and, even afterwards, when they were making tea for each other and kissing, something of that fear remained. Buried deep in Poppy and transformed into a sticky dread of conflict, a need to please, to plan the parties, to keep everyone smiling.

Which was why she would have said anything to quell the argument that ensued when Astrid and Eliot emerged from the lower deck. Igor had found them in the shuttle. They'd disabled it and, against orders, enacted their plan. Taking its life support apart and attaching it to the *Damocles*.

The entire crew were swept into a flurry of action after they realized what had happened. Poppy ran up to the communications deck, checking different channels to see if anyone had replied to their distress signal. Over the headset she could hear nothing but a vicious hiss of static, although a data file with a Russian title was loading on one of the monitor screens. Hope flushed through her. Was rescue coming?

As she reach over to grab the mouse, Harry burst into the room and shouted at Astrid, who was seated on the control deck opposite, transcribing figures from one of the screens.

Jesse ran in behind him, his face red, and grabbed Harry's wrist as if to hold him back. Harry twisted free. 'You realize,' he shouted, 'that it's an offence to disobey direct orders from your acting commander.' Igor and Eliot entered the room behind him. 'Igor said that you weren't to touch the service module. We were ordered to leave. To return home.'

'I know—' Eliot stepped between Harry and Astrid, his hands up as if to defend her. 'But we just couldn't.'

'Couldn't obey orders,' Fae said, her face pale. 'Back on Earth, this would be considered mutiny.'

'That's right,' said Harry. 'You'd be court-martialled.'

Astrid stood up. Poppy could tell that she was stunned by their reaction. It was the exact opposite of the one she had been expecting. 'But we saved you all.'

'Saved us?' Juno's voice was simmering with rage. They had all entered the room now, everyone but Commander Sheppard, who was still unconscious in the infirmary. It felt strange to gather like this without him.

'Do you realize what was about to happen?' Astrid asked. 'Do you realize what we were about to do? Leave this ship. Leave Igor – I mean, Commander Bovarin – and Fae and Cai and Sheppard to *die*. Go home. Only it's not home anymore. If we stepped out now, do you think we'd have a chance to go to

Terra-Two ever again? Do you think they'd choose *us*? All those years of work, everything we did would be wasted. Our whole lives ...'

'It will be wasted when we die here!' Harry shouted.

'Astrid was just doing what she thought was right,' Jesse said.

'No.' Juno slammed her fist against a desk. 'Astrid was just doing what *she* wanted. Being selfish and reckless.'

Astrid let out a cry of indignation, and stepped closer to her sister. 'Do you even want to be here, Juno?'

'What?'

'On this ship. On this mission. Did you ever really want to go to Terra-Two or did you just want to go because *I* wanted to go? Because you've never been able to stand being alone. You slept in my bed until you were twelve.' The expression of betrayal on Juno's face made Poppy ache. 'Maybe this is what this is about,' Astrid continued. 'You went to Dalton because you need me. Not because you have a higher purpose.'

'Oh, and you do?'

'There's a whole *planet* waiting for us, Juno. This is our only chance to go there. And you're all too cowardly to fight for it.'

'Die for it, you mean,' said Juno. 'Do you realize what you've chosen for us, now? The Russian expedition still haven't responded to our message. We only have a few weeks of oxygen left. They might not come in time. Or at all.'

'They will.'

'You better hope so. Because if you're wrong, it'll be *your* fault. You'll have all of our deaths on your hands.'

'We have three months of oxygen,' Eliot reminded them.

'No, we don't have three months,' Fae said. She sank down in the chair next to Poppy and put her fingers between her eyebrows as if she was nursing a headache. 'The volume of this ship is larger than the volume of the shuttle. So the partial pressure of oxygen will already be a lot lower. We have half that time or less, because once the oxygen is lower than 50 per cent of normal levels, we'll start to die.' Her words made dread and bile creep up in Poppy's throat.

'Remember what we learned in Sunday school about the Israelites?' Astrid said to her sister in a low voice, taking her face in her hands, willing her to recall it. 'Who trekked for generations in the desert, or the *Mayflower* pilgrims who crossed an ocean in the winter to found a new country. History will remember us. This is the day our descendants will sing about and rejoice.'

'The *Mayflower* pilgrims were religious nuts, and half of them died of scurvy, pneumonia or tuberculosis,' Juno listed on her fingers. 'And that land that they found—'

'What happened to your faith, Juno? Did you think this would be easy?'

'Can I be the first one to say,' Harry interrupted, 'that I have no plans to die here, or for this mission. Not now, or ever. And going back to Earth – going back home – would it really be so bad?'

'This isn't a holiday, Harry,' Astrid said, letting go of Juno and narrowing her eyes in disgust. 'It's not some ski trip you can return from when the going gets tough.'

'You made damned sure of that, didn't you,' Harry said, his voice low and deadly.

'Please stop,' Poppy pleaded and they all fell silent, bristling in the glacial light of Europa. Poppy's head spun with confusion. She didn't want to go back to Earth either, and the thought of leaving half of the crew to die on the ship had broken her heart.

'I'm glad they did it,' Jesse finally said. 'I feel like an idiot for not helping. I can't believe I thought I could leave Igor and Fae and Cai and Commander Sheppard to die here. Could you?'

'I know what you mean,' Poppy said quietly. 'Sitting on that shuttle a week from now knowing that our crewmates were suffocating to death.' Fae put her head in her hands, and Cai looked as if the thought made him ill.

'We're the senior crew,' Igor said. His voice was raspy, and he stopped a moment to cough into a handkerchief. 'This—' He coughed again. 'T-this is a choice that we made to give you the best chance.' Poppy noticed little petals of blood blooming on the cotton fabric in his fist.

'I'm sorry, sir,' Jesse said, turning to him. 'But it wasn't *our* choice.'

'It wasn't yours to make,' Igor said, his teeth gritted with fury.

'They've given up enough,' Eliot said. 'Igor gave up the rest of his life for this mission. Sheppard left his wife and baby behind. Fae clearly never wanted to be here in the first place.'

'That's right,' Astrid said, her eyes pleading for under-standing. She looked at Igor and then Fae and Cai. 'Please understand, Commander Bovarin. I know we're supposed to listen to orders. And I almost always do, but this time . . .' she took a shaky breath. 'This time there was too much to lose.'

'I've heard enough of this. I say we punish her,' Harry said, crossing his arms.

'How?' asked Jesse, looking to Igor, then back to Harry, whose fists were still clenched. 'Throw her overboard like pirates?'

'On Mars, the punishment for a serious offence, up to and including mutiny, is confinement,' Juno said.

Jesse snorted in disbelief. 'You mean lock her up?'

'That's exactly what she means,' Harry said, stabbing a finger at Eliot and Astrid. 'Both of them.'

'She's your sister, and this isn't a prison,' Jesse said, then turned to Juno. 'What happened to doing things differently?'

Juno folded her arms. 'We have to maintain the rule of law amongst ourselves. Otherwise, anything goes. She might be my sister, but we're all brothers and sisters here and Astrid *betrayed* us.'

'The rule of law.' Jesse snorted. 'Oh, this is about your plan to build a utopia by getting us all to follow a bunch of arbitrary rules you invented. Like that's never happened in human history before.'

'We have a chance to do it right this time,' Juno said, although she looked a little wounded. 'And I thought you believed in the Damocles Document. In making a better world?'

'I believe in *you*. But, don't you even realize what utopia means? It means – here's a fun fact – it means "no place". Somewhere that doesn't exist. There is no place where humans stop being humans. We're going to fight wherever we go, we're going to argue. In the future, we'll fuck our children up, and drill holes into the ground and spill oil in the sea. We'll make mistakes.'

'We certainly will with that attitude,' Juno said. 'There is no law up here, Jesse. So someone has to make it. We can't just go around treating each other however we want, hurting each other. One of us has to stop it.'

'And who made you the judge? Why does it have to be you?'

They were standing in a row now, Astrid and Eliot on the furthest end, Harry and Juno advancing on them, Poppy and Jesse in between. Poppy could see the fire and fear in Juno's eyes, and she looked around at the senior crew, hoping that they might put an end to the fight, but Fae was leaning over the dashboard on the communications deck in tears, muttering something like 'enough' or 'one thing after another' in German. Poppy knew that she hadn't slept for forty-eight hours. Neither had Igor, who was wheezing into his fist. Cai had never inserted himself into an argument before and he didn't now.

Disappointed, Poppy felt as if she'd leant over the seat of a lurching taxi to find there was no driver at the wheel. Who was in charge? On Terra-Two, the Betas were the people Poppy would have to make decisions with, would have to defer to and trust. Yet, at this moment, it seemed as if they hated each other.

'Okay!' Poppy shouted and raised her hands. Everyone turned to look at her. 'In light of the fact that Commander Sheppard is not here and this decision involves all of us, we should have a vote.' Fae lifted her head. Igor – who was leaning heavily against a desk for strength – attempted to straighten his back. 'Please can we?' she asked them both.

'Vote over what?' asked Fae.

'What to do next,' Poppy explained. 'I'm not saying that what Astrid and Eliot did was right, disobeying orders. But maybe it's right that with large decisions like this, life or death decisions, we should all be involved.'

'That's not how a ship works,' Igor said. 'Or any mission. There is a chain of command.'

'That's right,' Harry said. 'It's not a democracy.'

'Well maybe it should be,' Jesse said. 'Poppy's right. This is a chance for us to decide what kind of society we want to live in. How we make choices. How we deal with disagreement—'

'We can't *do* anything now,' Juno interrupted. 'Astrid and Eliot have sabotaged our escape shuttle. They made that decision without consulting anyone.'

'So let's vote on how to punish them,' Harry suggested.

'Whether or not to,' Jesse said.

'That sounds reasonable,' Igor said, exhaling heavily.

'It does to me too,' Juno said.

'Okay,' said Poppy. 'If Astrid and Eliot should be punished—'

'For disobeying orders and putting our lives at risk,' Juno interrupted, 'put up your hand.' She raised hers, and so did Harry.

'If Astrid and Eliot should be canonized when we get to Terra-Two for being brave enough to save the mission and everyone's life. . .' Jesse folded his arms. 'I don't think that Astrid should be punished for doing what she thought was right. When the Russians save us we'll be thanking her.'

'If,' Juno said.

Igor spoke. 'Both Astrid and Eliot should be stripped of their duties and responsibilities and confined to the infirmary.'

'I support this punishment,' Fae said. 'They put us all in danger. We're a crew; mutiny will destroy us as quickly as engine failure.'

'Me too,' said Cai from behind her. 'On Mars they would have been punished.'

'Obviously,' said Harry, 'Astrid and Eliot do not get a vote.'

'Which leaves one person.'

They all turned to Poppy. Five people were in favour of a punishment, one person against.

'I . . .' Poppy looked at Astrid's pleading eyes, but then turned to Juno and the rest of the crew. Poppy loved Astrid for her daring, but she was terrified of what would happen to them all now. 'I ... I can't decide,' she admitted, and when the rest of the crew remained silent she noticed a low but insistent noise coming from one of the computers on the communication deck.

A message. She ran to it and opened the attachment that had finally loaded. It was a voice file.

'What are you doing?' Fae leant over.

'Ultra-high-frequency radio communications,' Poppy said. 'Our transceiver picks them up sometimes.'

'*Eto Damoklov?*'

'Is he speaking—?' Juno began, but Poppy *shh*-ed her violently, and pushed the slider to increase the volume. Reduced some of the background noise.

'... *vash neschastnyy sluchay ...*'

'Our "misadventure" ...?' Astrid translated.

'Accident,' Poppy corrected. '*Neschastnyy sluchay* is accident. They're talking about the explosion on *Orlando*.'

'Who?' Fae leant over to read the signature.

'*Sputnik 17*,' Poppy said. 'The Russian station on Phobos. They heard our message. They say that their mission control has cleared them to send us a new service module. Engineers to come and fix our ship.'

Astrid dropped to her knees in relief, her eyes filled with tears. Jesse and Juno yelled in celebration.

'How long?' Fae asked, her eyes wide with renewed hope.

Eliot's brow wrinkled. 'Considering the acceleration of a VASIMR engine on a gen five Russian shuttle, and that we're about 2.5 Astronomical Units from Phobos right now ...' he swallowed, like a doctor delivering a miserable prognosis. 'About two months.'

'Eight weeks,' Juno whispered. 'And with this level of oxygen ... we'll be lucky if we make it.'

JUNO

13.02.13

1 A.M.

TEMPERATURE: 10°C
O_2: 86% SEA LEVEL
WEEKS UNTIL RESCUE: 7

IT HAPPENED FIVE DAYS later, when Juno was alone. Astrid and Eliot had been confined to the infirmary and so she and Fae moved their ailing commander into his own cabin. She'd been watching over him, reading in the half-light of his room, slipping into sleep herself, when the monitors started wailing. Her eyes flew open. Commander Sheppard was clutching at the duvet covers, struggling to breathe, gurgling and rasping, and Juno winced at the shallow sounds of his pain. She could see it in his eyes; the panic of oxygen deprivation, the fight in his clenching muscles. And, it was the strangest thing, she thought she could see the life drain right out of him. His face folded up on itself.

'Commander Sheppard,' she called out and began adjusting the machines, pulling at his oxygen mask, trying to save him, trying to keep him breathing, when she realized that he was slipping away and there was nothing she could do. She stared down at him in horror.

She didn't know what he could hear, but she grabbed his hand in hers and said. 'You were really good. You taught us everything you know. And you tried your best. You tried your best and you were really good.' Before she was finished, it was over. The man was still. His wide eyes looked as if they were made of glass and he seemed ... empty. He was still warm and soft but he wasn't there and with the blood draining from his face he didn't look like a person anymore, just a still thing.

She must have screamed, or shouted, or something, because the next thing she knew the others were standing in the door-way in their pyjamas and jumpers, pale and shocked.

'He's dead?' Jesse said. 'Poppy—' they could hear her feet coming up the hall, '—don't look.' But it was too late, and she let out a wail of despair.

Finally, Fae stepped forward and took charge, pulling the duvet covers up over Commander Sheppard's head and ushering everyone out.

Juno found herself in Jesse's arms, barely able to stand in the corridor, sobbing. 'I'm sorry you had to see that,' he said, softly, wiping a thumb across the tears in her eyes.

'I feel like such an idiot,' she said, swallowing, still shaking. 'Why?'

'I didn't realize until it was too late. It took me by surprise. I keep thinking about what I said to him – I feel so stupid.'

'What did you say?'

'I don't know, I just said the first thing that came into my head. That he was really good with us and really good at his job. I don't know.' She swallowed back another sob.

'Those sound like good things.' Jesse said. 'Those were good, kind things to say.'

'Really?'

'You know something my mother once told me?' he said. 'She was thinking about what it's like just before you're born. Babies can hear their mother's voices, they get distressed, they feel pain, even in their mother's stomach. They turn towards the light, like all of us. The womb, though, is the only world they have ever known. They can see all of it, the beginning and the end, and of course, they think there is nothing else. Can't even conceive of it.

'So, being born, being dragged out into the cold, into the searing lights and all the noise, must feel like dying – like their whole world disappearing along with every single thing they ever knew. Maybe dying is like that too; none of us know what's out there. But we've experienced something a little like it already. Being born was the best thing that ever happened to us. The world is bigger and more beautiful than we ever could have imagined and on the other side of it there were people we'd never met who already love us. They've been excited. They've been waiting.'

ASTRID

15.02.13

TEMPERATURE: 5°C
O_2: 79% SEA LEVEL
WEEKS UNTIL RESCUE: 7

THEY HAD ALLOWED HER to leave the infirmary only once, after the commander died. They held a memorial for him by the airlock, wrapped him in sheets and jettisoned his body into space. It was quick. No one wanted to talk much. '*Plenus annis abiit, plenus honoribus,*' Poppy said. 'He is gone from us, full of years and full of honours.'

Afterwards, they gathered in the kitchen, silently counting everything that they had lost. 'What are we supposed to do now?' Harry asked. Astrid had never seen him in such a state – unshaven and raking fingers through his greasy hair. 'With this mission? With what's left of our fucking lives?'

'Don't say that,' Juno said. She and Jesse sat at the far end of the room, her head in his lap. As their situation grew more dire, the two of them had folded in on themselves, in the eternal conspiracy of lovers.

'He's right though,' Eliot said, lingering by the window as

if he was distracted by something outside. 'You know they're talking about suspending the Europa Project?'

'Who?' Astrid asked.

'NASA.' Poppy nodded in confirmation. 'There were funding cuts after the 2008 recession. They never properly recovered and now, after this ...' She glanced out the window too, as if she could see the station there. 'It's pretty much guaranteed to happen.'

Astrid shuddered. 'Do you think that the Off-World Colonization Project would be suspended if *we* fail?'

'Maybe,' Poppy said.

There had been dissenters in the UK even before their launch. Astrid remembered that a few talk show hosts and columnists had called space academies such as Dalton 'a travesty'. Astrid had watched a video of a famous human rights activist on a politics programme saying, '*These children are too young to give their consent. They're trained from age thirteen, fourteen ... brainwashed, essentially. We talk about radicalization, but it is happening right here in these schools.*'

'Crew.' Igor entered the kitchen, looming large in the doorway, Fae behind him.

'Commander Bovarin.' Jesse looked up and nodded in acknowledgement.

Igor took a deep breath. 'We lost a friend on Wednesday. Commander Sheppard.' At the sound of his name Juno stifled a sob, and Jesse stroked her cheek. 'And before that the crew of *Orlando*.' Eliot turned to the window and bit his knuckles, his face clenched with pain. 'All of them surrendered their lives for their mission and, unfortunately, most of their work will be lost with them. What are those achievements worth when weighed against a life? Captain Omar Briggs, Dr Sie-Yan and their young crew – Cal, James, Kennedy. Commander Solomon Sheppard. A father, a husband, a friend. I hear you ask, what should we do now?'

Astrid flinched at the fresh cut of pain in his voice. Igor came to stand at the head of the table. 'When I, myself, chose to take part in this mission, people were shocked. "What about your children and grandchildren?" they asked me. "What about the things you will miss?" But, like Captain Briggs and Commander Sheppard, I pretended to laugh it off, then. Would they now? If they knew that this would be their end, long before their time, in a moment of fire and nothingness?

'For a long time I've wrestled with these questions. I think that we can find the answer in the lives they led. In their love for their work. Their hunger for discovery. Commander Sheppard was hoping that Terra-Two could be a place for his son and family to follow after him, a place where they would be safe from war and global warming. A second chance for humanity. And, in a different way, that is what Captain Briggs and Sie Yan were doing too. They knew the risks. I think they would have said, now, exactly the same thing they said then. When they were asked, "Will you embark on this journey?" they would have smiled, and they would have said "Yes!" I would say "Yes" again, too.'

AFTER THAT, THE LAST vestiges of her dream finally evaporated for Astrid. She felt as if, with Sheppard, every good thing had gone away.

She and Eliot were confined to the infirmary for what felt like a lifetime. Long enough for the regret to set in, and the guilt.

Astrid realized a few days later what a desperate situation she had sentenced them to. The fuel cells provided them with the oxygen they needed but, despite their efforts at conserving heat, the temperature dropped every day. A week after the accident, Astrid curled under her duvet and the cold hacked at her bones, chilling her right to the marrow. She felt as if she had never been warm and fought to remember hot baths of the kind she used to take at home, water so hot that when she lifted her arm steam curled off her skin. She and Eliot composed fantasy menus: boiling porridge and roast chicken with skin that cracked like leather, her mother's shepherd's pie, apple crumble with the saccharine custard they were served at Dalton. Many of the plants in the greenhouse had died. One night Poppy brought Astrid and Eliot their ration of food with a dessert bowl of canned peaches that had crystallized in the cupboard.

Already, the partial pressure of the oxygen on the ship was decreasing, the air growing thin. It was as if they were ascending a mountain at higher and higher altitudes. The manual listed a range of symptoms for them to look forward to: headaches, nausea, gradual loss of consciousness, high-altitude cerebral oedema, paralysis, coma. Death. Which, since they were unable to fix the oxygen tank, would likely occur within a few weeks, if not sooner.

Hallucinations were also amongst the symptoms; Astrid witnessed this one night when she woke to see Eliot in his bed opposite, fevered glitter in his eye, talking to his shadow. 'Get away from me,' he told it.

'Eliot?' Astrid rubbed her eyes, straining to see in the darkness of the infirmary. Eliot's face was oddly lit by Fae's desk lamp.

'There's someone out there.'

'Where?' But then it occurred to her. 'Eliot, you're dreaming.' She climbed out to shake him awake, and he looked at her, startled.

'What?'

'You had a bad dream.'

'Ara was here.' He scrambled out of bed and checked beneath it, grabbed at the metal bars of the gurney, checked everywhere. 'She was here in this room.'

'That sounds like a good dream,' Astrid said, turning away.

For her, sleep did not come easily. She lay awake most nights, torn up with regret for the choice she'd made. 'I'm sorry,' she said, her teeth chattering, rolling under the duvet, tears in her eyes. Sometimes she was on the edge of sleep, dreaming of drowning just off the shores of Terra-Two, her crew on the beach as she thrashed the waves, watching her die. Commander Sheppard, smiling the way he had a year ago on one of the early mornings when she'd found him singing to his son on the flight deck.

'I'm sorry,' she told him. Could he hear her? 'I made a mistake.' But the wash of the undertow swept her back into her own cold reality.

POPPY

IT CAME AS A surprise to Poppy, how hard Harry took Commander Sheppard's death. He disappeared after the memorial, and she spotted him heading down the corridor and into a room next to the cockpit. It was Solomon's room, with his name embossed on the door in silver letters beneath a pair of outstretched wings. Poppy often wondered if their commander had slept soundly, or if the burden of being captain of their lonely ship bore down on him, even as he dreamt.

The door was slightly ajar, and a thin stream of yellow light broke into the dim corridor. 'Hey,' she said, her breath misting in front of her. Harry was sitting on the bed, his back to Poppy. She lingered for a moment on the threshold. She could hear the melancholy wail of a clarinet through speakers, and over it the catch of a breath. 'Harry?'

She pushed the door open a little further. The room was only dimly illuminated by the lamp on the desk and the hot glow of Jupiter through a large window. Commander Sheppard's room was smaller than she had imagined it would be. It smelt of him, which, now, made Poppy feel a little creepy. She took a tentative step inside, her heart in her throat. The rug was soft and thick under her feet and Poppy noted everything as she passed. Solomon's uniform folded up on the easy chair. On his desk was an armillary sphere. Earth was a golden ball in the centre and the lamplight twinkled off the frame of delicate rings. Poppy ran her finger along the tiny engravings on the surface, lines of latitude, the tropics of Cancer and Capricorn. It was the most exquisite thing she had seen in a long time, and it gave her a thrill to try to imagine Commander Sheppard leaning over it late at night, tracing the constellations as they passed.

On the pin-board above the bed were photographs. Pictures of his son, his wife. She, feather-haired and smiling, his arm draped casually around her shoulders. Another, their wedding day, his hair grown out into an afro, his hand on her waist as they pressed a knife into luxurious white marzipan. Him playing the saxophone at sixteen or maybe seventeen, forehead scarred by acne. Him, pushing the British flag into the cracked surface of Mars. Seeing these pictures now was like peeling open a flower to find the vivid, surprising organs inside.

'Harry?' She glanced up and saw him hunched, face buried in one hand. Crying. 'Harry?' She put her hand lightly on his shoulder, unsure how to respond. She had never seen him cry before.

The accident in the space shuttle had left him scarred, lacerations along his forehead and temple, a patch of eyebrow where the hair no longer grew.

'I'll never be anything like him.' Harry's gaze followed hers up to the pictures on the pin-board. There was one of them on launch day – they looked younger to Poppy's eyes now, but she knew that was unlikely. Jesse had stood a little way away from them, and Solomon had pulled him over.

'Why does it matter . . . ?'

'Don't you realize . . . that's all that's ever mattered to me.'

'Really?'

His eyes drifted away for a moment as if he was looking inside himself. 'I guess so. Shall I tell you something stupid? Something this whole thing put me in mind of?'

She nodded.

'Years ago. Years and years ago, when I was – I don't know, young enough to hold my father's hand – we were walking from his office in Mayfair to get lunch. I was holding his hand and we were walking under some scaffolding when we heard a sound. Like one of the builders above us dropping something heavy, a hammer, or a pot of paint. The sort of thing that falls and crushes someone's skull. My dad *let go* of my hand.' Harry spread his fingers. 'Let go of my hand like it was on fire and ran for it, bolted ahead. Left me. And I stopped in the middle of the pavement, just staring at him. Thinking about what a coward he was. Thinking about those stories of people who jump in front of bullets for other people, mothers who lift cars to save their infants. And my dad, ducking for cover. I know it was probably just instinctive, fight-or-flight or whatever. But that was the thing that bothered me most. That it *was* instinctive. Him leaving me. Even then I thought, *I know*. He tried to laugh it off all the way to the brasserie but I thought, *Now I know*.'

'And Sheppard—' Poppy knew where this was going. 'At the moment it came to it, Sheppard saved you.'

Harry nodded. Poppy realized that this was one of the few times that Harry had ever confided in her or treated her like a friend. It hurt when she compared this intimacy to its imitation: late-night trysts in the games room, ten minutes pressed up against the bathroom stall being as quiet as possible. Perhaps, that whole time, this was all she had ever wanted from him.

'It'll be okay,' she told him.

'Will it?' Harry asked. 'They chose us because they think we're brave. Chose me to be the type of commander who can stare down death, leap in front of it to save my crew. Go down with the ship. Stay calm. But, I think ... maybe I was so good at it because I still thought that all of this was a game.

'Do you remember a question they used to ask us in the psych tests back at Dalton? There was this one they asked me once: "What would you die for?" I said something like "Great Britain" or "freedom". But you know what this whole experience has taught me? If they asked me again, "What would you die for?" *Willingly* die for? I'd probably say "nothing at all".'

ELIOT

16.02.13

TEMPERATURE: 2°C
O_2: 75.5% SEA LEVEL
WEEKS UNTIL RESCUE: 7

WHEN ELIOT AWOKE IT was the middle of the night, and the sound of his name echoed in the air like the final vibrations of a gong. His body ached with cold and the dark world had taken on a shimmery underwater quality.

He almost fell out of bed; his body was so clumsy and numb that he couldn't feel his fingers or toes and his lips tingled. They'd been locked in the infirmary for a week by that point. Fae had sealed the door, but there wasn't a door on this ship that Eliot could not open. He checked through the window to make sure there was no one in the corridor, then fumbled along the edge for the locking mechanism and twisted a paperclip in, a trick he'd performed before to save Astrid and Juno on the bridge. He pulled the latch and it slid right open to the corridor, lit in the deep blue of an artificial midnight.

'Eliot.' There it was again, a woman's voice. He froze and looked around, expecting to find Fae standing behind him, but no one was in the corridor and the cabin doors of all the senior crew were closed.

'Eliot!' It was louder that time, with a shrill panicked edge. He looked around in alarm.

'Who is it?' he said to the empty corridor. But no reply came.

He climbed through the next hatch and emerged on the lower deck, where most of the lights were off and the hum and whirr of machinery was the loudest. Eliot swallowed, noticing that his forearms were quilled with goosebumps. The games room was empty. After Europa, none of them wanted to spend much time there anymore.

The sound of banging made him start. It was echoing up the long hall just as it had that day when Harry locked Jesse in the airlock. 'Help!' someone screamed.

It was coming from the opposite direction to the airlock, behind the door that led to the greenhouse. Eliot ran along the corridor, opened the hatch to the bridge and entered. It was dank as a cave, the sound of his footsteps echoing all around. Broken glass crunched under his feet.

Further ahead, someone was splashing in the reservoir – the deep pond where the ship's water was stored. As he rushed there, he noticed the chemical smell of the agents they used to clean it. Someone was thrashing inside it, screaming 'Help me!', head surging up, then bobbing back under floes of blue ice that clinked against the sides of the pool.

Eliot whipped passed the trees and towards the water. 'Astrid?'

Who in the Beta could not swim?

He didn't have time to slow before he approached the reservoir, so he hit the water running. The ice on the surface was sharp against the soles of his feet, but that pain was nothing compared to the shock of the frozen water as it clamped like jaws around him.

It was only waist-deep, but the extreme cold tore through his body and his muscles seized. It was all he could do not to scream at the pain of it. Someone exploded to the surface again with a cry of horror, the water around her churned to foam from her panicked flailing.

Ara.

Her eyes were large and flashing silver with terror. He reached out his hand to grab her, buried his clumsy fingers into the folds of her vest, grabbed her waist and hauled her into his arms.

'I've got you,' he told her, pulling her close to him, pulling her head out of the water and wiping her long dark hair from her eyes. 'I've got you.'

She couldn't speak yet because she was coughing water up from her lungs.

'You came from outside, didn't you?' Eliot glanced up at the vault of stars above the greenhouse. 'I knew there was some-one outside.'

What was better than the weight of her in his arms? Her fingers were thin, longer than he remembered. He had forgotten so many details. The jasmine smell of her, the baby hairs that haloed her forehead and dusted the backs of her cheekbones, the eczema on her slender wrists and around her ears. Her legs, the birthmark the shape of Peru high up on her inner thigh. He'd forgotten other things too, like how big and dark her eyes were, like singularities; they seemed to suck all the light out of the room. His panic turned, then, to elation. It was possible to save her. He had saved her.

ELIOT

ELIOT WOULD RELIVE THAT final day so often that it took on a dreamlike quality in his mind. On the day before the launch, Ara had told him that she couldn't go through with it. They'd been in the back of the car, driving towards the British Interplanetary Society for the tree-planting ceremony.

'What do you mean you can't go through with it?' he'd asked, glancing up to the mirror to check if the driver was listening.

'Exactly that,' she told him in a whisper, leaning across the empty seat between them.

'Cold feet?'

She shook her head as the driver stopped at a traffic light. London's sunlit skyline flashed past her head, the dome of St Paul's gleaming like a Fabergé egg, jostling up against the modern monuments that pierced the clouds.

'Let's climb out and run that way,' she turned and pointed beyond the river, 'and just keep going. You and me.'

'What?' Eliot was unsure whether or not to laugh. 'Ara, we're just here for the ceremony. And then we have to get back to the space centre.'

'I'm not going back,' she said, and when she turned to him

her eyes were shining, the colour of iron. She took a deep breath, holding back tears, and clutched at her seatbelt. The car started up again, heading down towards Vauxhall.

'What if we get there and there's nothing?'

'Then we'd still have made it,' Eliot said. 'Do you think the *Apollo* crew looked up at the moon and asked, "What if we get there and it's just a rock?"'

'Maybe not. But no one is keen to follow after them. It's not as if they discovered America.'

'True,' Eliot agreed. 'But why are you saying these things?'

'Because I know something,' she said. Glanced up again at the driver's mirror. He was a quiet uniformed man who Eliot had not met before, keeping his eyes on the traffic.

'I know that we might not get to Terra-Two,' Ara said.

Later on, those words would toll like a bell in his nightmares, but that day he'd just shaken his head with confusion. 'What?'

'Do you remember anything about the Williamson Inquiry?' Eliot squinted at her. He vaguely recalled the name. 'The one commissioned by Save the Children to look into human rights abuses at space academies.'

'Oh ...' He waved a hand dismissively. He'd heard talk of this on the news for a little while, and the directors of the space agency and their teachers had only ever referred to it with contempt or vague amusement. A few months after, it had been suspended.

'My dad knows a lawyer who worked on it,' Ara said. 'And he told me ...' she took a deep breath, 'that they think we have a less than twenty per cent chance of making it to Terra-Two.'

'What ...?' Eliot's head was spinning a little. Ara blinked back tears and continued.

'It's lots of things. The skeletal support from the ground, the shortcuts taken by the UK Space Agency to win the race, the fact that Igor Bovarin's gravity-assist drive has never been tested on a manned mission. And he told me that—'

'No.' Eliot waved a hand to stop her. A dizzy wave of carsickness was rushing over him. 'That can't be true. Your dad's not a scientist.'

'No, but there were independent scientists and engineers and professors acting as witnesses for the inquiry. And they all said the same thing. That the mission is destined to fail.'

'No, you said twenty per cent.'

'Okay, it's eighty per cent destined to fail. That's a one in five chance of success. Not great odds.'

'Better than rolling a dice,' Eliot said.

'A die. Singular. Are you even listening to me?'

'Yes.' Eliot looked out at the water. 'I just don't believe you. It would be terrible if we failed. A humiliation for the UKSA. Why would they send out a ship with little chance of surviving?'

'Because, once we leave, it won't be their problem anymore. We'd reach Terra-Two in twenty-three years. But once we launch the gravity-assist drive and enter interstellar space, we'll be travelling at close to light speed. In Earth time, we won't reach Terra-Two for decades, not even including the time it takes for them to receive any messages from us. Do you remember the *Shēngmìng*? The Chinese generation ship that basically went missing. It was all about the launch for them. Showing the country's strength in the wake of the recession, and a year later they basically lost all contact with the ship.'

Eliot remembered the story.

'For them,' Ara continued, and by 'them' Eliot imagined that she was referring to the flag-waving masses, 'for them, the height of victory is tomorrow, the launch, when the whole world will be watching. They won't even care about the mission two months from now when the Olympics start. None of them will live to see us land. And, maybe we won't.'

'No.' Eliot turned away from her again, watched as a crowd of commuters waxed and waned at the crossing. They turned, over the bridge, past the busy tube station. 'It's not true. They're planning on sending missions of people after us. For people to join us. I don't believe you.'

'Because you don't want to,' she said, leaning across the gap between them.

'What do you want me to do with this information, Ara?'

'Follow me,' she said. The car headed down a familiar side road.

'You think that we can drop out?' he said, angry now. 'You think that's even an option?'

Ara shook her head. They both knew that, at this late stage, it would take more courage to leave the programme than it would take simply to go to space.

The British Interplanetary Society came into view, and within a few seconds they were almost there, heading into the car park.

'What's your plan?' Eliot asked her as the driver slowed. Ara looked at him for a long time, as if holding the knowledge in her fist, daring herself to speak.

JUNO

16.02.13

TEMP: 1°C
O_2: 75% SEA LEVEL
WEEKS UNTIL RESCUE: 7

THEIR SEARCH FOR ELIOT led them up to the greenhouse, where most of the lights were still off. Poppy called out his name in the darkness, and Juno followed clumsily behind her. They'd woken that morning to find the infirmary unlocked. Juno cursed herself for the oversight – of course Eliot knew how to unlock the doors. Though she was comforted by the fact that he couldn't have gone far, the short walk up to the greenhouse exhausted her. Nearly freezing temperatures. Low atmospheric pressure. She was beginning to feel it, the same heaviness in her body, the swollen face and hands that she'd experienced when first boarding the ship. As she and Poppy searched the greenhouse, Juno found herself stopping constantly to catch her breath, her pulse throbbing shallowly in her fingers.

'He can't have gone far,' Poppy said.

'I know,' Juno agreed. She felt as if she was breathing through a straw. 'Go ahead. I'll catch up.'

'We just need to make sure he's okay.' Poppy began to run.

In the darkness, the greenhouse was sinister and strange, plants covered in ice, the ground hostile and rough to touch. The cold pricked Juno's face and leached through the wool of her jacket. It felt as if every morning when she awoke the temperature halved, and now it was so low that water vapour had begun to condense into mists that curled around their ankles.

In the end, it was Poppy who spotted him first. The pale creature curled up amongst the leaves. His skin was white as moonlight, and the cold made the silver hairs all over his body stand on end. He looked as if he wasn't breathing. Juno only registered Poppy's scream a second later, by which point she was at Eliot's side, rolling him onto his back, checking for a pulse and pulling off her scarf to tie around his neck.

'Is he breathing?' Juno asked finally.

'I think so,' Poppy said, holding her arms under his shoulders, helping him to sit up.

'Leave me,' he mumbled, swatting her away.

'Eliot,' Poppy said, staring at him, 'you could die up here. Do you realize how cold it is?'

'That's what she wants,' he told her, his speech slurred in his confusion.

'Who?' Poppy asked.

'Ara,' he said.

Confusion, or hallucinations, Juno thought. Eliot must be in a worse state than she was.

'Look, Eliot—' Poppy's voice softened just a little. 'I know it's hard for you, but we've all got to try and keep it together right now. At least until the Russian shuttle comes. Doing things like this—'

'You don't understand.'

'Then explain it.'

Eliot squeezed his eyes shut, 'I c-can't. You'll hate me. And you're right to.'

'No one hates you,' Poppy said.

'You think I know, don't you? Why she jumped into the Thames. You think I know and I'm not telling you.' Poppy and Juno exchanged a frightened look. Nobody had mentioned Ara in months.

'Eliot,' Juno stepped a little closer to him, leaning on a branch, 'what are you talking about.'

'I'm talking about what she told me. The day she died. About the Williamson Inquiry and the Space Agency and Save the Children, all those things.'

'Okay.' Juno glanced at Poppy. 'He's clearly confused. We need to get him to Fae. And I don't know if I can carry him.'

'I know what I'm talking about,' Eliot insisted, his teeth chattering. 'She told me that we only have a twenty per cent chance of making it to Terra-Two.'

'Well, that's crazy,' Juno said. 'Where would she even get a number like that? What gave her that idea?'

'She said she knew things. Knew people who knew. I don't know. I didn't believe her then, but now . . .'

'Eliot,' Poppy's voice took on a scalding edge, 'are you telling us that you know why Ara committed suicide?'

Eliot let out a manic bark of a laugh. 'I know everything. The orbital period of *Orlando*, its perigee and apogee, I know all the code. I've recorded everything I've eaten for the past eleven and a half years.'

'Okay,' Poppy began, again struggling to get Eliot to stand

up. He was in his striped pyjamas, and the pale balls of his toes had taken on the waxy hue that suggested frostbite. 'Let's go.'

'No!' Eliot pushed Poppy so hard that she almost lost her balance, reeling backwards in surprise.

'I don't understand,' said Poppy. 'You're suggesting that Ara jumped because she thought that the mission would fail. But that makes no sense. If that is the reason then why didn't she just run away? Why did she have to . . . ?'

'I don't know,' Eliot said.

'Do you think we could have stopped her?' Juno asked. The question she asked herself every day, why she'd not just grabbed Ara at the BIS and begged her to stay.

'I don't know,' Poppy said. 'Ara wanted to die. Clearly. I mean – she must have. And if she did, I don't know if there's anything we could have done to stop her.'

'Is that your medical opinion?' Eliot asked

'What's that supposed to mean?'

'People want to die all the time, Eliot,' Juno said. 'It's a mental illness. Our first, most basic, instinct is to keep ourselves alive. It's innate, it's the reason we put clothes on our backs and food in our mouths and make penicillin. When that urge is gone then something is—'

'Broken?' Eliot let out a derisive laugh. 'You think we could have fixed her?'

'Maybe,' Juno said, but her voice came out thin. The effort of standing had exhausted her, but when she sat down on the frozen ground she immediately regretted it. It was cold as a mortuary slab.

'Maybe,' said Poppy finally. 'And maybe we'll never know.

We can spend our whole lives guessing and blaming each other but maybe we just have to forgive.'

'You think?' Eliot lifted his head to look at her. Poppy nodded. 'Say goodbye?' he asked and she nodded again. 'But . . . then I'd really be alone.' Tears seeped slowly from his eyes.

'No.' Poppy knelt down and grabbed his hand. 'We need you.'

'But . . .' He looked past her, at the shadows beyond the cracked spires, 'you know she's here with me.'

'Right now?' Juno's heart sank. It was worse than she had thought. Eliot was clearly suffering from some kind of delusion.

But Poppy simply continued stroking his hand calmly. 'She needs to leave.' She said it like an order, with a strength that Juno had never seen. Said it as if she could command him back from the world between the living and the dead.

Of course, Juno thought, *of course this is a conversation Poppy is comfortable engaging in*. Poppy, who had fought to find strength in the face of her own depression.

'Tell her. We need you here.'

Tears squeezed from Eliot's eyes. 'I don't think I can,' he said.

'I know,' Poppy soothed. 'It takes courage to be alone. But you have to tell her that she can't stay. Tell her that you forgive her but you have decided, today, to live.'

ELIOT

18.02.13

TEMPERATURE: -3°C
O_2: 68% SEA LEVEL
WEEKS UNTIL RESCUE: 6

FOR THE REST OF his life, Eliot's mind would always roam back to the edge of the Thames, and he would never properly understand what made her jump.

He'd left the Earth less than twenty-four hours after Ara had died. Had not seen her body again, after it had been carted away from Embankment. He had not attended her funeral, and the guilt of the abandonment crushed him.

When Juno and Poppy took him down to the infirmary, Eliot had been delirious with hypothermia. He'd thought that he could see Ara everywhere he looked.

His nerves had been on fire. Electric shocks arrowed up his toes and along the arch of his foot as Fae had tried to warm them. In his confusion, he'd thought he'd heard Juno and the doctor mention frostbite. 'I think he might lose them,' one of them had said.

Eliot cried so much that finally Fae injected something into his IV to put him to sleep, and in his dream he was walking through the ship, Ara's hand in his. Through the window, he could see that they were close enough to Terra-Two for him to discern mountain ranges.

'You can't come with me,' he told her. Her hand, in his, was heavy as a millstone.

'Of course I can.' She smiled the way she used to when they shared an inside joke.

'We used to go everywhere together,' he told her. He and Ara had grown up like two trees with their roots twisted together. Both of them liked to believe that, together, they were twice as strong. Although, silently, they knew that without the other they were crippled.

He saw them both, watching the long surf rise and fall near his uncle's house in Southerndown. Getting drunk in Brockwell Park, their blood sizzling with champagne, lying on their backs in the floodlit grass, talking about God and Terra-Two and the *Damocles*, which was shining above them even then.

In his dream, he wheeled through memories as they flashed like a life before his eyes. Her life. A surprise party in Ara's garden, their grinning mouths black with braces. Ara in her white school uniform, her shirt see-through and dripping from a water fight in the garden. The summer she bleached her hair candy-floss pink. By sixteen, Eliot and Ara were roughly the same height and their darkly lashed eyes and long hair made them look like long-lost siblings, their fingers entwined. Both of them thin and dour as refugees.

Ara's theory was that lovers had been conjoined twins in a past life, sentenced to look for each other in the next, bereft until they found the one person with a hollow in their chest shaped like the bump on their own.

'I can't go with you,' he said. And his own life flickered before him. His jaw growing square at twenty-three, etched with stubble. At thirty, sketching a new design for an updated VASIMR engine, improving on Igor's design. At forty, setting foot on Terra-Two, staring down at his hand as he touched rain. 'I remember this,' he'd say to himself. He saw it all, the abundance of the life before him, another seventy years perhaps. And he wanted it.

'I can't have both,' he told her as they approached the airlock. In the low oxygen, it took all the strength he had to haul open the hatch.

'Both of what?' she asked as she stepped inside the airlock, and waited for him to follow after her. For a moment, Eliot almost did. He stared at her bare feet on the ground, the way her hair floated around her head. His love for her cut like a knife, now. Caused him nothing but pain and so it was a relief, almost, to shut the hatch between them.

He reached over to the gearbox and found the emergency eject button. As he did, there was a banging against the porthole window, frantic pounding. Eliot saw that Ara was shouting his name in a panic. He froze, his mouth dry, considered again what this meant, a life without her. It was the only one he could have.

He remembered what Poppy had told him, that grieving for Ara would be like an uphill climb, a terrifying journey back to himself. This story, too, was a love story. It had only just begun.

WHEN HE AWOKE A day later, two of his toes were gone. But Eliot's chest was light with freedom. 'We had to,' Juno said, leaning down to examine the wound dressing. In the cold, her hands were shaking violently. 'They were too damaged.' Eliot struggled to sit up, his arms trembling under him.

'Does it hurt?' she asked.

Eliot turned to the window and pressed his hand against it. Looked for her in the blackness. 'She's gone,' he told Juno. And he actually laughed. The sound foreign but wonderful in his mouth.

'Who?' Juno asked. Behind the glass there was only the vacuum, and his own face. His own smiling face. 'Eliot, are you okay?'

'I'm . . . ?' He said it like a question, as if he was experimenting with the sound of it. 'I'm . . . okay? I am okay.'

ASTRID

20.02.13

TEMPERATURE: -9°C
O_2: 65% SEA LEVEL
WEEKS UNTIL RESCUE: 6

THEY RELEASED ASTRID FROM confinement after Eliot's accident. With Commander Sheppard gone, and Eliot sick, the crew needed all the hands that they could get. Astrid saw that they were all unravelling now, in different ways. The Russian expedition would not arrive for another six weeks. The temperature on the ship had dropped to below freezing, which meant that ice formed silver veins along the windows. If Astrid ever reached out to touch the walls of the ship, the cold was like a razor to her nerves. All but essential chores fell by the wayside. They spent long hours sleeping in their cabins, although the cold often woke them. Fae told them to check their bodies regularly for frostbite. After witnessing what happened to Eliot, Astrid was terrified of losing her own toes. During her time in the infirmary, she had scoured Fae's books on human physiology. Found the chapters on high altitude and hypothermia. Pages of medical photographs of frostbite, thumbs and earlobes black as coal, nails falling off toes, skin that looked like it had been burned by the cold. The pictures made her sick. And yet she could not stop herself from reading. She discovered that the slow reduction of oxygen would be accompanied by "inexorable deterioration of the body", a phrase that echoed in her nightmares. She discovered that some people acclimatised a little but that by the time the air pressure dropped below 40 per cent, they were all likely to be dead.

When she left the infirmary, the monitors in the control room and service module indicated that the oxygen levels had fallen to 65 per cent that of sea level. Which meant they were now all suffering from some form of altitude sickness. Harry, Jesse and Juno all complained of headaches so bad that during their morning conferences they would lean over the table, barely able to see for the pain. A few of them had developed a dry cough and they all stood at the top of the ladder, dizzy and winded with exhaustion from the effort of pulling their own weight up. Astrid woke often in the middle of the night in a sudden horror that she had stopped breathing. Cold sweat freezing the damp cotton between her legs, feet numb with cold even under two pairs of socks.

Astrid heard that while she had been in confinement, the rest of the crew had been attempting to trudge through some semblance of routine, eating silent meals in the kitchen, watching films together in the crew module. Astrid could not help suspecting that whatever positive feelings any of her crewmates might once have harboured for her had well and truly eroded. She'd sentenced them to this fate. In tearful corridor conversations, Astrid overheard them saying as much. There had been no messages from the Russian expedition that was apparently coming to their rescue, but Astrid kept running up to the Atlas module to search the skies for a sight of their shuttle, with the desperate regularity of a sailor waiting for landfall. Each time, she found nothing but the void.

One horrible morning, Juno did not wake at the sound of the bell. She was still in her bed after breakfast and when Astrid went to find her and pulled her duvet down, she saw that the side of her face was wet with vomit, only the whites of her eyes visible, lips purple.

Astrid cried out, panic darkening her vision. Stabbing her fingers under her sister's jaw, she detected a slow pulse. She scooped Juno into her arms, never mind the nail-varnish smell of her bile, and carried her to the infirmary. Juno was light as a bird, maybe seven stone or less, Astrid saw now, and it broke her heart. The hard edges of her pelvis pushed insistently above the band of her pyjamas. All this time, her sister had needed her help and Astrid had been too preoccupied to see it.

When she reached the infirmary, Fae looked down at Juno with a sad expression of inevitability, as if she was watching a vase topple from a great height, the predictable crack. She'd been waiting for this – knew it was only a matter of time before the low oxygen made one of them seriously sick.

She explained that it was likely Juno was suffering from high-altitude cerebral oedema, which occurs when a lack of oxygen causes swelling of the brain tissue. She tied an oxygen mask to Juno's face and gave her a dose of a drug to ease the swelling, but Fae didn't pull any punches when she gave Astrid the prognosis.

'People die of this,' she said, her voice grim. 'I've seen it in healthy men and women who climb mountains. Young people. They get a headache and then as the air gets thinner they get sicker and sicker. Many fall into a coma and do not wake up. I'm not going to lie to you. She could be dead in hours.'

Astrid could barely think through the steel vice of her own headache. She stumbled down the halls of the ship, fighting tears. Everything her sister had said about her had been right. Astrid had made this selfish, reckless choice, sentenced everyone to this death. The realization made her sick with self-loathing.

For the first time in her life the foundations of her hope began to crumble. For the past few years Terra-Two had been so wondrously close, so certainly in her future. And, today, she saw it receding from her even as she clutched desperately and foolishly for it. She felt like Tessa Dalton, dying alone at the edge of that fountain, the cold creeping in, her mad eyes fixed on the distant star where the planet spun, still believing that if she could just grasp a little further she could get there eventually.

That had been over a century ago, and here was Astrid – fool that she was! – doing the same thing.

When she entered the control room, Igor was there. Astrid began to cry. 'I've killed them all,' she said. Igor looked at her silently. 'My sister. All my friends. This is my fault, everything that's happened.'

'"Regretting the past is like chasing wind",' Igor said. 'Something we say in Norilsk. This is the situation we are in now.'

Astrid looked at the old cosmonaut. Fae had given him an oxygen tank, with a cannula that ran under his nose. He was already only surviving with the use of one lung; the plummeting temperature and oxygen pressure was sure to kill him soon. Astrid could not help the uncharitable thought that they would run out of all their supplies of medical oxygen sooner with Igor using it. The sound of his breathing made her wince, the sticky sound of fluid filling lungs, the muscles in his neck straining every time he inhaled. He, of course, had always known he was never going to make it to Terra-Two.

'How can you bear it?' Astrid asked, tears streaming down her face. 'Never going? How could Tessa?'

Igor looked at her as if she'd asked a foolish question, his eyes widened in surprise. 'You don't need to go there, to go there.' Astrid looked at the old man quizzically. 'This place, Terra-Two. This country that you dream of, that Tessa dreamt of. Perhaps you don't need to touch the ground, to smell the air.'

'I don't understand.'

'Perhaps that's what this new religion of yours is all about. New Creationists. Perhaps this thing you feel, this hope, this belief, is the only thing that you need. It is – what's the word? – transcendent.'

JUNO

WHENEVER SHE FELL ASLEEP time flew by.

The first night, she opened her eyes to see the solar system in miniature, the Earth cast in brass, spinning around the sun on spokes. It was Solomon Sheppard's armillary sphere, and in her fever it looked as if the sun itself was shining. She was in his old bedroom. Then in the infirmary where he had died.

When she awoke next, she was in a plastic tent. A hyperbaric chamber. Juno knew that if she could just work up the energy to roll onto her side she would find a clock on the far wall and then she'd be able to anchor herself a little in time. She would talk herself into it, steel herself for the task, but she'd drift back to sleep before she managed it. Finally, she gave up trying to move her limbs or to lift her eyelids and she tried to guess the time by the sounds on the ship. The muffled thump of footsteps outside, the voices of the others in the kitchen, Fae rushing in and out of the room, taking her temperature, scribbling notes.

Once she managed to cry out Astrid's name, her voice a pathetic rasp, and she felt a hand in hers, cool and firm.

'I'm here,' her sister would say, and Juno had never been so grateful.

'What's wrong with me?' she asked.

'The thing that's wrong with all of us. We're running out of air,' Astrid said, and Juno felt a tear splash against her wrist.

The pain, which came and went, made her cry out and clutch at her head – she thought someone was forcing a screwdriver through her temples.

Juno drifted in and out of technicolour interstellar dreams. She thought about God. Once, in class, her French teacher had pointed to 'le ciel' and said, 'You know, where they used to believe heaven was.' Juno had asked in shock 'Where do they think it is now?' She'd been on the edge of her seat at this new revelation.

'Where has it gone?' she asked. 'Where is it now?'

'I'm here, Juno,' said Astrid and Jesse, each holding a hand as she gasped in pain. This pain, it would grind the bones in her skull to salt.

Her mind was a kaleidoscope of fantasy.

Unhinged questions.

Why had Juno never wondered where all the gods disappeared to?

In astronomy, Jupiter was only a quiet giant in the sky, big enough to hold over 1,000 Earths but not as solid as one. She had never wondered what had happened to the god that shared its name. Jove or Zeus, the dispenser of skylight. What happened to Anat, knee-deep in blood, wrestling Ba'al's enemies. She saw now that they must have retreated somewhere, these defunct deities, and she thought she knew where.

'Terra-Two?' she shouted in her confusion. Only one answer.

'I don't think she's going to make it.'

Juno tried not to cry out again, but her head had been seared open. 'I can see everything,' she gasped, 'and it's beautiful.'

JESSE

21.02.13

TEMPERATURE: -12°C
O$_2$: 62% SEA LEVEL
WEEKS UNTIL RESCUE: 7

'JESSE?' HE'D FALLEN ASLEEP in Solomon's room again. He knew before Fae touched his shoulder and he opened his eyes because it was colder in there, and the smell of vapour rub and antiseptic clung to everything. He was too cold to feel his feet.

'Jesse?'

He straightened his back, pins and needles stinging his right calf and prickling his numb hands.

Jesse looked across at the girl he loved. For a while she'd drifted in and out of sleep, mumbling in confusion and shouting disjointed phrases. Often, she didn't recognize him. She had not regained consciousness for six hours. Though Fae periodically put her in a portable hyperbaric chamber, she'd stopped showing signs of improvement and Fae was wary about using up their supplies of oxygen. They would all need it, in the end.

'Have you eaten?' Fae asked.

Jesse tried to remember the last time he'd been in the kitchen, what time of day it was. 'I had breakfast.'

'That was twelve hours ago.'

'I—'

'You have to eat.' She touched the back of his hand with her mitten. 'Keep up your strength. I thought I'd try one last round in the chamber. Another dose of Dexamethasone. See if we see any improvements.' The word 'last' made Jesse's throat tighten. 'I'll keep her company. Go.'

Jesse stood with some difficulty. He was beginning to feel the weakness in his own body, pain in his head, a listing dizziness whenever he stood. Nightmares about drowning.

'I'll be back in a minute.'

'Take your time.' It sounded more like a plea.

Jesse squinted in the half-light of the corridor. Looked at the time on his watch and realized he'd already missed dinner.

Poppy was sitting at the breakfast counter when he entered, eating from a greasy bag of microwave popcorn. 'Guess what I found,' she said when Jesse entered, 'I forgot I packed these. It was Harry's idea: most junk food, least space. Oh, were you crying?'

Jesse felt the blood rising in his cheeks. 'No,' he said, 'just sleeping.'

'How is she doing?' Poppy asked.

'Bad …' He strained for a moment to catch his breath. 'Is there something to eat?'

Poppy looked around the room and shrugged. 'More mac broth – or else something from a tin. Nothing fresh left, obviously, since the garden died. The food in the water-based cans has frozen.'

Jesse sank down in one of the chairs, realizing that his whole body ached and that at any moment his constricted breathing might turn into sobs.

'You can have some popcorn for dinner. What do you prefer: sweet or salty or both?'

'I'm actually not so hungry.' Loss of appetite – another symptom.

'Jesse?' He turned to find Poppy's eyes wide and concerned. 'You're being super brave, you know that?'

'I'm not the brave one,' he said, thinking of how terrified he'd felt the previous night when Juno had woken up screaming, convinced that all the air had leaked out of the room.

'Oh, jeez!' Poppy swore under her breath. 'That was a stupid thing to say. I'm so stupid sometimes.'

'Don't say that,' Jesse said.

Poppy slid off the high chair behind the breakfast bar, rummaged through the cupboard and brought out a thin packet of something. 'I've been thinking about that, actually.'

'What?'

She walked over to the microwave and switched it on. 'I was thinking about the Beta.'

'Oh, yeah?'

'Don't you ever wonder about all this sometimes? Wonder why they chose us?'

'Because you guys were the best,' Jesse said automatically. His teeth were chattering.

'What does that mean?'

'You know, they tested us for years. We're smart, physically fit. We're of reproductive age—'

'Yes, yes. I'm not talking about any of that. Sometimes I think it was just some kind of sick test. All those fit-checks, the psych team on the ground. Doesn't it feel sometimes like instead of us experimenting on Terra, they're experimenting on us?'

Like the others, Poppy had lost weight, her cheekbones now sharply defined, and there were new hollows under her eyes. Her body was heavy with layers – working boots, a scarf, silver puffa jacket – but even so, as she stood, she kept stamping her feet to keep the blood circulating in her toes. Motes of frost stuck to strands of hair at the end of her ponytail, like sugar crystals.

'I just think,' she continued, 'we're all so . . . There's so much wrong with us.'

'I don't think so,' Jesse said. 'It's not us, it's this situation. There's nothing normal about this situation, about watching *Orlando* go up in flames and then half our own ship too. Watching Solomon die and then . . . and Ara . . . and . . .' He stopped, bit his lip.

Poppy ran her fingers through her long hair again. She was beginning to lose some of it; stray copper tresses caught between her fingers and pulled away from her scalp. 'I remembered Christina Abellard.' For a second the name drew a blank, and then Jesse recalled the tall olive-skinned girl who was on the debating team. 'And how when they started selections for the Beta we all knew she would make it.'

'Yeah . . .' he said, the memory coming back to him. 'Because she was amazing at everything.'

'She came top in all the tests. Eliot was the only one who beat her in astrophysics and mech. eng., and barely. Plus she was awesome at sports too.'

'Yeah, but there were loads of people like that. Dalton was that kind of school.'

'I know, but—' Poppy swore, spun around and stabbed the button on the microwave. The air was filled with the tang of burnt food and Jesse noticed the round black patch of scorched paper when she pulled the packet out, sucking on burnt fingers and hissing.

'You see,' she said, flinging the steaming bag of popcorn onto the counter, 'I'm useless.'

'Don't say that.' It was so cold that the steam plumed out of it in a kind of spectacular cloud.

'How did someone like me make it into the Beta, and not Christina?'

This wasn't new ground either, wondering how some had made it even through the first round of selections while others weren't offered an interview. 'It's luck, isn't it. Or I don't know, the professors had their reasons. Maybe—'

Poppy was shaking her head. 'Second round of selections, when they published that list of the fifty people who'd made it through ranked in order of how suitable we were. I was forty and Christy was forty-eight.'

'That didn't matter in the end anyway, remember, cos Christina dropped out. Her parents revoked consent. Said they didn't want their daughter going up into space when she'd do better on Earth as a surgeon or something.'

'Exactly.' Poppy stabbed a finger at Jesse.

'Exactly what?'

'I think they chose us because we're expendable,' she said.

Jesse's stomach sank. That couldn't be it.

'No,' he finally said. 'That's not right.'

'I was going through the records on Fae's computer, looking at our old test scores. Even in swimming there was not one test where Christina came below number twenty. She was in the top five for most things.'

'So . . . ?'

'So, in every way – on every scale they had – there was no way she was forty-eight out of fifty.' Poppy paused to open the bag of popcorn, steam curling up to her chin. 'It's not so bad,' she said. 'I can just pick the burnt ones out.'

'So maybe they have other scales,' Jesse suggested. 'Ones we can't see, and on those ones Christy ranked lower than you.'

'That's what I thought, but what would they be?' Poppy was flicking burnt popcorn from the bowl. 'And what's the point of having all those other tests, all those horrid hoops we had to jump through, getting up at dawn, doing those drills on the lawn, those fit-checks and holding our heads underwater until we choked, five-, six-hour exams – what was all that for?

'Well, I think that if you really were going to build a colony, a new country somewhere else, and it would take twenty-three years to get there, what would be more important than physical fitness or swimming badges?'

She shook her head. 'I don't know. What?'

'You'd want people who really *wanted* to be there,' Jesse said slowly. 'People who would give up their family, their future, a chance to be a surgeon or whatever and to travel across the stars for twenty years. Maybe those tests weren't about what we thought they were. Maybe they wanted to see how much we could sacrifice. How much we wanted to be in the Beta. Needed it. And the six of us wanted it the most. And maybe, on the last day, Ara didn't.'

*

THE SHIP WAS QUIET by the time Jesse walked back along the frosted corridor. The low rumble of a voice drifted through the half-open door of Igor's bedroom.

'Two funerals in one month . . .' He recognized Igor's heavy breathing,

'It's more than I can bear,' said Fae. 'I don't think she'll last the night.'

Jesse caught his breath and began to run down the corridor towards Solomon Sheppard's room. As he did, he struggled to shake away the thought of Juno dying, of wrapping her body in a sheet as they had for their commander and watching as she was jettisoned out into space.

Jesse fought against the clenching in his throat until he reached the bed where Juno lay, and dropped down to his knees and began to beg. He'd felt this way before, with his sister Morrigan, although he'd been a lot younger then. They'd been driving home from a cousin's wedding in Murang'a – rust-red roads, all the windows open, baking in the heat of the car – when his sister had slumped against him, her head hot with fever, and complained of a headache.

'Probably dehydrated,' their mother had said. What she always said when one of them complained of a headache.

The next morning she had not come downstairs for breakfast, and Jesse's mother had screamed when she found her, tangled in her bedsheets, her limbs thrashing, foaming at the mouth. Jesse remembered the feeling of the condensation on the cool marble under his bare feet, the sound of the fan whacking the hot air and the medicine man's prophecy coming back to him. That Morrigan would fall sick, but not leave this world. Like a talisman, he turned the old man's words over in his mind, even after she was rushed to hospital, even after she slipped into a coma, mouth half-open, dead to the world. The doctors had washed their hands of her but when she'd lived they'd said, '*Miujiza!*'

'Jesse?'

He looked up, brought back to his own body by a voice that sounded like Juno's. She was standing in the doorway for a moment, but then he realized. 'Astrid. It's you.'

The next thing he knew Astrid was standing next to him, her arms squeezed around her. This pain, he knew, they could share.

'Fae said that she doesn't think she'll make it through the night,' Astrid said.

'I heard . . .' Jesse said.

'So I thought . . . I wouldn't want to be alone.' She took off her glove and grabbed Juno's hand. Juno's breath was watery, as if her lungs were filling with fluid, coming in long, laboured gasps. And with every gap in between, Jesse wondered if she would take another breath, glanced at his watch, wondered if this was the moment.

'My grandma told me a phrase for that way she's breathing.' Astrid nodded towards Juno. 'They call it "climbing the mountain of death" in her language. They say that once you start to climb . . .'

'Do you believe in miracles?' he said. Astrid wiped an eye with the back of her wrist so that she wouldn't have to let go of her sister.

'You know that I do,' she said. 'I've been praying and praying but . . . maybe our luck's run out.'

Jesse looked at Juno's heartbeat on the monitor, blood

pressure, oxygen saturation. Astrid's head was blocking the lamplight so she was a dark shadow, slightly painful to look at.

'Maybe ...' said Jesse. He was thinking of the prayers of thanksgiving that the doctors had offered up to a merciful God. 'Maybe you can't just ask. You have to *give*.'

Astrid looked up at Jesse quizzically. 'Like, make a deal?'

'Like, make a sacrifice.' Jesse didn't believe in Astrid's God, but he believed in sacrifice. Remembered the Sunday school class in which he learned about Abraham and the son he took up a mountain to murder.

Astrid looked at her sister. 'You know, my mum once told me never to make a deal with God. It was the strangest thing she ever told me. She said that it's dangerous. That you should only make promises that you can keep.'

The thought frightened Jesse just a little. Reminded him that Astrid believed that God was not only the kindly father of her Sunday school songs, the one who held them lovingly in his hands, waiting in eager expectation for the moment that they would turn their faces towards him. To her, He was also the bringer of storms, the sharp hand of justice, an awesome force.

'What would *you* give up, Astrid? If you had to. What do you love the most? What would you sacrifice to save your sister?'

THEY AWOKE TO THE sound of the oxygen alarm. Jesse's eyes were too blurred to see the figures on the monitor but he knew what it meant. 'Astrid?' She'd been asleep too, but she started awake with a gasp.

'No ...' she cried, her voice light with horror. But Juno's mouth was hanging open and she was not breathing. Jesse pushed his hands under her neck to check for a pulse but couldn't find one.

Astrid screamed, dropped to her knees, tears pouring from her eyes. Jesse stepped back, his entire body numb, ears ringing, fingers trembling.

Then the ship was filled with the thunder of running feet, others rushing up the ladder. Fae dashed into the room, still in her dressing gown, and took in the scene. Poppy ran to embrace Eliot and a wailing Astrid, Harry and Cai lingered by the threshold.

'Poppy.' Fae pointed to Astrid. 'I can't work with this noise.' She opened a box and pulled out her stethoscope, pushed it against Juno's chest and said, 'Quiet.'

Jesse watched the concentration in her eyes, the way she frowned, shrinking away from the whine of the oxygen alarm. She was still for a long while, and then looked up at the monitor, pressed a button on the side and held it for a moment. It went blank, and in the silence all Jesse could hear was the sound of the blood throbbing in his eardrums.

'Juno . . .' Fae pulled off her stethoscope and switched on the main lights so they all blinked in the brightness.

The monitor in the corner of the room beeped, and then beeped again, then again, in the stiff regular rhythm of a heartbeat.

Juno opened her eyes, as if she'd just surfaced from deep water, dragging uncertain gulps of air and shaking all over.

POPPY

24.02.13

TEMPERATURE: -18°C
O_2: 59% SEA LEVEL
WEEKS UNTIL RESCUE: 5

SHE HAD TAKEN TO sleeping on the control deck, wrapped in
duvet covers, sitting in the pilot's seat and watching through the
wide window for any sign of the service shuttle. Sometimes she
fell asleep and imagined it twinkling in the distance, but then
opened her eyes fully and realized it was only her reflection in
the glass. She set the radio to tune and tune, the way Eliot had
showed her, and finally, one afternoon, a voice broke through
the static.

'*Mission Control*, Damocles, *comm check.*' Poppy leapt to her
feet on a floor slicked with ice.

'I'm here,' she told them, rubbing her numb cheeks.
'We're here.'

'*This is Commander Sheppard?*'

'No ...' Poppy said. 'It's Poppy Lane. I'm from the Beta.'

'*We received your distress call two weeks ago and my service team
is on its way.*'

'Right.'

'*We'll prepare to rendezvous in five days.*'

'Really? So soon?' Poppy glanced at the date on the dashboard. She'd calculated that, in the best-case scenario, the rescue shuttle could arrive in six weeks. 'That's amazing. Thank you . . .' Poppy strained to remember the name of the leader of the Russian expedition. 'Is this Vera Petrov?'

'*No,*' came the voice, '*It's Xiao Lin.*'

'*Xiao Lin He?*' Poppy repeated, hardly understanding what she was hearing.

'*Yes, from the* Shēngmìng. *We've been watching you. We've been wishing you luck on your endeavour. We're on our way to help.*'

JUNO

25.02.13

TEMPERATURE: -21°C
O_2: 58% SEA LEVEL
DAYS UNTIL RESCUE: 4

JUNO COULDN'T HELP FEELING as if the rest of the crew were avoiding her. She'd seen it on their faces when she opened her eyes, aware only of the beep of the machines as they indicated her heartbeat. Two days before they'd given her up for dead, and now here she was, staring back at them.

Sometimes she heard their voices outside the door as they trekked to the kitchen and she longed to be well enough to join them, but she was still too weak to get out of bed. It reminded her of the autumn that she'd broken her ankle falling out of a tree, and the interminable days that followed; watching her sister out in the garden collecting buckets of Cox apples, or carving pumpkins by the treehouse, haunting the town dressed as a ghost for Halloween, having fun while Juno was bed-bound and envious. Juno had watched the pumpkins rot on the windowsill, turn green and implode.

'Astrid!' Juno opened her eyes to find her sister slipping out of the room.

'I thought you were sleeping,' Astrid said.

'Sorry to disappoint you.' Juno didn't try to hide her resentment. 'I'm getting better,' she went on. 'Fae says the Dexamethasone must have worked.' She held up the arm that was still attached to the IV. 'So can everyone stop acting so strange around me now?'

'What do you mean?' Astrid asked, pulling her scarf tighter around her neck.

'You know what I mean,' Juno said.

'Well . . .' Astrid's gaze was still fixed firmly on the floor.

'Where's Jesse?' Juno asked. He had not come to see her since the night she first awoke. Juno wondered if everything would be different between them now that he'd witnessed her crying in the midst of her nightmares, feeble and confused and calling out for death.

'Maybe he's a little frightened,' Astrid said. 'We all are. I mean . . . you were dead.'

'You *thought* I was dead.'

'And then you opened your eyes.' Astrid shuddered. 'And for just a minute it was like it was someone else.'

'I *was* alive, you know? The whole time,' Juno said. 'It was just a machine glitch.'

'That's what Fae says.'

'But you don't believe her.'

Astrid looked down at Juno. 'You were dead,' she insisted. 'Jesse saw you. I saw you. You weren't breathing.'

'So you think, what? I came back to life?'

Astrid looked away again.

'That it was a miracle, like Lazarus,' Juno said, sneering.

'That I came back from the dead.' Astrid still didn't respond. 'I suppose it was a kind of miracle. The miracle of modern science. Like penicillin or—'

'Are you making fun of me?'

'What else can I do?' Juno sighed, and leant back in the bed, the old weakness coming over her. 'I didn't see my life flash before my eyes or a white light or the face of God.' Astrid flinched. 'I know I didn't actually die, but it *was* strange. I do feel as if . . .' She spread her gloved fingers out in front of her face and watched the lamplight seep through them. 'As if something happened to my body. As if I went somewhere.' She stopped herself. 'It's crazy, though. I know it's crazy.'

'It's not.' Finally, Astrid turned around to face her. Her cheeks were wet. 'I saw you Juno; you were dead, actually dead. Your heart stopped beating. I could feel it, then I couldn't. And your eyes, they were still open but they were . . .' She looked as if she was about to cry again. 'I've seen death before. I dragged Ara's cold body right out of the water, so I know.'

Juno looked away from her and tried to swallow the bile she could taste in the back of her throat. She wanted to make her voice sound light when she spoke. 'So that's why you're treating me like a leper?'

'Juno . . .' Astrid was going to cry.

'I'd have thought you might be a little happier to see that I didn't actually die.'

'I *am*. But . . .' she frowned. 'What if I told you that I brought you back to life?'

'I'd say no wonder everyone is worried about you. So what are you now? A magician?'

Astrid tried to laugh. 'I made a bargain with God.' She sighed and closed her eyes. Maybe she hadn't slept for a long while, there were shadows under her eyes and dirty tear stains streaked her hollowed-out cheeks.

'It was something Jesse said,' she began, 'about Abraham, and how he had to kill his son.'

'Don't tell me I know more Bible than you do. Abraham was told to kill his son and then God stopped him at the last moment.'

'That part doesn't matter. He was asked to give up the thing he loved the most. To make a sacrifice.'

'That part matters the most. What does this have to do with anything?'

Her lips were quivering. 'I've been thinking about the thing that I love most. My heart's desire, the thing that drove me to cheat the tests at Dalton. I had to give it up in order to save you.' A slow tide of dread rose up in Juno's stomach. She wanted to reach out her hand to stop Astrid before she could say something terrible.

'I have to give up Terra-Two ... and I have to go back to Earth.'

'I don't understand,' said Juno. 'You wanted to go the most. Out of all of us.'

'I know ...' Astrid swallowed. 'But I was thinking about Tessa Dalton. I always felt sorry for her. That she was the prophet. The woman who discovered Terra-Two but never actually went there. But then Igor said that maybe that was never the point. Maybe she never had to.'

JESSE

26.02.13

TEMPERATURE: -24°C
O_2: 57% SEA LEVEL
HOURS UNTIL RESCUE: 48

JESSE KNEW THAT IF it had not been for their profound luck –
crossing into the path of the *Shēngmìng* – they would certainly
have died before the Russians reached them. The captain of the
Chinese ship had agreed to send a resupply vessel with the spare
parts they would need to repair their service module, along with
two flight engineers. Jesse had asked Poppy to ask Xiao Lin the
reason for her generosity.

'*Out here*,' she had told them over the speaker, '*we are all fellow
travellers. Maybe one day, when we too reach Terra-Two, the crew of
the* Damocles *will remember our kindness and embrace our children
and grandchildren.*'

Even in the final two days before the engineers on the resupply shuttle were due to rendezvous with the *Damocles*, it felt as
if everything was falling apart. The cold was devastating and
drilled at their bones relentlessly. Although the Beta huddled
in the dim light of the crew module, wrapped in duvets, both

Harry and Eliot now had fluid in their lungs, and struggled to breathe without assistance.

Something about the helplessness of their situation roused dormant leadership qualities in Jesse. He found that he was the one who could remain calm in the face of death, did not check his body obsessively for the signs of it: frostbite, pulmonary oedema, hypoxia. He exhorted everyone to try to move as much as possible to keep their blood flowing, he cracked the jokes. A couple of days after Poppy had told them about the *Shēngmìng*, it was he who had gathered them all in the kitchen for the meeting.

'So,' he said, standing up at the end of the table, 'I'm sure you've all been counting down the hours until the *Shēngmìng*'s shuttle arrives, but in case you haven't, we're down to about forty-eight.'

Astrid clasped her mittened hands together. 'Thank God!'

'They're going to mend the service module and bring us some new medical supplies,' Jesse said. 'Once the repairs are done, we'll be back on course, to Terra-Two. In a couple of months we'll reach Saturn, Igor and Eliot will launch the gravity-assist drive and then there's no turning back.' The table between them was satined with frost, and their breath clouded the air. 'So, I'm offering everyone the chance to decide again. Do we, knowing all that we know now, all the risks, want to keep going? Does anyone want to return home, on our shuttle? With the help of the engineers, Astrid and Eliot can refit the life support system that they removed and anyone who wants to can return to Earth.'

Poppy's eyes widened, and she looked around at the rest of the crew. 'You're saying that some of us can still go home?'

'That's right,' Jesse said. 'But whether to stay or go: it's not a choice anyone can make for you.' They all shifted uncomfortably.

Not one day had gone by for Jesse without the keen pain of longing for the comforts of home. For the habitable envelope of Earth's atmosphere, for the safety of solid ground. He wondered who would say it first.

He looked around the table and his eyes met Harry's. Harry, whose scars were still hidden by bandages, one arm in a sling, voice slurred and slowed by the painkillers he had not stopped taking. Jesse had never believed that he could feel sorry for Harry when, for years, all he had felt was envy for the boy who seemed to have everything. But he'd abandoned it all on Earth; his parents' wealth and fame, the well-charted route his life could have taken. University, a graduate scheme, his father's investment company, doe-eyed wife and straw-haired kids.

'Well,' Harry said through chattering teeth, 't-this is the end of this hellish ride. For me. I-I want out.' Harry looked around the table for support, expecting a chorus of agreement. It didn't come. His gaze fell on Poppy. 'Don't you?' he asked.

Jesse would be sorry to see Poppy go. The crew needed someone like her. Someone who was gentle and empathetic, who resolved arguments and tried to understand everyone's point of view.

'You know,' said Poppy, 'I think if you'd asked me the same question a month ago, I would have said yes in a heartbeat.'

'And now?' Juno glanced at Poppy hopefully. It was almost as if the ordeal of the past few weeks had filled her with a new and clear resolve. Her storm-coloured eyes shone in a way they hadn't before.

'Now I have a family. Now, I have sisters.' She took Juno's

hand and squeezed it. 'Even if they can be stubborn. This place is my home.'

'And mine, also,' said Fae.

'Did you hear about it?' Poppy asked, glancing between Fae and the rest of the crew. 'Fae's fiancé—'

'Moritz, *meine Liebe*.' Fae smiled to herself, twisting her ring around her finger.

'We heard from the Russians that he's been chosen for *Die Ersten Vierzig*,' Poppy explained. 'The German group going to Terra-Two. A few people dropped out. After what happened to us and the *Orlando*, not so many people want to sign up to die in space. So Moritz was chosen from the backup crew.'

'We will be reunited on the other side. On Terra-Two,' Fae said.

'But you can be together on Earth too,' Harry said.

'Yes,' Fae agreed. 'But then what happens to you? When I was asked to come in Maggie Millburrow's place, for a little while, I have to tell you, I hated all of you. But now . . .' She shrugged.

'I think that's the closest Fae will ever get to saying she likes us,' said Poppy.

'Well, I do,' Igor said. 'You brave young people. But I was never going to leave. My mission is here.'

'Mine too,' said Cai.

Jesse didn't want the others to feel pressured to follow in their footsteps. He turned to Eliot and said, 'Well, if, like Harry, any of you would prefer not to continue, now is your chance.'

Jesse knew that they would need Eliot's engineering genius on Terra-Two. But, back on Earth, he could recover from his breakdown. Found a start-up with skinny-jeaned whizz-kids in Silicon Valley.

'But you need me,' Eliot said. He looked down at his wrist and pinged an elastic band against his skin. 'I made a promise to Ara that I wouldn't go to space without her. I've basically spent the past few months racked with guilt about breaking it. But . . . I don't want to end up the way she did. I don't want to go where she is.'

'We'd be glad,' said Jesse, 'if you stayed.'

'They'd be ruined if you left,' Juno said. 'I mean . . . they need an engineer.' She sat at the end of the table in her dressing gown, an oxygen tube hooked over her ears and under her nose. Jesse wanted her to stay more than anything. Wanted her practical way of thinking, her Damocles Document and her laws. He wanted to go to sleep with her every night, as he had only once, and wake up to the sound of her breathing.

Juno looked at her sister and said, 'This is the worst choice I've ever had to make. Go home and be with Astrid, or stay and . . .' She looked at Jesse, and he glanced away. Afraid that he might lose his composure and begin to beg.

'Astrid and I always thought we were only half-suited to this mission. That she's too naive and I'm too—'

'Cold?' Harry said.

'Practical,' Juno corrected.

'Hopeful,' Astrid said.

'I wish I were hopeful,' Juno said, her voice taut with long-ing. 'I wish I woke up in the morning kicking the covers off my legs, just ecstatic about the sun rising. I've been fighting a lot of conflicting emotions.' She paused and looked at her sister. 'Devastated that you're leaving and angry about the reason. But I've had a little while to think about it, and now I know that you gave up the thing that was most important to you to save my life. It's because you love me.'

She turned to Jesse. 'But then, I think about the world we'd be going back to. It's bloodstained history. How could I give up my chance to start again? To be part of something new. Something we'll try to make better. I'm excited to go,' she said to him. 'I still want to go,'

Then they all turned to Jesse, their future commander. He took a deep breath, and told them something that his father had liked to tell him and his sister. 'There's a story, a legend, that the Antarctic explorer Ernest Shackleton placed an advertisement in a newspaper, looking for men to accompany him on his expedition.' He paused, looked round the table, at every one of his crewmates, his friends, his family. 'The ad read: *MEN WANTED for hazardous journey, small wages, and bitter cold, long months of complete darkness, constant danger, safe return doubtful, honour and recognition in case of success.* Not everyone who read it would have applied for a position on the team, but the response was overwhelming. Perhaps because the triumph at the end would be all the sweeter because they'd know where they'd been. Perhaps because the men knew that nothing would be easy. Every day would hurt, but, when they came to the end of their mission, it would not be with regret but with rejoicing.'

JUNO

26.02.13

TEMPERATURE: -27°C
O_2: 58% SEA LEVEL
HOURS UNTIL RESCUE: 24

THE NIGHT BEFORE THE resupply shuttle arrived, Juno dreamed of Terra-Two for the first and only time. She dreamed of seeing it through the window of the Atlas module, as close up as Europa and then closer still when they swooped into low orbit over an alien sea. She saw Jesse's face, the light in his eyes as he took them down on the lander, as he steered them flawlessly through the most dangerous point – entering the atmosphere.

The crew tumbled from the ship, shocked and uncalloused as newborns. Wobbling under a different gravity, learning again to walk, to focus their eyes on new horizons and on the violet sky.

Juno dreamt of erecting a flag they had painted, together. Everyone's hands on it – Poppy's, Jesse's, Eliot's and Fae's – as they pushed it down into the sand. Giving their first gift to the land – a name, their country.

By the time they arrived, they had lived the journey so long that it was all they knew. Once they reached their destination, each of them flailed for a new purpose. The first night, Juno slept under the stars with Jesse, whose body she had come to learn by heart. She looked out at the sky and wondered if this had been worth everything she had given up for it. Could it ever be?

Now was the year to discover if her dreams of Terra-Two had been only dreams, and even as she beheld the twilit beauty of the planet, she realized that they had. Juno and her family had feasted, for two decades, on dreams alone. Now it was the time for the hard work.

They would face the first Terran winter unprepared. Welcome other expeditions as they descended from the sky, planted their own flags into the soil and fought in foreign tongues. An alien fever would wipe out two-thirds of the population and two members of the Beta. It would take generations to tame the land and even then – never completely. Their great-grandchildren would fell the ancient forests near the shoreline, build silicate towers and spill poison into the sea. They would remember, forget and remember again the lessons of their ancestors. But there would also be more to celebrate; Fae's wedding to Moritz, their long-held love preserved over time and distance. Eliot would play the guitar and Poppy would gather up wildflowers from the meadows and Moritz would place a crown of them on Fae's silver head. Juno's Damocles Document would become the foundation of a new constitution. They would sing songs and write plays, myths would flourish, vivid tales of the voyage, the void, the sacrifice and the loss of the old home their children and their children's children would never ache for. But they would still celebrate Landing Day with dance and fireworks. Once a year, they would cast their gaze up to the decommissioned *Damocles* as it twinkled in its graveyard orbit, making slow arcs across the sky.

When Juno opened her eyes, though, the dream was already forgotten. Nothing remained but a vague hope, and it gave her the strength to finally say goodbye to her sister. She was the one who helped to pull Astrid's helmet over her head, and she watched as the hatch, at last, slammed shut. She bit back her tears for the time it took for the shuttle to disappear from the porthole, and then when she finally turned around and broke down, Poppy, Jesse, Fae and Eliot all opened their arms to hold her.

ASTRID

12.05.2013

WHEN ASTRID STEPPED OUT of the shuttle the final time, it was just like the day that she left. Except that, this time, the sun was blinding. There was a sour smell of fuel on the air, and the scent of grass and sea was an assault on her senses.

They were not heroes, today. They were victims. The world believed that they had been barely more than children, brainwashed and abused, then hurled into the void to die. An inquiry was being held into the human rights abuses at space academies, experts questioning the ethics of filling students full of facts and then sending them off to found nations.

Harry was awarded a medal for bravery, for piloting the crew from the *Orlando* back to the *Damocles*.

Astrid and Harry slept off the weakness in quarantine, curled up together some nights clumsy and quiet as newborns, because they weren't used to facing the nights alone. One evening, Astrid woke to find Harry sitting on his bed opposite, sobbing. When he noticed her, he looked out the window and said softly, 'In my dreams, I'm still up there.'

ASTRID DISCOVERED THAT SHE'D been wrong about home. She thought her heart had abandoned it forever.

Her father had come to pick her up from the space centre, embraced her with tears in his eyes and helped her into the car. She had returned with nothing, no bags or belongings. As they drove through the city, Astrid felt as if she was seeing everything for the first time.

When they stepped outside in front of her house, she realized that her home was different from any place her feet could ever find. She had thought that the sight of her own street would be the greatest disappointment after circling the rings of Jupiter. She couldn't have known that the skin under her soles had never forgotten the feel of the cobbled path, the dandelions springing up between the stones. Her father's rough hand in hers. The dull sweetness of apples turning pink on their tree.

Astrid hadn't expected that when she blinked their front garden would be peopled with old ghosts; herself and Juno at five, six and nine making daisy chains with clumsy fingers or pressing their faces to the eyepiece of their father's telescope, jostling for another look at Terra-Two.

Their teachers liked to tell them in astronomy class that the light from the stars took years to reach their eyes on Earth. That the most distant stars could have burned out billions of years ago, but still their light brightened the night sky. Cosmic proof for the existence of ghosts. Ara had asked, 'What do they see, when they look back at us?'

Astrid used to think that home was wherever her sister was, but as she lingered before the front door, she finally understood that, somewhere in space, they were still together. They were still skipping stones across a duck pond at nine, devouring mint ice creams in Hyde Park, lying on the common looking for constellations. In the same way, Ara was forever dancing in the courtyard at the space centre, catching raindrops in her finger-tips and saying, 'What would you do, Astrid, with this day, if you could do anything at all?'

ACKNOWLEDGEMENTS

Every time that I ask him to listen to a chapter that I'm working on and he sighs or plays video-games instead of reading proof pages, I mentally cross his name off this list. But I owe so much to my husband, Benedict Douglas-Scott, my sixth-form sweetheart. He's an extraordinary man; kind-hearted, courageous and genuinely good. He inspires me every day and whilst this book could probably have been written without him, I would not be the woman I am without him.

I am indebted to everyone at Greene & Heaton, my agent and literary godmother, Judith Murray, and Eleanor Teasdale.

Sincere thanks goes to my editor, Anne Perry, at Simon & Schuster, Joe Monti at SAGA press and Fraser Crichton. After two years of your patient support, I feel as if my book turned up, like a prom date, at my door, shoes polished, hair brushed, ready to go to the ball.

To both of my mothers Dr Sheila Ochugboju and Philomena Agunbiade. All of my siblings, Ellakeche, Ruth and Che, whom I held hostage for a decade and forced to listen to every version of my story. And Pavalina Toukalkova for looking after all of us for years.

To my best women, and sister-friends: Natasha Dujkic and Dr Stella Collinson, who are good and loving and clever and strong; and to Ella Sparks whose integrity and all-round Junoness has inspired me since I was 16. And to Nanci Gulliver, my Anam Cara and creative soulmate.

I am very grateful to Sionaidh, Alexander and Venetia

Douglas-Scott, and to Anne Alfred and Michael Douglas-Scott. My friends Alice Lui and Jack Bowyer, Madhav Bakshi and Dr Thomas Eliot for his help with copy-edits. To Lauren Price-Evans for being such a lovely role-model and to Christopher King who has been the kindest and most supportive manager.

My father Emmanuel Ochugboju was the first person who told me that I could be a writer and KT Forster was the mentor who ushered me along that journey.

Thank you to all the women who have supported and encouraged me; my aunties Priscilla St. Leger, Dr Esther Horner, Joy Abang and Claire Asu-Adinye. And to my international aunts Dr Musonda Mumba, Dr Ebere Okereke and Ifeoma Dike. Special regards to Auntie Yvonne Adhiambo Owour, author of *Dust*, an inspirational mentor.

It has been my dream to write a book since I was a child. Four months before my agent sold this novel to Simon & Schuster, I knelt down, unemployed and discouraged, at the American Poet's Corner in the Cathedral of St John the Divine, New York. I had trekked across Manhattan alone, gotten lost in Harlem for hours, just to find it. And when I finally did, I unlatched my backpack, collapsed on the cold stone and asked God to believe me when I told him that I longed to be a writer. Three weeks later, after returning to London, I got an agent. For this book and for everything before and after, I will always thank God 'for he has crowned me with love and tender mercies and with all good things he satisfies me.'